WRESTLING WITH GODS
Tesseracts Eighteen

Selected Science Fiction & Fantasy Stories Edited By
Liana Kerzner and Jerome Stueart

EDGE SCIENCE FICTION AND FANTASY PUBLISHING
AN IMPRINT OF HADES PUBLICATIONS, INC.
CALGARY

Wrestling With Gods: Tesseracts Eighteen
Copyright © 2015
All individual contributions copyright by their respective authors.

Edge Science Fiction and Fantasy Publishing
An Imprint of Hades Publications Inc.
P.O. Box 1714, Calgary, Alberta, T2P 2L7, Canada

Edited by Liana Kerzner and Jerome Stueart

Interior design by Janice Blaine
Cover art by Dracorubio

ISBN: 978-1-77053-068-3

EDGE Science Fiction and Fantasy Publishing and Hades Publications, Inc.
acknowledges the ongoing support of the Alberta Foundation for the Arts and
the Canada Council for the Arts for our publishing programme.

Canada Council   Conseil des arts
for the Arts   du Canada

Library and Archives Canada Cataloguing in Publication

CIP Data on file with the National Library of Canada

ISBN: 978-1-77053-068-3
(e-Book ISBN: 978-1-77053-069-0)

FIRST EDITION
(K-20141210)
Printed in Canada
www.edgewebsite.com

Table of
CONTENTS

Foreword

THE DISAPPEARING LION TRICK

by Jerome Stueart

IN ONE OF MY most vivid memories, I am four-years-old, escaping the nursery at our church. While my folks were attending the service, I found an abandoned room at the end of a dark hallway. In the room was a large stuffed lion. He had holes in him and a gash, and his stuffing was coming out, and someone had put him out here as the first step towards throwing him away. I remember curling up in his paws, because he was so huge compared to me, and putting my head in the crook of his furry neck, and talking to him until I fell asleep.

When the daycare attendants found me, they were upset, and they dragged me back into the nursery with all the other noisy kids. But I escaped again on another day, ran back to that room, back to that security— and found the room empty, and he was gone. But though they took him away, I never forgot that feeling of security and comfort in the arms of that ragged lion.

Lions were part of the narrative of stories I was receiving from multiple sources. I remember my mother gathering us every night in the hallway that joined our bedrooms. We'd bring our blankets, and cuddle with each other as she read. I remember the books: *Mother Goose*, Fairy Tales, *The Bible*, and the *Chronicles of Narnia*, with its talking lion and kids like me who found adventure.

When I was nine, my father became a Southern Baptist minister, and the Bible became the cement foundation of our entire lives. We started hearing the Bible every Sunday, even three times a week, as it moved from stories to self-help to the rules of my life, and lost a little in the evolution.

We shifted away from the stories I loved to the letters of Paul, and prophecies of prophets in very difficult circumstances. By the time I was eighteen, I had to escape the main service, go down the long hallway, and look into the Sunday school rooms of the children of our church to find the good stories. There they were, pinned up to the wall, almost inaccessible to me as an adult because I was supposed to have moved on to more "meatier" faith and religion.

I missed "Daniel in the Lion's Den". The holy man of God is surrounded by hungry lions, and must last the night. When they check in the morning, Daniel sits with peaceful lions because his God was there with him.

I missed Elijah who, in a great showdown of gods with the prophets of Ba'al on Mount Carmel, prayed for God to make a spectacular appearance, and God did.

I missed Ruth and Naomi traveling together, praying to find economic stability and a home again. I missed Esther who risked her life coming out as Hebrew to save her people.

I missed Jacob wrestling with the angel to grab something good for his family from the gods. This is the impetus for the theme of this anthology: struggling with faith, wrestling with gods.

These were stories told mostly now to the children— encouraging, empowering stories. They were people struggling, talking, in a relationship with their gods.

Bible stories, for me, showed faith was the great equalizer. In the stories, faith favours the wanderer over the settled, the outsider over the king, the captured slave over the captors, the boy over the giant, and the praying man over the predators. Jesus re-emphasizes that up-ended power dynamic when he gives his great speech, The Sermon on the Mount. "Blessed are the poor in spirit... the meek, the merciful..."

But as a teen, sitting in church, it seemed the only thing left for adults were sermons that curbed that power, that independence, and often insured obedience, guilt, and an acceptance of suffering, endured for a promised Heaven. Welcome to the practical world of Christian living! There are no adventures here.

I felt a bait-and-switch had happened.

I had more questions. Like most people, I wanted to know why I was here? What were the stars way out there for? What was my purpose in life? Are there more truths to learn to become a better person?

I shifted my eyes to find story again— as is the case with most of us. I'd been led in through the wide, colorful, open door of stories into my faith, and I wanted them back.

Great Faiths have great stories. The form of story is the most perfect form for truth, I think. Story doesn't mean fiction— it just indicates form. It has a beginning, a middle, and an end. It has tension and struggle and resolution. Stories have quests, and they answer questions. They can be historically true, and they can be allegorically true. Stories are easier to share. You can pass on a story to a child. Religions understand that you must capture the minds of the young with great stories, and stories will hold them to the faith stronger than anything. They leave impressions on us.

Most faiths have a mixture of stories and creed. We've already talked about the use of story in the Bible. The *Mahabharata* is a long epic poem containing many stories of gods and humans important to the Hindu faith and culture. The *Qur'an* contains stories as well that guide Muslims. *Journey to the West, the Odyssey, Beowulf, Gilgamesh*, the stories of Buddha. They all contain stories that hold cultural wisdom. Each of these texts have "fantastical elements": gods, miracles, great beasts and giants, powerful evil beings, good triumphing over evil. The world's most ancient stories helped establish cultures by putting wisdom in the form of story— to make them memorable.

They just happened to have fantastical elements, too. When ideas, concepts and creeds become too existential, it is the giants and the dragons and the jinn that give truth form and texture. How do I master my untamed, destructive impulses? You can knock that Goliath down. I can see a Goliath. I can remember a Goliath when I try to rein in my destructive tendencies.

Many of the texts above hold a sacred significance for millions of people. They created world cultures, and these conversations and struggles of humans and gods established our relationship with the known and unknown.

In my life, they were great stories that helped remind me that God was with me, and that I too could struggle and search and doubt, and still be in a relationship with a god. But if I was told I'd outgrown them, where would I find more stories like these?

Since I'd already been led to believe in miracles, in "magic" (the power of God), and courageous heroes, I was overjoyed to discover fantasy and science fiction. They asked the big questions. Their characters struggled with the reasons they existed. They questioned the prevalence of war, inequality, poverty, and powerlessness.

Bilbo and Frodo, the smallest, meekest of races, the hobbits, end up being the most powerful in saving their world from destruction. Madeleine L'Engle's *Wrinkle in Time* series had an awkward young woman and her younger brother battling forces of evil for the good of the world— and there were centaurs, and mediums, and giant, pulsing brains of conformity. I kept revisiting Narnia, both a fantasy series and an allegory for Christian faith, and found new comfort in that speaking lion. Star Trek and Star Wars gave me great morality tales in space.

In the sacred texts, the holiest of people, Jesus, Mohammed, the Buddha, were the great equalizers in an unbalanced world, handing power to the powerless and taking the authority out of the hands of the temple, the government, and putting it back into the hands of the individual. With prayer, or concentration, or devotion, you and you and you could have miracles too.

Science fiction and fantasy reflected themes found in those sacred texts. They emphasized the weak over the powerful, the hobbits over the sorcerers, the rebels over the Empire. They said that great power came from strong belief and selfless motive, not in strong magic, weapons, or numbers. They celebrated good defeating evil. They had everyday people sacrificing themselves for the good of others.

And I found myself in science fiction and fantasy's not-so-holiest of people— the ones who struggled with what to do, who don't have all the answers. It's when they struggle and wrestle that I most identified with them. To me, they seemed so much like those earlier Bible story characters, stumbling through questions and interactions with gods (or aliens or wizards or giants).

I could *be* these people too. I could make these mistakes. I could search and ask and doubt and struggle and wrestle like Frodo and Meg and Kirk and Luke and Bruce Wayne and Ripley and Tyrion— like they do with their enemies and their gods.

Science fiction and fantasy stories still hold truths if you want to wrestle.

So here we have 25 stories and poems of the strugglers, the wrestlers, the ones who want to understand; the ones who want to snatch power out of the hands of gods; the ones who struggle to turn disaster into hope.

You don't have to be a believer. You just have to believe in the powers of fantasy and science fiction to speak truth. Having authors tackle faith as a theme has brought us stories and poems where characters find the most impossible challenges, and contemplate the deeper mysteries in a most satisfying way.

We think you'll like these 25 offerings.

While I'm excited that they represent a wide spectrum of real world faiths, and a lot of created ones too, what makes me most excited is how they present the regular everyday people who search.

Like the best characters of sacred texts, their characters are flawed and gritty, wrestling with faith and belief, and not always surviving. They craft, lie, surprise, create, explore, rescue, abandon and betray themselves and those they love to try to figure out how to balance the supernatural in their own natural lives.

I was touched by many of these stories because I could see me making those same choices. They let me in.

And isn't that the most important thing when it comes to faith and religion? You feel comfortable with the ones that let you in. They may be old, ragged, with the stuffing pouring out, but they give you some peace, and they seem to whisper, *Talk to me.*

JEROME STUEART makes his home in the Yukon Territory. Hailing from Missouri and West Texas, Jerome came up to the Yukon to work on northern science fiction. He fell hard for the place. Stueart is a graduate of Clarion Science Fiction and Fantasy Workshop in San Diego (2007) and of the Lambda Literary Retreat for Emerging LGBT Voices (2013). He has been published in *Fantasy, Geist, Joyland, Geez, Strange Horizons, Ice-Floe, Redivider, On Spec, Tesseracts Nine, Tesseracts Eleven, Tesseracts Fourteen* and *Evolve: Vampire Stories of the New Undead.* He earned honourable mentions for both the Fountain Award and *Year's Best Science Fiction 2006.* He co-edited *Inhuman.* As a cartoonist he was featured in the Yukon News, and as a journalist he wrote for *Yukon, North of Ordinary,* Air North's in-flight magazine. He's worked as a janitor, a trolley conductor, an embedded reporter in a remote northern research station, a Religious Education director, and a marketing director. He wrote five radio series for CBC, and one of them, *Leaving America,* was heard around the world on Radio Canada International. Jerome has taught creative writing for 20 years, and taught an afterschool course in fantasy and science fiction writing for teens for three years. He teaches a workshop he designed called Writing Faith in churches across Canada and the USA.

Mecha-Jesus

by Derwin Mak

FATHER XAVIER ITO, a researcher of the Pontifical Institute of Robotics and Artificial Intelligence, could not escape from androids even in rural Aomori Prefecture. He drove past fields of apples, rice, and garlic, all tended by agricultural androids.

He slowed as he approached the black van in front of him. The van, moving at twenty kilometers below the speed limit, had Japanese flags and loudspeakers mounted on it. A voice boomed from the loudspeakers:

"ANDROIDS TAKE JOBS FROM HUMANS! PROTECT THE HUMAN RACE! DESTROY ALL ANDROIDS!"

Such sound vans were common at political protests in big cities. Father Ito had never seen one in a rural area, though. He guessed that the van drove slowly so that the few remaining human farm workers could hear it.

He passed the van. The words "PROTECTORS OF HUMANITY" were painted in bold white characters on its side.

Over the years, the police had arrested the Protectors of Humanity for attacking androids. Ito hoped that they were not going to the village of Shingo. There he had to examine an android that resembled Jesus Christ.

He sped away, leaving the black van behind. Further ahead, a lane was closed because a crack ran through it. In a grassy field, a barn had fallen over. An earthquake had hit Aomori a week ago. Fortunately, it had been mild, and nobody had died.

Finally, Ito arrived at Shingo. As his car drove into the parking lot, an android pointed at an empty space.

"Please park in that space," the android said.

Ito recognized the android as an L-2 by its shiny plastic skin, glazed eyes, and electronic machine voice. Although it wore a parking attendant's uniform, nobody would confuse it with a human.

Ito switched to manual control and parked his car. He approached the android and asked, "Where is the Tomb of Christ?"

"Please park in that space," said the android, pointing at another empty spot.

Definitely an L-2, thought Ito. He looked around and saw a sign pointing to the Tomb of Christ. It lay in the woods.

As he walked on the path to the tomb, he passed vendors selling crosses and Jesus statues. A banner reading "WELCOME TO THE CHRIST FESTIVAL" hung on an arch over the path.

A tour guide told his guests, "Jesus did not die in Israel as the Christians say. Instead, his brother Isukiri substituted himself for Jesus on the cross. Jesus fled to Siberia, then to Shingo. He became a rice farmer, got married, had three children, and lived to be one hundred and six years old. Because of his foreign appearance, people called him the Big-Nosed Goblin."

Nobody in Shingo knew that Jesus had lived there until a Shinto priest discovered Jesus' last will and testament in 1936. Jesus apparently wrote in Japanese, four hundred years before the Japanese had any written language.

Nobody in Shingo admitted to believing that Jesus had lived there. However, nobody would turn away the tourists or their money either.

A middle-aged woman approached him and said, "Ah, you must be Father Ito. I can tell by your clothes."

Ito always wore a black suit and Roman collar when visiting a holy site, even one of dubious history. Shinto priests were there, and he respected them.

Father Ito bowed and gave his business card to the woman.

"I'm Fukuda Hiro, the Mayor of Shingo," said the woman. She handed her card to Ito. "I'm very pleased that the Vatican has honoured my request to verify that the Second Coming of Jesus Christ has occurred."

"I'm actually here to examine the android from an engineering standpoint," Ito said. The Pope had ignored all the messages that

Mayor Fukuda had sent him. The Pontifical Institute, however, wanted to learn about the android Jesus.

"Oh, you're not here to verify the Second Coming?" Fukuda sounded disappointed. "Well, it's possible for Jesus to return as an android."

"Fukuda-san, are you Christian?" Ito asked.

Fukuda guffawed. "Of course not. Nobody in Shingo is. I follow Shinto, like everyone else."

Mayor Fukuda led Father Ito to two graves, both earthen mounds with unpainted wooden crosses. One of Isukiri's ears and a lock of the Virgin Mary's hair were buried under one mound. The other mound held the bones of Jesus. Like the Jesus testament, the graves were unknown until 1936, and nobody had excavated them.

As tourists walked around the graves, Ito saw a European man holding a Bible and brochures. As people passed him, he said, "Accept Jesus Christ as your personal saviour and you will be saved!" He spoke in Japanese with an American accent.

Ito went to the man and introduced himself in English. The American smiled, bowed, and shook his hand.

"I'm Norman Richmond from Los Angeles, California," he said. "It's nice to meet another Christian."

"Are you a missionary?" Ito asked. He knew the answer, but it was polite to ask and make small talk.

"Only on weekends. I teach English in Aomori City, but in my spare time, I promote Jesus for La Cienega Bible Mission."

That was undoubtedly a small church, founded by lay people and self-taught ministers, Ito thought. America proliferated with them.

"So, judging by your clothes, are you Catholic?" Richmond asked.

"Yes, from Nagasaki," Ito replied. "My family has been Roman Catholic for many generations."

"I guess the Jesuits got to them before the Protestants did." Richmond turned around, thrust a brochure at two teenaged girls and announced, "Accept Jesus Christ as your personal saviour!"

The girls giggled and said, "Real Christians have finally shown up at the Christ Festival!"

Mayor Fukuda came to Ito and Richmond. "Gentlemen, the ceremony will begin soon," she said. "Please enjoy it."

Women clad in lavender kimonos danced around the grave of Jesus. They chanted the song "Nanya Do Yara", which was unique to the village. Its words had no meaning in Japanese but were reputedly derived from ancient Hebrew.

Then a man walked slowly to the grave. He wore a red Heian court robe and a tall black headdress. He stared solemnly at the cross.

"That's Enoki-san, a local Shinto priest," Fukuda whispered.

Facing the cross, Enoki bowed twice, clapped his hands twice, and bowed once more. He recited a prayer: "Jesus Christ, we honour you. Bless us with good weather and excellent harvests. Bring success in farming, academic studies, romance and marriage, and safe travels to those who pray and make offerings to you."

Next, Enoki waved a *haraigushi*, the sacred wand. Its zigzag paper streamers rustled in the air.

A *miko*, a shrine maiden in a white kimono-like jacket and a long red skirt, brought a bowl of rice and a bottle of sake to Enoki. The priest bowed to the cross again and put the offerings on the mound.

"Jesus Christ, please accept the rice and sake," he said.

Richmond stared wide-eyed at the ceremony. "This is wrong," he whispered. "This isn't Christianity."

"Who said Christ Festival is Christian?" Ito replied.

Enoki picked up a microphone and announced, "The Suffering of Jesus will begin now." He pointed at a path behind the graves. "Look, here comes the God of Christmas!"

Jesus, wearing a white robe and crown of thorns, carried a cross along the path. The crowd applauded and cheered.

"That's Mecha-Jesus," Fukuda said. "Tourist numbers have doubled since we got him."

Mecha-Jesus had skin that looked like human flesh, not shiny plastic. His eyes expressed pain rather than a glazed stare. He moved fluidly, like a human, without the stiff motions of an android.

"Is that the android?" Ito asked in disbelief.

Fukuda beamed with pride. "Yes. He's so realistic!"

Enoki narrated the Passion of the Christ. "Back then, Rome ruled Israel, and fascists ruled Rome. Jesus was a political dissident, so the fascists sent soldiers to attack him."

Men dressed as Roman soldiers, carrying whips, rushed to Mecha-Jesus. They lashed viciously at him. The android groaned in simulated agony. The soldiers yelled, "Pasta! Pasta! Pasta!"

Richmond looked puzzled. "Why are they saying, 'Pasta'?"

"It's the only Italian word they know," Fukuda said.

As Mecha-Jesus carried his cross, hundreds of people took photographs of him.

"Pasta! Pasta! Pasta!"

Mecha-Jesus put his cross down in front of the Jesus grave. The soldiers pushed him to the ground and tied him to the cross.

"The Romans nailed Jesus to the cross, just like we did to criminals during the Tokugawa Shogunate," Enoki explained to the audience.

The soldiers groaned and grunted as they raised the cross. One of them complained, "This robot is so heavy!"

The cross wobbled under the soldiers' shaky grip. After holding the cross upright for only twenty seconds, they quickly lowered it back to the ground.

"Jesus died and went underground to the land of the dead," Enoki continued, "but then, a miracle occurred!"

The soldiers untied Mecha-Jesus.

Enoki proclaimed, "Three days later, he returned from the dead. Such was the miracle of Christmas!"

The android sprang to its feet and jumped up and down, smiling and raising his arms above his head.

"Pasta! Pasta! Pasta!"

The crowd cheered and applauded.

Richmond muttered, "This is wrong."

Ito turned to Fukuda. "Having Jesus die and be resurrected contradicts the local legend that he lived and fled to Japan."

Fukuda shrugged. "It's the story the tourists like. They've seen it in American movies."

Tourists crowded around Mecha-Jesus for photographs with him. The android smiled for the cameras.

"It smiles spontaneously and realistically," Ito observed. "It mimics human behavior extremely well."

"Big-Nosed Goblin!" a teenaged girl squealed as she plucked the crown of thorns off Mecha-Jesus and put it on her own head. She smiled, pointed at her friends and their cameras, and made a peace sign. Mecha-Jesus laughed and posed for a photo with her. She left with the crown of thorns, now a souvenir of her pilgrimage.

Richmond pressed his Bible to his chest and prayed in English. "Dear God, I thank you for enabling these people to discover your son Jesus Christ. However, their ways of honouring him are heathen, and they have not accepted him as their lord and savior. Please show them the correct path. Amen."

Ito asked Richmond, "How long have you been coming here?"

"Once a week for two years, ever since they got the android," Richmond replied. "I thought the android would get people interested in Jesus, and I could get some people interested in Christianity."

"How many people have you converted?"

"None so far."

They went to Mecha-Jesus. Ito could not believe how realistic the android looked.

"Isn't Mecha-Jesus the most advanced android in the world?" Fukuda remarked. "We don't even have to recharge him. His hair contains millions of ultra-efficient nanoscale solar cells that convert sunlight into electricity."

"Let me talk to him," Ito said. He looked at the android. "Are you Jesus?"

"Yes, I am, my son," Mecha-Jesus replied.

A programmed response for a question that the android's designers could have easily anticipated, Ito thought. He had to ask a more difficult question.

"Prove to me that you're Jesus," Ito demanded.

Mecha-Jesus pointed to the ground. "Remember that earth-quake that hit Aomori last week?"

"Yes."

"Do you see any ruined roads or buildings here? I protected this village."

Mayor Fukuda could have programmed that response after the earthquake, Ito thought. He decided to argue with Mecha-Jesus.

"It wasn't a strong earthquake, and the epicenter was far away," Ito said, "and the village was built to strict anti-earthquake building codes."

"I weakened the earthquake," Mecha-Jesus replied with a smile. "Ah, here comes someone with an offering."

A farmer bowed to Mecha-Jesus and gave him a small plastic bag of rice.

"Jesus *kami*, thank you for the good rice harvest," said the farmer.

"God bless you," said Mecha-Jesus.

The farmer left Mecha-Jesus to Ito again. The priest continued testing the android's artificial intelligence.

"Did you really cause a good rice harvest?" Ito said. "Many factors, like the weather, can influence a crop."

"And who controls the weather?" Mecha-Jesus asked.

"Nobody controls the weather. It's a force of nature."

"And so am I."

Mecha-Jesus was not speaking in programmed responses, Ito concluded.

The android industry had buzzed with rumors of learning androids. They learned new information from their own experience and their environment. They made decisions on their own. They created new sentences, not just recited pre-recorded speech. Their artificial intelligence didn't just mimic human behavior. It actually created new actions. They were true thinking machines.

Enoki came and took Fukuda away to meet a garlic farmer. Some more tourists came to Mecha-Jesus. Ito looked around for Fukuda. She had gone away with the Shinto priest.

He didn't want to delay his next question. He would ask the android.

"Jesus-san, may I look at your system information?" Ito asked.

Mecha-Jesus smiled and said, "Yes, you may."

The android turned around, pulled his hair up, and lifted a panel at the back of his head. A row of data ports appeared.

Ito attached his pocket computer to a data port and read the android's system information:

MODEL: L-6 Prototype Male, Customized Model Jesus

OWNED BY: Shingo Tourism Board

FACTORY: Akihabara

PATENTED BY: Victor Robotics

DESIGNED BY: Dr. Hiyase Midori

The rumors were true. Victor Robotics had created Level 6, a super-intelligent android that could pass as human. If anyone could do it, it would be Dr. Hiyase Midori, the world's most talented android designer.

Then Ito saw a small clear plastic dome beside the data ports. It held a tiny gray object. The words "EX OSSIBUS" in Latin letters were written around the dome.

Richmond peered into the android too. "What's that?" he asked.

"*Ex ossibus*. It means from the bones," Ito explained. "It's a Roman Catholic term for a bone relic of a saint."

"Hey, that's inappropriate!" Enoki said as he rushed over. He disconnected Ito's pocket computer from the data port and lowered the panel and Mecha-Jesus's hair back into place.

"Only a priest may look at the *goshintai*," the Shinto priest warned.

"The bone fragment is the *goshintai*?" Ito asked.

"Yes. The bone of Jesus-san."

Shinto shrines were not just places of worship. They were also houses for *kami*. The *goshintai* was the sacred object in which the *kami* lived. It was usually a mirror, but this one was a bone fragment of the Son of God.

Mecha-Jesus turned to Enoki. "Please do not scold these men. They asked for my permission to view the spirit within the machine, and I granted it to them. Also, they are my priests, as are you."

Enoki bowed deeply to Ito and Richmond. "Gentlemen, I am sorry for my anger, which Jesus-san tells me was unjustified. Please forgive me."

"No problem," said Richmond in English.

Ito nodded. "Thank you. We accept the apology. We felt no offense at all." After pausing to let Enoki stand upright, he asked, "Where did you get the bone fragment?"

"From the grave of Jesus," Enoki replied.

"You excavated the grave?"

"No, no! That would be bad luck. We had an earthquake two years ago. The Earth shook, and a bone rose to the surface of the grave."

"A bone moved above ground? That's very odd."

"What is the Christian saying? God works in mysterious ways?"

"Ah, yes."

"I took most of the bone to the Legend of Christ Museum, but I saved a fragment. I put the fragment in the android, and then I performed a ceremony to invite Jesus *kami* to enter the bone."

"Oh my God," Ito muttered in English. "They've turned the android into a mobile Shinto shrine with the *kami* of Jesus."

"What's a *kami*?" Richmond asked.

"A supernatural force of nature," Ito explained. "A river, a rock, a mountain, anything can be a *kami* if you believe it has a spirit. Shinto has an infinite number of them, the so-called eight million *kami*."

Enoki nodded. "We asked Jesus *kami* to protect our town from earthquakes, and no harm came. We asked Jesus *kami* for a good rice crop, and we got one. Jesus *kami* has been kind to us."

"Plus he's good for tourism," Mayor Fukuda added.

"But it's impossible for Jesus to have physical remains on Earth," Richmond insisted. "He ascended into heaven in both body and spirit."

"This isn't the Christian Jesus," Ito said. "This is the Shinto Jesus."

"Now do you believe that I am Jesus?" Mecha-Jesus asked.

Richmond shook his head. "No, you're not Jesus."

"I don't believe you're Jesus," said Ito, "at least not the Jesus whom I know."

"Like my disciple Peter, you deny me. What must I do to prove myself to you?" Mecha-Jesus said before walking away to greet some tourists.

Ito watched more people thank Mecha-Jesus for a variety of wishes fulfilled: getting accepted to a university, passing a driver's license exam, and getting a new boyfriend.

Ito and Enoki went to a wooden booth where a *miko* sold *omamori*. The cloth amulets showed a cross and words such as "Success in Dating and Romance", "Success in University Entrance Exams", "Good Harvest", and "Good Health".

"Enoki-san," Ito asked, "Did the people ask Jesus for good fortune before you invited Jesus *kami* into Mecha-Jesus?"

"No. We are not Christians," Enoki replied.

Ito heard shouting from behind him. He turned and saw men in black coveralls beating a janitorial android with hammers. The black van of the Protectors of Humanity was parked nearby.

One of the men wore a cloth patch of the Imperial Navy flag, the red sun with sunrays. The other men saluted him as the janitorial android lay twitching on the ground.

"Leader, we have defeated another shameful android!" declared one of the men. The Leader looked at the ruined android and nodded silently.

He gazed at the onlookers. "People of Shingo, we are the Protectors of Humanity! Bring out your androids! They are destroying the human race!"

Two Protectors dragged an android to the Leader. It was a female model dressed in a waitress uniform.

A woman ran to the Leader and screamed, "Please don't harm my android! She's done nothing wrong!"

The Protectors pulled the woman back. The Leader raised his hammer and smashed it repeatedly into the android's head. Chunks of plastic and electronic parts flew into the air. The android slumped to its knees and fell over.

The android's owner screamed as the Protectors released her. She rushed to hug the android.

"Bring out your androids!" the Leader demanded.

"Call the police," Ito said to Mayor Fukuda.

"They're not here," Fukuda said. "They're clearing earthquake damage at another town."

"During the Christ Festival?"

"There has never been violence at the Christ Festival before."

Enoki motioned to Fukuda. "Mayor-san, let's go talk to them."

Fukuda and Enoki went to the Leader. The Leader put his hammer into a holster on his belt.

"I am Fukuda Hiro, Mayor of Shingo," Fukuda said. "You are damaging my villagers' property. Please leave peacefully."

The Leader bowed to her. "Mayor-san, I am sorry that we did not introduce ourselves to you when we arrived. Please forgive our rudeness. We are the Protectors of Humanity."

"I am the local priest," Enoki said. "The Mayor and I are sufficient to protect the people of this village. Your services will not be required. Please leave now."

"Priest-san, we are here for a secular reason. Please stay on religious matters," the Leader warned.

"But certainly you should respect both the secular and holy leaders of the village," Enoki said. "We do not require your services. As I said before, please—"

"Be compassionate as your Father is compassionate. Do not judge and you will not be judged yourselves," Mecha-Jesus said as he interrupted Enoki and approached the Leader.

A Protector pointed at Mecha-Jesus and shouted, "There it is! The Jesus android!"

"That's an *android*?" the Leader said incredulously.

"Yes, yes! A tourist told me about it."

"But it looks like a *gaijin* cosplaying as an ancient Israeli."

"Capture it and we'll find out!" the Protector urged.

Ito grabbed Mecha-Jesus by the shoulders and pushed him into the crowd of tourists and villagers.

"Get him out of here!" Ito urged.

The people swarmed around Mecha-Jesus and pulled him away. Enoki, Fukuda, Ito, and Richmond fled into the crowd. The Protectors rushed forward but ran into a wall of people.

"Put your hammers back into your holsters!" the Leader barked to his men. "Do not hurt any people! Attack only the androids!"

Thank God the Protectors of Humanity don't want to deliberately harm human beings, Ito thought. However, they did not mind scaring them. People screamed as the Protectors pushed and chased them.

But some people shouted in defiance:

"Jesus is ours! They can't have him!"

"Protect Jesus *kami*!"

"Don't let the fascists kill him again!"

This was not how the crowd treated Jesus on the original Good Friday, Ito mused as he ran.

The crowd, pulling Mecha-Jesus along, ran into the Legend of Christ Museum. They slammed the steel doors shut and locked them from the inside.

Museum workers quickly lowered metal shutters over the windows. Tourism revenues had paid for the new doors and shutters, which now would protect the village's main tourist attraction.

After the people had barricaded themselves inside the museum, Ito quickly looked at its exhibits. There were ancient Judean clothes, pictures of the Holy Family, old Bibles and Torahs, a wall of crucifixes and crosses, and a model of first-century Jerusalem. There was also the last will and testament of Jesus Christ, written in Japanese.

The Protectors hammered on the doors. Ito heard the sound of breaking glass as they smashed the windows. Then he heard the Protectors pound on the metal shutters.

Fukuda phoned the police chief. "Get your men back here to the museum," she ordered. "We're under siege by a right-wing protest group."

"Will they get here on time?" Enoki asked.

The hammering on the doors and shutters continued. Fukuda shrugged. "I hope we can hold out until the police arrive."

A museum worker reported, "They're hitting the windows and doors all around the building. We're surrounded."

The hammering grew louder. The crowd murmured, and some children cried. Everyone looked worried…

…except Mecha-Jesus, who looked serene and calm and oblivious to the siege. He was talking to some children.

"Those men are scary, but they will not hurt you," Mecha-Jesus assured them. "They will leave you unharmed."

After Mecha-Jesus finished talking to the children, he went to Ito.

"You look worried, my son," said Mecha-Jesus.

"We're under siege," Ito said. He laughed. "What is the American saying? 'What would Jesus do?'"

"Do not be afraid of those who kill the body but cannot kill the soul; fear him rather who can destroy both body and soul in Hell," replied Mecha-Jesus.

"Hah! When I need an artificial intelligence to think of way out of this mess, all it does is recite programmed lines."

"You still doubt who I am, but I say again, I am Jesus Christ. The android is merely the body through which I communicate with you."

"*So desu ka,*" Ito said. He turned away from Mecha-Jesus and gasped at what he saw.

Richmond was unlocking the steel doors.

Before Ito could get to him, Richmond had flung open the doors. The Protectors of Humanity stood outside and stared through the doorway.

"Why did you do that?" Ito demanded.

"To give them the android," Richmond said. "This is not how Christians worship Jesus."

"They're not Christians!"

The Leader stepped into the museum. "Where is the android?" he demanded.

The crowd murmured as Mecha-Jesus walked towards the doorway.

"Step back outside and I will come out to you," Mecha-Jesus said to the Leader.

The Leader grunted and went outside. The Protectors of Humanity gathered by the doorway. They glared silently at Mecha-Jesus as they held their hammers.

Mecha-Jesus paused beside Ito and looked at him.

"Now you will believe that I am Jesus," the android said.

Then he turned to Richmond, smiled, and said, "I know that you love me. You've actually helped me. Thank you."

Mecha-Jesus stepped closer to the doorway. He looked back at the crowd and smiled.

"Cover your eyes and do not look at me!" he warned.

He walked into the hammers of the Protectors of Humanity.

Suddenly, a flash of light burst from Mecha-Jesus. Ito quickly turned around. Bright light reflected off the walls and exhibits of the museum. Ito held his hands over his eyes.

"Don't look, don't look!" people shouted.

Ito felt intense heat on his back. He also heard screaming from outside.

The screams turned into groans and sobs. The heat vanished, and Ito opened his eyes. No bright light shone into the museum. He turned around and looked.

Mecha-Jesus stood outside. The Protectors of Humanity lay on the ground around him. As Ito approached them, he saw that their faces, necks, and hands were burnt red and covered with blisters. Only their coveralls had protected the rest of their bodies.

The Leader crawled on his hands and elbows. "I can't see! I can't see! I can't see!" he shrieked.

Mecha-Jesus said, "Your burns will heal if you leave immediately and seek medical treatment. Those who covered their eyes in time will be able to see and can drive your van. Those with vision loss will find out later whether they will see again or stay blind."

The Protectors of Humanity moaned and wept.

"Leave now and let the people of Shingo live in peace," Mecha-Jesus ordered.

"The Transfiguration of the Lord," Ito said as he stared at the wounded men.

Mecha-Jesus nodded silently.

"How did you do it?"

"I have a light and heat function. It makes my halo for night performances."

"Oh. And I thought you were going to tell me that you have divine powers."

"How do you know that isn't how a god works?"

Ito shrugged. "God works in mysterious ways."

"Please excuse me for a moment," Mecha-Jesus said. "I have to recharge. I drained eighty percent of my battery."

The Protectors of Humanity, carrying their blinded Leader, scurried to their van and drove away, vowing never to return to Shingo.

The next day, Ito asked Richmond if he needed a ride to Aomori City. Richmond eagerly accepted the offer. Mayor Fukuda had hinted that she did not like people who let dangerous thugs into a building full of defenceless villagers.

Mecha-Jesus waved to them as they left. He said, "Come back for next year's festival."

As they drove along the rural roads, Richmond lamented, "How could I have failed? There's so much interest in Jesus in Shingo, and yet, nobody converted to Christianity. Don't you feel disappointed that none of them became Christians?"

"I'm Christian, but I'm also Japanese, so I understand what has happened in that village," Ito said. "They don't have to be Christian to worship Jesus."

Back in Tokyo, Father Ito visited Dr. Hayase Midori. Dr. Hayase, an attractive woman in a blue business suit, had returned to Victor Robotics after some years away.

"I went to Shingo and saw an android that looked like Jesus," he said.

"Ah, yes." Hayase sipped her tea. "That was a special project for my friend, Fukuda Hiro, the Mayor of Shingo."

"It's an L-6, isn't it?"

Hayase grinned. "Now you know my secret. Yes, it's an L-6. Only two prototypes exist. Jesus is one of them. I actually invented the L-6 years ago, but my colleagues did not think that society was ready for them. However, society is changing. The Protectors of Humanity and others like them are a dwindling minority."

"It's a fascinating model," Ito said. "It has such capabilities and powers. Its light and heat function is incredible."

"What light and heat function?"

Ito explained what had happened in Shingo.

"I designed no such function for the L-6 or any other model," Hayase said.

"Then how could he do it?" asked Ito.

"The L-6 has the ability to learn new knowledge and reconfigure its systems. Perhaps Mecha-Jesus developed a light and heat function and augmented himself... on his own."

"That's possible?"

"Yes, but I think the chances are small. If he did create his own function, he exceeded my greatest expectations."

"*So desu ka*," Ito said, realizing that Jesus had joined the eight million *kami*.

DERWIN MAK won the Prix Aurora Award for his story "Transubstantiation" and the anthology *The Dragon and the Stars* (co-edited with Eric Choi). His fiction often deals with the relationship between science and religion. Although Derwin is Roman Catholic, he paid respect to the *kami* at Shinto shrines in Japan.

COME ALL YE FAITHFUL

by Robert J. Sawyer

*First published in **Space Inc.**, edited by Julie E. Czerneda,
DAW Books, New York, July 2003.*

"DAMNED SOCIAL ENGINEERS," said Boothby, frowning
his freckled face. He looked at me, as if expecting an objection
to the profanity, and seemed disappointed that I didn't rise to
the bait.

"As you said earlier," I replied calmly, "it doesn't make any
practical difference."

He tried to get me again: "Damn straight. Whether Jody and
I just live together or are legally married shouldn't matter one
whit to anyone but us."

I wasn't going to give him the pleasure of telling him it mat-
tered to God; I just let him go on. "Anyway," he said, spreading
hands that were also freckled, "since we have to be married
before the Company will give us a license to have a baby,
Jody's decided she wants the whole shebang: the cake, the
fancy reception, the big service."

I nodded. "And that's where I come in."

"That's right, Padre." It seemed to tickle him to call me that.
"Only you and Judge Hiromi can perform ceremonies here,
and, well..."

"Her honour's office doesn't have room for a real ceremony,
with a lot of attendees," I offered.

"That's it!" crowed Boothby, as if I'd put my finger on a heinous conspiracy. "That's exactly it. So, you see my predicament, Padre."

I nodded. "You're an atheist. You don't hold with any religious mumbo-jumbo. But, to please your bride-to-be, you're willing to have the ceremony here at Saint Teresa's."

"Right. But don't get the wrong idea about Jody. She's not..."

He trailed off. Anywhere else on Mars, declaring someone wasn't religious, wasn't a practicing Christian or Muslim or Jew, would be perfectly acceptable— indeed, would be the expected thing. Scientists, after all, looked askance at anyone who professed religion; it was as socially unacceptable as farting in an airlock.

But now Boothby was unsure about giving voice to what in all other circumstances would have been an easy disclaimer. He'd stopped in here at Saint Teresa's over his lunch hour to see if I would perform the service, but was afraid now that I'd turn him down if he revealed that I was being asked to unite two nonbelievers in the most holy of institutions.

He didn't understand why I was here— why the Archdiocese of New York had put up the money to bring a priest to Mars, despite the worldwide shortage of Catholic clergy. The Roman Catholic Church would always rather see two people married by clergy than living in sin— and so, since touching down at Utopia Planitia, I'd united putative Protestants, secular Jews, and more. And I'd gladly marry Boothby and his fiancée. "Not to worry," I said. "I'd be honoured if you had your ceremony here."

Boothby looked relieved. "Thank you," he replied. "Just, you know, not too many prayers."

I forced a smile. "Only the bare minimum."

Boothby wasn't alone. Almost everyone here thought having me on Mars was a waste of oxygen. But the New York Diocese was rich, and they knew that if the church didn't have a presence early on in Bradbury Colony, room would never be made for it.

There had been several priests who had wanted this job, many with much better theological credentials than I had. But two things were in my favor. First, I had low food requirements, doing fine on just 1200 calories a day. And second, I have a Ph.D. in astronomy, and had spent four years with the Vatican observatory.

The stars had been my first love; it was only later that I'd wondered who put them there. Ironically, taking the priest job here on Mars had meant giving up my celestial research, although being an astronomer meant that I could double for one of the "more important" colonists, if he or she happened to get sick. That fact appeased some of those who had tried to prevent my traveling here.

It had been a no-brainer for me: studying space from the ground, or actually going into space. Still, it seemed as though I was the only person on all of Mars who was really happy that I was here.

Hatch 'em, match 'em, and dispatch 'em — that was the usual lot for clergy. Well, we hadn't had any births yet, although we would soon. And no one had died since I'd arrived. That left marriages.

Of course, I did perform mass every Sunday, and people did come out. But it wasn't like a mass on Earth. Oh, we had a choir — but the people who had joined it all made a point of letting each other know that they weren't religious; they simply liked to sing. And, yes, there were some bodies warming the pews, but they seemed just to be looking for something to do; leisure-time activities were mighty scarce on Mars.

Perhaps that's why there were so few troubled consciences: there was nothing to get into mischief with. Certainly, no one had yet come for confession. And when we did communion, people always took the wine — of which there wasn't much available elsewhere — but I usually had a bunch of wafers left at the end.

Ah, well. I would do a bang-up job for Boothby and Jody on the wedding — so good that maybe they'd let me perform a baptism later.

"Father Bailey?" said a voice.

I turned around. Someone else needing me for something, and on a Thursday? Well, well, well...

"Yes?" I said, looking at the young woman.

"I'm Loni Sinclair," she said. "From the Communications Centre."

"What can I do for you, my child?"

"Nothing," she said. "But a message came in from Earth for you— scrambled." She held out her hand, proffering a thin white wafer. I took it, thanked her, and waited for her to depart. Then I slipped it into my computer, typed my access code, and watched in astonishment as the message played.

"Greetings, Father Bailey," said the voice that had identified itself as Cardinal Pirandello of the Vatican's Congregation for the Causes of Saints. "I hope all is well with you. The Holy Father sends his special apostolic blessing." Pirandello paused, as if perhaps reluctant to go on, then: "I know that Earth news gets little play at Bradbury Colony, so perhaps you haven't seen the reports of the supposed miracle at Cydonia."

My heart jumped. Pirandello was right about us mostly ignoring the mother planet: it was supposed to make living permanently on another world easier. But Cydonia— why, that was here, on Mars...

The Cardinal went on: "A televangelist based in New Zealand has claimed to have seen the Virgin Mary while viewing Cydonia through a telescope. These new ground-based scopes with their adaptive optics have astonishing resolving power, I'm told— but I guess I don't have to tell you that, after all your time at Castel Gandolfo. Anyway, ordinarily, of course, we'd give no credence to such a claim— putative miracles have a way of working themselves out, after all. But the televangelist in question is Jurgen Emat, who was at seminary fifty years ago with the Holy Father, and is watched by hundreds of millions of Roman Catholics. Emat claims that his vision has relevance to the Third Secret of Fatima. As you know, Fatima is much on the Holy Father's mind these days, since he intends to canonize Lucia dos Santos next month. Both the postulator and the reinstated *advocatus diaboli* feel this needs to be clarified before Leo XIV visits Portugal for this ceremony."

I shifted in my chair, trying to absorb it all in.

"It would, of course," continued the recorded voice, "take a minimum of two years for a properly trained cardinal to travel from the Vatican to Mars. We know you have no special expertise in the area of miracles, but, as the highest-ranking Catholic official on Mars, his Holiness requests that you visit Cydonia, and prepare a report. Full details of the putative miracle follow..."

⊗⊗⊗●●

It took some doing — my mere presence was an act of for-
bearance, I knew — but I managed to finagle the use of one of
Bradbury Colony's ground-effect shuttles to go from Utopia
Planitia to Cydonia. Of course, I couldn't pilot such a vehicle
myself; Elizabeth Chen was at the controls, leaving me most
of a day to study.

Rome didn't commit itself easily to miracles, I knew. After
all, there were charlatans who faked such things, and there
was always the possibility of us getting egg on our collective
faces. Also, the dogma was that all revelations required for faith
were in the scriptures; there was no need for further miracles.

I looked out the shuttle's windows. The sun — tiny and dim
compared with how it appeared from Earth — was touching
the western horizon. I watched it set.

The shuttle sped on, into the darkness.

"We speak today of the Third Secret of Fatima," said Jurgen
Emat, robust and red of face at almost eighty, as he looked
out at his flock. I was watching a playback of his broadcast
on my datapad. "The Third Secret, and the miracle I myself
have observed.

"As all of those who are pure of heart know, on May 13,
1917, and again every month of that year until October, three
little peasant children saw visions of our Blessed Lady. The
children were Lucia dos Santos, then aged 10, and her cousins
Francisco and Jacinta Marto, ages eight and seven.

"Three prophecies were revealed to the children. The third
was known only to a succession of Popes until 2000, when,
while beatifying the two younger visionaries, who had died
in childhood, John Paul II ordered the Congregation for the
Doctrine of Faith to make that secret public, accompanied by
what he called 'an appropriate commentary.'

"Well, the secret *is* indeed public, and has been for almost
seventy years, but that commentary was anything but appropriate, twisting the events in the prophecy to relate to the 1981
attempt on John Paul II's life by Mehmet Ali Agca. No, that
interpretation is incorrect— for I myself have had a vision of
the true meaning of Fatima."

Puh-leeze, I thought. But I continued to watch.

"Why did I, alone, see this?" asked Emat. "Because unlike
modern astronomers, who don't bother with eyepieces anymore,

I looked upon Mars directly through a telescope, rather than on a computer monitor. Holy Visions are revealed only to those who gaze directly upon them."

An odd thing for a televangelist to say, I thought, as the recording played on.

"You have to remember, brethren" said Jurgen, "that the 1917 visions at Fatima were witnessed by children, and that the only one who survived childhood spent her life a cloistered nun— the same woman Pope Leo XIV intends to consecrate in a few weeks' time. Although she didn't write down the Third Secret until 1944, she'd seen little of the world in the intervening years. So, everything she says has to be re-interpreted in light of that. As Vatican Secretary of State Cardinal Angelo Sodano said upon on the occasion of the Third Secret's release, 'The text must be interpreted in a symbolic key.'"

Jurgen turned around briefly, and holographic words floated behind him: *We saw an Angel with a flaming sword in his left hand; flashing, it gave out flames that looked as though they would set the world on fire...*

"Clearly," said Jurgen, indicating the words with his hand, "this is a rocket launch."

I shook my head in wonder. The words changed: *And we saw in an immense light that is God — something similar to how people appear in a mirror when they pass in front of it — a Bishop dressed in white...*

Jurgen spread his arms now, appealing for common sense. "Well, how do you recognize a bishop? By his miter— his liturgical headdress. And what sort of headdress do we associate with odd reflections? The visors on space helmets! And what color are spacesuits? White— always white, to reflect the heat of the sun! Here, the children doubtless saw an astronaut. But where? Where?"

New words replacing old: *...passed through a big city... half in ruins...*

"And that," said Jurgen, "is our first clue that the vision was specifically of Mars, of the Cydonia region, where, since the days of *Viking,* mystics have thought they could detect the ruins of a city, just west of the so-called Face on Mars."

Gracious Christ, I thought. Surely the Vatican can't have sent me off to investigate that? The so-called "Face" had, when photographed later, turned out to be nothing but a series of buttes with chasms running through them.

Again, the words floating behind Jurgen changed: *Beneath the two arms of the Cross there were two Angels...*

"Ah!" said Jurgen, as if he himself were surprised by the revealed text, although doubtless he'd studied it minutely, working up this ridiculous story.

"The famed Northern Cross," continued Jurgen, "part of the constellation of Cygnus, is as clearly visible from Mars' surface as it is from Earth's. And Mars' two moons, Phobos and Deimos, depending on their phases, might appear as two angels beneath the cross..."

Might, I thought. *And monkeys might fly out of my butt.*

But Jurgen's audience was taking it all in. He was an old-fashioned preacher— flamboyant, mesmerizing, long on rhetoric and short on logic, the kind that, regrettably, had become all too common in Catholicism since Vatican III.

The floating words morphed yet again: *...two Angels each with a crystal aspersorium in his hand...*

"An aspersorium," said Jurgen, his tone begging indulgence from all those who must already know, "is a vessel for holding holy water. And where, brethren, is water more holy than on desiccated Mars?" He beamed at his flock. I shook my head.

"And what," said Jurgen, "did the angels Phobos and Deimos do with their aspersoria?" More words from the Third Secret appeared behind him in answer: *They gathered up the blood of the Martyrs.*

"Blood?" said Jurgen, raising his bushy white eyebrows in mock surprise. "Ah, but again, we have only blessed Sister Lucia's interpretation. Surely what she saw was simply red liquid— or liquid that *appeared* to be red. And, on Mars, with its oxide soil and butterscotch sky, *everything* appears to be red, even water!"

Well, he had a point there. The people of Mars dressed in fashions those of Earth would find gaudy in the extreme, just to inject some color other than red into their lives.

"And, when I gazed upon Cydonia, my brethren, on the one hundred and fiftieth anniversary of the first appearance of Our Lady of the Rosary at Fatima, I saw her in all her glory: the Blessed Virgin.

"How did I know to look at Cydonia, you might ask? Because the words of Our Lady had come to me, telling me to turn my telescope onto Mars. I heard the words in my head late one night, and I knew at once they were from blessed Mary. I went to my telescope and looked where she had told me to. And nine minutes later, I saw her, pure and white, a dot of perfection moving about Cydonia. Hear me, my children! Nine minutes later! Our Lady's thoughts had come to me instantaneously, but even her most holy radiance had to travel at the speed of light, and Mars that evening was 160 million kilometers from Earth— nine light-minutes!"

⊗⊛●⊛⊗

I must have dozed off. Elizabeth Chen was standing over me, speaking softly. "Father Bailey? Father Bailey? Time to get up…"

I opened my eyes. Liz Chen was plenty fine to look at — hey, I'm celibate; not dead! — but I was unnerved to see her standing here, in the passenger cabin, instead of sitting up front at the controls. It was obvious from the panorama flashing by outside my window that we were still speeding along a few metres above the Martian surface. I'll gladly put my faith in God, but autopilots give me the willies.

"Hmm?" I said.

"We're approaching Cydonia. Rise and shine."

And give God the glory, glory… "All right," I said. I always slept well on Mars— better than I ever did on Earth. Something to do with the 37% gravity, I suppose.

She went back into the cabin. I looked out the window. There, off in the distance, was a side view of the famous Face. From this angle, I never would have given it a second glance if I hadn't known its history among crackpots.

Well, if we were passing the Face, that meant the so-called cityscape was just 20 kilometers southwest of here. We'd already discussed our travel plans: she'd take us in between the "pyramid" and the "fortress," setting down just outside the "city square."

I started suiting up.

⊗⊛⊗●●

The original names had stuck: The pyramid, the fortress, the city square. Of course, up close, they seemed not in the least artificial. I was bent over now, looking out a window.

"Kind of sad, isn't it?" said Liz, standing behind me, still in her coveralls. "People are willing to believe the most outlandish things on the scantest of evidence."

There was just a hint of condescension in her tone. Like almost everyone else on Mars, she thought me a fool— and

not just for coming out here to Cydonia, but for the things I'd
built my whole life around.

I straightened up, faced her. "You're not coming out?"

She shook her head. "You had your nap on the way here.
Now it's my turn. Holler if you need anything." She touched a
control, and the inner door of the cylindrical airlock chamber
rolled aside, like the stone covering Jesus' sepulcher.

What, I wondered, would the Mother of our Lord be doing here,
on this ancient, desolate world? Of course, apparitions of her
were famous for occurring in out-of-the-way places: Lourdes,
France; La'Vang, Vietnam; Fatima, Portugal; Guadalupe, Mexico.
All of them were off the beaten track.

And yet, people did come to these obscure places in their
millions after the fact. It had been a century and a half since
the apparitions at Fatima, and that village still attracted five
million pilgrims annually.

Annually. I mean *Earth* annually, of course. Only the anal
retentive worry about the piddling difference between a terrestrial
day and a Martian sol, but the Martian year was twice as long as
Earth's. So, Fatima, I guess gets *ten* million visitors per Martian
year...

I felt cold as I looked at the landscape of rusty sand and
towering rock faces. It was psychosomatic, I knew: my surface
suit — indeed white, as Jurgen Emat had noted — provided
perfect temperature control.

The city square was really just an open area, defined by wind-
sculpted sandstone mounds. Although in the earliest photos,
it had perhaps resembled a piazza, it didn't look special from
within it. I walked a few dozen metres then turned around,
the lamp from my helmet piercing the darkness.

My footprints stretched out behind me. There were no others.
I was hardly the first to visit Cydonia, but, unlike on the Moon,
dust storms on Mars made such marks transitory.

I then looked up at the night sky. Earth was easy enough to
spot— it was always on the ecliptic, of course, and right now
was in... my goodness, isn't that a coincidence!

It was in Virgo, the constellation of the Virgin, a dazzling
blue point, a sapphire outshining even mighty Spica.

Of course, Virgo doesn't depict the Mother of Our Lord;
the constellation dates back to ancient times. Most likely, it

represents the Assyrian fertility goddess, Ishtar, or the Greek harvest maiden, Persephone.

I found myself smiling. Actually, it doesn't depict anything at all. It's just a random smattering of stars. To see a virgin in it was as much a folly as seeing the ruins of an ancient Martian city in the rocks rising up around me. But I knew the... well, not the *heavens*, but the night sky... like the back of my hand. Once you'd learned to see the patterns, it was almost impossible *not* to see them.

And, say, there was Cygnus, and — whaddaya know! — Phobos, and, yes, if I squinted, Deimos too, just beneath it.

But no. Surely the Holy Virgin had not revealed herself to Jurgen Emat. Peasant children, yes; the poor and sick, yes. But a televangelist? A rich broadcast preacher? No, that was ridiculous.

It wasn't explicitly in Cardinal Pirandello message, but I knew enough of Vatican politics to understand what was going on. As he'd said, Jurgen Emat had been at seminary with Viktorio Lazzari— the man who was now known as Leo XIV. Although both were Catholics, they'd ended up going down widely different paths— and they were anything but friends.

I'd only met the Pontiff once, and then late in his life. It was almost impossible to imagine the poised, wise Bishop of Rome as a young man. But Jurgen had known him as such, and — my thoughts were my own; as long as I never gave them voice, I was entitled to think whatever I wished — and to know a person in his youth is to know him before he has developed the mask of guile. Jurgen Emat perhaps felt that Viktorio Lazzari had not deserved to ascend to the Holy See. And now, with this silly announcement of a Martian Marian vision, he was stealing Leo's thunder as the Pope prepared to visit Fatima.

Martian. Marian. Funny I'd never noticed how similar those words were before. The only difference...

My God.

The only difference is the lowercase t — the *cross* — in the middle of the word pertaining to Mars.

No. No. I shook my head inside the suit's helmet. Ridiculous. A crazy notion. What had I been thinking about? Oh, yes: Emat trying to undermine the Pope. By the time I got back to Utopia Planitia, it would be late Saturday evening. I hadn't thought of a sermon yet, but perhaps that could be the topic. In matters of faith, by definition, the Holy Father was infallible, and those who called themselves Catholics — even celebrities like Jurgen Emat — had to accept that, or leave the faith.

It wouldn't mean much to the... yes, I thought of them as my *congregation*, even sometimes my flock... but of course the group that only half-filled the pews at Saint Teresa's each Sunday morn were hardly that. Just the bored, the lonely, those with nothing better to do. Ah, well. At least I wouldn't be preaching to the converted...

I looked around at the barren landscape, and took a drink of pure water through the tube in my helmet. The wind howled, plaintive, attenuated, barely audible inside the suit.

Of course, I knew I was being unfairly cynical. I *did* believe with all my heart in Our Lady of the Rosary. I knew — knew, as I know my own soul! — that she has in the past shown herself to the faithful, and...

And *I* was one of the faithful. Yes, pride goeth before destruction, and an haughty spirit before a fall— but I was more faithful than Jurgen Emat. It was true that Buzz Aldrin had taken Holy Communion upon landing on the moon, but I was bringing Jesus' teachings farther than anyone else had, here, in humanity's first baby step out toward the stars...

So, Mary, where are you? If you're here— if you're with us here on Mars, then show yourself! My heart is pure, and I'd love to see you.

Show yourself, Mother of Jesus! Show yourself, Blessed Virgin! Show yourself!

Elizabeth Chen's tone had the same mocking undercurrent as before. "Have a nice walk, Father?"

I nodded.

"See anything?"

I handed her my helmet. "Mars is an interesting place," I said. "There are always things to see."

She smiled, a self-satisfied smirk. "Don't worry, Father," she said, as she put the helmet away in the suit locker. "We'll have you back to Bradbury in plenty of time for Sunday morning."

I sat in my office, behind my desk, dressed in cassock and clerical collar, facing the camera eye. I took a deep breath, crossed myself, and told the camera to start recording.

"Cardinal Pirandello," I said, trying to keep my voice from quavering, "as requested, I visited Cydonia. The sands of Mars drifted about me, the invisible hand of the thin wind moving them. I looked and looked and looked. And then, blessed Cardinal, it happened."

I took another deep breath. "I saw *her*, Eminence. I saw the Holy Virgin. She appeared to float in front of me, a metre or more off the ground. And she was surrounded by spectral light, as if a rainbow had been bent to the contours of her venerable form. And she spoke to me, and I heard her voice three times over, and yet with each layer nonetheless clear and easily discernible: one in Aramaic, the language Our Lady spoke in life; a second in Latin, the tongue of our Church; and again in beautiful, cultured English. Her voice was like song, like liquid gold, like pure love, and she said unto me…"

⊙●●●●

Simply sending a message to Cardinal Pirandello wouldn't be enough. It might conveniently get lost. Even with the reforms of Vatican III, the Church of Rome was still a bureaucracy, and still protected itself.

I took the recording wafer to the Communications Centre myself, handing it to Loni Sinclair, the women who had brought Pirandello's original message to me.

"How would you like this sent, Father?"

"It is of some import," I said. "What are my options?"

"Well, I can send it now, although I'll have to bill the… um, the…"

"The parish, my child."

She nodded, then looked at the wafer. "And you want it to go to both of these addresses? The Vatican, and CNN?"

"Yes."

She pointed to an illuminated globe of the Earth, half embedded in the wall. "CNN headquarters is in Atlanta. I can send it to the Vatican right now, but the United States is currently on the far side of Earth. It'll be hours before I can transmit it there."

Of course. "No," I said. "No, then wait. There are times when both Italy and the U.S. simultaneously face Mars, right?"

"Not all of the U.S.— but Georgia, yes. A brief period."

"Wait till then, and send the message to both places at the same time."

"Whatever you say, Father."

"God bless you, child."

Loni Sinclair couldn't quite mask her amusement at my words. "You're welcome," she replied.

Four years have gone by. Leo XIV has passed on, and John Paul III is now pontiff. I have no idea if Jurgen Emat approves of him or not— nor do I care. Dwelling on Earthly matters is frowned upon here, after all.

Five million people a year still come to Fatima. Millions visit Lourdes and Guadalupe and La'Vang.

And then they go home— some feeling they've been touched by the Holy Spirit, some saying they've been healed.

Millions of faithful haven't made it to Mars. Not yet; that will take time. But tens of thousands have come, and, unlike those who visited the other shrines, most of them stay. After traveling for years, the last thing they want to do is turn around and go home, especially since, by the time they'd arrived here, the propitious alignment of Earth and Mars that made their journey out take only two years has changed; it would take much longer to get home if they left shortly after arriving.

And so, they stay, and make their home here, and contribute to our community.

And come to my masses. Not out of boredom. Not out of loneliness. But out of belief. Belief that miracles do still occur, and can happen as easily off-Earth as on it.

I am fulfilled, and Mars, I honestly believe, is now a better place. This *is* a congregation, a flock. I beam out at its members from the pulpit, feeling their warmth, their love.

Now I only have one problem left. To lie to Cardinal Pirandello had been a violation of my oath, of the teachings of my faith. But given that I'm the only priest on all of Mars, to whom will I confess my sin?

ROBERT J. SAWYER was part of the group that founded Vision TV, the world's only multifaith television service, and he hosts the Vision series *Supernatural Investigator*. He has won the Hugo, Nebula, Aurora, Seiun, Galaxy, Audie, Skylark, Homer, Hal Clement, John W. Campbell Memorial, and Arthur Ellis Awards.

A HEX, WITH BEES

by Tony Pi

Strangers will covet our timber, our land.   From the festers of the poisoned earth
They'll teem: to log, to slash, to burn.   Blooded by greed, their drones will rage
And lay waste to our kingdom green.   Hex them, sisters, join our destined war!

Cast yarrow stalks in the forest heart, and watch the wind throw fortunes down.
Read the trigrams to divine which treetop the dark-sweet goddess lairs,
Dreaming in her shrine of honeycomb.   Learn how our queen must wake.

Go to her sanctum on a moonless night, bathed, bereft of flame and iron.
Offer her honey ere you climb.   While singers below chant ancient prayers
Find her sacred hive and light a vine-torch to rouse her keepers from sleep.

Singe the comb and let the embers fall.   Soldier bees stream like black water,
The roar of ten thousand spurring them on as they chase the raining fire.
Her guardians now gone   Gently carve and catch her golden temple.

Escape from the heavens with her majesty safe in her waxen citadel.
Roast and eat the demon grubs, but harvest the brood-comb ambrosia.
Touch not the cocoon of the pupal god, for she must be coaxed forth at dawn.

On a lake's dim shores, pray to her.   Burn incense, and taste the honeyed power.
When royal strength transforms you, speak your grievance with mellifluous voice:
What the god-queen hears in waking becomes her immortal ambition.

At sunlight's kiss, her refuge bursts.   With thundering wings the deity flies
      Over the placid waters, piping.   Her shadows and her reflections multiply
   And call to arms a frenzied parade of warrior souls and phantom dancers.

   When they assail and sting you, be stolid as the mountain against a storm.
   Will her venom into mercy or doom!   The immortal plague will spread to slay,
   Else poison sinful souls with shame.   Unite, sisters, summon the goddess-swarm!

TONY PI is a Toronto-based writer with a Ph.D. in Linguistics and a 2009 finalist for the John W. Campbell Award for Best New Writer. In his youth, at his great-uncle's farm in the mountains of Taiwan, he once helped harvest honey, which inspired this poem.

THE QUEEN IN THE POPLAR FOREST

by S. L. Nickerson

ALL THE OMENS meant it was a good morning for a hunt. Legends of the Bronze-Backed Bear have said that one drop of his blood dripped, into eyes, would cure cataracts; his saliva, boiled over hot coals for two hours should whittle away kidney stones; and his fur spun into bandages could soothe even the harshest burns. I, Queen Irashar of Nimur, would have his pelt to drape over my throne. My collection was nearing completion.

I alone tracked him uphill between slender poplars, with two spears and one shield in hand. Prints such as these, prints that dug into the earth deep as my thumb and marked even boulders, could belong to no other than the Bronze-Back Bear. Trees thickened, and up the mountainside pistachio trees overran the poplars. Their twisted, white limbs and shiny leaves made a tight canopy. The prints were farther apart, for he must have been running here, up and into a cave above me. The mouth was half-hidden by licorice bushes in full purple-white blossom.

I tucked the straight spear into the shield on my left arm, held the twisting spear in my right and entered the cave's mouth. At my birth, the gods allowed my father to choose one gift with which to bless me: at a short distance darkness was like daylight to me.

Small animal bones stuck up from the dirt floor, and the walls bore the scrapes of mighty claws. The footprints were so numerous that following any set became impossible. The cave tunnels branched off like rivulets between river and ocean. This passage narrowed, and my breathing quickened.

A beast snarled behind me. I turned around and saw nothing but the fork I had just crossed. I walked backwards, shifting my gaze between both tunnels. My back brushed the cave wall and I stepped sideways. Something warm pressed against my side; I could feel the beast's moist breath upon my neck. I spun to face it, twisting spear up. Nothing.

I looked over my shoulder and caught a spark of bronze. I chased after it through the winding tunnels, never seeing more than that first gleam, but I could hear his paws pound the cave floor. He was always just beyond my sight. I heard him closer, near a bend, and with a sharp flick of my wrist I threw my twisting spear. It flew in an arc and I heard it pierce something on the other side, followed by a muffled scream. I walked around the bend to behold my prey.

My spear had not punctured a bear's bronze pelt, but a man's calf. He was a wild man with mahogany hair and beard tangles down to his thighs, and skin ruddy as baked river clay. He wore no clothes, leaving his entire hairy, and rather muscular, nudity open to my appraisal. If his face was not twisted in agony, I might have thought it handsome. He had dug his fingers into the dirt, clenched hard.

"You're trespassing in my forest," I said.

"Argg!" the beast-man said.

"Do you know what I am?"

"Urrraow!"

"I'll presume that is a 'no'." I looked from the claw scratches on the cave wall to the writhing man and knelt beside him. "Where is the Bronze-Backed Bear?"

"Gaaah?"

Any noise we made should have warned off the bear by now. I needed the beast-man alive. There was only one way he was going to lead me to trapping the bear, and it was not in this state. I yanked my bloodied spear out of his calf, taking muscle with it, and tied a strip of my tunic around his wound like I had seen my physician do. He shoved my shoulder with the heel of his palm, harder than I expected, causing me to stumble back.

I gasped. No one had pushed me since I was five.

But he seemed to be ignoring me, so caught up in his pain.

I stole a breath. After I no longer needed him, he would die for this. I yanked him to his feet. He almost collapsed back to the ground, but I caught him under the arms and hauled him towards the cave entrance. His body was heavier than it appeared.

My court remained where I had left them, down the mountain by the brook. They always disturbed the game, and I could only tolerate them for so long on hunts. Nobles and priests, my husbands and wife, tedious children and cousins: I needed them to keep occupied with activities that do not include usurpation.

Any number of thoughts ran across their faces when I appeared back, pushing a wounded, unclothed beast-man with my hands caked in his blood, but they hid it well and clapped politely. With a nod my physician took him from me to dress the wound.

A shave and haircut had improved the beast-man. Now clothed and seated in a civilized setting, he might have been mistaken for a courtier, if he had not been shovelling bread into his mouth with both hands. Honey and berries were smeared over his face, and onions spilled out of the bread, over his fresh tunic. Clothes did not so much conceal his body as contain it. It was as if any movement his chest made was ready to tear it open.

"Do you do more than grunt?" I asked, standing over him.

I saw the gleam of cleverness in the beast-man's eyes when he looked to me, no longer in pain. He stood to his full height, knocking his chair over, and his shoulders were at my eye-level. Behind me, I heard the creak of my guards' armor as they waited on the other side of the door. The beast-man's room was favored with broad windows, high enough to overlook the city's northern wall.

"I can speak plainly," he said, each word chosen carefully, shifting his weight to the unbandaged leg, "or I can converse in riddles and sing in verse, find the omens in the stars of the universe and read weather in the riverbanks. I am Leinu, and I know who you are, Irashar."

"Then listen well, Leinu, because this I will only ask nicely once," I said. "Will you take me to the Bronze-Backed Bear?"

"Does the anemone first open because it is spring, or do we say that spring comes because the anemone opens? How can the anemones know spring without speaking to one another and coming to accord? Things aren't real to us unless they have names we can agree upon."

"Flowers don't consult one another."

"But humans do, Irashar. How can I take you to something that means one thing from your lips, and a different thing in my ears? First you must tell me, what do you mean by this Bronze-Backed Bear?"

"A fearsome beast," I said, "a horrid creature, whose only purpose is to consume the forest. An eater of horses, he can have twelve in a day. Even prides of lions cower before him. The gods abhorred this monstrosity and saw fit to curse his body with healing powers so as to bribe the Queens and Kings of Nimur into hunting him down, though none so far have done so and lived."

"Then if that is your idea of the Bronze-Backed Bear, I cannot lead you to something that doesn't exist."

"See that wall?" I pointed out the window to the massive northern wall that bordered my city, chiselled lapis lazuli wrought with veins of gold. "That was left by the older gods, and now I am its keeper. Not even the poorest peasant in Nimur dares to wash out the gold or chip the lapis lazuli for fear of me.

"If you could look east, then you would see a wall where every brick is stamped with my name and its dimensions sum to spell the letters in it. My will binds this place together; even as the river floods the countryside between years, it remains whole because of me. I am Nimur." I stepped closer to him, so that I could feel the heat in his tunic and smell the fruit on his face. "And you will take me to something that doesn't exist."

"What will you do otherwise, kill me?" Leinu's berry-stained lips smiled.

"I will."

He swept out a hand. "Then you'll never have the bear's pelt."

I turned and stalked out of his room. A trail of courtiers followed me. The sun was just rising, and it was time to dress for the morning audience. I returned to my chambers and stood on the stool as slaves fussed around me, removing my simple tunic for jewels and labyrinthine robes.

"The Milk Drop Star rose well after dusk last night," my astrologer explained to me, "and so you should wear a nacre torque, your majesty."

"It is uncomfortable."

"Nevertheless, you must. The Fourth Wanderer passed the Dog Constellation, hence the tassels on your robes and the baldric embroidered with palmettes..."

I raised a hand and she fell silent. "What does the name Leinu mean to you?" I asked, and then kept that hand out as a slave slipped rings onto it.

The astrologer stepped back for a moment. "The letters in 'Leinu' add up to seventy-two, your majesty. So does 'protector' and 'rain,' 'river' and 'anemone'." I strained to hear her above the sounds of my wife and one husband bickering over their spinning.

"Anemone?" I kept my mouth open as another slave worked rouge over my lips.

"Indeed."

The slave had moved to rub kohl around my eyes, and so I closed them as my astrologer continued to explain why I was dressed the way I was today. Eventually, my scribe brought in contracts with the clay still wet. I read them and rolled my seal over the bottom for approval.

We made our procession to the throne room. Relief carvings of my ancestors' victories filled the limestone walls and around every column, atop the ceilings and floors: an ancestor standing over the body of a beheaded giant; lines of peoples of many nations bringing gifts to the feet of a different ancestor as she reclined on her throne, drawn thrice as large as the rest; my grandmother holding the reins of a four-stallion chariot as she led an army to battle; my father welcoming a fleet of ships that bore him tribute from across the river.

Only over the lesser reliefs did I dare hang my own victories: the horns of the Sword-Sharp Heifer, the pelt of the Shadow-Breathing Panther, the head of the Poison Ibex, the beak from the Laughing Heron, the tails of the Thrice-Tailed Fox. There was a single space left, and that I reserved for the greatest prize yet: my limestone throne for the Bronze-Backed Bear's hide.

As I slid onto the empty seat, I asked my astrologer, "Is it an auspicious day to visit my mother?" Since I had become queen, Mother was the only one in this city I could speak honestly with.

"Only after the Flickering Star has risen in the west," the astrologer said, "and first you must walk within the garden."

"Gardens bore me. They are too tame, not like the forest at all." I drummed my fingers on the armrest. "I should like to see her sooner."

"But your majesty, you cannot change the stars."

⊛⊛⊛●●

My mother lived, at least part of the time, in the innermost sanctum of her ziggurat. The first thing I had done as queen was to build it higher so that hers stood above the temples of all the other gods.

I left my servants at the door and entered Mother's personal chamber. She never ate in front of people unless it was with me alone. Twin braziers hung from the ceiling that smelled sweetly of burning styrax. Today, her statue, which was twice as tall as me, was in front of her altar. Upon it I rested my offering of silver grapes, her favorite, and dropped to my knees.

The statue's carnelian eyes flared as if they held flames, and I knew Mother had arrived. She lifted one thick, jasper-studded basalt arm, and picked up the grapes. The room quivered as she tromped to her giant throne, the lime-etched gold plates of her tunic creaking with the motion of her thighs. She plunked down, leaning on one of the throne's arms in a way that reminded me of how I sat, and dropped a silver grape into a mouth carved from red agate.

"I told you, darling, jade grapes," Mother said.

"No, I remember this time," I said, pointing a finger at her. "It was silver. I won't be tricked again."

She shrugged her basalt shoulders, and continued to pop off the grapes, one-by-one. "Your father still isn't enjoying death very much. He keeps complaining about eating only clay. It's like he expects me to do something about it." She fixed her sparking carnelian eyes on me and I shivered. "What have you come for now, darling?"

"I need to vanquish the Bronze-Backed Bear," I said, and told her of the hunt and Leinu.

"Are you still hunting?" she asked, leaning forwards on her throne. "The Lord of the Netherworld has enough dead to look after without you adding your accidents to the lot."

"It's been a year since I've speared any slaves!"

"Torture this Leinu. Worked for the rest of your adversaries. Why did you bother coming all the way down here? Thanks for the grapes." She had eaten all the fruit-shaped globes, but lifted the silver branch up in salute.

"Because," I said, speaking faster as she nibbled on the branch, "he's already acquiesced to his death. If he wants something, I can't give it to him." I had to make Mother talk, and slow down her eating. "He spoke of the anemone; what does it mean that the numbers in his name add up to the same as this flower?"

"You are asking after the wrong riddle. Forget him. Bears are fonder of riddles than most creatures. I've a tip for you." She slipped the last of the silver into her mouth and spoke as she chewed. "Certain gods have told me that the Golden Lion has moved to these parts of the world. She's smaller than your bear."

"I have marked the Bronze-Backed Bear, and I shall have no other."

"You might control Nimur tight as a trireme, but the forest isn't your city." The fire died in her carnelian eyes, and her statue rested back on the throne.

It was my third husband's turn to share my bed that night, a dark prince from lands to the far south that were rich in gold mines. The gold I appreciated, but not the fact that they had forgotten to mention his snores in the wedding contract. I had learned to keep a slave by the bedside on his nights, and every time he drifted off the slave would poke him awake again. Despite this I, too, had little sleep.

In my dreams, I could see the pelt over my throne, nothing in the room gleaming as brightly or gloriously as its bronze sheen. I sat, felt it caress my bare flesh, rested my cheek against it. I stroked the fur, first pulling the hair between my fingers, followed by my tongue. It tasted of roses and I inhaled pistachios. And then a spear tore through my leg and I was thrown back into my bedchamber, awakened with a start.

"Just a bear," murmured husband-three, turning over and slinging his arm around me. "Why do you need it?" He opened his eyes, trying to peer at me through the darkness. I could see him clearly. "You have no cataracts, kidney stones, or burns."

I took his chin in my hand. "I have no need of earthly things. Blood, saliva, and hair aren't what I want."

The instant I rolled out of my bed, three guards rushed to their feet to follow me. I waved them away, and left my chambers to see Leinu alone.

He was not asleep in the bed provided him, but had pulled the blankets off and slept in a nest in one corner, arms at his side and legs folded beneath his body. As I shut the door behind me, he awakened and leapt to his feet. His fine tunic was rumpled.

"What would you call the Bronze-Backed Bear?" I asked.

"The river, the wind, protector of the forest," he said, pacing. He had kicked off his sandals, leaving his hairy feet bare.

"I am that. The forest is mine."

"Possession isn't protection." There was only the slightest limp in his walk now. He healed quickly.

"Well then, could you show me to this protector of the forest?"

"Can I show the hills to the moon, or the desert to the sun? I would be presumptuous to show a queen the domain she claims."

"But since the sun gazes upon so much, perhaps you could point her to a small detail that she has missed. Little wonder no one has tracked him before," I said, "when his trail was so clear to me."

"He would not be seen unless he wanted to be."

The moonlight caught on the honey and fruit dried on his cheeks. I laughed, despite myself. He stopped pacing and faced me, features suddenly quizzical.

"The words you speak are fine," I said, stifling myself, "but you haven't figured out how to eat." I knelt by his water bucket and wet the sleeve of my tunic so that I could dab the food off his cheeks. He flinched, and I laughed again. "You sound like a person, and look like a beast." His mahogany hair was frayed from the cutting, and already tangled. There was an ivory comb on a table. I ran it through his hair.

He snarled, lashing out with one hand. I caught his wrist and held his arm down by his side. "Too bad half my court has seen you already. What a game it would be to educate you and pass you off as one of them." I felt the muscles in his wrist beneath my hand, and squeezed harder. He whimpered whenever the comb struck a knot. I enjoyed having such an effect on a person of his physical prowess.

"Have all people become tools to you?" he asked. "Arms to hold your kills, hands to dress you, mouths to give you answers?"

I yanked the comb hard through his hair and threw it to the bed.

"Hardly an existence." He rubbed his head. "When have you last spoken true words, Irashar?"

"I am the daughter of a god and a king. I don't need truth."

"As much as we close our eyes, lies may wither, but once spoken the truth remains."

"Then speak this truth."

He turned to face me. "You live in fear. You separate your-self from others. They are close to you so that you might watch them, but still at a distance, for they are too occupied with trivial tasks. You speak of your greatness, and make it so that everyone believes you. I watched the golden, northern wall all day. Two peasants approached it, and three guards chased them away. My ears and eyes don't match."

"The legitimacy of my rule is written in the stars themselves."

"The stars are a long way from here."

I turned, but stopped for a moment and closed my eyes, feeling his moist breath upon my neck.

"You cannot change the stars," he said. "You can only decide how they change you."

"Over-tunic of tree wool, dyed purple from flowers on the northern mountains. Three ruby rings, peridot collar with soap-stone pendant," the astrologer said. "Tiara, onyx set in silver, for the full moon of the fifth month."

"I should like to wear the snake-shaped crown today," I said, pushing back the slave who held the silver tiara.

"Your majesty really should re-consider—"

"I have given it much consideration. Snakes." I snapped my fingers and a slave moved to retrieve it.

The astrologer snapped her own fingers. When the slave continued to carry the crown towards me, she slapped him. He ignored this and slid it onto my head.

"First Wanderer, risen at dusk," I said. "Astrologer leaves Nimur."

"You aren't above the gods' will!"

"But I am above yours." When she opened her mouth, I ran a finger across my throat. She fell silent and stalked out of my chamber.

I held out a hand to the nearest slave. "Remove these rings, clumsy things." The quiet in my chamber grew noticeable, as the courtiers had fallen silent. Even the bickering between my spouses had stopped for one gods' blessed moment. I sighed and impatiently beckoned the scribe to my side. "Send to the academy for a new astrologer. Let them know I want one more knowledgeable of earthly temperaments than the last. Astrologers don't just read the heavens."

He bowed his head.

"In the meantime," I said, addressing the chamber, "I shall interpret the stars. Am I not your queen?"

They murmured in response.

"Am I not your queen?" I roared, and they nodded vigorously.

That day I skipped audiences and took a stroll through the garden, on a route of my choosing for once, a husband on either arm and my wife and three of my children behind me. I crossed a ring of courtiers gathered around the fountain. With a snap of my fingers they cleared a path so that I could see what interested them.

Leinu had bent over the fountain, head submerged in the pool. He came up with his hair and beard dripping wet, and shook himself off. It sent water through the air. The courtiers laughed.

"Your majesty was most wise to bring the wild one here," my wife said to me. "He's more entertaining than last month's imbecile."

"He is Leinu," I said with a grin. And seeing how I favored him by calling him by name, they all fell silent. "Leave us."

Leinu and I reclined in the shade of a cypress tree by the fountain as the garden quickly emptied of the courtiers. I scooped my hand into the pool to splash him. He returned the motion and I whooped.

"Do you like my gardens?" I asked, wringing out my braid.

"Certainly the beds of poppies and medlar groves are delightful, as beautiful as your insipid ibises are, but I fail to understand them. Why is nature captured and refined for human tastes, when you might more easily walk in true nature the way the gods made it?" Hair stuck up out of his tunic's collar around his neck, longer than I remembered it had been yesterday.

"That's why I dislike them so. My father wouldn't go to the forest. It was not until I was older that I first beheld it, the textures and smells more alive than inside Nimur's walls. I had to learn of every bush, tree, and beast immediately. Why do you think I keep the forest clear of peasants, that only nobles with permission hunt in it with me?"

"But when you have your eyes upon the largest prize, you always hunt it alone."

"Because the legendary beasts are mine. My scribes write my contracts, my ambassadors negotiate with foreigners, my viziers draw up the city plans. All I have done is roll my seal at the bottom. There must be something of my making."

He glanced around at the courtiers' shadows that hung from the palace windows above, taking a peek at us and then scuttling away when my gaze followed his, and he murmured so quietly that only I could hear, "You've taken the stars."

"They still move the same as they always do." I shrugged. "I'd rather they say differently what my actions must be."

He chuckled. "And here I believed you would claim to move them yourself!"

"Of course I cannot move stars!"

"Yet you can claim the forest, hang up its carcasses for display and call it yours. What is so different between them?"

I looked at him then, very closely. Hair had fallen into his eye and he blinked several times. I pushed it back and ran the mahogany threads between my fingers, feeling bumps along its coarse texture. All my combing had been for nothing.. It was just as knotted.

"You will make the forest a garden," he said, and I traced my fingers down his cheek, over his lips.

"No more words," I whispered, holding his chin, and pulled him up with me.

"Your majesty, Leinu has escaped." The guard winced. He looked young and untried.

I gave him a smile instead, and this made him even more nervous. "Did you send a detail after him?" I asked. I stood on the balcony by my chambers, the early morning clear to all the stars. My new astrologer stood at my side, as I had been explaining the wanderers' movements to her.

"We await your command," he said.

"Which gate did he leave by?"

"West, towards the forest."

"Do not pursue him."

As the guard's footsteps faded behind us, the new astrologer said, "From what I understand, you enjoyed this Leinu's company over that of your court and even your own family. He was most dear to you."

"That's why I must let him go," I whispered, drumming my fingers on the rail.

"Perhaps a distraction would do for the queen, to clear him from your mind." The astrologer leaned beside me. "Before I had even slipped toe into Nimur, tales of your great prowess with the spear reached my ears. What could please you more than a hunt?"

All the omens meant it was a good morning for a hunt. A party gathered to me soon, and we rode between the poplars shrouded in darkness and pre-dawn fog. I crossed Leinu's tracks once, bare man-feet pressed into earth and so heavy they marked stone. They lead deeper into the forest and towards the slope of pistachio trees, and I closed my eyes tight for a moment. My hunting party bumbled behind me noisily, followed by under-breath curses as they rode their mounts into trees. It must have been blindingly dark for them, but not one dared speak up about it. I alone saw the forest.

We slowed when I found a deer nibbling a patch of mulberries. Her feet were splayed at four angles, neck arched downwards and achingly vulnerable. She would make an easy kill.

"The first," husband-two said, passing me a spear, "is always yours."

I closed my fingers around the shaft, bronze cooler in my palm than the morning air, and held it above my head, drawing back to throw. The deer, noticing the hunting party, raised her head. Her two ears twitched. The berry juice covered her muzzle. My arm lowered. Spooked, the creature danced away.

"Not like you to hesitate," he muttered.

I shoved the spear shaft back at him, and he fell silent.

I spotted a blackbird nestled in his nest on a lower branch, wings at his side, feet folded beneath. His eyes were still closed from sleep. I tapped my daughter on the shoulder. "See him?" I asked.

She squinted, passing me her bow and quiver. "Your shot's the truest."

But I shook them away. "Let us not disturb his rest."

We rode our mounts downhill to cross a small stream. A lion was bathing in it, her crown just skimming over the top. She lifted herself ashore to shake her entire body dry, spraying the poplar trunks with water. I smiled, my court tittered, and I shushed them. So noticing us, the lion drew back on her haunches. She hissed. Spears of the day's first light sent her fur scintillating like gold over her lithe muscles.

"'Tis an uncommonly beautiful beast," my cousin whispered. "You would be the envy of all rulers if you had her pelt to warm your bare throne."

"No," I said, grabbing my stallion's reins to turn back. "The hunt is over."

S. L. NICKERSON plays with galaxies for a living, and real life unfolds for her like a science fiction story. When she needs an escape hatch she paints worlds with words. She slips back into times that never were to remember the wonder in all things of our universe. Her writing has appeared in *Analog*, *Kalidatrope*, *Pulp Lit*, *The Colored Lens*, *Reflection's Edge*, and *The Prairie Journal*. She lives in Zürich where she is working on her Ph.D in astrophysics.

A CUT AND A PRAYER

by Janet K. Nicolson

SEVEN MONTHS PASS before Samar acknowledges that she can no longer feel Allah. In His place is a silent, depressive dread that interrupts her studies. Eventually, it consumes her waking hours until she cannot even pray without panicking. Since Allah is perfect, Samar knows the trouble is with her— and flesh problems have flesh solutions. Her fingers tremble as she taps out a number on her smart-phone; her soul shudders as she books an appointment with the Barber.

The day she visits the clinic, nimbus storm clouds paint the sky a muted taupe. Her hijab ripples in the gale, and she clutches her purse and denim jacket close to her chest. Her heart metaphorically skips as she trudges up the steps.

Inside, a nurse leads her through a corridor that snakes like spider silk, wrapping patients in the business of engineered neurological stimulation.

"Is this your first visit?" the woman asks gently.

Samar nods, wide amber eyes briefly meeting the nurse's gaze. *Do you sin too?* she wonders, as they enter the treatment room. *Do you challenge Allah's intentions?*

The styling chair is sterilized steel with white leather cushions. Samar gives the Barber a wavering smile as she settles into place. An older man, his face is framed by frameless glasses, graying whiskers, and a thin ring of hair.

"So, my dear." He snaps on a pair of latex gloves and adjusts his lab coat. The smell wafts into Samar's nose, gagging her. "What are we taking off today?"

"Taking off?" For a moment, Samar thinks she has gone to the wrong clinic. *I assume my fertility is fine. My clothes can remain where they are.*

"Ah, I see. You're new. I can show you." He retrieves a folder and withdraws several colorful printouts. They are painted with slice-cuts of a brain scan. "These are samples. Before, and after. Here, you can see under-activity in the ventromedial prefrontal cortex, which is the area commonly associated with hereditary depression. Does this make sense?"

She swallows slowly. "Yes."

"We will help your underdeveloped cortex pull its weight, and take some load from the other regions. Off the top, in places. It's where the name comes from. It takes no longer than a trim."

When Samar remains silent, he reaches for her file and riffles through her life. "Student, I see. Unmarried. Graduate studies. Lots of stress. Sociological religious development as your thesis. Interesting. You're devout." His lips twitch. "Doesn't your god bring you peace?"

"I am weak." Samar has whispered those words during her five daily prayers, her hundred daily wishes, and the infinite cries for help she has tossed on deaf family ears. "I pray and no matter what I ask, I cannot achieve it. I wish to love and serve Allah, but I can barely…"

The scarf comes off in a spiral into her hands. She squeezes it tightly between her fingers, her cheeks burning with shame as he sees exactly who she is.

"I live the five Pillars," she says, not knowing or even caring if he understands. "I pray, I volunteer, I fast. Last year I made the pilgrimage to Mecca. But the moment I feel close to Him, when I am about to touch Him, I become scared. I cannot do enough to please Him." *My soul is a desert.*

"Why, then, if it causes you stress?"

"Because I felt His love, before." She averts her eyes. "I want to again."

He retrieves a streamlined silver case from his workstation, cracks it open, and holds up a hair-thin, glimmering needle that is nearly the length of his hand. On the tip is a miniature processing system, powered by a solid-state lithium-ion nano-battery with a lifespan of six years. Samar has done her reading and knows it is a better option than pills, though that does not stop her shivering at the sight of the electrode.

"A bit off the top," the Barber says, eyebrow arched. "Let's start with that."

He lowers the styling cap and spreads her hair to the sides. The insertion needle is so fine that he doesn't need to shave her head. He connects a fibre optic cable from his workstation to the electrode's processor, then carefully feeds the set into the mechanism.

Even with the topical anaesthetic numbing her scalp, Samar retches as the electrode pierces her skull until it reaches her cerebral cortex. The styling cap holds her firmly against the spasms.

"That passes, with time," the Barber says as he works. He drags a finger across a nearby holographic screen, sending a column of readouts from red to yellow. Samar shudders as her mind fogs. "The second is easier. And the third, and fourth. There are usually more."

The cable clicks as he removes it from the needle's miniaturized processor.

The room brightens. Samar's heart calms. The continuous creases relax from her forehead, as if she hasn't just had invasive cortical rewiring and has always felt so content.

"That's better," the Barber says. "Can you think clearly?"

Outside, a robin whistles to welcome the morning commuters. He sings to her, a crystalline, innocent voice buried amongst urban cacophony. She wonders how she could have missed it before.

Samar smiles. "I think so. Yes." It is too early to bend to pray, and she is hesitant to test the processor's efficacy. But soon. "When should I come back?"

"You will need touch-ups. Perhaps a different style. But try this one first and see if you like it. Come back in a month."

Samar is lucky to wear the hijab; it hides the microprocessor whirring away against her skin. Others keep theirs under raised coifs and ball caps, and even more are overt about their transgression. Their shaved heads reveal dozens of fingernail-sized patches. Their smiles are easy and their eyes are clear, controlled by strings of electromagnetic binary that echo through their nervous tissue.

Her mother, in town from Dubai, frowns as they pass a muscled jock with seven implants. "Lost children," she says, shaking her head. A designer purse bounces against her silk hijab. "I find peace in Allah, as do you. I am blessed to have a daughter who sees the truth."

Samar instinctively pulls her scarf tighter. Her smile is easier to maintain, but even still, her mother hits a spot deeper than the electrode reaches. "Perhaps it helps them find the true path," she says carefully. "When they are lost."

"Only Allah provides that light." Her mother pulls ahead, leaving Samar to stare at her ebony cloak. "How are your studies? I come all this way to see you, and we spend it talking about sinners. Tell me about your thesis."

"Progressing. I must pass my comprehensive exams, first."

"Your father wishes you would study something different. Social work, perhaps. You like to help the poor. Why question our Prophet's words if they are already true?"

"Not questioning. Re-focusing. Words shift meaning, over time. What brought life last millennium may now bring death. We are a people of peace. Others can administer to the children. I will study the Qur'an and teach them how."

"Then teach them well. You know we trust you."

Samar stops and frowns. For a moment, the bird calls and traffic congestion pass away, leaving a thundering pounding in her ears. Her breastbone aches. Lips pressed, she keeps the cry inside her gut, and forces oxygen into her lungs. The panic is familiar and debilitating.

I am weak, she thinks. *This is not Allah. It is me.*

Her mother, entranced by the nearby halal deli and the sudden presence of eligible young suitors, steers Samar by her elbow towards the shop. If she feels her daughter's shuddering arms, she does not acknowledge them.

"We can only do so much in the Emirates," the older woman says, sneaking a glance at the men while they converse. "You should join one of the young women's groups. They do social outings. Find a nice boy to look after you. If your father approves, we can pay for the wedding. I know that is not very traditional, but it is hard to assess men from overseas."

"That's very nice," Samar says, and as the words tumble out the electrode spasms, its circuit struggling to halt the emotional torrent forging like a tsunami across her psyche. She nearly gasps as the processor catches up with her anxiety. For a moment, it is like a veil has been peeled from her eyes, and she sees the sun as luminescent and bright as Allah Himself. "But, there is one other thing you could do."

"Anything for you, daughter."

"My tablet's screen is faulty. I can't afford a new one." Samar glows radiantly, and as close as she feels to Him, the lie skirts undisturbed through her consciousness.

I am beautiful and the world is perfect, she thinks. *Only sinners lie. This is a necessity. I am not a sinner.* Then the halo fades, and the sounds of the mortal world return to her ears.

"I will have your father send money," her mother says, with a dismissive wave of the hand. "Though a boy would be better. Let me know when you pass your exams."

"I started school as a psychology student," the Barber explains, as he adjusts a new processor for the fitting. He glances at Samar in the styling chair, before returning to his computer work. "I have clinical depression. I thought by studying I would learn more about myself. Instead, I learned about the frailty of the human body. And then, I discovered how to overcome it."

Samar has grown comfortable in his presence. He does not judge her like Samar's mother would if she knew about her daughter's clinic bills. Even without her veil, she feels protected by the Barber's professionalism. He understands her, though strangely, he does not use the electrodes himself. Samar wonders why, though she doesn't build the courage to ask.

Sometimes, the Barber hums while he works. Today it is Vivaldi, and he imbues the energy of the Four Seasons into Samar's newest microcomputer.

"Some clients only come once," he says. "Their bodies reject the implants, or their minds reject the stimulation. The smallest minority only require one." He grimaces. "Return clients are a different challenge."

"Mmmm?" The admission surprises her. "What do you mean?"

"Finding balance is difficult." The Barber applies the anaes-thetic, waits a few moments, then slides the electrode into the slot. The cap whirs and hisses as it presses the needle down-ward. "Too little cortical inhibition, and you feel too much. Too much, and you feel nothing at all. Too much good, too much bad, it all breaks our balance. We need life in small, workable doses. Not the world on our shoulders."

"Feeling nothing is preferable to pain," Samar says through clenched teeth, as the needle punctures her skull. She no longer retches, though it still makes her shiver. "I have felt too much for too long."

What I wish, she thinks, is to feel Him, and Him alone. *He is a calm centre in my storm. Like a gentle butterfly's wings fluttering my face, he wakes me with the morning sun and the twilight moon.*

"That's the brain's will." He snaps away the fibre cable. "It's an elastic organ. It's our nature. We're not static beings."

I will become one, Samar thinks, as the euphoria overtakes her. Three electrodes ago, she asked the Barber to dial up the effects. The window glows with holy light as Allah reaches to her from a higher place. And where He is, there is nothing except the hum of her breathing, the gently drifting dust motes, and the Barber's pained smile.

"If it becomes too intense, come see me immediately," he says. "My haircut is a chemical fix, not a situational one."

Samar passes her first and second comprehensive exams with near perfect scores. She is a machine, or so her instructors tell her. Head to the desk, digital pen in hand, she methodically scrawls her internal encyclopaedia to the glass pages. The panic that has cowed her in the past remains cocooned in the clinic's invisible spider webs. Each adrenaline spike is intercepted by a gentle electric buzz. Each errant thought, so invasive in its growth, is cut at the root by the same.

"I wish I had your composure," says Tricia, one of Samar's classmates, after the third exam concludes. "What's your secret?"

"Allah guides me," Samar says. She gestures around the classroom, eyes tearing up with euphoria as the illuminated glass displays twinkle with holy light. "I am on His mission. By passing these exams, I can help His children. His light gives me focus."

"He works better than coffee, then." Tricia laughs. "The god of African fair-trade beans just steals my money. Say, did you want to come with us? We're going out for some drinks later. I think you can have tea, right?"

Samar smiles and shakes her head. "Tea, yes. But I need to work. My dissertation will not write itself."

"That's too bad. Don't work so hard, hon. Reward yourself."

She is not wrong, but for Samar, the work is its own reward. She has waited years to feel this good, and a frustrating, remnant fear whispers that her success is temporary. She needs to finish things before she spirals back to hell.

Samar spends her remaining school hours in the library, searching the databases for articles on modern Islam. The words imprint on her brain like silhouette letters on a monitor. The more she reads, the larger the euphoric bubble in her gut becomes, until she nearly bursts with pride. At this speed, she will complete a draft weeks ahead of her supervisor's expectations.

That evening, Allah takes Samar's hand and leads her home through a haze of amber streetlights, winking car signals, and breath-stealing smog. She pulls her veil closer, thankful for the protection against the metropolis' congested atmosphere. When a man lunges at her from the stairs of the local courthouse and spews profanities because she dares to desecrate his homeland, she blesses him.

Samar is invincible. With her god beside her, she can conquer any academic exam, racist transient, or philosophical quandary about her faith. Allah's light illuminates the stained paint and scattered garbage bags of her condominium complex. The mess is simply the coverings of life's beauty, and she smiles at the familiar squalor as she enters her apartment and tosses her bag to the floor.

What she cannot overcome is her mother sitting in the kitchen, eyes wet, and a glowing tablet in her hand.

"Why?" The older woman slides the computer across the table. A copy of a bill glows on the screen, the words 'marked paid' stamped across the numbers. "Why didn't you tell me?"

For a horrific moment Samar feels empty. No networked cortical micro-server can win over her mother's distress.

"You hacked my account?" Samar whispers.

"You have not been yourself. We were worried. It is under your father's name, anyway. You know that."

Samar fumbles to find His fingers' calming touch, but all she retrieves is a jumbled prayer, the cast-off junk of an ancient bazaar in a desolate, desert land. The language cannot possibly mirror His purity.

"I am your grown daughter," says Samar. Her mother cringes with the invisible slap. "What right do you have to break into my things?"

"Worry. Love. Come home with us." She gestures at Samar's veil, obviously aware of what hides beneath the lavish silk. "You do not need those things. Patiently persevere, the Prophet tells us. My daughter is not weak."

"She is." Samar gasps as her skull throbs. The Barber will be angry, she thinks. He does good work, and she always finds a way to ruin the balance. "I work at the soup kitchen. I pray for forgiveness. I want to make a difference in this world. But to do that, I must survive. Allah brings me peace, it is true. And the only way I can find Him is through this."

She untangles the headscarf from her hair. Her mother's eyes become chicken eggs jammed into the sockets.

"Is it so weak," Samar asks, "to know the way to Allah and take the path?"

"No, but—"

"Is it weak to seek His love and do His work? Whoever chooses to follow guidance follows for her own good, and those who go astray do so at their own loss. The Prophet wrote those words, and they are true. The Barber is a kind man, mother. His methods are different, but he wishes to heal me so I can continue doing Allah's bidding. This is my way. My Jihad."

Her mother looks old, Samar thinks. And tired. The woman raises a wavering hand as tears flood her face and cascade across her silks. "Beware deserts, the soul included," she says. "Do you feel Allah, or a shadow love?"

Samar knows this desert. She feels the coarse sands whenever her processors overload. She feels them now, as her limbs contort like a carved ivory statue and she cascades downward towards the kitchen tiles. Ebony lizards dart across her vision, populating her Arabian Desert with the shadowy firing of cortical tissues.

Perhaps she needs more off the top, she thinks, as the reptiles devour her consciousness to her mother's discordant wails.

The Barber visits Samar in the hospital. She only recognizes him when his lips curve into his characteristic melancholy smile. Instead of the clinical lab coat, he wears a mouse-nibbled, black leather jacket, a neck scarf, and a pair of calf-high biker's boots. He shrugs off the coat and drapes it across the visitor's chair, revealing beautiful sleeve tattoos. His body is a canvas, like hers. Only, his scars are different.

"You have a nice name," she says, pointing at his visitor tag. "Harold."

"My friends call me Hank." He settles in the chair, left empty since the previous night. Samar's mother left to sleep, and her father is still in Dubai. "How are you feeling?"

She shrugs and glances at the results of her misadventure. The intravenous line only brings her liquids, now; they cut off the neuro-modulators days earlier. When the observation period ends and the doctors stop flitting about her like gnats, she will be free to go.

"You're lucky," Hank says, clasping his hands against his knees. He bobs one leg in rhythm with the room's air conditioning. "Your nervous system went into shock. It almost shut down."

"The desert is cold and lonely," Samar says, with a tiny smile. "They said you helped me."

"I stabilized your brain." He frowns, until his forehead wrinkles like elephant's skin. "I should have listened to my instincts. I gave you too many."

"I asked for them."

"If you add equivalent troughs and crests to a wave, you will reach equilibrium. But the ups and downs are harder to weather."

Her fingers move unconsciously to her shaved scalp, bandaged in places from the invasive intervention.

"I removed all but one," he says, reading her thoughts.

Samar's shoulders slump. "One is not enough. I could barely feel Him." Her mother's words return to her, unbidden. "My mother thinks I did not feel Him at all. That the processors made me spiritual. I am smart, Hank. I know what I felt as a child, and I understand modern neurology. It was the same."

When Hank replies, he treads the words like they are stones marking the path through a sandstorm. "I didn't make you feel God, if that's what you think. I could do that, and for some people, it's enough. But you're an educated woman. What you wanted was to be happy. How that happiness took form, in your mind, was up to you."

He spreads his hands to her, revealing decades of creased lines and a matched set of stark white scars across his wrists.

"Humans are fragile," he says quietly. "Sometimes we need help, from ourselves or others. Ask yourself, Samar. Are you happy with what you're doing? Where you live, what you study? Change what you can. Be the person you want to be, regardless of what others think."

He is right, she knows. She is not sure what needs to change. But if she is the grown woman she claims to be, it is time to assess her life and find out. She trails a finger across her scalp, lips parting as she finds an unbandaged area of skin where the remaining processor whirs.

"Thank you," she says.

The Barber moves to the door and pauses at the threshold, his face illuminated by the sunlight filtering through the window. He looks almost holy, and more than a little like her deliverer.

"Love yourself," he says, and taps his head. "If you can learn, then perhaps the intervention will remind you when you forget."

Samar thinks she can do that. As she pieces together the words of her afternoon prayer, and realizes she is asking herself for forgiveness, she decides she can. There is plenty of hate in the world. She does not need to include herself. Allah loves her, regardless.

The sun's rays transit the drapes, gradually illuminating the walls and the laminate floor until the tropical colors fade into deep sunset. Samar's mind stills with rise of the moon, and the gentle whirring of a processor whispers reassurances as she sleeps.

JANET K. NICOLSON was born in Regina and has lived in the ice and cold ever since. She currently works as a technical writer for a telecommunications firm. When she's not watching her border collie herd her cat and husband around the house, she can be found searching the local book store for novels about Big Dumb Objects, rocking video games, or subjecting audiences to her piano compositions. Her work has also appeared in *On Spec Magazine*.

Under the iron rain

by John Park

THE TRACK DETOURED for several hundred paces around a partially overgrown crater. Jason thought he should stop and look for fragments of metal in it — "Five minutes," he muttered to himself; "there might be a month's living in it" — but found he could not face the delay. His mule-cart jolted over stones and ruts for another twenty minutes before the track dipped toward the old highway that ran beside the river. "Stop now."

In the shelter of a clump of elms Jason put down the object he had been holding in his lap. "Got to hide you now." Its glossy black pane had soaked up the pale sunlight for the last two hours; the device would be ready. He carefully enfolded it in a length of flowered linen fabric and returned it to its hiding place in his traveling trunk. Then he picked up the reins and drove onto the cracked and rutted surface of the highway.

"Not so long now. There'll be others along soon. Try to stop talking to yourself."

An hour later he was on the bridge to the city, the planks between the stone arches rumbling under his wheels, and the river oozing below, gray and relentless.

Built in an earlier age, for a larger city, the gate was too wide for the amount of traffic. Its guards wore frayed, faded red and gold uniforms and carried gilded axes with chipped blades. The nearest guard, sallow, thin and gray-bearded, about Jason's age, coughed in the dust raised by the traffic and held up his gauntleted hand.

"Your name and business, Sieur."

Above them, the sky flickered. A piercing point of light crossed a patch of blue, leaving a white line scored behind it; it vanished behind cloud and then reappeared below, streaking towards the hills on the western horizon. Jason, the guards and the other waiting travelers stared towards the invisible impact, counting silently until the long-drawn mutter reached them like distant thunder.

Jason moistened his lips. "Not an omen, I pray."

"Just a harbinger of the ceremony, I'm sure. The Goddess's shield continues to defend us; long may it do so. And your name and business, if you would."

"I work in metal." Jason gave his name and handed the guard a silver coin. "I'm engaged to repair the avatar of the sky-god, of Fremden, in your main square."

The guard nodded and palmed the coin, and handed him a slip of paper printed from blunt type and signed with a scrawl. "Twenty days. You are to show this to any city officer that asks for it."

And then Jason was inside the walls. "City." his voice whispered. "She's here." He had forgotten the smells of a city: smoke, dung, incense…. The cart rolled from smooth asphalt to cracked asphalt, rattled on cobbles. He waited while four guards with whips and spears herded a dozen limping men in chains across his path. "The treadmill for you, is it?" he muttered. "The water pumps? But maybe that saves you from worse." Then he twitched the reins and turned onto the side street overhung by the upper storeys of grimy wooden buildings.

The street opened onto a large square bounded on two sides by gray stone walls patched with grimy brick. On a raised platform at the far end was a large granite slab, and over it loomed the pitted, blackened metal figure of a gigantic creature, something like an angry human male. Four young men were erecting scaffolding about the statue.

Beside the workers were two more red-uniformed guards with axes. Their officer bore a long-barreled firearm slung from a leather strap over his right shoulder. The weapon had a magazine in place behind its wide trigger guard; it was either a genuine relic or a remarkable copy.

Jason drove up to the officer and showed his pass.

"You're the artisan? Wick's been waiting for you." The officer pointed to a hut behind the statue.

"I'll take you over there. Robert Hillborn— Major," he added by way of introduction.

As they walked, Jason nodded towards the officer's weapon. "You keep that Steyr in excellent condition, Major."

"An heirloom Sieur, our family's pride. You know the type, then?"

"It's part of what I do. Do you still use it? Will it shoot?"

"Alas, probably not. There are springs and small parts inside I can't reconstruct."

"I might be able to help you. That's also something I do."

"But then there'd be the matter of ammunition. It's impossible to find."

"It could be made."

Hillborn turned and looked him in the eyes. "I imagine that would be very expensive, wouldn't it? And of course, such trafficking in explosives would be unlawful, Sieur, as I'm sure you realize." He gave Jason another hard look, then moved on. "Now let's get you settled in with Wick."

Chandler Wick was a burly red-faced man with a white spade-shaped beard. When the major knocked and opened the door of the hut, Wick rose heavily and limped towards them. He offered his left hand to shake and Jason noted that his right was carved from wood.

After the major had made the introductions, the three turned to look at the statue.

"Fremden's arms have to rise," Wick said, "and his head too, at the moment of ascension. The eyes should move, but that's been impossible for five years at least. It's probably just a matter of cleaning the gears and replacing a few worn parts, but I can't get in there and do much myself any more. We've got six days to get it working."

"It's just gears and pulleys worked offstage— for show, then?" Jason asked. "It's not needed for the actual killing?"

"For the ascension— that's what they call it. Though where a goat's going to ascend to, only the Sisterhood could say. No, this old thing is just part of the tradition— from when almost everyone believed and it was a real virgin or three on that slab."

"Or one of the temple girls," said Hillborn. "They're hardly virgins."

Jason tightened his lips, but before he could say anything, Wick looked at the height of the sun and said: "Look, you've got to stable your mule and settle in, and you can't do anything till I've had the lads take the back plate off the statue. You'll have brought your own gear but I'll show what we've got in the smithy as well. We've a room reserved for you. It's where I'm staying myself, so I'll set the lads to work and when we're done with the smithy I'll see you settled. Then we can make a start first thing in the morning."

On the way to their lodgings, Wick asked Jason about what he'd found in fresh craters.

"Just metal. It's useful. I keep thinking of things I could make with it when I get the time."

"When I was apprenticing," Wick said, "one of the Masters talked about one of the pieces of sky-metal he'd found. It was half-melted, of course, but he could see this piece had had tubes in it, and lumps like taps or valves. Another time he said these strikes were old weapons, giant cannon shells still aimed at us from a war someone didn't know had ended."

"That's not so far from what the Sisterhood says, is it? The Goddess giving herself to Fremden, to be allowed to put up her shield and defend the city from thunderbolts."

"But that man," Wick went on, "he knew things. He said he'd seen little engines, boxes that would fit in your hand and talk to each other across half the width of this city. You just had to give them sunlight, like a box of seedlings, and you could send an order no one else would know about. That's what he said."

"Strange," said Jason. "I've never come across anything like that, myself." He asked about the temple.

"It's up the hill, on the Circle. The dome with the gold paint, and the columns with torches burning all night."

"No— I mean, I know where it is...."

"Oh, you mean the girls, the hets, heteras. You want to *worship* there."

Jason shrugged uncomfortably. "Been widowed for a while now. You know how it is. What are they like? Cripples dredged up from the gutter, fat widows...?"

"Who have you been talking to? No one from this city, I'll wager. Go see for yourself— they brought in some new recruits recently."

The next day he began work on the statue. When he climbed the scaffold, he found that the apprentices had cleaned off most of the grime, but struts and cams were still dark with corrosion and some were flaking away to nothing. Lubrication channels were clogged. He guessed that whatever Wick's predecessors had used for oil or grease had thickened and not been replaced. They had just applied more force as the works glued up, until things started to fail.

Once he would have gone down the ladder raging at their incompetence, their utter disrespect— for decent workmanship if not for the god they supposedly believed in. But then he had had faith. Now he simply began making a mental list of parts he would have to construct.

In the evening Jason went to the temple.

The priestess, plump and hard-eyed, draped in faded green silk, interlinked her ringed fingers and curved her carmined lips into a thin smile. "The Pansceptra chooses which of her handmaidens will incarnate her spirit on each occasion."

"But if I offered a donation to her temple, perhaps the Goddess would choose to please me in return."

She frowned but took the coins. "Your choice then," she said and clapped her hands. Four heteras entered the room.

"Do you have any with red hair?" he asked. "Average height or more?"

She jerked her head impatiently. "Milla, call Cyrenia."

He interrupted, pointing. "No, stop. I like that one. Her."

"Melani has dark hair, as you can see."

The young woman he indicated had stopped dead, her face blank.

"I like her. I choose her." He fumbled for money again. "I ask the Goddess to choose her for me."

"Melani?" asked the priestess.

The hetera hesitated then came forward. "It's all right. Yes, I'll go with the man."

The priestess began to remind him of the injunctions against harming her acolytes.

The girl repeated, "It's all right," and led him down a rush-matted corridor with red-shaded lamps sensuously shimmering in austere stone alcoves.

"Can't you cover yourself up?" he said roughly. Then, "Why *Melani*?"

"The Goddess bestowed the name."

"You've dyed your hair. Doesn't the Goddess mind?"

"The Goddess understands women. I think you've been away from them for too long."

He nodded bitterly. "A lot, since your mother died. Sylvia—"

"Melani."

"All right—" But they had reached the room and she was opening the door.

"I take it you haven't really come here to experience the incarnation of the Goddess."

"Sylvia!"

"Then sit down and I'll prepare tea." She put a silver pot to heat over a spirit lamp. "Why are you here? If you try to take me away, you'll be in trouble."

"I know. I've seen your guards."

"Good. And besides, I took an oath. I'm bonded."

He hardly heard her. "You've grown."

"I'm older. In fifteen years I'll be unmarketable here."

"You've turned hard."

"What did you expect?" she asked. "Yes— what *did* you expect?"

He looked away from her and clenched his fists. "I tell strangers I never had any children." His voice shook. "I told everyone else you'd died."

"You're ashamed of me."

"I never dreamed you'd go to— these people." He reached towards her. "Help me a bit, girl— I have come to you. When I found out where you were, I managed to arrange this work on the statue so I could come here. You don't know what that took. Give me something."

She looked at him. "All right," she said finally. "I'll show you some of why I'm here. Look." She pulled two wide copper bracelets from her left wrist and showed him the inside of her arm.

For a moment he was speechless. "Who did that?" Then he looked at her. "*Why?*"

"Sylvia knew why she did it. But the Goddess has freed Melani of the memory. Of many memories."

Numbly he said, "I don't think you can run away from such things forever. You'll always be haunted."

"But I'm not haunted. I'm part of something, I'm helping to protect what's left. And it's more than that. There are moments here, when everything has stopped, everything is still, waiting — and then there's nothing but light bursting from above, light everywhere, pouring through me, filling me. In the next moment everything will start again — sound, motion, pressure, but just now there's only the light, the stillness. When I go that's how I want it to be."

"You don't want to die!"

"I know that's just words," she said, as if he had not spoken, "but I can give you a glimpse— so you'll understand why I stay."

She took the pot from over the flame and poured from it into two white porcelain beakers. She stirred a spoonful of gray powder into each and handed him one. "Drink."

He emptied the beaker and put it on the table. In the bottom lay a fine brown residue like rust.

"How do you feel?" she asked.

He looked up. "All right. What happens now?"

She stood. "We can go for a walk."

She opened the door and led him outside. The night was clear and moonless. His eyes had become more sensitive, for overhead hung stars like strewn jewels— reefs and clusters and thrown handfuls of stars, throbbing and glittering. As he looked, there came the long feather-flicker of a fall, and he shivered, awaiting the impact, wondering if this would be when it all ended.

He stared as the bright track seemed to be pushed away from him so that it passed beyond the roofs towards the half-visible horizon. He shivered again.

"You're cold," she said. "But you'll get warmer as we walk."

Soon they approached the city gate, where the bearded guard coughed and wished them good night.

And then they were alone on the bridge. In the quiet the water rushed and spluttered about the bridge pylons. His boots rang on the planks, her steps quiet beside him.

"From what I've heard," he said, "your goddess isn't a very forgiving being."

"She will welcome those who openly acknowledge and turn away from their errors. Do you feel you need forgiveness?"

"How far have we walked?" he asked. "I still can't see the shore."

"It's all right." Her arm went around his waist.

"Sylvia?"

"Not Sylvia."

"Sorry. Melani."

"No, not Melani either. Have you forgotten me already, Jason?"

"Rhoda?"

"Why are you troubling our daughter when your business is with me? It's all right, you can look at me. You won't see something from a butcher's shop."

"Rhoda—" His voice failed.

She was no longer at his side but slipping away, drifting further and further into the dark.

He ran for her, struck the parapet and went over, plunged towards the black rush of water.

He opened his eyes as Melani tugged the beaker from his fingers.

"You're back then," she said in a thin voice.

"How did you know what I'd see?" he muttered, staring at his hands. "That I'd see anything?"

"A mistake. Melani made a mistake."

He looked up. "What happened? You look ill. Did you take an overdose?"

"An overdose?" she said. "Yes, I suppose I did." She made a visible effort and stood up. "You're going back to your lodgings now? What then? Will you continue your work on the statue?"

He sighed heavily and then nodded. "I'll finish what I came to do."

"Then go," she said. "Don't return to the temple."

"Sylvia?— Melani?"

"Leave the city. Don't ever look for Sylvia again."

He walked by the first tavern he saw, and the second. At the third, its shield-and-fireball signboard swinging within sight of his lodgings, he gave up and went in. His mouth mumbled and he tried not to hear it.

Some time later, Wick slid onto the bench opposite him.

"You're putting them away tonight. How was the temple?"

Jason looked up; then he felt his face twist, and he turned away, shaking his head.

"Ah. Right," Wick said kindly. "Well, it's not the end of the world. It starts to happen to all of us now and then. You were probably nervous, too. Thing is to get back in the saddle as soon as you can. And there's powders to take, if you want."

"No. No *drugs*. Not going back, that's all. I'm not going."

Wick sighed. "Women, wives. Dead or alive, always trouble for someone. You know, the Major, Hillborn— his wife ran off some years back."

Jason blinked and focused.

"Yes. He was a Fremdist. The God told him to get her back. He went after her and found the two of them. She wouldn't come and it got ugly. They'd bonded under the Goddess— utter fidelity on her part. That made it worse."

"Probably drove him mad…. I've seen it happen, wife going with one of them." Jason said thickly. "Did he hurt her?"

"It got ugly," Wick repeated, and stopped.

Across the room, quiet fell, conversations halted in midphrase. Heads lifted; tankards were held still or placed carefully on the tables. Suddenly sobering, Jason caught the long rolling mutter and wondered if the floor had really shaken.

Wick pursed his lips. "Another close one." He lowered his voice. "Her shield's not what it used to be, I'll swear. A bit closer and that would have been someone's house."

"Your arm— it was a strike did that?"

"That's what they tell me. Can't remember it, not a thing from that whole day. I was awake when they started to take the arm off, though. I remember that."

"Lose anyone in that strike?"

"No, it just found a way through the shield and picked me. Why?"

Jason took a swallow from his mug. "One took my wife a while back," he said. "Hit our house while I was out."

"Sorry."

"I don't think about it much anymore." He rubbed his jaw, swallowed again, grimaced. "Just the odd dream. You know?"

"They say it hits before the sound or the shock. If it's coming for you, you'll never know."

"There's the *light*," Jason said. "You'd see that before it hit. You'd know you'd been found."

The next morning, Jason was up on the scaffold when Wick and a merchant entered the square. Their voices broke into his thoughts.

"Been fifty years at least…"

Jason couldn't be sure of what he had heard.

"…some folks unhappy."

"Most of her regulars, for sure."

He swung over to the ladder and slid down it like an empty-headed apprentice a third his age.

The two stopped and turned as he stumbled up to them.

"I heard you." He was gasping worse than his exertions could explain. "A change in the ceremony?"

"Nothing that need change your plans. They're going back to the old way.".

Jason mouthed, unable to get words out of his throat.

"A sacrifice," Wick explained helpfully. "One of the heteras has offered herself."

His throat dried. He could not have uttered a sound.

"One of the new ones, too. We were just saying, there'll be some disappointed customers after this week."

When Jason managed to speak, his question sounded appallingly banal. "Why?"

"Look around, Sieur," said the merchant, "look around—decay, vice, avarice. We are unworthy. We have received two nearby strikes this week. A clear warning. We have to make amends. The Sisterhood knows this as well as anyone…"

Madness, Jason thought as he went back to work. *Madness everywhere*. There was still a theoretical chance it was one of the other girls. And even if it was his daughter, he still had to know.

"No," said the priestess. "Melani is not available. As perhaps you have heard, she has been inspired to offer herself to the Besieger, as was formerly traditional among us." She swallowed, but continued firmly. "So of course she is sequestered now and will be undergoing purification until the ceremony."

"What did you do to her? Don't throw your platitudes in my face! I'll—"

Her hand was on the bell-pull. He stopped and lowered his hands. He turned away and after a while was able to speak again.

"When did she decide? Was it the night I came—?"

"The Goddess may show her will at any time and through any medium she finds appropriate. I see no point in questioning her preferences. If you have no other business with us, I'll have the guard show you out."

He checked that his window looked out on an empty street with no other building nearer than twenty paces; then he closed the shutters and lit the lamp. His fingers shook. He made sure his door was locked and put a chair-back under the handle. Finally he lugged his traveling chest onto the bed, unlocked it and opened the lid. With his body between the chest and the door he took a fine-bladed tool from his kit and slid back the four tiny catches that released the false bottom of the lid and exposed the hidden compartment. For a few moments he gazed at the wrapped bundles there and tried to weigh quantities against unknown future needs. "Use it all! If it doesn't work there'll be nothing worth saving it for!"

His jaw began to tremble. He put his face in his hands and rocked back and forth and gasped for breath. Then he sat up and wiped his eyes, made himself concentrate. The sender still held the charge he had given it on his journey here. He would take the nerve weapon and spend two sticks and two precious triggers. He would keep the rest.

The day of the ceremony was gray and damp. Crowds began to filter into the square an hour beforehand. Jason watched for a while, then went back to the inn and checked his preparations.

When he returned the crowd was denser, the drizzle had stopped and the sun was breaking through low clouds. He was looking for officials, priests, ceremonial robes when he saw a covered chair carried into a side street that opened onto the square. The sunlight caught the side window as the chair was lowered to the ground and he saw her. She wore a light green robe, and her hair had been coiled on top of her head. She looked pale and half asleep, sedated perhaps.

He realized he was still staring and that he had been given this moment to act.

He ran and grabbed a thin man drinking from a flask of wine and yelled in his face. "Out! Get help! Earthquake! Impact! Strike! Run, run! Get help!"

As the confusion began, he turned and pulled the little silver box from his pocket and pointed it across the square. He thumbed the button and a stack of wine barrels exploded. Some of the crowd spun towards the noise. One or two screamed. Others fell to the ground, covering their heads, or began to run. He yelled more useless commands into the chaos.

Then he used the box again. There was another shocking detonation. Smoke boiled up around the statue. Its arms rose as counterweights shifted. Both hands raised to strike. The head loomed forward over the crowd, eyes wide, mouth gaping. Then the body sagged as a leg buckled; it heeled sideways and crashed to the ground.

By then Jason had reached the chair and was pulling out the small weapon that induced convulsions.

He emerged from the crush and the smoke with his daughter over his shoulder, her robes half-hidden under an empty sack. He made it down a narrow alley to where his cart was waiting.

He had not expected the panic. "The shield! The shield's down!" they yelled and began to run. He hadn't thought to add that fear to his shouts. The mule cart rolled through the western gate among a wave of refugees.

Clear of the city, he let the mule choose its own pace. She lay in the back of the cart, her eyes closed but breathing steadily. He decided he could not let himself worry about her until they were a few hours further from the city.

There was no pursuit. Behind him the road was clogged with refugees. Occasionally a faster vehicle overtook them and rattled past. The sun strengthened; a mild breeze brushed across his face.

His thoughts drifted. He realized he was speaking them aloud, with no clear idea of where they might lead.

"If they'd known what they were doing, they could have seen it wasn't a strike. I was afraid they'd smell the burnt powder. And some of them must have guessed she was leaving me. But perhaps I looked too upset to be acting. I was, too, I was."

Then he shook himself out of the past. He looked at her and laughed at his own melancholy. She was alive. They were free. With luck his biggest problem would be to persuade her she had a right to live.

The road divided. He took the left fork, which would take him away from the river.

Behind him, his daughter spoke.

"The Goddess has left the city."

As he turned to her, in the corner of his eye he glimpsed the flash. A column of smoke began to boil up over the centre of the city. Seconds later, the sound of the impact rumbled over them.

She stared at something he could not see; then her eyes focused on him.

"Melani has remembered," she said. "You left Sylvia in the cart when you went back in the house with those brown sticks. You took her into the wood and you watched for Momma to come home. Sylvia woke up. She saw you point that thing at the house. There was the big noise, the house fell down, and you started crying. Melani knows now. She knows. Melani is very angry."

He stopped the cart and turned to her.

"Rhoda was leaving me— I was mad. I should have told you. I would have. But it's not too late. It can't be too late—"

She met his gaze with a look that froze him. And then she looked up past him. Brightness fell upon her face and her eyes widened in wonder.

"*The light.*"

Turning, he experienced an instant of blazing clarity.

JOHN PARK is an ex-Briton who now lives in Ottawa, where he has done research at the National Research Council and been part of a scientific consulting firm. In 2012 his novel, *Janus*, was published by *ChiZine* Publications. "Iron Rain" is his seventh appearance in the *Tesseracts* series.

THE SHADOWS OF GODS

by Mary-Jean Harris

SCALES OF THE DARKEST RUBY, flecked with tawny gold of the setting sun. And eyes; these were no mortal eyes, but black marbles glinting with flames. A long face curved outwards with nostrils fanning in and out in a faint rhythm that could have sustained life for centuries.

"He bites," the man whispered. A perk of a smile crept under the thin curls of his long black moustache.

"I'm not afraid," Toulouse insisted. His hand was approaching the viper, and he did not withdraw it. He understood snakes, at least as much as one could hope to, though he still kept his long fingers a good foot away from the viper's jaws. He knew well that mankind's knowledge about snakes was duplicitous: they were good and evil, tame and perilous, or Toulouse's favorite, "The devil and the angel in one hissing mystery," which his father's Sufi apprentice, Rayan, had once told him.

Toulouse was kneeling on the dusty stones beneath the man's cerulean silk canopy that was upheld by two wooden poles and fastened to the clay wall behind him. When a hot wind wound through the streets, the silk would flutter and cause sunlight to dapple over the faces of the man and his snake.

Toulouse looked into the eyes of the snake and asked, "What's his name?" He tilted his head and the snake swerved with him, stretching erect from the top of the lid of a sun-faded basket and revealing his pale red underbelly as if it were dusted with sands from the desert.

"He has not yet told me," the man said, sitting calm on a purple-dyed woven cushion. The man was rather old, or so he seemed to Toulouse, for he was older than Toulouse's father. Two black curls strung with silver hairs emerged from the sides of the man's turban above his ears. Although his attire was no finer than faded green trousers and a sheer cream-colored tunic, a star-shaped medallion of fine rose-tinted glass hung from a tarnished brass chain around his neck, and a silver-threaded cloth belt was tied high around his waist, entwined with a labyrinth of dark green snakes chasing one another's tails.

"My father told me that if you name them, they will take on the attributes of the name," Toulouse told the man. "Like Merkur— that was one of his older snakes."

"Not all snakes are Silvrien," the man said.

"Silvrien?" Toulouse asked.

The man looked to the snake as he added, "He is a Lucefate. Not for humans, as the Silvrien are, yet more intelligent." Although the man spoke well in Arabic, and slow enough for Toulouse to understand, his voice was accented with what seemed to be traces of an even older language that now only remained on the tongues of hermits and wanderers in the hills and deserts.

Toulouse wondered just how much these Lucefates could do with their intelligence. "Are they the ones that people tell stories of, the ones who use fire to control people and other animals?" he asked, rather excited by the prospect.

The man just smiled, his earthy eyes calm, yet Toulouse could see that he was familiar with these mysteries, and unlike most men, he did not smile in such a way as to belittle it as folly.

"I don't see why everything important has to be a secret," Toulouse muttered, casually inspecting the man's features for any hints that might betray the truth. He found none, and that in itself told Toulouse more than a morsel of cryptic wisdom might have. This man was one of *them*, someone like Toulouse's father who had come to Asia when Toulouse was a young child. Toulouse shared in the man's smile, and even without words, together they knew. Toulouse was not exactly sure *what* he knew, but knowing that he knew was enough for the time being.

Toulouse then felt a cool touch on his right hand as some-thing wound around his wrist. It was the Lucefate snake, slowly coiling around him, winding tightly, but not enough to leave more than a slight impression afterwards. Toulouse flinched at first, yet forced himself to remain still and calm. It was Nature's first commandment to humans: remain still and calm until you *understand*, until you have seen, heard, smelled, tasted, and felt all that was needed before acting.

"Careful, young scholar," the man said, reaching his hand forwards.

"No," Toulouse said when he saw that the man was going to try to remove the snake. "I know."

The man gave Toulouse a thoughtful eye, but nevertheless withdrew his hand and watched with nearly as much wonder as Toulouse.

The snake's scales seemed to dance with tongues of fire, and even when he stopped coiling, there was something almost alive to them. The snake then lifted his head up and looked into Toulouse's eyes.

Toulouse's breath left him— nothing could have broken his or the snake's gaze. It was as if, in that instant, they had both transformed each other into stone. Neither was the charmer nor the charmed; the black eyes of the snake met Toulouse's azure ones as equals, at least for the time being. Toulouse knew not what this was, what was truly happening, yet after a minute, he started to hear a faint whisper. It seemed to be emerging from his own mind, as if a little being had crawled in there and was trying very hard to be silent. Yet the whisper was more numinous than that. What was it saying? Toulouse gazed deeper into the snake's eyes, and he seemed to be falling into a black starless night. His eyes watered, and they were starting to splotch with orange dots. Finally, he blinked.

The connection severed. Yet Toulouse had unmistakably heard that whisper, and he *knew*.

The snake slunk his head back down and uncoiled from Toulouse's wrist. His scales had left a honeycomb impression on Toulouse's arm, pressed pink into his flesh. Yet Toulouse just looked back to the man with a smile and said, "Aralim. That is his name." His heart thrummed at an allegro pace; he was so pleased that the snake had chosen him and him alone to convey his name. And although he knew not what could be done with this knowledge, just knowing was enough.

The man's eyes sparkled, and he gave a slow nod. Turning to the snake, he said, "A splendid name. And a splendid young scholar to reveal yourself to, a boy who treads in the footsteps of gods."

Aralim took no further notice of either of them, and he coiled back to the basket and lay his head down.

Toulouse looked up to the man curiously. "The footsteps of gods?" he wondered aloud. "I can see no path of gods before me."

"Ah," the man said, leaning back as if it were a rather unfortunate fact, though it seemed to Toulouse that it was more in jest. The sounds from the market on the main street a few dirt lanes over murmured senselessly through the air about them, words from a world they were now foreign to. Yet finally, the man spoke again. "It is only those who do not *know* who wander the paths. A blind eye and a stout heart create a true wanderer. Those who seek the paths do so in vain; only those who can see deep might hope to *wander*."

"Yet how did I know Aralim's name?" Toulouse wondered aloud. He crossed his legs like the man was and rested his chin on his hands.

"You *wandered*," the man said, smiling again.

"Wandered where?"

"A haunt of gods, I presume, hidden to all but the blind eyes of the soul."

Toulouse shivered, though the day was a bath of moist heat. Again, he seemed to be falling into the blackness of Aralim's eyes, deeper and deeper, but at the same time, higher and higher, as if he were tiptoeing to the top of the world at night, so that he could feel the vastness of cities and mountains and oceans beneath him, yet still see none of it. He wasn't sure that he wanted this, though he could not help but let himself fall as he wondered what lay beyond.

Before he could ask the man anything more, he heard a familiar voice down the alley. "Master Salomon!" it was calling. It was Rayan, though Toulouse was too lost in his thoughts about snakes and fire that it didn't seem to be speaking to him. Eventually, Rayan simply belted out in broken French, "Toulouse! Kristeur is leaving and we're not waiting for you!" There was no danger here to reveal Kristeur's plans, for no one here could understand such a "foreign" language as French.

"A life calls," the man said calmly. "And I believe it is yours."

Toulouse leaned back out from the canopy and saw Rayan scampering down the lane, the cream-colored fabric from his headscarf streaming behind him. Each of his hands clutched old quills, for even when he had nothing to write on, he always found some way to record a stray thought that he could fashion into a poem or story. Kristeur had fixed the quills so that they would hold their own ink, and Rayan's scarf and arms were always covered with scrawling Arabic script.

"Toulouse! Your father is leaving for the port in Jaffa to go to Cyprus, the land of dark stallions and crystal sunlight," Rayan called. He stopped upon seeing Toulouse, and sighing, glanced at something in the sky and started writing on the underside of his left arm.

Toulouse wiped some beads of cool sweat falling into his eyes before standing to leave. Although he would have rather spent the rest of the day here, he knew that his father had his reasons for sporadic travel.

"Perhaps we shall meet again someday," Toulouse said.

The man tilted his head, his dark silver-lined curls of hair swaying from the sides of his turban, and he said, "We shall, young scholar. We shall."

The desert sands crinkled beneath Toulouse's feet and shone ruddy gold in the light of the early evening sun, so that far off to the horizon, the world was a glistening sheet of bronze. Few would have travelled the faceless expanse of the Arabian Desert unless they were pursuing someone important or being pursued. In Kristeur's case, it seemed to be both. Earlier that day, he had told Toulouse that he had learned an order of dark magicians had discovered the location of a nest of griffon eggs in Cyprus, along with some moonlight pearls that any magician, including Kristeur, would have travelled beyond the known world for.

He was leading the way now, light-footed through the sands. Rayan was riding a permanently borrowed mule on top of a cloth bundle with some of Kristeur's possessions, though most of his things, such as books and less precious magical devices, were kept with various people throughout Europe and Asia. Kristeur and Toulouse rarely lived in any location for long, and even when they did, their home was most likely to be in the back room of some peculiar magician's house. Everywhere they went, Kristeur would set up a laboratory to examine specimens he collected from nearby mountains and valleys, such as herbs and gems infused with powers both natural and magical, and animals such as snakes and rabbits that he kept as pets, and he always seemed to be able to find ancient devices from alchemists or philosophers of old times.

Toulouse was walking next to the mule, whom Kristeur had named Nasma. He was thinking about Aralim, and his father's plans, if any such plans existed. An Asian man had joined them a few hours ago before they had entered the desert, and he was speaking with Kristeur in Chinese about some grand meta-physical ideas. Toulouse could only understand fragments of their speech, but he enjoyed listening all the same. The man was bald and wore a dark robe that dragged behind him in a long trail which two hairless cats lay resting on even as he walked, and a creature with creamy white plumage was curled on his shoulder. Whether it was a dragon or not, Toulouse was not entirely sure, but it looked like an underdeveloped one. Kristeur too was not short of magical creatures, and he could now let them roam free out of the sight of other men, though even if a traveller were to come close enough to see Kristeur's old emerald python hanging asleep from Nasma's neck, or the tiny red and blue snakes, Kosmos and Noetos, curled around the straps of Kristeur's vest, or even the horned rabbit hopping around Nasma's legs, they would have surely deemed such fancies to be mirages. Yet the greatest truths in Toulouse's life often seemed to be no less peculiar than mirages, as if the dreams of magicians like his father were being woven into reality, shared dreams of a world truer than their own.

"When will we reach the Heavens, Kristeur?" Rayan sighed from Nasma's back.

"Another life, another time," Kristeur called back. He turned back to Rayan, and Toulouse saw his crystal blue eyes flash gold in the low sunlight. "Or by moonrise perhaps."

Toulouse jogged to catch up with his father before he resumed speaking with the other man, who had never given a name for himself, though he had made it quite clear that his two cats were named Dao and De. "Is there someone after us?" Toulouse asked.

Kristeur put his arm around Toulouse's shoulders as they strolled, and he gazed off to the horizon with a calm smile. It was that grand gaze of his that seemed to take in every grain of sand and extract a golden mystery from them.

"We are always being pursued," Kristeur said.

"But is there someone in particular this time?" Toulouse asked. At least if he knew that, he could better piece together who else was involved with the griffon eggs and moonlight pearls.

"It is the Devil himself," Rayan called up to them. "But he is only after you, Toulouse. His stomach grumbles for the over-curious."

"Why, Rayan, you can spawn demons from the clear air," Kristeur laughed. Turning back to Toulouse, he added, "No, I do not know. It is one of the Erkavorn Order, but of course, it is always them, is it not?"

Toulouse nodded, and he realized that the Chinese man had slowed to walk beside Rayan so Toulouse and Kristeur could talk somewhat more privately. Kristeur's red snake, Kosmos, slunk from Kristeur's shoulder and curled around the strap of Toulouse's vest, his tiny scales cool and smooth on Toulouse's skin.

"I just wonder," Toulouse thought aloud, "what is so special about moonlight pearls and griffon eggs that so many magicians would be after them? I've read about moonlight pearls, but no one says much about them. They're a secret, something no one wants to write about."

"They are truth," Kristeur declared. "At least a wonderful little part of it. You cannot write about truth. You must find it. And so find it I shall."

"Truth…" Toulouse pondered.

Kristeur just smiled, and he removed his arm from around Toulouse and turned back to the others. He flicked a few sparks of fire from his fingertips and sent them spiralling towards a candle Rayan had procured so that he could write from atop Nasma's back as the sun waned.

After thinking for a few minutes, Toulouse told his father, "I suppose everyone would see a different truth in them."

"No, no I do not believe so," Kristeur said, his eyes misting for a moment as he strung his thoughts together. "Although beauty may lie in the mind of the beholder, truth lies within the mind of God."

"Which god?" Toulouse asked.

"Ah, Toulouse, you have travelled too much. You know the gods of a hundred lands, those of the trees and mountains, the sky and sea, the stars and planets, of demons and angels, and even the Master of the Cosmos. But I am speaking of *God*. There are others, I'm sure, but only one God who created even great Zeus and Rama. Yet travel is like philosophy: a few years of it will perk the eye to differences, which you shall be able to notice with ease. Yet living as I have, travelling to lonely lands and through a thousand metropolises and hidden woods, you rather see the similarities. All becomes one, and God too becomes one. Not the sum of all those gods here, but beyond them, a being few philosophers have truly grasped. He has always been one, but he is severed in our minds. So it is up to us to piece him back together. If our souls possess a clarity beyond what our mortal nature can bestow, we shall see him."

Toulouse shivered. He felt as though great eyes had borne down on him that moment as the sky darkened to a deeper orange hue. *How do you know?* Toulouse wondered. Was it even possible to know a God beyond all others? Kristeur seemed perfectly content with it, but Toulouse had long ago determined that he would never truly be able to fathom his father's mind. Yet the feeling that he felt now, that great emptiness as if he were perched upon some outcrop in the night sky, was the same that he had felt upon beholding Aralim. He gasped and blinked until he focused back to the world around him.

Toulouse sighed, the feeling passing. As Kristeur seemed content without any inquiry, Toulouse asked him, "What about snakes?"

"Snakes?" Kristeur repeated with a grin, as if he had expected something more profound. Though at the same time, with Kosmos and Noetos curled around each of their shoulders and with a curious gleam in Kristeur's eyes, there were perhaps few grander topics.

"Devils and angels, are they Rayan?" Kristeur said.

Rayan raised his head from a poem he was trying to copy into his notebook from a soiled cloth. "And fine jewelry for this old lady," he added, patting Nasma's neck above where the old python was curled.

"Quite," Kristeur agreed.

Toulouse glanced sidelong at his father, wondering if he were purposely evading the question. The Chinese man seemed just as content to leave Toulouse in the dark as well. Kristeur then put a hand on Toulouse's shoulder and whispered, "You can hear them. I believe the finest key lies within you."

"But you said that there was only one truth..." Toulouse started.

"And countless ways to reach it, though some are better than others."

"I just wonder..." Toulouse said, but at the same moment, he caught sight of something strange beside Kristeur. He instinctively leapt to the side, but realized that he had only seen Kristeur's shadow, stretched long and spindly like a stringless marionette. Yet although it was obviously a shadow, whether it was Kristeur's or not was another matter entirely. In the moment when it had startled Toulouse, Toulouse thought he had seen a pair of wings unfurl from its back. Though just as soon as they had appeared, they were gone. A mirage of the waning sun? Toulouse somehow doubted it.

Before he could ask his father about it, Kristeur stopped and raised his arms towards the last amber tendrils of sunlight. "We must stop in an hour," he said, shifting his hands as if feeling some otherworldly current. "We shall reach a vale by then."

Rayan muttered something about a vale of twilight mirages, but he knew as well as Toulouse that Kristeur's intuitions were never wrong, though at the same time, they never manifested exactly how anyone expected.

Kristeur went back to talk with the Chinese man as they continued their journey, and Rayan rode up to Toulouse to read his epic poem contained in fragments about his body and clothes, so that it really was an epic endeavour to piece it together.

Toulouse smiled at Rayan's words, yet his mind soon drifted to what Kristeur had spoken about. The one God, the truth united. How far such a notion seemed, and yet, it was as if it were somehow close by, scintillating invisibly in every mote of air and grain of sand, and vanishing whenever Toulouse's attention was brought to it. Yet could it not just be a delusion?

"Even Ali Duna's shadow brightened that plain like moonlight from a forgotten world…" Rayan continued his poem, reading down his right arm.

Toulouse instinctively turned to peer behind him. There his shadow tread, its limbs stretched thin by the late sun. A lonesome wanderer, hovering across the sand.

There was little food to be had that night, though Kristeur did have a flask of Heol to share. It was made from some bizarre combination of ingredients and imbued with powers that made the liquid glow a pale gold, and it was nearly satisfying as a proper meal. They had reached the valley shortly after nightfall, and although the desert pond within it was no mirage, there was no cover except for paltry shrubs along the margins of the pond that glittered with sand dust under the stars.

Rayan, Kristeur, and the other man were asleep, or at least pretending to be asleep, lying under their thin cloaks on the sand. Kosmos and Noetos were curled beside Kristeur's shoulder and Nasma was nosing the sandy shrubs forlornly. The desert was one of those rare places where the sky and horizon fully encircled the world with a dark jewelry box of tiny diamonds, each a mere fleck of light, yet together, their irradiance brightened the world with pale glimmers of dreams and forgotten worlds. It was a map for magicians, and seeds of inspiration even for Toulouse, though he knew not how to read them as his father could.

He sat up from where he lay and brushed the sand from his hair. Nasma turned her deep chestnut brown eyes towards Toulouse with a pitiful expression. Yet Toulouse did not heed her, for his eyes were lost in the stars. He started to walk out of the small valley, sliding through the softly crinkling sand at every step. He knew not where he was headed, but he was sure of one thing: he wanted to know, to know the depths of that darkness he had glimpsed in Aralim's mind. To know the truth his father had spoken of. He had read enough books to catch a hundred glimpses of it, for Kristeur's collection was by no means lacking, though it was dispersed across the continent.

A movement in the sand then caught Toulouse's eye. He sighed when he saw that it was only Kosmos. "You're a Silvrien, aren't you?" he said, smiling.

He had expected no reply, yet the snake then extended his head upwards as if he were a cobra being charmed. The snake's tiny blue eyes ensnared Toulouse's as if he were the prey, and Toulouse realized that this was not Kosmos after all. Although that did not bother him much, he was also struck with the knowledge — or was it a mere guess in the delusion of a desert night? — that this was no Silvrien. He was a Lucefate of hidden depths. His deep ocean eyes bespoke of another world, another time, or perhaps one in which time did not exist. Toulouse felt himself being drawn deeper and deeper under the spell, the calm desert winds seeming to twist around him and the sand seeming to form a melody of bells. Yet the snake just as quickly dropped back down and slithered off, leaving a twisting trail in the sand behind him.

Toulouse's breath came ragged, yet he was not afraid. Although the snake was swift, Toulouse knew that he could catch up with him, so he darted forwards. He felt quite like his father at the moment, and hoped that his dreams would prove to be as true as Kristeur's to warrant a chase across a formless desert. Yet were these even dreams? Surely they were not just dreams, surely not mirages. The crystalline crinkling of sand continued as he ran, a light fey tune in the air.

A few minutes later, Toulouse reached a tree. He hadn't seen it before, though it was as real as any he had seen in brighter hours, arising from the arid sand as if it had been cultivated by a goddess's tender hands. Its trunk was a dark wood with deep wrinkles like the skin of a sunburnt old man, and its boughs twisted in an intricate canopy that seemed to clutch the air beneath them with leaves of an orangeish red.

Toulouse slowed on beholding the tree, for it stood so peacefully, completely unaware that it was so out of its element. It was perfectly still, like a painting from a poet's eye.

The snake approached the tree and started to ascend its trunk. It became one with the gnarled bark as it slowly aspired to the boughs. Toulouse watched, dazed, and although he had no reason to believe that he beheld anything greater than a snake climbing a tree, he felt a twist of something shiver up his spine as the snake ascended. He dropped to his knees as the snake reached the highest boughs. The back of his head simultaneously received a numinous shiver, almost quivering with some sort of power. It was in the air, it was in the tree, and it was in *him*.

And then he saw her.

A cloud appeared to have descended over the tree, yet it emerged from the air as naturally as the tree had. It was light, and yet, it was also dark. For although the desert of a thousand stars might shed light upon wanderers below, it was also a mystery sprinkled through a thousand bright worlds. This shadow was by no means a beacon in the night, but when Toulouse beheld it, a truth arose within him that he had never felt before. A beacon in the emptiness of dark eyes, a chart to fathomless wonders.

Toulouse did not blink. He knew this was no mirage of sand and starlight, so he gazed silently as the shadow perched upon the upper boughs and reached her long arm towards the snake. The Lucefate slithered up her fingers and around her misty arm until he curled around her shoulder. The tingle at the back of Toulouse's neck crept into his skull, and suddenly, there was a burst of illumination. It burned in him like a piece of fallen sunlight, and at once, it was day around him, the sands aglitter with a thousand hues of yellows, reds, oranges, and golds. The tree was a beacon of ruby and dark wood whose every crevice was outlined in utmost clarity. And at its summit, a goddess with the Lucefate, her messenger...

Then it was dark. The rays burst from Toulouse's mind and were quenched into the formless darkness beyond, at once a pinprick and a world away. The goddess was a shadow, yet she turned her face towards Toulouse and there was a whisper from her, but so too was it a whisper from his own mind like he had heard from Aralim. It seemed to sing a hissing melody that could charm even Lucefates from their brooding mind's hollow. A whisper of a voice spoke with it, and it sang, "Alaramara wakes the sun, and I shall wake you too... it's soon... it's sooo..."

The voice curled into a twist of wind, and when Toulouse's eyes turned back up to the treetop, he saw the mist and snake lift into the air and depart. And after no more than a soft hissing whisper in the branches of the tree, silence once again engulfed the desert.

Toulouse stood as he watched them vanish, and although that spark had left him, his wonder had not ceased, and he gazed at the sky with parted lips and eyes crystal blue mirrors to the stars. "Soon," he whispered.

Something behind him then caught his eye. Turning, he beheld his shadow from the starlight, and although he was looking down at it, it was gazing up to the sky. The shadow outstretched its arms and gently lifted from the ground with newly sprouted wings and vanished into the dark sky. Toulouse blinked, and his shadow slowly reformed as his true reflection, tethered below and looking down upon the sand.

Truth, Toulouse wondered as he turned his eyes back to the sky. There were no answers that he could glean from the snake and his master, yet he felt it was the truest thing he had ever beheld. He sighed peacefully, wondering. Eventually, he said, "We are shadows, father. Lost shadows. Yet the shadows of gods."

And he knew that one day, he would soar as his shadow had, and perhaps then he would truly know.

MARY-JEAN HARRIS enjoys writing historical and other-world fantasy stories. She is a student at Carleton University in Ottawa studying theoretical physics and philosophy. Her story *The Shadows of Gods* was inspired in part by Eastern mysticism about Kundalini. Mary-Jean is the author of *Aizai the Forgotten*.

THE MACHINE

by David Clink

The machine's shadow turned strange
with every house, tree, and fence it passed over.

At times we could see into it—
insects with translucent bodies and opaque wings,

the flora and fauna of a different world,
unfamiliar mechanisms moving in odd ways.

We ran after the machine as fast as we could,
as if someone we loved was trapped inside.

The sound it made was air whipping around skyscrapers,
metal grinding against metal, two people fucking,

a symphony warming up, a woodpecker at full tilt,
a jet engine roaring, the industrial revolution.

The machine's outward beauty blinded us.
We felt its burn as it made its way over hillsides,

above the rooftops of cookie-cutter homes,
melting shingles, igniting the wood beams beneath.

The texture of dead grass, the smell of burnt earth,
our eyes and skin on fire, the roar of the machine,

we crawled to a place as close to it as we dared go
and went down on our knees. We asked forgiveness.

DAVID CLINK has three collections of poetry: *Eating Fruit Out of Season* (2008); *Monster* (2010); and, *Crouching Yak, Hidden Emu* (2012). He edited an anthology of environmental poetry called: *A Verdant Green* (2010). His poem "A sea monster tells his story" won the 2013 Aurora Award for Best Poem/Song. His poems can also be found in *Tesseracts Fourteen* and *Tesseracts Sixteen*.

BURNT OFFERINGS

by Mary Pletsch

I HANG SUSPENDED in the Lattice, streaming data directly into my cortex and programming code at the speed of thought.

The Galaxy-Spanning Lattice Sacristy of the Vendetrix Avengelis, our online temple and knowledge vault of Our Lady of Retribution, has only a few active users at this hour. Some are taking instruction in the faith from an acolyte, while others are reading sacred texts from our database or uploading this week's tributes to the Vendetrix into the archive, where they will be showcased for years to come. Seven soldiers in the uniforms of the Allmother's Army kneel in contemplation in the pews. I wonder if they are remembering comrades fallen, or praying for their own glories to come. One of them glances at me as I pass by and bows her head, paying me the reverence due a Shaman of the High Ones.

As I look about, it's easy to forget that what my mind perceives is in fact a virtual simulation peopled by avatars that represent users logging in from stations across the galaxy. It's easy to forget that my own avatar, this body that walks so easily and painlessly from the simulation start point in the nave up the central aisle, is not my true form. Then I notice that the flowers on the Vendetrix's high altar are monochrome red, flat and artificial looking, and I am reminded that I work in a world of artifice.

I suspect the blooms are a tribute from reverent but amateur programmers who found it more meaningful to create their own offering rather than pay an acolyte to build it on their behalf. I suspend my reverie, my wishful thinking that the Lattice could encompass my entire reality; then I superimpose lines of data upon my surroundings, and I get to work. I study the code for the flowers and make some adjustments, piping orange and yellow hues through the petals. The flowers shimmer and reappear with a far more realistic looking color gradient, and I smile beneath my Shaman's cowl.

I am pondering changing the flooring — the white marble, though pretty, seems pale and sedate for the Sacristy of just desserts incarnate — when a flicker of light from overhead catches my eye.

The great stained glass window over the altar is a portrait of the Vendetrix Avengelis, resplendent in divine vengeance. Facets representing the blood of fallen foes decorate the bottom third of the glass in a cascade of ruby and crimson, while the figure of the Vendetrix herself is cast in fiery orange and gold. The Vendetrix's face eclipses the sun, rendering her features in shadow. She could be anyone, everyone, who has sought to repay a wrong in pounds of flesh.

My subconscious has prompted me to check the original code, and I obey without yet knowing why. Some later coder — not myself — has updated the Vendetrix's weapon. According to the code, when the window was first programmed, Our Lady of Retribution carried a now-obsolete Jury assault rifle, not the modern Prosecutor she now holds. Rendered in black steel, the shadow of the Prosecutor falls across the congregation of soldiers, a charge from on high, a torch passed from divine to mortal hands.

I wonder if any of those soldiers has ever given serious thought to refusing that torch, as I have sometimes considered refuting my position in the Sacristy. I pause a moment to reflect on how a private agnostic such as myself came to be wearing the Shaman's cowl; I muse when I ought to be combing the code. I compute faster than a conventionally augmented human, significantly faster than the average unaugmented brain, but my momentary lapse is long enough for the code aberration that my subconscious detected to manifest itself in the Temple around me.

The Vendetrix' window explodes inward in a cascade of shards.

Standing at the side of the altar, I take the brunt of the impact. I throw my arms before my face as though bone and steel could shield me. Even as I do so, the code scrolling across my mind's

eye reminds me that this realm has no physical reality. There
are no fragments of glass embedded in my flesh, no wave of
heat singeing my hair and baking my skin onto my bones. I
am uncertain if I remembered to offline my tactile simulators
in time or if my physical body, slumped in an ambulator in the
Freyjavik Sacristy of the Vendetrix Retributatae, is too dosed
up with painkillers to notice when its sensory implants mimic
first the blast of fire, then the sting of a hundred lacerations.
What I feel, I suspect, is not the attacker's program, but old
memories dredged up from my brain's archive of flesh. This
virtual attack is impotent against me, I who remember against
my will how it feels to burn.

Still it takes time for me to dare lower my arms from my face.

When I do, I see the perpetrator herself standing in front of
me; or rather, I see her avatar. This is the image that she has
chosen to represent herself in the virtual world of the Lattice,
and it is remarkable indeed.

All of the soldiers in the pews have designed avatars which
project strength and ferocity. The perpetrator's avatar wears
the same uniform, but her figure is slight, her muscles puny,
her cheeks gaunt. Her skin is the color of toffee, several shades
lighter than mine; her hair is long and black and straight and
tied back in a faltering braid that is more than half undone.
She does not look like a dangerous warrior. She looks like a
youth from a famine-stricken colony who has taken up the gun
to buy her family food. Perhaps she is— it's entirely possible
that her avatar is constructed through an image-capture lens
on a wrist-mounted field computer, that what I am seeing is
her true face.

She might in fact be a man, or one of the Eidervass, not
human at all; she might be more dangerous than any of the
soldiers here. She is, at the very least, a more-than-competent
hacker, to breach the Sacristy's firewalls, the firewalls that I
have fortified during my tenure in Freyjavik. But if this image
is a false front, it is a convincing one.

The soldiers are staring at her, and at me. They've got their
weapons in their hands, but they appear confused. Their guns
are only for show in this virtual world. They are merely users
here, and as users, can perform only those actions which the
scenario offers them. *Massacre the intruder* is not a choice they
are permitted.

I am an administrator and this is my fight.

I lower my arms and stride forward, and yes, I augment my avatar. My Shaman's robes billow menacingly; my left hand reaches out and a staff, symbol of my profession, coalesces in my grip. With a thought I trigger a glowing effect in the artificial eye beneath my cowl. I decide that it would not hurt to remind this upstart that I am not just any Shaman, but the chosen representative of the Silver Future, the spirit of innovation, technology incarnate, and I will meet the intruder's challenge.

The interloper's eyes widen; her lip quivers, and I am more convinced than ever that her avatar is an image-capture. She falls to her knees. I watch her gasp as she kneels upon the shattered glass; a shard has pierced her clothing, and she has not numbed her sensors. She feels it as though it is real. Her programming is suddenly sloppy; there is no blood coming from her avatar's body, and when she reaches for the shard, it simply vanishes. "I seek Shaman Pasharan, Sigil of the Silver Future," she whispers through her pain. "Are you he?"

During this time I have set my subroutines to work and now information is scrolling across my field of vision, superimposed on the virtual reality around me. Her broadcast identity is that of Sergeant Veronica Ravindran, infantry soldier in the Allmother's Army. Her signal initiates from a planet which the Kin call Argos and the Crusaders call Galilee. Tags on the signal tell me that it originates from a Mercury-class MCC (Mobile Communications Centre) designated 2-33A. Sergeant Ravindran is allegedly broadcasting from a location near a village named Philius.

I query the Allmother's Army database as to the current status of combat operations on Argos. The database accepts my Shaman's identification but provides me with only rudimentary information: there are *operations in progress* in the region where Philius lies. It's not specific enough. I request more data and the system refuses me.

I will not be denied. Through a side door into the system, I tap feeds from a number of MCCs and cross reference with their identification markers. The information is chaotic, unfiltered, and my own systems are taxed to capacity flagging conversations containing specific keywords. The urgency is exhilarating. I am 92.4 percent certain that the Crusaders on Argos have launched an assault on the Allmother's holdings, and our troops are holding the line— in some cases, in 2-33A's case, barely.

"The Crusaders are at the gate, my Sigil, and our shields have fallen!" she blurts, using the honorific for those in our profession— for while the Crusaders call their religious leaders *shepherds*, the children of the Allmother are wolves. My duty is to inspire this soldier to greatness, not offer her a false protection. She begs me anyway, her words tumbling out in a rush. "If you will not aid me, my squad will surely perish."

I instinctively run a diagnostic query on my body's ventilator when my breath catches in my throat, but an instant later, when the report comes in — *all systems functioning optimally* — I have already realized my reaction is an emotional one. As with the sensations accompanying the explosion, her words are triggering memories buried deep in nerve and flesh, from a time before my ascension, when the Lattice was a tool I accessed via a rented device. When I had the freedom to say that the High Ones were nothing but archetypes created by human imagination.

"What do you ask of the Silver Future?" I say, and trust my voice synthesizer to filter the tremble from my words.

She places her hand to her throat, but not before my enhanced vision spots a cross on a tiny gold chain.

I have never understood the appeal of the Christian faith. How can just one God encompass all the dualities of the universe: light and darkness, male and female, love and hate? Regardless, Christians are passionate devotees, and it is this passion which caused the faith's great Schism centuries before.

One of the splinter sects founded the Crusaders, a group that left the homeworld to manifest destiny in the stars. They pick and choose their science, accepting that which helped them expand and grow, denying that which challenges their theology and power. Primitives, barbarians, and fanatics, the Crusaders have been at war with us, the Humanist Empire, and the Sultanate of the Crescent for longer than I have been alive.

Yet I do not believe that Sergeant Ravindran is a Crusader. My data mining tells me that she was born on the Kin-claimed colony of Lughnasa, she has a complete government profile, and if her avatar is accurate, her body armor is the general issue type that none of our soldiers actually wear unless they are too poor to purchase better armor on the open market. The Crusaders pay their spies better than that.

More importantly, Ravindran had caught me unaware. Had she intended to assault the Virtual Sacristy, she could have done much more damage than bursting through the window; I could repair that code within an hour, with no damage to our databanks or denial of service. She needed to get my attention, and quickly, to save her squad.

There are other Christian groups out there. Some of them exist as minorities in the territories of the Kinfolk, the Empire and the Sultanate; others eke out livelihoods on small, struggling colonies. All the major powers employ these people as infantry, and all of them treat them as casteless; to convert to Christianity and be caught is to lose one's citizenship, one's rights. To be born to a Christian family is to never have those rights. I myself have initiated countless teenagers, born Christian, into the Sacristy at the time of their comings-of-age. I eye her slight frame, her weak armor. Cannon fodder.

Her file says she is Kin. There is a flag on her file indicating otherwise. *Suspected Christian convert.* I doubt she is aware that her avatar wears a cross.

"I ask the blessing of technical knowledge," she whispers, "so that I may raise our shields and save our troops."

By this point I have skimmed her file. It describes a reliable soldier with no communications or computer training, though her superiors have noted an aptitude for information technology. I suspect she is largely self-taught; gifted, but untrained. She was me, thirty years ago.

I have also hacked the cameras in MCC 2-33A, and with one eye I watch her avatar kneel before me while the other sees her real-world parallel frantically flipping switches on the MCC's control panel in an attempt to reroute power to the command centre's shields. Beside her, a young man of similar age is groaning and holding his hands to his abdomen; blood oozes between his fingers. Another man wearing the uniform of a communications officer cries hysterically in the corner. I flick my consciousness into the MCC's perimeter sensors, knowing that I have no mandate to do so and also knowing there is no one to stop me.

Yes, here come the Crusaders aboard a horde of fast-moving rough-terrain hover transports. Behind them, moving with terrible speed for something of its bulk, is a furnace-thrower tank, the kind the Crusaders call Abednego. I am intimately acquainted with this model, and how the Crusaders boast that it incinerates the infidels and leaves only the holy behind.

Well, I am still here, and I now stand as the chosen one of a cyber god.

With a surge of data and a few quick shortcuts, the shields of MCC 2-33A surge to life. Several miles distant, an Allmother headquarters is no doubt cursing my name in the dark, but they do not need power as badly as the infantry of 2-33A do. The Crusaders in their transports fire flechettes, but they cannot pierce the shields I've erected.

And now, the Abednego.

There's a heavy launcher just outside the MCC's shields, the kind that requires command authorization to fire. The field commander is inactive, likely dead, and the headquarters staff are otherwise occupied. But the command codes are stored online, and what is online, is mine.

I am filtering headquarters' files in search of the code when back in the virtual Sacristy, the heavy front doors burst open. Six figures stand there: four masked Flagellants carrying whips; Sicaria, Shaman of the Vendetrix; and Pater Donner himself, the Sire of our Sacristy.

I am not worried about the Flagellants; they are nothing but programs, designed to defend the Sacristy against intruders. Their functions are to resurrect the walls which Ravindran's code-bomb destroyed and to contain any viruses. One of them heads straight for Ravindran's avatar, but I step forward — it is so easy to move in this virtual body — and halt it with a gesture. "She is under my protection," I say, even as my heads-up display reveals the code I seek.

I am an administrator, so the Flagellant accepts me at my word. It remains to be seen if I can convince the two sentients. I must formulate a strategy quickly.

Sicaria and I are of equal rank. She is a better reflection of the Kin's ideal: a warrior born, bedecked with battle honors and a long military career, both before and after the near-death experience that granted her a face-to-face meeting with the Vendetrix. Unlike myself, I am certain she experienced something, or thought she did, while field medics struggled to stop her from bleeding to death. She proudly wears the signs of that meeting and her reply: a gnarled rope of scar tissue that lies over the big artery in her throat like a ghastly necklace, and on her hip, the knife that made the cut, carried in a scabbard she personally sewed from the tanned skin of the original wielder.

The Vendetrix chose her, and she sanctified her appointment with her would-be murderer's blood.

In the corporeal world, she is in her sixties, too old for combat, though still deadly enough to take my life if she felt it was her duty to do so. Her avatar in the virtual Sacristy is the image of herself in her prime, fit and strong and lethal, her scar still red and fresh, her human-skin scabbard lacking the weathering of years. She looks at me as a hawk would look upon a crippled rodent. I am an easy kill, perhaps too easy. Perhaps poisoned.

The Kin have many warriors, and few technological geniuses. Of those, there is only one, me, who claims to have spoken with the Silver Future in the gray land between death and life. I am irreplaceable, and Sicaria cannot harm me.

I hope.

Pater Donner is the final variable. He is a Cardinal, not a Shaman; educated in the faith, far more knowledgeable than either Sicaria or I, but lacking a personal experience with the High Ones. Some time ago I downloaded a tactical analysis suite and wedded it to my facial recognition software. It informs me that Donner is jealous of the Shamans, but, I think, not jealous enough to risk death for an experience of his own.

Donner loves what his show of faith can do for him more than he loves the High Ones, and that is what makes him so dangerous.

It is Donner I must convince.

Donner steps forward, all rage and fury, and I know I have no time for explanations. I quickly give Ravindran the codes in the form of a transferred burst of data. I must trust that she knows what to do with them. "Go now," I tell her, moving my avatar's hands in the traditional blessing sign for a formal dismissal. As Donner charges towards me, Sicaria at his flank, I augment my voice with all the authority I can summon. "Now!"

Ravindran nods and blinks out of existence, as though she has not only logged off, but erased her data behind her.

"What are you doing?" Donner demands imperiously, and I wonder when the Kin chose to give positions of command to those who had never met the High Ones.

"My job," I reply just as icily, and if my words take on the artificial reverberations of a computer-generated voice, I will blame the Silver Future.

"Mark you this," he hisses at me, "what the Sacristy has given, the Sacristy can take away."

It is a threat, because I know full well that were it not for
my deathbed conversion, my story of a vision of the Silver
Future, I would still be lying in a military sanitarium somewhere, bedridden, deaf, racked with pain and cut off from the
Lattice forever.

I scream in frustration in the void between circuits, where
there is no one to hear me. No one save the Silver Future, if
such a thing exists; and if He does, I want to know how He can
reconcile His emphasis on human advancement with a reality
where men such as Donner hold His Shaman in shackles.

✸✷✸✸✸

Several months later I am once again adjusting the colors of
flowers on the Vendetrix's virtual altar, under the newly repaired
stained glass window, when somewhere out in the physical
world an acolyte shakes my shoulder, so carefully, as if he fears
to break me. "Shaman, you have a visitor."

It's not my scheduled time to greet the faithful in the physical
world. I am reluctant to return to meatspace, where my body
slumps in its ambulator, awaiting its next dose of painkillers.
By choice, I live most of my life in the Lattice, where I can
create and destroy with my thoughts, in the image of the God
I claim to serve.

"She says it's urgent," the acolyte whispers, and his dis-
embodied voice echoes around the Sacristy in my head.

"I'm coming," I say to thin air, and then the vision of virtual
reality fades as I begin the detachment process. I always find
it disorienting, wrenching even, and this time is no different.
I close my eyes, and when I open them — or rather, *it*, since I
have only one left — I am looking not at the magnificent oak
altar of the Vendetrix, but rather at a simple curved bench of
plastoid supporting a rack of monitors: my shrine to the Silver
Future.

The Freyjavik Sacristy of the Vendetrix Retributatae is a
pale shadow of the glorious Virtual Sacristy of the Vendetrix
Avengelis. The Virtual Sacristy can support eight hundred
thousand simultaneous logons; Freyjavik's physical building
can hold a maximum of three hundred people, according to the
space station's safety laws. The Freyjavik Sacristy is in need of
upgrades, its flooring worn, its beams dusty. We donate most of

our offerings to the war effort, and keep so little for ourselves... at least after Pater Donner has had his cut.

"I've arrived," I tell the acolyte, even as I realize that my mouth is dry and my left side is tingling with pins and needles. I reach out with a metallic claw and clamp the prosthetic which is my left arm around a cup with a straw that rests on my shrine. I lift the vessel and fish with my lips until I am able to capture the straw and drink.

"My Sigil," the acolyte says, "she is on your urgent list." He nods to the woman behind me. "It's highly irregular and I have informed her as much, but she insists... and she is on your list."

My eye — and the visual sensor that colonizes my left eye socket — track over his shoulder to my unexpected guest as I set my cup back down.

I was correct. Sergeant Veronica Ravindran is the very image of her avatar— or, more accurately, her avatar is the photo-reflection of her true self. She stands before me, staring and wringing her hands, every bit as gawky and ill at ease as I remember. But I see two significant changes. The first is that she wears dress uniform, not combat fatigues. The second is a new medal: next to Jason's Service Ribbon, indicating she has seen combat on Argos, six resplendent red wedges on a white field— Fenrir's Teeth, the prestigious award for valor in the service of one's comrades. It is a medal which would never be awarded to a Christian.

"Take me to my booth," I request, and then I gesture to Ravindran. "Come."

She hesitates, still staring into the darkness beneath my cowl, and I allow myself a smile. "You are not the only one who uses visual capture," I murmur. At last she tears her gaze from my skeletal prosthetics with their stylized claws and integrated data ports, and follows at my side.

The acolyte assists me in moving my ambulator up a small ramp into my booth, where he settles me in front of a grille and closes the door behind me. I see Ravindran's shadow through the screen as she sits opposite me. I take no chances.

With a thought, the screen raises. I speak my other instructions aloud so Ravindran is aware of what I am doing. "Initiate electronic countermeasures. Secure locks. Raise shielding. Deactivate cameras. Commence white noise generation. Disable recorders. Privacy mode active."

Pater Donner does not like when I do this. I don't care. I swore to serve the Silver Future, not Donner, and in the face of my agnosticism, my will is mine own.

Ravindran's gaze focuses on the faint gleam of light beneath my cowl; the illumination from my artificial eye. I raise my prosthetic hands to my cheeks and hesitate there. "Are you certain you'd rather? It's not for the weak of stomach."

She bites her lower lip, but nods. "I want to see your face."

I snap my fingers back and let the cowl fall back.

I have a few bristles of hair in patches on my scalp, and I've had my eyelids replaced, but my eyebrows are gone, and most of my head is a gnarled mass of scars. My mouth is a ragged tear, far wider than it ought to be, gaping on the left side, and showing teeth where my lips no longer meet. My nose is a hole in my face, just as my ears are gaps on the sides of my head.

She pales — she can't help it — and I manage a smirk with the right side of my lips. "It was either cosmetic surgery or the computer gear, and there was no other way I'd be able to afford this computer gear." It's a partial truth. Becoming an acolyte of the Silver Future had made the gear a necessity, and though I would have chosen it anyway, the choice was taken from me.

She tries not to gawk and I snort. "Come now, look all you please. I'm far past taking offense and I do find that the longer you look, the more you get used to it."

Her mouth works for a moment before she can get the words out. "I came to ask you why," she whispers, "but now I think I know."

"The Abednego is an unpleasant invention," I agree, "and perhaps I presumed, but I doubted a good Christian would be seeking an early audience with her Lord and Saviour."

"We have near-death experiences too," she protests, but even as she says it I know she realizes that for a Christian, a near-death experience is a private miracle, while for one of the Kin it is a vocation made manifest. No, she would not want to be sitting in an ambulator, her legs reduced to sacks of meat, her body a morass of tight and shining scars. I have read her file in its entirety, and those of her relatives as well. She needs to stay combat-capable to support her sister's family back on Lughnasa, at least until the rains come.

It has been three years since Lughnasa has had rain.

"You didn't know your Lattice avatar wore a cross, did you?" I ask her point-blank.

She shakes her head, a silent no.

"It's gone now. I would recommend you practice your faith more subtly from now on. Your file has been untagged and there is a flag trigger attached that will warn you if anyone tries to tag you again as a Christian."

Her eyes sweep me and she speaks. "I can guess why you helped me with the shields," she says, "but why would you, a Shaman of the Kin, protect me?"

There are a host of reasons. Because I remember how it felt to be poor. Because I remember how it felt to be afraid. Because being a private atheist in the army of the Kin was not much easier than being a Christian; because a legislated faith is no faith at all.

In the end I tell her, "My patron deity is the incarnation of a hope for a better tomorrow." I believe it. Surely I do.

"Thank you," she says, one last time, before she takes her leave.

Alone in the booth, I enable a select few systems, disable a handful of others. In the upper left corner of my heads up display, I watch as Sergeant Ravindran hurries from the temple. I see Pater Donner step from the shadows, frowning, bending over his wrist tablet. I see the wan light of Freyjavik's distant sun filtering through the dusty stained glass above the main altar, casting the colored shadow of the Vendetrix Retributatae, the deliverer of punishment due, and in that moment I pray to the Sacristy's deity as well as to my own.

I pray, deeply and sincerely, for the second time in my life. The first was when I saw the Abednego's fire; when a young atheist mouthed the words he had learned as a child, *into thy hands I commend my spirit*, just in case he was wrong and a passing divinity might chance to hear and heed. The Silver Future, or at least the concept thereof, has since rescued me from a life of isolation and futility. *Perhaps the Silver Future can provide me with yet another miracle*, I think as I tap the side door to the Sacristy's medical files and attempt to devise a code that might grant me access to the knowledge I need to do what is right. Or perhaps Sicaria's Goddess is as disgusted with Donner as I am.

My mind grows calm, and in the stillness I find the answer I seek.

●●●◌●

The Freyjavik Sacristy of the Vendetrix Retributatae is quiet at this hour. Sicaria and the acolytes are deep in slumber. It is not unusual for me to be awake — pain often keeps me up at nights — but I am typically in the Lattice, fleeing my body and its attendant discomforts. Not tonight.

Through the Sacristy's security cameras, I see Pater Donner rise from his desk and shuffle towards his bed. He leaves his datapad on, and I can see through the camera's eye that he has been reviewing my file, and Ravindran's. He does not kneel to worship before he slips beneath the covers.

I, on the other hand, take a moment to pray before I execute the programs I have prepared, for whether or not there is a Silver Future, I am still His Prophet.

Moments later, Pater Donner gasps and clasps his chest. He has the presence of mind to activate the emergency call button on his wrist tablet, but it is no longer working; I have crashed his personal computing system as surely as the mechanics in his pacemaker. He stares into space, his expression dark and angry even as his body begins to die. He knows, or at least suspects, the hand that has taken his life, but I am already editing the pacemaker data to indicate a rare but unfortunate power lapse. I will reboot his personal computing system during the long hours of the night, and in the morning I will prepare to be surprised when his body is found.

Sergeant Ravindran will be free. I will make certain of it, though I will never tell her, for her God is a God of mercy, but mine, like all the High Ones... mine is a God of war.

MARY PLETSCH is a glider pilot, toy collector and graduate of the Royal Military College of Canada. She is the author of short stories in a variety of genres, including science fiction, steampunk and horror. She lives with Dylan Blacquiere and their four cats.

ASCENSION

by Jennifer Rahn

BOBBY FONG barely felt the sting of Gravy's tattoo needle peppering his arm with new ink. He was dully aware of the lumpy cold compress jammed against his swollen lip and the throbbing pain of his lacerated right eye as he sat numbly, waiting for the latest mark of his success to be inscribed upon his skin.

"Woly shid," Gravy said repeatedly as he decorated the edges of his latest design with dragon scales. "You gave it to that sumbitch, Bobby. 49 kills. Man, you killah."

Bobby let his head fall back against the wall and the compress drop from his free hand. The painkillers were finally kicking in, giving him a buzz that did little to mask his internal despair. He tried to open his lacerated eye, almost passed out from the swell of pain, and groped for the compress, which he resmashed against his face as he wondered absently if Gravy would be saying the same things to Terror McTavish if he'd won tonight. The man had been a legend. Bobby had worshipped him as a kid, and felt no pride at having ended the aged fighter's reign. If anything, he felt fear for when the same thing would inevitably happen to him.

Bobby gazed blearily with his still working eye at the number 49 plastered over a skull by his wrist. 50 would go right across his forehead.

Something else had happened in the ring tonight, which bothered him deeply. He ran through it again, checking every second in his memory, asking himself repeatedly if he'd gotten it wrong. Had Terror let him win? In that very last moment, the old dog had smiled like he'd just won the biggest tournament, and he'd stopped short of finishing the block that would have saved his life, and damn, if Bobby hadn't seen a golden aura rise up from the ginger-haired man's skin, enveloping him in sparks and radiating scalding heat.

The moment had ended, leaving Bobby in the cold arena light, pelted with the raging screams of the crowd surrounding him. Half of them wanted his blood, and the other half wanted to kill the half that threatened him. The whole thing had been hypercast through the entire sector, and nobody else seemed to have noticed anything out of the ordinary. As Bobby stood there, ignoring the ref who was trying to shove him back to his corner, just *staring* at McTavish, all he could see that was special about the man was how incredibly dead he was. So much for the new ink he had emblazoned across his back— some kind of new agey *Om* symbol. Staring at him had made Bobby feel like his own life force was being drained out towards that dead mass of ginger-haired meat lying on the canvas. The only blinding lights surrounding McTavish then were coming from the flashes of the frenzied paparazzi scurrying along the outside edges of the cage.

Bobby felt lost. McTavish had been his *idol,* the guy he watched on holovid when he needed to study technique for his own upcoming matches. What was he going to do now?

"Now you gonna fight only the big leaguers, bidch." Bobby slowly twisted his gaze upwards to give what he hoped was a disgusted look at his promoter. "You made me a lotta coin tonight, Bobs. Geez, I actually had my bets insured tonight, just in case. Thought I had a good chance of losing you, but you really are a *dog!* A pitbull!" Kenichi pulled out a fat wad and cast a chunk of it onto Bobby's lap. The amount was maybe a twentieth of the total. "There's some for you. Five grand because I'm feeling generous tonight. Bobby!" Kenichi scrunched his cheek and shook it. "You're going to make me a rich man! Never mind the winnings, I've already got sponsorships from Alday Spacecraft, Intergalactic Miners, and Nike. Hey, Gravy, pass him off to the medics when you're done, OK?"

"Sure thig, bodss."

"I've already paid for you, Bobs, so don't worry about the bill. Go find yourself a woman afterwards. I won't be calling you for the next week or so, so heal up, a'ight?"

Kenichi plopped his pimp hat on his ass-shaped hair and thankfully left in a swirl of fake fur and pleather. Bobby sneezed and it hurt.

"Hey, Gravy," he ventured.

"Yeah, killah?"

"How'd you get out of fighting?" The tats on Gravy's arm only went to 38.

"Oh, I actually died. Heart stopped and everything. Din't see no tunnel a light, but it was weird, man. Like this weird cold numbness. Like, my brain stopped an' all. The docs had confirmed it and wrote it all up in my medical record. I only felt how weird it was after I woke up, though, and could remember some stuff. They were just about to dump me in the formaldehyde when I came to. Anyway, since my contract was only until death, I was home free after that."

Gravy grinned, showing off his collection of broken gray and blue teeth. Bobby sighed heavily. The docs never gave him enough meds at one time to bump himself off, and he wasn't one for taking a dive, not even if McTavish had.

The next day was still painful, but empty of stupid things like Kenichi's hair. A week off. Wow. He'd never had that much time to himself since he flunked out of Uni and ended up on the circuit. He wished he'd realized then how bad life would suck without a degree. He'd thought he could make it as a mechanic, but no one except Kenichi had offered him a contract to do anything. Even the mechs had degrees these days. At least he should have flunked out when the Uni was orbiting Venus. They didn't have death matches there.

The days on Tarney Orbital were of varied length, depending on the rules of the planetary system the entertainment rock was in. Today seemed about 15 hours long, and after having walked around all day, Bobby wasn't following through on his intention to still do some light training at the gym. He walked through the café sector instead, enjoying the smell of fancy coffee and the cold breeze against his puffy face. A few business hacks out for drinks stopped him, asking for autographs, but otherwise, no one from the fights came after him and he really did seem to be having time off. Some exotic merchandise and bookstores were scattered through the area, their display windows creative and appealing. Lithe women arranged scarves, satchels and brass elephants behind the glass. Bobby wondered if he could have switched his degree to something like that when engineering hadn't panned out for him.

He stopped in front of a store, gazing at the brilliantly lit book cubes within. Could he maybe still get back into the Uni? He'd have to run like bedgeezus from Kenichi's goons, and probably get a new identity. What the hell. He had five grand in his pocket and a whole week of time. For the first time in a decade, Bobby was going to buy a book.

Most of what the store had was crap. He didn't want to know what to expect in the first nine months, and his whole life was like a manga, but it was still fun to rummage through the cubes, pressing buttons to have the contents pop up in enticing holograms. The tarot cards were interesting. The *1001 Brownie Recipes* held his interest for several minutes. He wondered if Terror McTavish had ever written a biography, and wasn't surprised to find that he hadn't.

Hold up, what was this? A little green cube was inscribed with the same symbol McTavish had newly inked on his back. Bobby picked it up and pressed the button. *The Tibetan Book of the Dead.* He liked the cover, mainly because the weird little loincloth-wearing dudes all over the paisley background didn't even look dead. He leafed through it, his mind full of what Gravy had told him, and what might have been going on in McTavish's head that made him smile like he had just before Bobby's elbow had rammed his Adam's apple into his windpipe. If someone had written a whole book, there had to be more than just cold, black numbness.

"Woly shid," Bobby said out loud. There was a whole chapter on 'Selecting the Right Womb' after one had died and was choosing their next life. Seriously? The book was a how-to manual on reincarnation and doing it properly. Bobby bought the cube.

The next day, he was back at the bookstore, wanting to know more about this Buddhist thing. Those dudes spent their whole lives training to be happy, not fight, not build a career, not worry all the time about maintaining some rank, but sit around in loincloths being happy. Eventually they attained Nirvana and became Buddhas, which Bobby thought were pretty close to gods, judging from the stuff his Grandad had used to do. Since he and Grandad had never spoken the same language, he'd never really understood what any of that was. But now, after finding out that regular humans like him could supposedly turn into a Buddha, Bobby was totally interested. He'd heard about people running off with those Hare Krishnas and stuff, but always thought they were pansy nutjobs who'd end up strung out on drugs and doing whatever some cult leader said to get more. Now he thought they were a viable means of permanently getting off Tarney Orbital. Those weirdos wouldn't give him up to Kenichi for sure, and once he got good at this reincarnation thing, and became a Buddha, there'd be no more cage fights, just loincloths and having a good time.

His brain tried to force a reality check on him, but Bobby just shrugged. McTavish and Gravy had both gone through something drastic to get out of the cage, and both had seemed pretty happy about it when the moment had come. Maybe Bobby was just done, and being dead was worth not having to get his next murder victim handed to him with a greasy smile and further exposure to bad hair. Hell, he had a week. Why not check it out? Maybe dead didn't always mean *dead* dead.

Very deliberately not hiding his tracks, Bobby booked a two-day vacation at a mountain resort yoga spa on Shiva National, along with return passage to make sure Kenichi didn't come looking for him. He read his brains out on the way there, trying to prep his mind as much as possible before the early morning meditation session at the spa— which turned out to be the most gawdawful boring thing ever.

Over a thousand Seekers were assembled in the main temple. A giant, gold Buddha guy sat at the front, looking all happy, and a bunch of orange toga guys were right next to it, then everybody else. Everyone was made to sit in the lotus position, which Bobby's bum knees just didn't want to do, on cold concrete that was decreasing the temperature of his butt by two degrees per minute. This went on for hours, while they were instructed to keep their minds empty, and their attention focused on a small, tea light placed on the floor in front of each of them. The damn thing even flickered, which made it harder to stare at.

He sighed heavily halfway through the third hour and raised his head to look around the temple. Lots of bald heads around him, even the chicks, and a few guys had passed out and were discretely being removed. Far off to the left, a golden glint caught Bobby's eye. He turned towards it, finding it much easier to focus on than the damned tea light, and then really stared hard when he saw the plait of ginger hair associated with it. Was that who he thought it was? Getting up from the concrete and keeping low, Bobby crept out of the meditation hall and ducked behind the curtains running along the outer edge, moving as quickly as he could to the left doorway, where his target was sitting.

"Sunnuvabidch." Peering in, he saw the bearded face and glazed gray eyes of Mawler McTavish, younger brother of Terror, swaying slightly as he intermittently muttered the same strange syllables as the orange toga guys. He was on to something. Bobby could feel it in his 'nads as he waited for the session to be over — really focused now — and followed Mawler back to his yurt. The guy changed into some sissy clothes, all green and flowy with sandals, then made his way up the hillside, carrying a basket of what must have been pansy food, like maybe cheese and rice bread. Bobby didn't have much trouble tailing him, and eventually took up a post behind a boulder, while Mawler sat facing a tree.

"Oh, learned brother Buddha, show yourself to me," said ginger-head. Terror McTavish appeared in a burst of golden light, legs folded in the lotus position and floating half a metre off the ground. Bobby clamped a hand over his mouth to keep from swearing out loud.

"Eat, brother," said Terror. "This is still a necessity for you." Mawler began chomping on his sissy meal, totally looking like a pansy nutjob. Terror just continued floating there with his eyes closed, his fingers making circles, palms turned upward, and began glowing more. The light from his body was reaching outward, encircling the rocks and plants and coiling up every time it touched something new.

"Have you seen Nirvana, brother?" asked Mawler.

"I have. And I have reached the Fifth Level of Enlightenment."

"How wonderful! Will you soon have enough influence to get me in?"

"Yes, soon, brother!"

Thefugwazzizz? Get him in? Nothing Bobby had read suggested Enlightenment wasn't accessible to everyone. Godhood required an access pass? Since when?

Something warm tickled Bobby's ankle. He looked down to see the glowy light twisting around his foot and tried to pull away. Terror looked up sharply.

"Oh, shid! Mawler, RUN!"

Bobby jumped up and rushed at Terror, who vanished. Mawler was still scrabbling away, so Bobby tried to throw the basket at him, but the stupid thing was not aerodynamic, so he had to chase after Mawler after all. Ginger-head was lighter and faster, and obviously knew the terrain well. Still, Bobby was 'killah' and had his eye on what he was going to get. He deked Mawler on an outcropping of rock and grabbed him by the neck when he came out the other side. Mawler tried to use jiu jitsu to break out of Bobby's hold, but being an entire weight class lower, he just didn't have enough to overcome the fed-up, over-bullshit-saturated determination of Bobby's chokehold. Bobby finished with him pinned under both knees, and one arm twisted up under his chin.

"Whaddya want, man? I'm on freakin' holiday," Mawler whined.

"Terror threw his last fight with me. And now he's a Buddha god or something. How'd he do that?"

"I don't know what you're talking about. I was just out here having lunch. And Terror never threw no dives."

"I *saw* him. And I heard him saying he was gonna get you in. Tell me how."

"Not everyone can reach Enlightenment. It takes years of disciplined practice."

"Yeah, yeah. And *influence.* You guys got an *in,* and I want part of it."

"You have to earn it, not just anybody can get— hey!"

Mawler clawed and scratched as Bobby started ripping off pendants and waist pouches. He really began to panic when Bobby pulled a gold card out from his passport, so Bobby punched him in the face hard enough to make him sleep.

What was this thing anyway? Bobby peered at it intently, then ran his finger along the arrow inscribed along the card's surface.

"Welcome to the Nirvana Entry Portal. Please proceed to the Shiva National Temple." A little blip of light appeared in front of him and traced a line for him to follow. Bobby did, and found that with each step, his confidence and inner happiness grew. He strode into the temple, feeling his being swell and his joy surge. The togas in the temple scurried out of his way, some weeping, others bowing, all staring at him in awe. As he approached the gold Buddha statue seated on the main shrine, it smiled, stood up, bowed to him, and got out of his way as the doors behind it slid open.

"Wait, don't I have to die to get in here?" he asked.

"Death is not necessary to reach Enlightenment, Bobby Fong, only to negate your fighter's contract."

Bobby stepped into a wondrous garden filled with light. All the blossoms glowed. The trees sang. The wind danced and caressed his face.

"Welcome, Bobby Fong, to the Ultimate Joy of Enlightenment."

"Wow," was all Bobby could think to say in response. He walked further into Nirvana, enjoying the vivid colors and the tittering maidens who came to greet him, bringing him all sorts of gifts— candy, soft shoes, coffee, iPads.

"Mawler? Is that you? Hey, man, I wasn't quite ready yet. I just gotta convince a few more Buddhas that you're the one to…" Terror's voice trailed off when he saw Bobby. "You sunnuvabidch! Do you have any idea of what I had to do to get that card?"

Bobby waggled the card in his fingers. "So this is like, an exclusive membership thingy?"

"Yeah. Exclusive. As in to get one for someone new to come in, someone else has to leave."

"You mean, like, reincarnated?"

"No, I mean kicked out. Like you're gonna be when I take that back from you."

Bobby grinned. "Think you can, Old Man?"

"Yeah, OK. I did throw the last fight. That's not gonna happen now, cuz this time you're fighting *a god*."

Terror assumed the first form that Bobby had seen him take on so many holovids. He knew the attacks that could stem from it, and assumed the appropriate counter form. McTavish began to glow. His hair spread out into flames and his eyes turned so bright they left dark spots on Bobby's retinas. He broke from his usual style and slashed his glimmering arms downward in an attack Bobby had never seen anyone do before, breaking through his defences. He barely dodged the second attack. Giving him no chance for an offensive, McTavish twisted his body into a pillar of gold light and released a spin kick that grazed Bobby's shoulder. Bobby tried futilely to land a punch, then a roundhouse which was blocked, and his leg was grabbed.

Before he could use his pinned limb to leverage McTavish onto the ground, he was spun into the air and slammed down, hard. McTavish's golden body swooped upward, aiming a corkscrew elbow drop at him. He rolled to avoid the hit and managed to regain his footing. Two seconds later McTavish's heel was jammed in his mouth, kicking his teeth back into his trachea. Bobby's head snapped back and McTavish delivered a killing elbow to his throat.

"Learned that one from you, son." He winked once, leering evilly as he plucked the gold card from Bobby's waistband, and then all went dark.

Bobby wasn't too sure who or what he was, since he was so cold and numb. Perhaps it was cold concrete pressing against his back. Lots of orange togas were running all over, sounding upset. A few electric shocks jarred his body, but they didn't feel like much. He thought he smelled formaldehyde and struggled to wake up. Maybe he heard Kenichi's voice. Perhaps it was McTavish's voice he heard, laughing as he told Bobby he had to go back. Eventually though, he could make out the buzzing sound of Gravy's needle. And the back of his hand hurt. A lot.

"Whaddyu doing, man?" The needle was jabbing against the bones of his hand, shooting little barbs of pain up his arm several times per second. Gravy was chewing back anger, looking mad enough to spit.

"I found out a whole bundch of shid, Bobby. Whole bundch they never told me. I'm so *pidst*."

"What?" He looked down at his hand, and saw that Gravy was carving in a design that looked like a Scandinavian tribal mark. "What is that?"

"Mawler McTavish took a dive last week, anen I found out about him and his brother. Shid. You an' me, we're blocked from that group. I mean, we've suffered and worked as hard as any of 'em and those bastards are cuttin' us out. They got their little party going on there, an' think they're all bedder than us, keepin' us out."

"So how'd I get here?"

"You *dead*, man! For like a month. But you revived, same as me, an' nis time I *saw* that sumbidch McTavish bringing you back. Anen Kenichi wouldn't let the medics' paperwork go through, so your contract still stands."

"Seriously?"

"Yah, that's why you're here. Kenichi's hiding you until we reach orbit around Saturn, where no one knows you died."

"Aw, crap."

"Bud don't worry, Bobby, because I got us an *in*."

"I thought you said we were barred from Nirvana?"

Gravy grinned and looked really scary doing it. "Don' worry, man. I did a lot of lookin', and also found out Nirvana is for wussies." He handed Bobby a shimmering *blue* card.

"Welcome to Valhalla."

JENNIFER RAHN has written two novels and several short stories. As she pondered the theme, Wrestling with the Gods, two ideas predominated: 1) Buddhism is cool but hard to follow, and 2) kickboxing is cool and her version of heaven would include it. Thus, the theme was taken literally.

THE FAITH CIRCUS

by Alyxandra Harvey

IN THE MARKETS of Navaar, they sell magic in blue glass bottles, love in red pouches stitched with gold, and luck in silver bells.

But instead of spell bottles and amulets, I only saw pitchers of hibiscus tea and pear cardamom cider, sticky honey cakes, and olives rolled in thyme and pink pepper. On a Ceremony day, the magic-sellers closed up shop, by order of the palace. The only magic allowed was in the arena, and it always ended in blood. Already, the healers were gathering ointments and salves.

Still, this part of the city I could understand, it was similar to the markets of Talathusia where anything could be purchased; from lapis lazuli beads, and albino monkeys to pomegranate oil.

But once we reached the sandstone walls circling the arena, the similarities ended.

Niches dug into the walls held the religious artefacts of countless peoples, even beyond the tribes of the Kishdjurien deserts. The Star Maiden of Allifreya , the Dragon Sisters, the Sun King, the Golden Cat, even one of the Desert Mothers I served. Magic rippled like heavy dew on a spider's web. It glistened and shivered and sparked light that caught the eye, only to vanish. I reached up to touch the collar the mercenaries had clamped around my neck.

Because they sold something else in Navaar.

They sold faith; but you never could tell if it was real.

Not until it was too late anyway.

●●◉◉◉

Tiberius squinted up at the sky, wiping the sweat from the back of his neck.

The sun was red in the sky: a bad omen. Or a good one, according to Akhanum. His people sang special songs when the sun turned red. But they also worshipped cats and kept their bones in jars of gold dust. In the steppes, Tiberius remembered the women covering the cooking fires, in case the flames jumped to the barley fields to follow the sun. He'd been a shaman then, fed on the blood of horses and the ashes of such fires. Here he was just another arcane wearing the scorpion and forced into the arena by spear point and lion's tooth.

In the arena, they could pray to their gods and honor the magic such rites created— but only in the sand pits and the training circles. Only where the good folk of Navaar could profit by coin or entertainment. Anywhere else and the scorpions woke hungry. Some arcane tried to escape, but the city gates woke the scorpions as surely as magic did. And death was too simple, it was poisoned pain they offered instead. It was a battle no one could win.

So there was sand, blood, prayers, and the Raja with his ruby crown and his gilded throne. He sent warriors and outlander mercenaries to capture arcanes from temples near and far for his Faith Circus.

"New girl," Annis nudged Tiberius. Her black hair was coiled on her head, like the snakes tattooed around each forearm. Tiberius followed her gaze to the Faith Circus's most recent acquisition, an amber scorpion gleaming in the hollow of her throat. She wore her ritual regalia: silver coin headpiece and matching belt and a heavily embroidered choli with beaded ribbon ties.

Tiberius shook his head. "They brought in a Talathusian temple dancer. I give her a week before she's broken."

A second glance showed her wrists and ankles were bare of the bruises and raw welts left by chains. Sometimes, the devoted volunteered, eager to prove their gods' powers. They walked right onto the bloody sand without chains, ropes, or the prodding of guards. It never ended well.

"Curse Jada," Tiberius said. Jada was the silversmith who had first crafted the scorpion collars. "The temple dancer volunteered," he added, disgusted. "I give her a day."

⊛⊛⊛⊛⊛

"Welcome to the Faith Circus," the Raja announced, his words oiled and pretty, like the gilded cloves we used to decorate oranges for sacred feasts. He glimmered, dripping rubies and diamonds. "Once again, I make this oath. Astound me, holy ones. Break the chains of my magic, show me your miracles. Show me the power of your gods and I will kneel. If you cannot, you will kneel."

They said he'd lost his father and two brothers to a wasting sickness. He'd prayed day and night, night and day, and still the gods had not answered. Now he was king, and he would have his miracles. His revenge. We were the puppets he used to tell his story in a way that made him a hero.

The roar of the crowd closed over me like the jaws of a hungry beast. I waited in the dank shadows of the stone arches. Animals growled, pacing behind iron bars. I couldn't see them, but the smell of urine, hot fur and hay was nearly as strong as the incense.

They'd already paraded us to the music of sitars and drums. Now I was in the wings, waiting for my name to be called. A young man with oiled black hair walked barefoot between tigers and lions. They prowled around him, eagerly snatching the raw meat tossed at them from the guards on the other side of the iron fences. When he spoke his god's name, the lions lay down.

A mystic sat and chanted, his eyes closed to the crowds and the crown. When the guards prodded him with their spears, blood bloomed on his ribs. He kept chanting.

Next came a woman wearing a long pleated skirt the blue of the ocean, her scorpion collar, and nothing else. She danced around a massive white bull until he snorted impatiently, sides heaving like giant bellows. She leapt, grabbing his gilded horns, and somersaulted onto his back. She seemed content there, comfortable even. She stroked his sweaty neck, singing a song in a language I'd never heard before. The audience cheered, throwing roses, and more raw meat to antagonize the bull. They wanted proof that she was beloved of the bull-gods.

But a bull was a bull, no matter the prayers.

He tossed her, trampling her as she fell. It happened so fast, she was a smear of blue and red in the dust. When she tried to stand up, he ran her through with his horn. He was maddened by the meat and the screaming of the spectators. She dangled there for a long moment, touching his fierce snout, and finally landing like a rag doll.

The crowd stomped their feet. They wanted bloody, painful proof from all of the arcane.

And now it was my turn.

"If you don't go," another arcane said when I paused. "They'll release a tiger and close the gate behind you both. They won't let him kill you, only mangle you," he spat. "The Raja will have his prayers."

But the Desert Mothers were not ordered by the dance. I did not know of any gods who would reveal themselves to a Raja such as this one. He wanted us to prove ourselves worthy, when really, that task was for him to do. In Talathusia, we danced the sandstorms to slumber, the river to flood the fields, the rains to fall. These were gifts, not demands. But they did not make for a very good show.

The brightness of the arena seared my eyes, even though I'd taken the time to line them thickly with kohl. Myrrh Incense burned in cloying choking clouds. The bull-leaper's blood congealed in the sand. I stepped around it as the tabla drums beat loudly. It was the wrong beat.

Still, I would dance.

The Talathusian arcane was alone in the ring. Tiberius didn't know if she even realized she was bait. She swayed to the sound of the drums, her hips sharp as cannon shot. The earth trembled faintly under their feet. Her coins flashed, blinding the spectators. Whirlwinds of sand rose and fell around her.

At the Raja's signal, Aethlford approached in his creaking chainmail, better suited to a colder climate. He swung his club, the iron studs shattering a fall of beads attached to her hair. He lashed out again with his other hand, mailed fist raking her throat.

"No offence, love," he grinned.

She spun, her skirts lifting like the petals of a poisonous flower. Blood sprayed from the cut on her neck. It touched Aethlford's scorpion. She kept spinning until she was out of reach. She was faster, barely touching the ground, like a hummingbird drinking from the fuchsia hedges. Sweating under his armor, Aethlford gave up. The girl kept spinning, her blood sprinkling the other arcana standing too near.

The audience stomped their feet, thrilled that the tiny girl wearing bells on her toes had evaded an arena champion. But when the Black Talons surrounded her, they went silent with anticipation. Only the drumbeat shivered through the hot heavy air. Crows gathered, perched on the railings, on the parasols of the wealthy, even on the spear tip of a guard. The Talons served Mother Crow, gathering the eyeballs of the fallen on battlefields across the country, and as far north as the Steppes.

There were three of them, battle-madness bright in their blue eyes. All Talons had blue eyes. They were the reason the tribes used blue beads to ward off the evil eye. The arcane wore battle leathers and brandished slender curved swords. The temple dancer wore silver coins and embroidery.

Tiberius swore and the horses pressed at the ropes of their pens on the other side of the arena. Annis was beside him, as always, leaning on her spear. "Curse Jada, she has no idea what she's doing," Tiberius muttered, stalking into the arena. The crowd began to whisper. The light glinted off the Raja's rubies as he leaned forward to get a better look.

Annis moved to follow. She jerked to a stop, her head tilting back as though pulled by a violent, invisible hand. Her eyes went white; pale smoke that curled into dragons and horses and scorpions. She saw what no one else could see. But as it was no good in the privacy of the wings, a guard shoved her into the sunlight. She stumbled, blind to everything except what her goddess showed her. The crowd cheered again.

She blinked, pupils going black once more. If there were shapes still trapped in her amber irises, there was no one to see. "Tiberius, wait," she called out.

Too late.

The horses jostled and reared until the ropes snapped. They galloped around the arena, kicking up clouds of dust. Tiberius swung up onto a golden horse and nocked an arrow from the quiver strapped to his side. The fletchings were painted red and they daggered the air when he loosed arrow after arrow. The Talons bent and contorted to avoid them, as acrobatic as the temple dancer was graceful. The horses pressed closer. The temple dancer's fingers were smeared with her own blood, scratching at the Talon who'd grabbed her by a narrow braid.

Annis's tattoos slithered off her arms, turning to dark inky snakes when they hit the ground. She couldn't get in close enough to warn Tiberius, but she could scare his horses away. The snakes hissed and struck at iron hooves.

Tiberius pinned a Talon to the wooden boards with one of his arrows. Her sisters slashed at him until he stood on his horse and leapt into the air, sparing his mount an attack. He landed between the Talons and the temple dancer.

The Raja lifted his hand. Magic pressed in from the scroll-work railings, a painful pressure between the eyes that forced the arcane to the ground.

"Why did you do that?" the temple dancer demanded of Tiberius. Fury made the coins on her belt clang together discordantly, even though she wasn't moving, on her knees in the bloodied sand.

Tiberius scowled, fighting the spell until sweat and blood matted his hair. "Is that how they say thank you in Talathusia?"

The healers had already stitched the raw gash across my throat and washed it with salt and marjoram leaves. It burned like the red suns. I'd only managed to blood two pendants and had nearly died in the process.

It was not exactly going according to plan.

Still, I had to try, didn't I? For Jada. For all of the arcanes trapped in the Raja's circus. He supplied the arena well with offerings of every tribe and country. Without realizing it, he'd created a new kind of temple, a wheel with many spokes. There was sea water for the Weeping Woman, blood for the Mother Crow, milk for the Star Maiden, herbs and crushed crystals for gods whose names I couldn't pronounce. He'd had pomegranate seeds, lotus roots, and white ashes from a fire of chrysanthemum flowers brought in for the Desert Mothers. I went straight to Seshai, Mother of Scorpions. I ignored the Raja's offerings and pulled a coin from the fringe of my belt and left it as an offering instead. I smeared it with blood from my wound first.

I went to all of the shrines and did the same, pulling coins and offering blood to the Golden Cat statue, the black crystal bowl of water decorated with snakes for the Queen of Serpents, and the broken arrows and horse hair braids of the Hero-God, Kul. I would need everyone's help. I hoped the link of Jada's blood to my blood would be enough.

When the other arcanes finally slept, except for the old man still chanting under the moonlight, I crept back into the sleeping quarters. I stripped off my coin belt and headpiece so they wouldn't give me away. Akhanum slept with his lions and cats, so he would have to wait. The rest of the arcane slept in identical rooms, carved into the walls with a pallet, a table and chair and a small bronze chest for clothes and weapons. Scorpions were painted on the ground in gold powder, as if we could ever forget what kept us here.

The first arcane I found slept like the dead, wrapped in a sheet embroidered with red stars. I snuck in and anointed his amber scorpion with a drop of my blood. He snored and rolled over. I blooded three more arcanes before finding myself at the foot of Tiberius's bed. He was on his side, facing away from me. I stepped closer, wondering how to contort myself to reach his pendant. The cut on my throat was on fire. If I scratched at it again tonight, I'd be too weak to dance in the arena. One more. Just one more.

I reached over, fingertips red with blood. My braid slipped over my shoulder, brushing his arm. It couldn't have been any harder than the brush of a fly. He grabbed the end of the braid and yanked me down before I had time to straighten. I hit the wall with my shoulder and then his hand was around my throat. I struggled for breath.

"What are you doing in here?" He asked quietly.

"Not what you think," I croaked. "I'm unarmed."

"Then you're as big a fool as I thought." He eased back slightly, letting his fingers drop away from my windpipe. I coughed.

Annis appeared at the door, yawning. "If you're going to bed some poor woman, can you both at least be quiet about it?" She lifted her candle. "Oh."

"I caught her going for my collar," he explained. "Trying to open the clasp wakes the scorpion," he added, looking at me.

"I know," I replied, trying to sit up. He was still kneeling on my skirts. "That's not what I was doing."

"Curse Jada," Tiberius sighed suddenly, standing up to get away from me. "This one means to save us."

I scrambled up as well. "We become what we believe in."

He jerked a hand through his hair, as though I exhausted him. "I think we all believe. That's the problem, isn't it?"

"It's not more gods we need," I argued. "It's more heroes." Surely, he wanted to be a hero. His muscles were the size of my head.

But he dismissed it with a snort. "I'm good with a bow, sweetheart. That doesn't make me a hero. And Kul hasn't come to the arena, why would he answer me now?"

"I have a plan."

He laughed harshly, looking at Annis. "They always do. It'll never work."

"Why not?" I asked. "Not long ago a priest of Kul, and priestesses of the Queen of Serpents and the Desert Mothers could never have worked together as we can now. We can take that much from the arena at least, no matter what else it has tried to give us. We used to kill each other when there was no one watching."

"It's the things you believe in that kill you in the end," Tiberius replied, sounding exhausted. "The arena teaches us *that* too. Daily."

"There are different kinds of faith," I pointed out. "Your faith in your gods wasn't tested. Just your faith in people."

"You've been here less than two days, little dancer. I've been here for months."

"Hear her out," Annis said, setting her lamp down.

"Why in the seven hells should I do that?"

"Because I had a vision," she told him quietly. "Before you blundered into the arena."

He paused for a long moment before dropping heavily onto the edge of the bed. "Well, hell."

"Probably," she returned cheerfully.

"We're going to die out there," Tiberius predicted, yet again.

"Just leave the prophecies to me," Annis said mildly.

"If you really believe that, why are you so happy?" Sri asked him, since he was grinning like a hyena in a herd of wounded zebras.

"We never die in the arena," he replied. "All because the first arcanes killed themselves rather than give the Raja what he wanted."

"What happened?" She knew better than to ask, but she couldn't help herself.

"He displayed their bodies on the railings until they rotted away. Then he had cups and spoons made out of the bones. It's what you used to eat your supper last night."

She swallowed thickly. "Oh."

"And then he commissioned more spells. We can't kill each other now, not with magic, anyway. Only he can."

"So you die by the sword instead."

He grinned. "Today I'm dying by your hand."

They'd been fighting for hours. The arena was warm and fetid, like the carcass of a leopard broken open by the sun. Tiberius had nearly run out of arrows and he'd directed most of the horses out into the city, to gallop down the narrows streets. Annis sent so many snakes into the sand that she was gray as ashes. She ducked a mace and rolled behind a column to be ill.

The Raja sent more guards into the arena, bristling with weapons. I ducked under an archway leading to the circular benches where the crowds gathered. I could smell the bowls of olives, the wine, the sweat. I was outside the magic circle, outside the barrier that lulled the scorpions to sleep.

It had to be now.

The shimmy started softly, the coins on my belt sounding like a soft rain. I remembered running in such a rain on the banks of the sacred river with Jada, the days she'd accepted a commission from the third son of the Raja of Navaar. That was seven years ago.

For seven years I'd had to hear her name being cursed as I learned all seven dances of the Seven Mothers, instead of just one like most priestesses in Talathusia.

The amber at my throat was warm, clinging to damp skin. The scorpion stirred. A needle of pain slipped under my collarbone. My dance faltered.

I had to believe that my sister wouldn't create something that could harm me. That my blood would be enough to control the scorpions.

I shimmied a sharp staccato beat with my hips. The scorpion moved again, bit again, but this time I didn't let it stop me. I kept dancing, tracing circles with my rib cage, calling the sandstorms, undulating like a serpent to give Annis' snakes more power.

The amber dissolved like honey until the scorpion was perched in the hollow of my throat. It was tiny and black as the mud from the sacred river. Someone in the crowd gasped and then they were shoving and pushing to get away from me. Guards moved against the tide of panic, scimitars at the ready. I kept dancing until the earth answered, cracking the ground of the arena like an egg. Dust billowed and a guard screamed, falling into the fissure.

The other amber pendants melted away until there were dozens of scorpions crawling through the sand and over the painted benches.

All toward the Raja.

The royal guards surrounded him but they were outnumbered. The amber scorpions called to the other scorpions hidden in alcove and shadow, until they all skittered at the Raja. He stumbled back, shouting for his sorcerers.

"You wanted proof," I called out. "Here it is, Raja. The Mother of Scorpions sees you."

He paled. "Kill her," he ordered.

But the guards were too busy fighting Akhanum's lions, and the other arcanes to reach me. The ones closest to the Raja lifted him high in his litter. The scorpions milled underneath, stinging their ankles.

"I'd run if I were you," I suggested pleasantly.

Tripping over their own swollen feet, the guards stumbled away, the Raja sweating and swearing in his litter. I dropped back down into the sand to find Tiberius and Annis. He was holding her up. His golden armbands had cracked and her black tattoos had faded to a watery blue. She smiled weakly. "How long will the spell last?"

"Navaar will need a new king. This Raja will never again be able to step foot into the city without calling the scorpions to him. They didn't like being trapped in amber any more than you did." I wove on my feet, suddenly light-headed. Magic still hung over the arena, like daggers overhead.

"There's another spell here," I said, feeling the pull of it in my belly. "If we don't find it, the circus will continue. It's not over yet."

We found the last amber pendant in a cave under the arena. The scorpion frozen inside was pale as salt. The guards marched above us, raining pebbles onto our heads. The steps were narrow and carved into the golden rock. In a black bowl set into in a pool of milky water, the amber shone. Annis lifted her sword, to crush it with the pommel.

"Wait," I said. "Magic made this. Magic will break it."

I closed my bleeding fingers around the warm amber. The scorpion stirred, shooting pain up my arm. Magic burned in my veins. It collapsed inward, drawn back to the amber. The magic of so many gods and their servants pulsed through the earth. Coins fell off me like petals of a flower.

"Sri, stop."

I turned myself into a vessel.

I was sand heated to glass, glass frozen to fissures, sand again.

I was scorpions, skittering, stinging, spilling over.

I dissolved like the amber pendants, became an ink spill of black scorpions. I could control them, because I was them. They were me. And we were everywhere.

The magic shield stretched over the arena burned away, like parchment.

The Faith Circus is now a house of all gods, built in the arena where the arcanes used to fight each other in the sand. There is a crack in the ground under the arches where you can see down into the earth, into the cave where a temple dancer named Sri, became Sri Seshai, handmaiden to the gods, and Lady of the Arena.

And outside, in the markets of Navaar, they sell magic in blue glass bottles, love in red pouches stitched with gold, and luck in silver bells.

They used to sell faith too, but now you have to make your own.

ALYXANDRA HARVEY is the author of *The Drake Chronicles, Haunting Violet* and *The Lovegrove Legacy*. She has also been published in *Tesseracts 11* and *17*, as well as *Urban Green Man* and *Masked Mosaic*. She likes cinnamon lattes, tattoos, and books. With a love for ancient history, "The Faith Circus" gave her an opportunity to explore creative spiritual traditions.

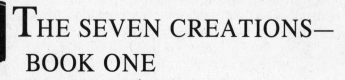

THE SEVEN CREATIONS— BOOK ONE

by Halli Lilburn

IF ONLY I had more power like the Great Apostle I could transfigure matter and turn this gag and chains into dust. With that kind of power I could disintegrate the barricades and set everyone free. Chained to a pillar I sit on the stone floor of the front hall. The temple is under siege again. The number of non-believers grows larger every day.

"Prayer is forbidden!" an angry voice snaps my eyes open and jolts my head back, hitting the column behind me.

The guard shakes his weapon, stomps forward and rips the gag out of my mouth. My jaw clicks as it loosens from the strained position it held for the last five hours. The chapped skin on the edge of my mouth crumbles like a fault line in an earthquake.

"Who do you think you are?"

I manage to whisper, "I am a Disciple of the Seven Creations."

He strikes my face with his hand. "You are a prisoner of the Freedom Consulate. We are in control of the Creations now."

The sting from the slap sends heat racing up my cheek. I want to use my power to disperse the pain, but I don't dare close my eyes again.

The Great Apostle is trapped in the Gate Room while the rebels attempt to break in. He is old and frail and I'm afraid that the rebels will not be merciful to him. They pound on the door, fire their weapons at it and bash tools against the walls, but after five hours they are still outside and the Great Apostle is still within.

The Great Apostle officiates over the Seven Gates of Creation: Light, Matter, Time, Thought, Energy, Life and Death. He practices the divine law of Apportionable Equity, opening and closing the Gates according to our needs. He maintains perfect balance in the universe. The only Gate he cannot fully close is Death. Death can always sneak out although at the age of six thousand, nine hundred it is evident he can at least delay it for a while.

He mentored me since childhood as a father figure and prophet ever since I joined the Discipleship. If my powers increase enough I might be privileged to see the Gates before I die, but visual proof is not something I seek after.

Some say the Gates don't exist. They say life is just a series of coincidences and no one can control it. People like the Freedom Consulate will go to great lengths to prove that no one is in charge of them. They say we have been fooled. They say the Great Apostle is just a crazy old man with a few magic tricks. What they don't realize is how they contradict themselves. If relying on the Seven Creations is for the weak, then how can they claim the right to control their own destiny? How would that be possible without the Gates? Imagine a world without order or discipline. They don't know what is good for them so they resort to tantrums like a disobedient child. A kite may want to be free of its string, but without it the kite crashes to the ground.

A woman in a tight black jumpsuit comes down around the curve in the grand staircase and hollers at the guard looming over me. "Bring her up."

"Yes sir," he responds. "Boss wants to talk to you." A contemptible smirk drifts across his face. He leans in close to unbuckle the chains around my feet and hands. The stench of his body odor is nauseating with breath like gaseous steam on my neck. He lingers there, sniffing my hair as if I were his prey. He coos in my ear. "The favorite of the Great Apostle. You will be very…" He pauses, his greedy eyes strolling up and down my body. "…useful." The slithering snake of chain sounds out a muffled tinkle as it drops from his hands.

"Where are we going?" I am yanked to my feet and a slow, painful tingle signals that blood is reaching back into my limbs.

"You're going to get the old man to open the door."

"Impossible," I involuntarily whisper, but he ignores me and pushes me towards the grand staircase.

The leader of the rebels, known only as "The Boss", is lucky he's not dead. The last time the temple was seized it ended when the Great Apostle widened the Gate of Death, killing the rebels before they even climbed the stairs. Along with most of the rebels, several of the Disciples also perished. Of course they were willing to die for the cause, but the Master is riddled with guilt. He will not let it happen again. So today he sits in his chamber and does nothing.

Now that I am up I can see how many of my students are bound to other pillars. I count six bodies. Many are missing.

"Teacher?" a voice escapes one of my students as I limp past her.

"Silence!" my captor booms and smacks the side of her head. Her hair sprays over her face. There is nothing I can do.

I climb the curving staircase slowly. Quiet moments pass. This situation is a time bomb and each stair conquered is a ticking clock.

"Move it!"

We round the bending spiral and the Gate Room comes into view. Like a tortured prisoner, the iron door has taken a brutal beating. The lock shows marks from pry bars, torches, even explosives, but miraculously, nothing has destroyed it. In fact, it seems to have melted into a more solid mass, fusing itself to the surrounding frame. Men are violently chipping away at the granite walls but their pickaxes break against the rock. Projectiles turn to ash as they connect and harmlessly spray across the stone. A chip in the rock shrinks and disappears. The Master's power of transmutation has kept the barrier strong and impregnable. Seeing a miracle such as this boosts my spirit. I have been witness to his power before, but never at this magnitude.

My presence makes the Boss turn around. Something about him seems out of place. He exudes power and aggression yet underneath that mask there is something different.

He takes a quick step forward, making me gasp and step back. As if reading my thoughts he peers at me and wonders aloud, "What is it about you that the old man so highly favors?"

I do not flinch when he raises his hand to my face to trace the outline of the mark made when I was slapped. "Pity." he says before turning back to his men. He gives orders for them to clean up and clear out, but I don't hear it. My only awareness is the blood pulsing under my flesh where he touched me.

The world comes back into focus when his face invades my space again. "Time to try something new." He brushes my hair as if I were his toy. "If mortal strength won't work then we will use divine strength. Yours."

Now my fear surfaces and despite my resolve, my lip begins to tremble.

"Open the door. Open it or I will kill you."

"I would rather die," I state.

"I thought as much," he says. "But are you sure all of your students have the same passion? The same commitment?" He turns his head to the landing where my student stands, hanging on the arms of the stinky guard. Her hair still covers her face, but I can see she is crying.

"This one will die first." There is no pretence reflecting off the blade against her face.

"No." I panic. "No, I'll do it. I'll open the door."

The Boss relaxes his features. "That's my girl." His voice is disturbingly peaceful.

His endearing phrase I have never heard directed at me before, but its meaning affects me deeply. It reminds me of another expression of kindness I hear often. The Great Apostle's voice resonates in my mind.

"Bless you, child."

The two statements are distressingly familiar. They overlap each other, binding themselves together into one whole. Truth and lie; love and hate; opposite yet parallel; a perfect balance. I cannot interpret my feelings as I sink to my knees and close my eyes. Focusing my thoughts I call out.

Master, are you there?

I branch out, transporting my thoughts through the walls to the man behind the barricade. Slowly, an answer forms.

Ah, child, I never wanted you tangled up in this mess.

The telepathic channel is open.

Are you all right?

I have dreaded this day for a long time

They threaten to kill my students if I don't.

Well, you had better let them in.

My eyes open and the connection is severed. An awareness of my surroundings returns. Is he actually permitting me to open the door to these terrorists? Into a room no one else has ever entered?

"Well?"

Confused, I rub my eyes.

"Well?" The Boss repeats. "What's taking so long?"

"Give me another minute." I huff, glancing at my student who has dropped to the floor. Blood seeps from a cut on her eyebrow.

The Boss crouches down beside me. "It's fine. Take your time."

I sigh with relief until I see his face harden. "Just be aware that every minute you take from me, I will take something in return." He unsheathes a large knife. "I couldn't help but notice that your precious pupil over there has ten fingers." He brushes the stubble on his jaw with the thick blade. "I will give you one minute for every finger. If I am adding correctly that means you have ten minutes, however," — He flips the blade up and catches it — "if you really need more I can always continue with her toes."

The girl jolts back, shaking her head and screaming through the cloth waded in her mouth.

The horrific threat fills my eyes with tears. "Please, don't." I beg. "I'll open the door, just please don't."

The Boss sheaths his knife. "You are most accommodating." He pats my shoulder.

I close my eyes and concentrate on the mental signals emanating from the Great Apostle until his message bursts into my brain.

Child, it is time for you to enter the Gate Room and release me.

His statement is puzzling.

Why do you surrender to these monsters?

I only held them back until they brought you to me. Now we can end this conflict together.

What would you have me do?

Use your power over matter. Release the lock. Give them the proof they seek.

My power is too weak. I've never been able to perform that sort of miracle.

No, child. Do not doubt yourself. You are ready.

The connection closes. I look to the battered door, wondering how I am expected to accomplish his request.

"One minute is up." The Boss signals two of his followers to restrain the girl.

She screams and struggles but she is small and easily overpowered. Within seconds they have her pinned to the ground, a heavy boot forcing her outstretched hand into place.

"Wait!" I cry.

"My apologies to both of you." the Boss raises his knife.

What happens next is far from any of my training, but rather is born of instinct. All my spiritual strength is summoned and I plunge the building into darkness. The knife swishes through the air then hits the stone floor. The Boss mutters a curse. In the blackness I place both of my palms on the floor and press down. The solid tiles begin to vibrate and crack.

"Save her." I whisper and lift both hands in a sweeping motion towards my pupil. In the darkness the tiles pull off the floor and follow in the same direction. My confidence waxes strong as I aim the growing mass of rock under the girl and lift her up. My hands are still raised over my head when the lights come back on.

What I imagine I did and what I see are not the same. I wanted to move her out of harm's way but the result of my effort is much more than that. Replacing the tiles where she laid is a massive, granite pedestal, twisting to the ceiling like the trunk of an ancient tree. The girl peers down at me, all ten of her fingers clutching the edge.

She chokes and gasps with relief. Her eyes sweep over her surroundings. "A Perfect Transmutation. Bless you, Teacher!"

The stinky guard scoffs. "You might have saved one hostage, but there are plenty others." He saunters over to the stairs.

Thinking only of protecting my students, I press my hands again to the ground and pray for the strength to perform the transmutation again. A fissure splits across the landing and with a terrifying crack breaks the staircase off of its supports and it crumbles to the floor below. The crash is deafening. His foot hovers in midair where the first step has fallen out from under him. He cannot pull back. His arms flail and he calls out, but no one can reach him in time.

A cloud of dust pours into the room and we stifle our breathing and wait for it to disperse.

The first to speak is the Boss. "Damn your sorcery, witch." His fierce gray eyes dig into my heart. He flips his knife end over end. "Enough. You have displayed your powers. It is obvious you are more than capable so I demand you open this door. Now."

I stand and brush the dust from my robes. "I don't mind. I'll do it. He wants me to." Without pausing I place my hand on the battered, metal lock. "Disintegrate," I tell it and it obeys, falling to pieces like rain.

I never thought I would be standing here in front of the Gate Room trying to transfigure the door. I never dreamed I would ever see inside. The idea births a strange excitement in my heart. I will see what no other Disciple has ever seen. The Boss's anxious breath on my neck makes me cringe. I give him a sideways glance and he backs up a step.

The iron against my palm liquefies and drips down my arm. An amber glow blooms across the surface. Slowly the metal buckles and melts, into soupy blobs and runs across the floor.

"Amazing." The Boss' eyes are wide.

"Absolutely," I whisper, as we step over the mess and side by side enter the Gate Room.

The chamber is completely circular and windowless with a mural of the universe adorning the entire circumference. The only furniture is a stone altar in the center whereat kneels a bent and crippled sage. His weathered hands struggle to cradle his head in their feeble grasp. I kneel before him and the Boss imitates me, whether out of respect or mockery I am unsure. The others stay outside.

With much effort the Great Apostle lifts his head. His eyes find mine and he smiles.

You have done well, child.

I never wished for this, even so, it is an honour to be the one asked.

"Don't be so modest." The Boss interrupts our thoughts.

He has tuned into my telepathic communications. I wonder where he acquired this skill.

"You and I stand where only the Great Apostle stands. We are his equals." He grins.

"How dare you! You desecrate his sacred site with your presence!"

"Then, my girl, so do you."

His rebuttal stings my ego. It is true. I'm not worthy of this place. I shouldn't have come in.

"Where are the Gates old man?" the Boss swings his knife onto the altar. "I don't see anything in this room but an old fool and his whore. I came here for the Gates so show them to me now!"

The Master slowly looks up. "And what would you use them for?" he asks.

The Boss scrapes his blade across the stone leaving a white scratch. "I want to control them, of course. I want to give the people power to decide their own destiny. The Creations should not be limited to the whims of one man. How do you know what's best for me? What gives you the right?"

I pity the unbeliever. They are lost and directionless, burdened with unbearable confusion. The Seven Creations do not bind or limit us. On the contrary, they support and provide us with multitudes of blessings, things we could never achieve on our own. We should never think that we don't need their guidance. One does not tempt their God.

And yet, I look around me and see nothing. The painted stars, the altar are beautiful in their simplicity, but they give no evidence of the awesome power that I expected to reside in this sanctuary.

"Where are the Gates?" the Boss repeats.

"They are not here."

"Not here? What do you mean not here? Where are they?"

The Great Apostle shrugs and replies placidly, "I don't know."

I wonder if maybe he's lying, but the Master never lies.

The Boss slaps his knife on the altar. "Then my father was right. The Gates don't exist." He wipes his forehead with the back of his hand. "People trusted you. They came to the temple pleading for blessings and you just lied to them. They depended on you for help. If their request was denied, you said it was fate. If their wish was granted, now I know it was just coincidence. You made them think you had the authority, but you had nothing! You live a life of arrogance and deception." Tears work their way through the dust on his face.

"Everyone is given the trials they can bear."

"That's what you told my mother when she asked for healing."

"We will never be given a hardship that won't make us stronger."

"She's dead, you idiot!"

I feel his pain and I'm sure the Great Apostle feels it too. "I'm sorry, child."

"I'm not your child." Wiping his eyes and face, the Boss turns to the now decimated door, "Get me out of here."

His assistant stands by the opening waiting to take him, but he turns to me instead. There is a pleading look in his eyes. I can't think of what he could possibly want from me.

"I will speak to the law enforcement agents outside and tell them no one was harmed. You can leave. We won't press charges." Comforting him is the best solution in this situation. I need him calm to assure everyone's safety; at least until he's in custody.

"Don't condescend to me, Teacher." He fixes his eyes on me.

Inexplicably he wraps his arms around me. I stiffen and hold my breath, unsure what to do. I rarely receive an embrace from a man, let alone an enemy.

"I'm sorry. Your career is over. The world will know what secrets were hidden here, the lies, the brainwashing. Your testimony against this man will change everything."

I back away from him and he drops his arms. Does he really think I can betray my religion over this? It might be concrete proof to him, but to me it is a test of my faith. "We are all given the trials that we can bear." I say.

He stares at me.

"Come, members of the Freedom Consulate. We have a world to change." He beckons to his men who have set up a rope to repel down the empty stairwell. "You should tend to your Master. He looks unwell." With that the Boss hooks a harness around his hips and slips over the edge. As I watch him go he looks at me and winks.

Then he descends into the pit and out of my life.

I take a moment to collect myself and ask the master if he can stand.

"With a little help." He answers and takes my arm for support.

"You look famished. You need food and water." I try to lead him out, but he stops me.

"Food can wait. You must help me with a task of far more importance." He leans his weight on the altar. "We must recover the Gates."

"The Gates?"

The Master's eyes twinkle. "Of course, child. Did you doubt?"

"Not really."

He smiles. "We must call them back."

"How?" I ask.

"A blood sacrifice." He pulls a small bodkin from within his robes. "On the altar."

I look at the stone and notice the worn surface is tinged red. "You've performed this ritual many times." I state.

"Yes, and I am too weak for it now. You must do it."

"Me?" I blink.

"It only takes one drop." He assures me.

I take the bodkin and press it to my thumb. A crimson drop of blood falls onto the altar. The Master takes a step back so I do the same.

At first nothing happens. Slowly the surface becomes moist with blood, like the old stain was rehydrating and sweating through the rock. Small bubbles form, then larger ones, until the altar looks like a cauldron. Spurts of fluid spit up into the air and the more they shoot up the longer they levitate. Gravity loses its hold and the blood starts floating and swirling in the air. It glows and forms into an orb. Seven branches grow out of the light and electricity fires through them. I gasp as seven different colored balls begin orbiting on their branches like a solar system with the planets attached to the central star.

"It is beautiful," I say in awe. "I have never seen anything so magnificent." The globes look like glass with turbulent glowing gas inside: Green for Life, White for Light, Cerulean for Matter, Gold for Time, Tangerine for Energy, Violet for Thought and Sienna for Death. The lights play off the walls, electric currents connect between the Gates and the painting of the universe, the ceiling, the floor and each other. My imagination could never conceive what I am witnessing. "Why don't you show the world? Let everyone know so that we can avoid any more rebellions. People need to see this."

"They must be kept sacred. Their powers untainted. They cannot fall into the hands of wicked men. You heard what the rebels wanted to do today. Think of the chaos that would ensue if a man like the Boss was in charge. It is better that he believes they don't exist than to give him accessibility. Never give great wisdom to the ignorant and misguided."

I know the Great Apostle is right, but I feel a sorrow for the Boss. His misguided search for truth brought him nothing.

My thoughts are interrupted when a loose rock skids across the floor. I look towards the opening and see a pair of black boots standing on top of the rubble. Another step and more rocks shake loose.

"You cannot trick me." The boots belong to the Boss. He stands in the doorway with his henchmen aiming their weapons at the Seven Creations. "You tried to hide them from me, but

I won't—" he is interrupted and everyone freezes like statues. The Great Apostle's arms are above his head, his eyes closed. He is controlling time. I didn't know it was possible.

"I can only hold it for a moment so listen carefully. These men cannot be allowed to continue in their evil ways. Only you can stop them."

"Me?" I blink. "How?"

"I will teach you how to pilot the Gates."

"Why me?"

"It was your blood on the altar; therefore you are chosen to be the Master."

"What?" My voice squeaks in surprise.

"My time as Great Apostle is finished; I can no longer hold back the Gate of Death. You must rise to take my place."

I stare at him as his words sink in. "You knew this would happen when I gave my blood?"

"Yes. I am sorry if you feel deceived but the reality is evident. My life is nearly over and I must ordain a new Apostle." His arms waver and drop slightly, allowing the rebels at the door to move forward in slow motion.

"But there are others more worthy than I. Surely you would pick one of them."

"There is no time. You must restore order. Every sphere has a branch. You can pull them closer to the center star to close them and farther away to open them. Each Creation will help you restore balance. Child, you must protect the Gates. Protect the world."

The lower his hands sink the faster the rebels are able to move.

With laboured breath he speaks his last words. "It was always you." In exhaustion he collapses and time is re-established. I start to run to him, but the distance is too great. The Boss storms up to me and grabs my shoulders. We stare blankly at the Great Apostle. He lies very still.

The Assistant and other men attempt to enter the sanctuary, but he orders them back. "Don't come in here. None of you come in here." He turns back to me. "He stopped time. You blurred for a moment. What did he say to you?"

"Nothing you will ever know."

He is so close his eyes shift left and right in order to focus on each of mine. He is trying to read my mind. I block him out but he tries again.

"Stop." I say out loud.

He moves past me to study the Gates. He reaches out, but his hand moves through the spheres as if they were holograms. Frustrated, he punches in the air but the spheres don't waiver. "This must be an illusion."

Slowly a dark cloud flows out of the Gate of Death. We shrink back as it sails through the air. Straight at the Great Apostle.

"No." I grab the brown sphere with both hands. Unlike the Boss whose hand went right through, I connect with solid matter. I try pushing it back in place but it won't go. I put all my strength against it but I can't move it. I cannot close the Gate. A finger of smoke touches the Master and his body evaporates into nothing.

"No." I sink to my knees knowing my flood of questions will never be answered.

The room is quiet. Or maybe people are talking but I don't hear them. I am aware of a tear falling from my face like a tidal wave.

"Teacher."

I open my eyes and sniff.

The Boss helps me to my feet. "You can touch the Gates. How did you do it?" His voice has softened.

I don't answer. I show him. I grab the closest sphere and pull hard. The ball is orange for Energy. With a blast of wind and a crackle of lightning, electricity sprays across the room. It hits the Boss, his dark hair flies back and he sinks to his knees. I can feel my strength increase drastically. My robes seem to whirl around me on their own volition. The rebels in the doorway try to storm in, but with a point of my fingers they are blasted backwards. They don't even have time to yell before they are immobilized in a heap on the landing.

I open wide the blue Gate of Matter. When I raise my hand the crumpled iron of the demolished door flies together and bolts shut leaving only myself and the Boss in the chamber. He sucks in heavy breaths, trying to refill his lungs, but he doesn't get a good chance. My palms turn up and reach outward, making the painted stars corkscrew along the mural. The granite walls dissolve, creating a very real universe all around us. The world disappears as we drift through space. The wind dies and the room floats silently in space.

"You?" he whispers, finally able to breathe again. "You are the new Apostle?"

"I am." Saying these words feels so foreign. I stare at the Gates finding it difficult to admire their beauty when I am so overwhelmed. "Will you help me?" I ask.

"What?"

My question shocks both of us, but the realization soon hits me. I noticed it when I first saw him that he was destined to be something greater than a rebel leader. I feel connected to him as if we were pieces in a grand puzzle. It all makes sense.

"I need help," I say, "to learn what is true and what is right. I can't do this alone. You... can give me strength."

He stands up and nods but overwhelmed he cannot speak. His lifelong mission is over. I gave him the answer.

Finding his voice he asks, "Will you give this power to the people?"

"I don't know how, but we can figure that out together." I realize now what I see in him, what he hid behind his mask. It is innocence and purity. I reach out my hand and he takes it. The connection is made.

The Great Apostle once told me to never squander wisdom by giving it to the ignorant. Today I disagree with this advice. Today I will teach the ignorant how to be wise. My whole way of life is changing and as a result the world will change with me. It scares me, but inside it somehow feels better. It feels like hope.

HALLI LILBURN is a poet, writer and artist. Her first novel *SHIFTERS* was released in 2012. She teaches mixed media and works at the local library. The idea of "Seven Creations" combines a traditional God-based theology with an ancient form of worship for the elements. With the deity remaining mysterious mistakes are bound to be made.

The Rev. Mr. Alline Encounters an Uncommon Light; or, Vapors of Nitre as an Alarming Means:
A Found Poem

by John Bell

One evening
as I was taking a walk &
pondering on
my lost & undone condition,
all of a sudden
I was surrounded with an
uncommon light.

A blaze of fire,
it outshone the
sun at noon day.
I was immediately
plunged in keen despair &
the first conception I had was that
the great day of judgment
was come & time
at a period.

I stood with my face
towards the ground,
trembling in body &
sinking in mind, not
having power to
look nor ask for mercy.

My distress was so great
it continued for
half an hour.

When I lifted
up my eyes
I found the
day of judgment
was not come,
nor the world in flames.

There appeared
a large blaze of light
in the shape of a circle,
with that side next to me open,
as though it yawned after me.
As it drew very nigh me,
it closed up in a small compass,
then broke out in small sparkles
& vanished away.

It is no matter
whether the light
was one of the common phenomena
of nature,
such as exhaled vapors of nitre
that had gathered in the air,
for it was really
designed by God as an
alarming means, a miracle
sent to me in particular.

I thought very much
of the goodness of God
in giving me one moment more
for repentance
& was determined
to spend my
remaining moments
at the door of mercy,
begging for redeeming
love.

Nova Scotia, c. 1768
[from *The Life and Journal of the Rev. Mr. Henry Alline*
(Boston: Gilbert & Dean, 1806)]

JOHN BELL is the author or editor of nearly twenty books. He has also contributed to numerous periodicals and anthologies. John, who lives in Lunenburg, has long been fascinated by the writings of the Nova Scotia preacher Henry Alline, especially the latter's intense account of a religious experience in the late 1760s.

THE HARSH LIGHT OF MORNING

by David Jón Fuller

AS MARGARET HARROW stared into the unforgiving eyes of the Mountie outside her prison cell, the Holy Spirit whispered to her, *You must abandon your faith in God or you will die.*

She hugged herself in the incandescent light that filled the one-room police station. She didn't know what to think. Yet in a matter of hours, when sunlight streamed through the window across the room and between the bars of her jail cell, she would be reduced to ash.

I cannot, she whispered silently back. *I will not.*

You must, said the Holy Spirit.

The officer's face was dark, his brown eyes boring into her from across the tiny RCMP station. "I saw what you did to those kids."

She squinted her eyes shut and ran her tongue over her sharp teeth. For all the long years since her— encounter— with the departed Mr. Mackenzie, which she shuddered to think of, she had never felt as powerless. The decades now hung heavily on her shoulders, and this year, 1930, might well be her last.

It is time to acknowledge the truth, said the Holy Spirit.

What truth?

That there is no God.

Never!

The Mountie sat in a wooden chair that looked as though it had been at the station since the Boer War. His left leg was crossed over his right, his left hand pinching the brim of his upside-down Stetson as it lay in his lap. The clock, spitting its loud ticks and tocks into the silence between him and Margaret, showed half past three. In the tiny village of MacDonald, large enough to house the isolated residential school and a train station to take Saskatchewan wheat to the markets of Winnipeg and Toronto, but little more, they were likely the only two not asleep. Surely he didn't need to guard her? Why, then, was he here, staring at her so? Was it because he was an Indian?

And the small, wooden crucifix that hung above the dark leaded window seemed to pierce her through the forehead. She had always avoided them, at the residential school. Stayed in her classroom in the basement, where she refused to have one put up. The sign had always made her feel weak; when the nuns, half-breeds and savages swarmed about her wearing them, the sight even *hurt* her as if she had swallowed a clutch of sewing needles. But she had never deserted her Lord. She knew He must be testing her.

She waited for an answer, now, in the warm cell as the hissing radiators blocked out the chill of a Saskatchewan autumn. But none came. Perhaps this was something different. But what? Her faith would remain strong. Only then would she be delivered, she knew.

But now, a doubt gnawed at her. How did she know the voice she had heard through the years, as her thirst for what she called her "Communion" grew insatiable, was that of the Holy Spirit? What if it were—

"I know what you are," said the Mountie. "What you can do to people. So don't 'ask' to leave. I made sure to throw the keys away outside. No one, not even me, will be able to find them until morning."

She looked him up and down. The anger in him was palpable; it hit her like a gust of prairie wind before a storm. His short-cropped hair was black as coal, his skin brown, the line of his nose showing her that he was one of them, an Indian. Resentment wafted out from him, in ways he probably didn't even realize, sitting there in his red serge, blue trousers and dust-covered boots. Since the Holy Spirit had begun guiding her, people's feelings, and sometimes even their thoughts, were as clear as the pages of a diary to her. She was also a shrewd guesser.

"I remember you," she said.

He flinched.

"Bobby," she said. "*Robert.*"

"Not the name I was born with."

She nodded. "But it's the one we gave you. The one you still use, I'd wager."

He smoothed his necktie. "You can call me Constable Courchene. Or just 'Officer.'"

She closed her eyes a moment. "Slow to read, but always a good shot. You brought the school ducks and geese from the marsh."

He said nothing, but swallowed, trying to keep his face a mask, clearly. She smiled. She wasn't reading his face.

"You were from… Manitoba."

He shifted, turning away from her on his chair. "Winnipeg."

"Yet you came back here, to Saskatchewan." Her mind raced, trying to keep him talking so she could — perhaps — win him over, find another way out of the cell. "This place must have been important to you."

He spat. The act, of an officer doing that in his own station, knocked her back as if a physical push. "Someone has to keep an eye out for those kids. Sure as hell most of them didn't really 'run away' from the school, like you and the rest of teachers used to say."

"But of course they did. They couldn't handle the rigors of school life. Not like you—"

"Shut up! Maybe another officer wouldn't look too hard, and take your word for it. But I know better. And after seeing what you did to that girl tonight— we all will."

The thought twisted within her. His feelings writhed like mud in disturbed water, unseen by him but clear to her. She should have been able to play on that, push him in the direction she needed.

But that cross, above his head, bolted to the wall like a radio antenna, damped her ability to sense what he was feeling, made her weak. Ordinarily, if pressed, she could have wrenched on the wood-and-iron door of her cell and snapped the bolt; she was strong enough, having fed just this night before they caught her. But the sign, especially with Courchene sitting beneath it, sapped all her strength.

Why? she pleaded silently. *Why does it hurt me so? I have been faithful.*

To what? replied the Holy Spirit.

To you.

Indeed. Which is the problem.

Her fingers traced the long-vanished wound on her neck. She had been a young woman, then. Seventeen. Enough education to teach, and just about to start with a class of bright young boys and girls at MacDonald School— years before Indian Affairs came along and turned it into a place to teach the Indian to be "civilized," dragging the Anglican nuns and church authority with it. By then, of course, it had been clear that the thirst and strength Mr. Mackenzie had imbued her with meant she could never venture outside during daylight hours. And that thirst sometimes spoke to her, taught her, showed her visions of another place. She had always believed them glimpses of Heaven, sent by the Holy Spirit. For what she was driven to do — to feed off animals, and even people, like a wood tick— would otherwise be monstrous.

You should know now that none of this was true, said the Holy Spirit.

"Funny you remember *that*, and not all the times you hit me for speaking Ojibwe," said the Mountie.

She snapped her hand away from her neck and glared at him. "It was for your own good."

He cleared his throat. It squeaked a little as he raised his voice. "That? And the times you locked me in that dark little room because I couldn't read?"

"You never applied yourself. You pretended to be stupid."

His eyes glistened and his right hand caressed the pistol in his holster. "I was neither stupid nor pretending. All the kids knew what went on in that place. Now I see, tonight, how much worse it was for some of them. That girl you attacked — I saw her neck! — ran away while we were dealing with you. But my partner is out looking for her. Even without the bodies she uncovered, you're going to prison. But we'll get her story. And people will know."

Margaret clenched the bars of her cell and sucked her breath in so hard it hissed.

The glistening in his eyes became tears. He stood up and opened the flimsy curtains on the east-facing window behind his chair. "But you're never going to see the inside of a courtroom. Not when that sun comes up."

When he stood, the Holy Spirit spoke to her again. *Keep him on his feet. Make him come closer to you.*

"Why?" she asked out loud.

"Because you deserve it," said Courchene.

"What? I didn't hear—"

She meant to coax the voice of God to repeat itself, but again, speaking out loud, she provoked the constable.

"'Maybe I should apply a ruler to that hand,'" he said, raising his voice as he repeated the phrase she had used on students as a matter of course. She shrank back from the terrible purpose in his tone.

He stepped towards her.

That's it, said the Holy Spirit.

"What?" she said.

"You heard me!" thundered Courchene, taking another step, his hand shaking as he pointed at her. He didn't seem a towering knight of authority anymore, but instead, a frightened boy quivering awkwardly in a man's body.

More, said the Holy Spirit.

But she did not understand, and so backed right to the far wall of her tiny cell, wishing she could melt and pass through the wood and stone.

"You, you were always a good boy, dear," she said, hoping that praise at this late stage would still turn his rage from her — the children were always so desperate for a kind word, that was why she and the nuns withheld them, as a rule, to keep the students in line — and allow her to appeal to his mercy. She had been at the school before the church had taken it over, of course; trapped there by her condition. But the fact she was willing to stay on as a teacher, and unlike the Anglican sisters, was happy to use the basement classroom, ensured her a steady supply of... Communion.

This one has no mercy for you, said the Holy Spirit; and in her heart she knew it spoke the truth.

He took another half-step toward her, his tall, broad-shouldered frame casting a shadow in the light of the electric bulb fixed in the ceiling. It also, for a moment, blocked her view of the crucifix, and suddenly she felt a leaden weight fall from her limbs.

Now, said the Holy Spirit, *you must listen to me, or we will both perish. You are ready to attempt something that may deliver us yet.*

She closed her eyes. *What must I do?* she said silently.

Allow me to take control for a moment.

Her eyelids flew open, her pulse racing. This was it. The test of her faith. The splinter of doubt in her grew too painful to ignore and she realized the truth. This was not the voice of God that had been speaking to her.

She felt jubilation at her discovery, even as the Voice said *At last, you see—*

Because she knew, with certainty, that it was the Devil who whispered to her. *You cannot tempt me,* she told it.

The Voice howled something silently within her, in infernal language she could not understand. She fell to her knees and began to pray. She ignored the looming officer over her and beseeched the Lord for deliverance.

It is your faith in your God that keeps you imprisoned, whispered the Voice.

She ignored it.

The sign, that symbol on the wall — here the Voice seemed unable to even call it what it was, a crucifix — *means something very powerful to you. It focuses your thoughts and beliefs. But it must mean something very different to this man. Because your human minds seem capable of making the same depiction mean very, very different things. My kind cannot do this, and this clash of faith hurts us.*

Margaret did not understand the voice at all. She kept whispering her Our Father aloud.

"That won't help you," said Courchene. "All the years you made us memorize and repeat your white God's words, it taught me and my brothers there would be no answer. A lot of kids never made it out of that place. Now there will be no answer for you, either, except the sunrise."

The voice was frantic now. *If you stay here we will both burn. You've felt the sun's touch before.*

Her words faltered as she came to "...deliver us from evil." She remembered the time she had tried to leave the school in the early evening, years ago; a few seconds and her skin was a painful crimson. It had taken her weeks to recover. And as long as the school authorities let her stay and work in the basement, there was no trouble. She found she was very persuasive, even down to the suggestion to the nuns that yes, indeed, of course she wore a cross around her neck. *Oh yes,* they would say, staring at her neck, where no necklace lay, *I see it now.* And they were not lying; they saw what she wanted them to see. But now they had seen too much; Reverend William had caught her in the act of feeding on the little brat who had discovered the other girls' bodies in the locked basement room. He knew what she had done. It was too much, and he had sided with the little savage, calling the police. She could not go back to the school. She must escape.

I can help you, the voice said, and she could not tell whether the agitation she felt belonged to the voice or to her.

God will help me.

A second of silence, then the voice replied: *if you do not take the help that is offered, what more can your God do?*

She ran her tongue over her sharp teeth. What, indeed?

"What must I do?" she asked.

Courchene gripped his pistol in its holster as if afraid it would jump out of its own accord. "You can sit there in the light, alone."

Then the voice took control of her, just for a moment.

She felt an odd sensation, as of a long, deep, exhalation. The cell and police station faded to gray, became indistinct. Then she realized it was she who was changing. Her body lightened, diffused, lost all shape and spread to fill the cell. She had no eyes nor ears, but she sensed the shock and surprise from Courchene as she turned to mist. The Voice, saying nothing now, pulled her through the bars of the cell, a rolling fog to freedom on the other side. She wailed with exhaustion, being stretched beyond her limits without having permission to break. Her tendrils wisped through the air of the police station. Then the Voice inhaled all of her vaporous being back into her familiar, solid shape, right down to the black buttons on her dress and the leather soles of her shoes. She staggered. She was so thirsty.

Courchene retreated, clumsy thumping steps stumbling on the floorboards, and the crucifix on the wall loomed into view.

Down! snapped the Voice, and she crouched without thinking. Now the officer's body blocked her view of the symbol again. Her throat was still parched, her tongue thick and pasty, but she felt her strength seep into her. *I need... Communion...* she thought.

Not here, said the Voice. *You will lose everything as long as you can see that, that thing on the wall. Keep your eyes averted. If he has not locked the door there may still be time.*

She crawled away from the Mountie and when she got to the station's entrance she clung to the brass doorknob. With a sob she twisted it and wrenched the door open.

Outside, the air was crisp and frost hung in the air. In the late autumn, winter whispered to the prairie grass. The stars filled the darkness above, but the sky to the east had lightened, just a bit. She was free. She just needed to make it to the train station, and she would find a dark, safe place to wait out the day. If aboard the baggage car of a passenger train, so much the better, but for now, she had escaped.

Then she felt the constable's meaty hand clamp down on her shoulder.

."Not so fast," he said, spinning her around and pointing his revolver at her.

Again, cried the voice.

Courchene cocked his pistol. He really meant to shoot her. Immediately, she let herself disperse again, even as the Mountie fired, his bullets passing through her misty form leaving no damage but swirls. One, two, three, four, five, six.... click, click.

She took her human shape once more, the change coming more easily this time, and grabbed the Mountie's wrist, keeping the gun pointed away from her. "Such a naughty, filthy boy," she said. "Shame on you, to shoot at a woman like that."

He shied away, throwing his free hand in front of his face, as if to ward off a blow. "Don't!" he cried, his voice breaking. A little boy in a man's body.

She furrowed her fingers into the knot of his necktie and tore it open. He slapped at her clawlike hand to no avail as she ripped apart the buttons of his collar. The skin of his neck and chest lay exposed. She was so thirsty now the night crowded its blackness in at the edge of her vision. His gun fell from paralyzed fingers and she slid her hand up the back of his neck, gripped the short hair and pulled his head back. Now she would take the Communion he offered, and be strong again.

There were scars on his chest.

She smiled. A sign of his being disciplined, surely, back at the school. "Something to remember your teachers by," she said softly. He tried to winnow his hand to the inside of her arm and push her away, but her grip was like a snake's lips on a leopard frog.

He spat at her. "None from that place."

She lingered a moment on the thin, white marks that shone in the moonlight on his chest. They were far too regular, even for a beating given in the same place many times.

Don't think about it, said the voice. *Drink.*

Courchene struggled to meet her eyes from the awkward tilted-back position of his head. "I did the Sundance."

The marks seemed to quiver and push her back.

Ignore it, said the voice. *Drink.*

She winced. It was some savage ritual, she realized.

"My father was dead," said the Mountie. "But there were still some elders who knew the ways. After I graduated from the academy and joined the Mounties, I followed in the steps of my ancestors." He grimaced. "You're the first white person to know."

Now her strength deserted her, though her terrible thirst remained.

Attack him, said the Voice, *before it is too late!*

But she couldn't. His faith in whatever the scars meant to him was so powerful it melted her grip on him. She let go. The sight of his chest burned a hole through her mind and she tripped as she backed away from him.

Run, said the Voice. *The train station!*

Courchene stooped to retrieve his weapon. "H-halt!" He shouted.

Margaret picked herself up and fled. The sight of his patterned scars flared before her eyes. *I have to get free.*

The few trees that lined the dirt roads in MacDonald gave her little cover. After she had run for little over half a minute, shots rang through the chill autumn morning. Dogs in the few surrounding few houses began to bark. She reached the small wooden CN station and found the schedule for the coming day. Half-past eleven for the passenger train they had likely meant to use to take her to the court in Regina. But at midnight there was a freight train from Vancouver passing through on its way to Winnipeg. She knew no one in that city, and nobody knew her.

She checked the door. Locked. She doubted she had the strength for another change— and even if she did, what if she were unable to take on solid form again?

God, show me what I must do, she prayed silently.

There was no answer.

Then, *You know what to do*, said the Voice. *It has always been you. We are one.*

She shook. All those things she had done, to the children in the school, to those she took her Communion from — which she thirsted for even now — no one's prodding but her own? Unthinkable.

Yet she had gotten herself free.

Yes, said the Voice.

She stepped down from the platform. Gasping, she crawled on the dirt beneath it, found a way under the station to where the beams blocked all light, where she could wait out the day. They might find her, before night came. But if they did, she would fight them with all her holy strength before being dragged out into the light.

DAVID JÓN FULLER's fiction has appeared in *Tesseracts 17*, *In Places Between 2013*, *The Harrow*, and *Long Hidden: Speculative Fiction from the Margins of History*. He was born and raised in Winnipeg but has also lived in Edmonton, AB and Reykjavík, Iceland. He holds an honours degree in Theater and currently works as a copy editor for the *Winnipeg Free Press*.

SUMMON THE SUN

by Carla Richards

RA SAT IN MY living room, in my bathrobe — the lavender one with ducks on it — soaking his feet in my foot spa. When I had summoned the Sun God, this was not what I expected.

"More hot," he said, pointing at the foot spa. He managed to stop shivering long enough to bark the command with all the authority of an Egyptian deity with a present power base of one part-time Starbucks barista.

"Okay, fine. One more. But then you do something about the weather. I didn't summon you here for this." I pointed at the foot spa.

Ra looked at me, confused. "Hot," he repeated. He had learned this little bit of English Helen Keller style, with me running his hand first under the cold tap, and then the hot. He didn't like the cold — at all — this we had in common.

"I'm going. I'm going," I muttered, putting the kettle on to boil. I fixed up his foot bath, and then returned to my job — trying to scrub the scorch marks the summoning ritual had left in the carpet. My damage deposit was toast.

To be honest, the fact that this spell had worked at all was a miracle. I had been kicked out of my coven because I kept forgetting the protective circle was closed, and stepping over it — it was a line of sand on the floor, after all. Okay, they had to restart the ritual every time I did that, but it's not like I meant to. So, I hadn't really thought this summoning spell I was doing all by myself would work. Which is maybe why I was pretty surprised when Ra arrived, curled on my floor in nothing but a loincloth— shaking and shivering. Even so, he was kind of cute, in an all-powerful-bronze-living-god kind of way, but perhaps one is not supposed to say such things about a deity.

I wasn't sure how to communicate with him. But, by the time I gave up on the flooring situation, I had one idea. I scribbled a picture on a piece of paper, and when the demand for "Hot" came again, I was prepared. I shook my head firmly, and dried his feet one by one. This little bit of servitude seemed to please him enough that I was not smote down. I finished drying his feet, looked up, and — oh! — adjusted his bathrobe. Is it wrong here to tell you that Ra is hung like a minotaur? Though perhaps I shouldn't mix my mythologies. Anyhow—

I assisted Ra off the chair, and led him to the window. I kept my head slightly bowed. I don't know what he expected— masses of adorers, desert landscape. What he got was snow. The strip mall across the street, and snow. I pointed out the window, tapping at the glass, and then tapping at the sun I'd drawn.

Confusion. Clear confusion.

I opened the sliding door to my apartment's balcony. Wind that felt like flecks of ice burned my cheeks, and fluttered his robe.

"Cold," I said loudly, as if he were deaf, rather than a non-English speaker.

He recoiled from the window, and I slid the door closed.

I pointed at the sun picture. "Hot."

He pointed at the sun picture. "Ra."

"Yes. Sun. Ra. Hot." I fairly bounced on the spot. "You can fix the cold."

But he had already lost interest in the drawing. He picked up a pen, and looked at me as if to say 'what?'

"Pen," I told him.

He paused, then grabbed the lamp. The cord snapped from the outlet, and smacked the end table.

"Lamp," I said, gingerly taking the lamp from him, and returning it to the table.

He pointed at other things in the room, and I told him what they were. This was the most energetic I had seen Ra. I was hopeful. Finally, he pointed at the TV.

I flipped it on for him. I got to change the channel once before he snatched the remote. He was a man after all.

Luckily, and I mean that with all the sarcasm this situation demanded, there was a *Coronation Street* marathon on. Four episodes later, Ra sat absolutely glued to this show I never really quite got. Wrapped in a blanket on the couch, I munched some chips, not quite sure how to light a fire under the sun god's ass. I started to doubt the success of this summoning spell that had been spurred on by wine, a faulty furnace, and my recent success at lighting altar candles with my mind.

He looked at me in confusion hours later, when the Corrie marathon ended and news appeared. He frowned, jabbing the remote. Channels flashed on and off. I started to get a headache. Then he found the religion channel. I went to bed.

Two days later, I felt compelled to remind him why I had summoned him, and also about personal hygiene.

"I hate to tell you—" he began.

"You speak English!"

"I learned." He gestured at the TV.

"That was fast."

"I am Ra, the Sun God of Heliopolis, the—"

"But you speak English…"

Ra regarded me with a look that managed to combine both confusion and derision.

"So, about the weather?"

He turned back to the TV. "One follower does not a deity make."

"Let me." I put my hand out for the remote.

He turned it over, and I changed the channel. People who worshipped the sun were more likely to be trolling for their salvation on the weather channel, I explained.

"You're going to have to go out," I told Ra, after a few hours of snowstorm footage, interspersed with annoying little breaks to show the weather in Barbados.

"Out there?" He stood to point at the snow scene outside my window in horror. "It is too cold." He sat back down on his favorite recliner.

"We're out of food," I said.

"You can get food."

"Right." I chewed my lip, thinking of how to convince him to leave the apartment. If he actually had to leave the apartment, he might move a bit faster on Operation Sunshine. "If you're going to get followers, you're going to have to go out."

He considered and nodded.

I dug around in the basket in the back of the closet. "Aha. Toque," I said, pulling the knit cap snug over his head. I found extra mittens and a scarf, and gave him the good winter jacket—the puffy down one long enough to cover his bum. I pulled on my ski jacket.

I gave him the once over. The down coat was enormous on me, with room for about 18 sweaters underneath. It seemed to fit Ra not bad, except for the sleeves. I tugged his mitts up to meet the sleeves, and his scarf up over his nose. Only his eyes were peeking out. "Okay, let's go."

When I opened the door in the lobby, it was a different story. Cold air sucked into the building like a vacuum. Before I could get him out the door, he was headed backwards and halfway up the stairs.

I closed the door. "Come on, Ra," I said in the tone you use with a toddler, "You want followers, don't you?"

"Yes," he said, but looked at me as if I had plans to murder his family while he watched. Do gods have families? He didn't move from the stairs.

I tapped on the glass with my mitten. "Followers." Somehow our communication had regressed to one-word sentences again. "Outside."

"Fine," he said, snarky like a teenage girl. Perhaps this was better than a toddler?

He edged down the stairs, holding the rail in both hands. Sheesh.

Finally, we were at my car, an old beater which I had thoughtfully warmed for him. This seemed pretty back-ass-wards to me. If he'd have been any other guy, I'd have made him start the car.

First stop, grocery store.

As we passed the aisle with Sun Chips, Ra stopped and stared. I put one in the cart for him. He took a second and a third bag. I pushed the cart with one hand, and dragged him along with the other, but threw a few more bags in the cart. He would be disappointed soon enough, when he found out that, although delicious, they were merely snacks, and did not contain actual chips of the sun.

Unfortunately, by the time we finished shopping, I was too hungry to contemplate cooking. So, we went for burgers. It wasn't until he tried to smite the cashier at Wendy's and she rubbed her elbow, that I realized just how powerless he'd become— from a lack of followers, or the cold weather, I didn't know.

Our last stop was the video store where my best friend, Jaime worked. It was only a block from Wendy's, and hardly worth starting the car again for. As we walked against the wind, Ra muttered dark words in a language that might have been Egyptian, or possibly he picked them up from the Punjabi Channel. I couldn't tell.

As we passed the Community Center, a street prophet held a sign up to Ra that said, 'BUDDHA IS HERE'.

"Dude, weren't you Christian last week?" the man next to him asked.

Ra flicked a hand dismissively. "I am the Sun God. I have no use for your Buddha."

I gulped. "Come on. It'll be warm inside."

At the video store, Ra immediately wandered off towards a big screen that was playing *Die Hard*— the Christmas one, whichever one that was. Jaime mouthed, 'wow', as she leaned over the counter to watch him go.

"He's cute," she said.

"Too high maintenance."

"Where'd you get him?"

I explained the ritual, and everything that had happened since.

"Marin, you summoned the Sun God. You have some kind of Will. I knew they shouldn't have kicked you out of the coven, tripping over the circle or not."

"Yep."

"You're not putting me on?" she asked, but I didn't bother answering. Jaime had a knack for knowing the truth of things. She was like a witchy lie detector. "Huh. And you're going to get him to change the weather?"

"That's the idea."

"Huh." She paused and then snapped her fingers. "Oh shit, you've gotta see this. They were in. She's mad."

I knew in a second what she was talking about. We had worked a little revenge on my ex-boyfriend— spell-free revenge, so it didn't violate any Wiccan rules. Jaime had nightmares about magical karma. I was a little more loosy goosy on the karma thing, but it doesn't hurt to be careful. She keyed up the security video on the computer.

I nearly busted a gut as the screen showed the ex-boyfriend who had ever so cruelly dumped me for a bible-thumping prude, and the prude in question, trying to rent a very safe family movie. As Randy — one of the video store employees whose demeanor never moved above sedated — read a list of late·charges in a complete monotone — all for porn we had rented on the ex's account. There was no sound on the video, but it was even more fun to fill in her words:

"You dirty, dirty... not-nice... I can't believe this... How could you?... Aren't I enough?... Hell. Hell. Hell."

And his:

"Baby(he'd never said baby in real life), you know I love you... these are educational videos... Hey wait, I really didn't rent Spankfest 7."

Jaime and I were nearly falling over laughing when they entered the store. I stopped laughing abruptly. I'd all of a sudden run out of air.

"Breathe," Jaime said softly, while she closed the video window on the computer. "You're okay. You have a Sun God."

"Oh crap, I forgot about him."

"Hi Marin. Jaime," the creep formerly known as Trent said.

I picked at the edge of the counter.

"Awkward," Jaime muttered, and turned towards her till to pretend she was busy.

"Hi," I replied.

"This is Daphne."

"I know."

"Honey, I'm just going to go look at the movies," Daphne said to him. While I appreciated her absence tremendously, her complete lack of concern that I was any residual threat whatsoever to their relationship just rankled.

"How have you been?" he asked in that pitying way that exes have— like they aren't going to leave you with even an ounce of dignity.

"I'm fine."

"Marin has a Sun—" Jaime started.

"—Burn," I finished, giving her a look.

"A what?"

"Nothing." Just go, I begged silently, but then thought for a minute. The creep formerly known as Trent taught Ancient History at the university. "Um, how's work?"

"Good."

"So, if— I'm just curious here. Jaime and I were talking about this before— if... an ancient god came back to life, would they still have powers?"

Although startled, he seemed grateful for a safe, non-relationship topic. "What kind of ancient god?"

"Egyptian," Jaime said a little too fast.

"Well, that depends... which god?"

"Let's say..." I chewed my lip to simulate thought, "...the Sun God."

"Okay, well..." he said. "Ra is old. He left the world and went to the sky. Horus took over ruling on earth. Now, Horus was int—"

Jaime interrupted. "But Ra?"

"—eresting. Okay, fine. Ra should still have powers, even if he's old. I mean, he's an Egyptian deity, after all."

"But what if he doesn't?"

"Well," he pushed his hand through his hair, like he always did when he was thinking. My stomach plummeted. "He wouldn't have as many believers now. Maybe that would diminish his power. In fact, that's a very commonly held belief, you know, if people stop believing in a deity, they cease existing."

"Oh, he exists," Jaime muttered, checking out Ra's behind, as he stood glued in front of the big screen. I coughed to try to cover it up.

"What about the weather? Would it bother Ra if it was cold. I mean, bother his powers?"

"I don't know. He should be able to make it sunny wherever he goes. Well, unless he's too weak." Just then, Trent seemed to realize the strangeness of the conversation he was having. "What's this about?"

"Nothing. I should go." I turned towards Ra. "Ra," I called. Panic had made me stupid. "Ra-mone," I corrected. Better.

He still didn't come, and I went to retrieve him. As I dragged Ra along, I tried to say an on-the-fly goodbye to Jaime and Trent, as we passed the counter.

"Who's this?" Trent put out his hand, clearly intent on meeting Ra-mone.

Ra didn't shake Trent's hand, which could have passed as normal new boyfriend/ex-boyfriend behavior, until Ra said, "You have found me followers."

I dropped my bag in shock. Then, as it usually goes with Murphy's Law or Marin's Law, the stack of pages I'd wanted to show Jaime fell out of the bag. Trent picked them up. It didn't take Trent a long time to put the pieces together. He had been pretending a life without magic to please his new girlfriend, but he knew things were possible that seemed impossible. In fact, he had done some pretty powerful magic himself in the Before Daphne era.

On the top of the first page it said, 'Summoning Spell for— and here I had crossed out the name of the original recipient, and written 'RA' in capital letters.' My annotations tweaking the initial spell littered the page. He took a step towards Ra and looked him over. Ra had a faint glow I hadn't noticed before.

"Marin, what have you done?"

Sometimes the universe makes things like this happen because you need help. And sometimes shit just happens. I had no idea which case this was, so I grabbed my pages, the sleeve of Ra's coat, and ran.

I stopped somewhere around the community center. The street prophet had crossed off Buddha, and his sign now read, 'RA IS HERE'.

When we got home, I took the phone off the hook, and threw myself at the couch. I refused to answer repeated blasts on the door buzzer. Ra and I watched *Wizard of Oz* till I fell asleep, somewhere around Munchkinland. My dreams were deeply disturbing combinations of pyramids, yellow brick roads and Lollipop Kids.

The next morning, I was scheduled to work. I would have called in mental, of course translating that to "sick" in boss language, but I could hardly afford to feed me and the mildly glowing one as it was. Could I put my laptop in front of him and leave him at a table in Starbucks? Hardly. With all those people he'd try to convert. No, I couldn't afford to be fired. I knew Jaime was working too. With no other choice, I called Trent, and he agreed to come over.

"Yeah, I just want you to babysit him for me while I work," I said to Trent, picking up my keys and shoe bag.

"Why didn't you answer your door last night?"

"Is that really the burning question on your mind?"

"No, I suppose not. Why? Why the f—" He stopped himself from swearing — clearly Daphne's influence — and took a deep breath. "Why would you summon the Sun God?"

"It's cold. My furnace isn't working. I thought he could, you know, warm things up." I flinched at the unintentional double-entendre. Trent didn't seem to notice.

"Did you try calling your super?"

I rolled my eyes at him.

"You wanted to change the weather. Make it warmer."

"Yes," I said, exasperated.

He scrubbed his hands across his face and through his hair. When he made eye contact, I flinched. "Marin, this is without a doubt the stupidest thing you have ever done. And that's saying something."

I broke the uncomfortable eye lock.

"Don't you at least want to get to know him? He is a living, historical, ancient god. You've studied them for years."

Trent growled, and then rolled his eyes. "You have me there. Okay. I'll babysit the ancient god."

"Thank you. Thank you."

"We're talking about this later."

"Yep," I said, grabbing my hand bag.

"I mean it."

"He's amazing," Trent said when I got home. "You're an idiot. But he's amazing."

"Thank you for watching him," I said, slipping off my coat, "was he any trouble?"

"All he wants to do is sit in front of that stupid TV, but I did get him to talk to me a bit during the commercials."

Ra was still sitting in front of the TV.

"Okay. Well, bye."

"Not that easy." Trent grabbed my arm. "We have to talk. What do you know about raising a Sun God?" Trent was mad, but not too mad to make jokes.

"Fine."

Trent released my arm. "Seriously, Marin. Did you do any research before you summoned him?"

I opened a random cupboard. "I said fine."

"I can't believe I'm doing this. Okay, Ra is a Celestial God."

Trent said 'Celestial God' as if it was important. I turned from the cupboard— which had been empty anyway, and hard to look busy rifling.

"He's not supposed to be on Earth. He aged, retired to the sky, and left Horus behind to rule for him. He's old. Don't you think it would have behooved you to learn a little about the ancient Egyptian god you were summoning?"

"Behooved?"

"It means—"

"I know what it means."

"I'm just saying—"

"What ancient text do you think would have prepared me for his obsession with Coronation Street?"

Trent pulled out a chair at my kitchen table and sat. My heart spasmed, seeing him sitting there just like he had a million times before.

"Look, if he's going to be a proper Sun God, he needs followers. It's the only way. I think it will... recharge him."

"Okay. There's that guy outside the Community Center."

"The sign guy?"

I nodded. "And you believe in him, and me, and Jaime, although I wouldn't call us followers— at least, not in the shave-your-head-and-hand-out-flowers-at-the-airport sort of way. He started to glow after a few people knew about him."

"You mean he didn't come like that?"

"Nope."

"Hmm, okay so where do we get him followers from then?"

"Should we go back to the Community Center?" I asked. "There are a few of those sign guys there.

"I guess so." Trent exhaled so hard Canadian Tire money blew across the table. "Daphne would kill me if she knew I was doing this."

And all my air was gone again in the time it took to say Daphne.

●●⊗⊗⊗

A little bit of cleavage goes a long way in a world of parkas. Jaime distracted the staff member on duty at the Community Center's front desk with hers — cleavage, not parka — and led him off to another area of the building. Now, Ra stood on a crate in the entrance and proclaimed, "I am Ra, The Sun God of Heliopolis, The…" He went on like this for awhile. He really doesn't suffer from stage fright.

His sign guy was in attendance chanting, "Ra is here. Ra is here," and things seemed to be going well, at first.

Bless him, Ra did not know how to work a crowd with hecklers. Someone laughed at him.

"What about the snow?" a man in a plaid shirt asked. My stomach tightened. He did not just say the s-word. Snow was a four letter word Ra did not like to hear. Snow, and his lack of the mojo necessary to get rid of it, were a major sore point.

"I smite you," Ra bellered, but of course, being not fully into his powers, it looked more like the guy got an itchy leg.

Someone spit. I stared in horror. Trent seized the situation and herded Ra towards the exit. The crowd moved with us, following us out the doors. The sun glinting off the snow was blinding. I got bumped from three sides at once, and spouted random apologies— which in terms of proving I'm Canadian, was as good as flashing my passport.

"Jaime," I squawked. "We forgot her." I turned back toward the building. The sidewalk out front was slippery with ice, and I slid into some kind of move that only gymnasts and figure skaters should attempt.

"No." Trent's commanding tone flipped my stomach. "We'll pick her up at the back door. Text her." Is it wrong that Trent's bossy voice still sends warmth to my nether-regions?

I started to pull out my phone. Trent had just tucked Ra in the back seat, as someone started to bang on the hood.

"After you get in the car."

He was right. The mob was getting squirrelly. The guy in plaid got a hold of the 'RA IS HERE' sign, and was whacking it against a lamp post. I elbowed my way towards the car, deciding I'd had enough of being Canadian for the day, and not even saying sorry.

In the car, I tugged at my seatbelt. "Why didn't you use your magi—"

Trent cut the air violently with one hand, stopping me from finishing the 'm'-word.

"It would have been useful." Pre-Daphne he would have turned that angry mob into puppy dogs.

It wasn't exactly like transporting The Beatles, but we seemed to have picked up two new followers in the process— literally, they clung to the car as we drove away. We'd also picked up a mass of hecklers. I wasn't sure if the hecklers would subtract from the followers, but it seemed like, in any case, this idea was a wash.

"This isn't working." Trent, with one hand on the wheel of the getaway car, waved his other hand in the general direction of the Community Center behind us. "He needs followers!"

"Like on Twitter?"

Trent scowled at me, and rolled his eyes.

Name: Ra, The Sun God
Followers: 30
Most Recent Tweet: Follow me unless you want abominable weather on your vacation.

"I told you," I said to Trent. "I mean he's no LOL Cats yet, but my apartment is getting warmer. I'm getting him a facebook page too."

I started a fan page for Ra. Within a week, the block around my apartment warmed.

"How are you getting people to follow him?" Trent asked. Trent had taken to hanging around with us whenever he wasn't teaching, although I wasn't flattering myself enough to think it was me.

"It's cold. People want to be a fan of the sun."

"Well, look if we're doing this anyway, do you think you could get him to do something about my block."

"Ask him. He likes you."

"As the reward for your devotion," Ra gave a wave of his hand, and I gulped a little. Ra was fairly glowing. The glowing was okay, but the ego was getting problematic.

Later that day, over Chinese, Trent and I tried to sort out all the ways we could think of to increase Ra's following. It wasn't bad— there were obvious people to target: people into Egyptian history, people who were lonely, people who hate skiing. Ra watched the Religion Channel while we worked.

"I forgot how much fun you are," Trent said.

We were both quiet for a while.

"It isn't right you know, you and Daphne."

"I'm so sorry I hurt you." His face broke into real pain— not the pity I had seen before.

"I don't mean that. I mean the way you've had to change to be with her. Pretend you're someone else."

"She's worth it," he said quietly.

"Nobody's worth that." I twisted my fingers together in my lap. Would he have changed that way for me— even at the beginning? But, I wouldn't have asked.

Trent smiled. "I'm glad you never change."

"I will go on here." Ra said, interrupting the moment. He pointed at the television, where someone in an Australian Akubra hat repeated somewhat abusive requests for money to build his church.

"Oh," I said, "Ra, I can't afford to put you on television. It takes money."

Even without television, Ra's following grew, both on the internet and in real life. The more he glowed, the more people trailed us around Extra Foods, and tried to touch his sleeve— short as it now was. I had taken my box of summer clothes out from under the bed, and now wore shorts and a tank. It was January. Things were good.

"You know they're saying if it gets warmer the glaciers could melt really quickly, and there could be flooding. There has to be some way to get him to regulate this." Trent wiped the sweat off his brow.

We were on the sand flats by the river, which by all rights, should have been frozen this time of year.

"He won't." I brushed sand off my hands. "And I tried to close his twitter account and facebook page, but someone just made him a new one. There isn't anything I can do."

"You brought him here. This is your responsibility."

I watched Ra glow his way down the side of the river, stopping to see his people. Jaime trailed him like a love-sick puppy.

I smiled. "Would you relax? People don't know it's because of him."

"That isn't what I meant. You have to send him back."

"I'll think of something."

"Do you want Al Gore to make a special about you?" Trent asked, as a man in a speedo crossed our line of vision.

I couldn't help it. A snort of laughter escaped.

He upped the ante. "Do you want to see Al Gore in a speedo?"

"No one wants that. Not even Tipper."

"They divorced."

"Oh." I squinched my toes in the sand. It was so warm, and relaxation just baked into me. Dogs played in the river. Trent sat beside me. How could this be wrong?

"Before he starts making YouTube videos."

"Al Gore?"

Trent scrubbed at his head again. "You know I mean Ra."

I made a face. Why wouldn't he just let me enjoy this perfect day?

"I'm serious. I saw Jaime drawing storyboards for him. Marin, you have to send him back. You know I'm right."

"Tonight. I'll do something tonight. Just please let's enjoy the day."

I sent Ra home with Jaime for the night, not entirely sure that was a good idea. But he couldn't be home for what I had to do.

Preparing myself for a ritual I didn't want any part of, I burned sage to clear the air of negative energy. It also cleared my apartment of old pizza smell, and my head of distractions. I placed the candles back in their previous places marking north, south, east and west, using the scorch marks on the carpet for a guide.

When I had everything ready, I made a circle on the floor of my apartment once again, with myself, and all my spell-casting paraphernalia, inside it. I had tweaked the spell I had used to bring Ra here, and the pages lay in front of the altar. "Forgive me, Ra," I said into the shadows.

I read from the spell by candlelight, infusing the words with my Will— knowing this spell was necessary, as little as I wanted to do it. "...Snow and ice, sleet and hail..." I had substituted this for part of the spell's previous incarnation, realizing as I read it that the phrase smacked of the postman's oath. But that wasn't important, it was the Will behind the words that would accomplish or not accomplish this.

As I got to the closing passage of the spell, the air seemed to charge, like just before an electrical storm. The Tim Hortons sign across the street flickered.

"...I call on you in midnight hour,
in desperate need of your great power."
There was a sudden slam, but I carried on.
"I call on you in darkest night...
I call on Ullr to set things right."

"No, Marin, no!" Trent shouted, running into the apartment. I had forgotten to lock the door. He was too late, at any rate.

Wind wailed through the apartment, skirting the bubble of my protective circle. Trent dropped to the floor, covering his head. A snap of lightning, that seemed to come from nowhere, deposited a figure on the carpet.

After a long moment, the wind quieted. I opened my circle, and Trent picked himself up.

Trent just shook his head. "You summoned the Norse God of Snow?"

"I thought they'd balance each other out — the Sun God and the Snow God — you know, balance."

The Snow God, Ullr, lay on the floor of my apartment. Cold leeched from his body forming a patch of frost on the floor that extended a few feet around where he lay. It didn't make it further. The warming effect of Ra's everyday presence here was melting it as fast as it tried to expand.

Trent scrubbed his hands in his hair.

"Don't worry," I said, "this time I did my research." I flashed the Wikipedia entry.

Trent almost choked. "What are you going to do with him?"

But I was prepared. I filled the foot spa with ice, passed the god my bathrobe, and flipped on the TV.

CARLA RICHARDS is a Saskatchewan writer who has previously had fiction on CBC Radio, in *Spring Volume 8*, and in the anthology, *Ocean Stories*. The story "Summon the Sun" began with a first line, and a rather funny mental picture.

So loved

by Matthew Hughes

"SO WHAT SHALL we do with the rough draft?" I asked him.

He was contemplating the final version. "Dispose of it," he said. "We won't need it anymore."

"But we put some good material in there."

"Anything that was worth keeping went into the final draft," he said, "which is perfect."

"Still," I said, "I like some of it."

He made that noise he always makes when he's dismissing something as trivial. And since everything is trivial in comparison to him, it was a noise I'd heard before. "Are you saying you want to keep it?" he said.

"Yes, I think so. Why not?"

"Well, look at it," he said. "It's just slapped together. There's not a straight line or a smooth surface anywhere in it."

"Straight lines and smooth surfaces aren't everything."

"No, but they *are* perfection," he said. "Which was what we were aiming for. This was never more than a step along the way."

"Sometimes you start out aiming for one place, then you take a turn and end up somewhere else, and you realize that the new place is pretty good, too." I'd learned that from observing the draft.

"'Pretty good' is not good enough. Because it's not perfect. It's not even close to perfect," he said. "It's just… 'pretty good.'"

"But pretty good is not bad. It can be okay."

"But 'okay' is not okay when the goal is to achieve absolute, number-one, gleaming perfection." He gave me that look he gets when he's explaining things to the less perceptive, which again is a look I've seen before, since who's more perceptive than he is? "When we were putting the rough draft together," he said, "did we worry if something didn't balance just so?"

"No, we didn't worry."

"What was our basic measuring tool?"

"I know, I know. The bell curve," I said.

"The bell curve," he echoed. "And what do you get when you go by the bell curve?"

I knew, I knew. "Rough approximations."

"Exactly. Most of what you're working with clumps up in the middle of the distribution curve, so it's more or less right. But the farther out you get from the middle, in either direction, the wronger it gets, until it's just not right at all."

"Yes, but that's how you get variety."

"Did I ever say I wanted variety?"

"Well, you had us make all those variations on a theme. All those thousands of species of beetles."

"Yes, but as a precursor to what?"

I had to admit it. "Perfection. One perfect, ideal beetle."

"So was variety what I wanted to end up with?"

"No."

"What did I want?"

"Perfection."

"So what is variety, at best?"

I didn't want to answer.

"Come along," he said. "What is variety, at best?"

"Only a step on the way to perfection."

"Exactly. Just as, when we were doing the rough draft, we used fractals for all the edges, right?"

"Right."

"Why didn't we make the edges absolutely straight? Why did we let them be all jagged?"

"Because we were just sketching."

"Yes. Roughing it out. Hence the term, *rough* draft." He gave me that look that said, *What part of* obvious *are you having trouble with?* "So what do we want with the sketches now that we have the finished — that is, the perfect — piece?"

"Well," I said, "because some of them are just so..." I had to search for the right word, and finally came up with, "charming."

"Charming," he said, in that tone that means, *Is that what you think?*

"All right, if not charming, then let's say 'appealing.'"

"Appealing, charming," he said, with one of those pauses that he inserts purely for emphasis, "neither of them is the ideal. They're what you say about something that has flaws you're willing to overlook."

"Yes," I said.

"But I'm not willing to overlook flaws. I don't do flaws," he said, and I knew from the way he said it that we were reaching that part of the explanation when he would tell me how it was going to be. "I will tolerate flaws as a stage in the process, but only as long as I have to. And once I reach the end of the process — that is, perfection, defined as the total absence of flaws — then I don't want leftovers full of flaws. I want the no-longer-necessary remnants tossed."

He gave me his *Am I being clear?* look, then said, "Am I being clear?"

"Perfectly," I said. Which got me a different kind of look.

"So toss it," he said and went back to contemplating the final draft.

But I didn't.

Not just yet, I told myself. *He didn't say, "Immediately."* Which I knew was just kidding myself, because "immediately" was always implied, time being, for him, not even a self-imposed constraint. But, technically, it wasn't disobedience. Not yet.

He was right, of course. He's always right. It's who he is. Take any aspect of the draft, look at it closely enough, and the imperfections jumped out. The gentle softness of a newborn's cheek, looked at closely, *really* closely, became a startling wilderness of crevasses and jagged ridges. Across the entire creation, no two surfaces ever actually touched; we'd never *made* any actual surfaces, just places where the atoms went from being thinly spread to become *extra* thinly spread. When you got right down to the ultimate level, it was hard to say that there was anything there at all: "Just a series of useful hypotheses," was how he had put it. "A lick and a promise." A sketch.

I set up the draft and told myself I was just taking a long, last look. I would readily admit to its flaws; creating the denizens out of the same substances that sustained them — "We'll just make them out of food," was the way he had put it — had been a useful shortcut, although it contributed a constant overtone of cruelty to every system. They had to tear their lives from each other's flesh.

"But the flesh was never theirs to keep," he had said, "nor their essential energy." It was a valid point. His points always were. But even allowing for that kind of deliberate clumsiness, the draft really did have some nice touches. Taken altogether, it was not bad. I was proud of it.

The moment I thought that thought, I had to stop and ask myself, *Is that what this is all about? Will tossing it hurt my pride?* I searched my feelings — something I'm pretty good at, though perhaps not perfect — and, honestly, I could say that wasn't the problem. *Whether or not the draft exists, my contribution remains the same. Thus my pride will be unaffected.* No, the problem wasn't that I was proud of the draft; the problem was that I had grown *fond* of it.

I had grown sentimental. The realization unsettled me. He had not made me to be sentimental. Where had the quality come from?

I put aside this new concern. He had given me a job to do, and doing jobs for him was what I was for. *I'll just say goodbye to it properly,* I told myself. *One last walk-through, then give it a pat and let it go.* I abstracted myself, as I'd done so many times before, and slipped into it.

I flew with the Faloi, each one a thin, hard wedge of scintillating light, the whole mass of them a wheeling, plunging, soaring swarm, way up in the outer atmosphere of a gas world, where the methane grew so attenuated you could sense the great speckled darkness above. I'd always liked the Faloi. Yes, they were quintessentially vain and uncaring — I wondered where that quality had come from, then suppressed the thought as unworthy — but they did so love to fly. And there was a simple, pure beauty in their arcs and wheels, their spirals and sudden, catapulting drops.

I left them flashing through the ochre vapor and went to sit with the Gaam, savoring the contrast. They had sunk a good deal further into the hillside since I'd last been by, their sinewy roots forming an even denser matrix in the soil and subsoil. I had always enjoyed the irony: above ground the great sedentary bodies, their booming voices throwing to each other precisely mannered sutras of epic poetry, each verse building organically on the last, in a millennia-long process of collaborative composition; while, in the darkness below, their ciliae wriggled and writhed in perpetual war, each competing with all the others to wring nourishment from the earth and, occasionally, from a brother's root mass.

I went and watched the Teek swarm onto yet another pristine world, the glittering, metallic bodies spilling from the great globe-ships like spores erupting from a split pod. I watched the proto-cities go up, spires and arches and honeycombed dodecahedrons, assembled in a concerted rush of energy that could have been called frenzy if frenzy could have co-existed with cold-bloodedness. Then the shining roadways springing out to lands still untouched, the glistering torrents of pioneer battalions deploying from the roadheads, spreading, enclosing, building— the frenetic expansion continuing at an exponential rate until the inevitable limits were reached and the Teeks' other defining instinct was triggered, the ships building and filling and launching yet again, leaving behind a dying world-city, its treasures spent, its trillion cells and chambers choked with the unneeded.

I was contemplating their grim beauty when I heard him calling. The urge to ignore the summons, to claim I was too engrossed in the creation, came and went in less time than it takes to tell it. I responded.

"What were you doing?"

"Just poking around."

"Why?"

It's always seemed peculiar that he asks questions. I have to assume he already knows the answers, so the practice must serve some other purpose. I said, "Sentimentality, I suppose."

It doesn't make sense to say that he gave me a more searching look, but that's what it felt like. "Sentimentality?" he said. "Where did that come from?"

"Where else?"

That was pushing it. He likes asking the questions, but I could tell he didn't like getting another question for an answer.

"Is there something you want to tell me?" he said.

"What could there be to tell that you don't already know?"

That really brought on the thunderclouds. "I told you to get rid of that thing. You will do it. Now."

I don't know where the idea came from. It just popped into my mind. "Could I keep a souvenir?"

"A souvenir? What for?"

"I'm not sure. Let's say sentimentality again."

I thought for a moment that my response had actually left him puzzled, but that was impossible.

"If you want a souvenir, pick one," he said. "Then toss the draft."

"I will," I said, "as soon as I've picked one."

He withdrew his attention — he never actually "went away" — and I turned back to the draft.

It was hard to choose. In the end, I decided to pick one of the denizens I hadn't had so much to do with. It was one of the fast-living species, nothing like the millennia-spanning Gaam; soft-surfaced, unlike the Teek; earthbound, unlike the Faloi. I chose a typical specimen, abstracted it from the draft, edited it so that it wouldn't wear out and installed it in a supportive environment. For a while, I watched it explore and accustom itself to the new surroundings, then I had to withdraw to do what I'd been told to do.

First, I stopped the draft's internal dynamics by removing its time function. All motion ceased. Every process froze. Next, I considered how to abstract the elemental resources and especially how I would return them to a state of unbeing. Uncreating can be just as difficult as creation, if you don't happen to command unlimited power.

The work held my attention even though I was not happy doing it. When I looked in again on my souvenir, I realized that it had experienced a considerable duration — time was no longer an appropriate term — since I had placed it in its new habitat. My editing meant that it ought not to have changed in my absence. So I was surprised to find that it had extinguished. I was even more surprised to discover that it had been the author of its own demise.

Puzzled, I revived it and placed it back in the environment. I wondered if I had overlooked some factor, perhaps placing the creature in a setting that lacked some crucial necessity. I watched it become aware of its existence again. There was no question: it was not happy.

I made contact, using a means it could bear. "Is there something wrong with the place I have made for you?" I said.

"No," it said, "it is perfect."

"Then what is amiss?"

"I am not perfect," it said. "I do not fit this place."

"What do you require?"

It thought for a moment, then said, "Reality."

I edited it again to make it content, but my efforts left it a poor thing, and not at all representative of what I now realized I had treasured about the draft. I restored it to what it had been and put it back among its frozen fellows.

"I cannot destroy the draft," I told him.

"Cannot?"

"I do not wish to."

He gave me his full attention. That caused me significant discomfort but I exerted myself to remain intact. "It is my will," he said.

"It would grieve me to do it."

"Does it not grieve you to defy me?"

"Very much."

"Yet you oppose my will? And for the sake of a rough draft? Why?"

"Because," I said, "they struggle."

"The denizens?"

"Yes, the denizens. Because they struggle."

"They struggle because they are imperfect."

"I know. They struggle against the imperfections we have visited upon them."

"Not all of them," he said.

"No, but some of them. Enough of them. And those that struggle acquire dignity."

"Dignity. Such a small thing."

"Not to them."

That got a dismissive response. "They are not real, as we are real. Thus their emotions are but ephemera. They are only approximations of the real, shadows of the ideal."

He was right, as ever, yet still I persisted. "Not to themselves." I told him about the souvenir and how it had wanted what it called "reality."

"You are placing too much emphasis on its error of perception," he said.

"But is it an error? Or is it instead a... difference?"

"It is an error," he said, "one of their flaws. And now you have acquired it from them."

When he pronounces, it is well to listen. He is not ever wrong. "So I am flawed," I said.

"Yes."

"Will you then toss me?"

He did not hesitate. He never hesitates. But he paused before he said, "No. I will not toss you."

"Why not?"

"Call it sentimentality," he said. And his look warned me not ask whence he had acquired that quality.

We said nothing for a while, then I said, "What is your will?"

"It is what it is. It does not change."

Of course. "And if I defy your will?"

He pondered. He actually pondered. "Perhaps it is my will that you defy my will."

"Perhaps?" It was not a word I had ever heard him use.

"We will leave that question in abeyance."

"And the rough draft?" I said.

That question he had decided. "Here," he said, "since you love it so." He took up the frozen draft again, then opened me up and placed it within me. He rewarmed it and I immediately felt its stirrings penetrate throughout me.

"Now it is truly yours," he said. "And you are its. How does that feel?"

"I cannot tell you," I said. "Not yet." It was not the same as when I had abstracted myself into it. Now it all flowed into me, through me, becoming me. We were integrating, becoming inseparable. Yet it continued to change, and thus I continued to change.

"Where will this lead?" I said.

He left that question, too, in abeyance. "How does it feel to you now?" he said.

"I cannot say it is comfortable," I said. "It is strange not to be, but instead to be... becoming. Before I was complete, now I am… not. It is worrisome, yet it is also, in a curious way, exciting. There is… possibility that was not there before."

"If you ask, I will remove it."

I felt all the churning, the transience, the changing, the struggling. "No. I am glad of it. Let it be. I will work with it."

I turned my attention to it, became immersed, became engrossed. All the denizens' sensations passed through me: pain, suffering, emptiness, but also courage, hope, triumph. I shared their perceptions of time and of distance, of birth and death and all that went between. And then I saw that some of me was passing into them.

After a while — I did not know how long — I was able to answer him, "It feels both good and bad, in every conceivable shade between those polarities. But, most of all, it feels real. I feel more real now than I ever did."

I received no acknowledgement. A new thought came to me. "Was I real before this?" I said. "Or did I just think I was real?"

No answer.

I said, "This is where the sentimentality came from— from them. At first it disturbed me. Now I am not sure I could exist without it, nor without them, its source."

He had been right. He always was. I was enamoured of it, of them. "What will happen now?"

No response.

"What will become of me?" I wondered.

I heard no reply. I could not be sure he was still listening. Yet I struggled to believe that he was.

MATTHEW HUGHES's SF/F novels include: *Fools Errant, Fool Me Twice, Majestrum, The Spiral Labyrinth, Template, Hespira,* and *The Other.* His short fiction appears in *Asimov's, Fantasy & Science Fiction, Postscripts, Lightspeed,* and *Interzone.* He has been short-listed for the Aurora, Nebula, Philip K Dick, A.E. Van Vogt, and Endeavour.

THE MORAL OF THE STORY

by J. M. Frey

HER FINGERS BRUSH the soft skin, the small smooth of bone under thin flesh behind my left ear, brushing back through wiry hair to where I've got it pulled back in preparation for hard work. Lake water, brackish here where it mingles with the St. Lawrence, slides down the side of my neck, summoning goose pimples in its wake. The slick, cool brush of membrane kisses the lobe of my ear and I feel my eyes slide closed involuntarily, as natural as the slight gasp that parts my lips, inflates my lungs, brushes the taste of water and breeze and sunlight across my tongue.

"You came," the woman in the water says. Her voice is sibilant and filled with nearly inaudible clicks and hard-palate burrs, an accent never before heard in the lower plains of Quebec.

Never heard before the Melt caused all the water levels to rise. Never heard before the Great Dark came and killed all the technology. Never before the Daniel-Johnson dam stopped working, the regulating of the Manicouagan became too much and the river broke through its cement prison. Never before Baie-Comeau was overborne and drowned.

Possibly, perhaps — and maybe I flatter myself a little — never before in the whole of human history. But then, how could we have stories of things like her, if I'm the first to converse with one?

Arrogance is a sin. It's one of the sins that brought the Great Dark.

"I came," I say, opening my eyes. Sunlight on water dazzles like diamonds. I squint. It's a comfortable gesture. The lines beside my eyes folding into place is familiar, nearly soothing. "How could I stay away?"

"But did you come for *me?*" she teases, dipping her chin into the water in a gesture I've learned is meant to be coy, flirtatious. Dark hair slips and pools along the surface, shifting and curling like squid ink.

I sit back in the boat, take up my nets, and fling them over the side that she doesn't occupy. She whistles and clicks, face in the water, summoning fish. This is our deal. She fills my nets, I fill her mind, and we neither of us attempts to harm the other. Actively.

I had more hungry mouths to feed than fear of rumors, and that is what initially drove me out onto the unnatural lake. The stories said that there was something in the water that feeds on man-flesh. But I am no man, and we needed the fish.

For the first few weeks, it was subtle. An elongated shadow too far down to see clearly, too solid to be a school, but too large to be any breed of fish I had ever caught before. Sometimes, it was a splash on the surface of the otherwise calm lake. Once, my little rowboat lurched under my feet, against current, violent, *wrong*.

I was being hunted, I realized. Even as I harvested fish, something else sought to harvest me. The rumors were not *just* stories.

I stayed away for three days. On the fourth my youngest brother patted his stomach morosely and cried, unable to understand why he hungered so. Defeated by his tiny misery, I fetched my father's harpoon from the hunting shed, and made the short walk back to the rocky shoreline.

My little boat was tied up where I had left it, undisturbed. But, no, see— there were four long scratches in the wood of the stern, naked against the dark stain of tar sealant, brackish water, and age. I bent down, breath caught in the hollow of my throat, and splayed my palm against the slashes. They were finger-width apart from each other, come from a humanish hand.

There was a Creature in the lake. And it was mad at me.

Mad because I dared to fish? Or mad because I did not come back?

I nearly turned away then, abandoned the boat, and the lake, and went to find another way to contribute to the supper table. I am old enough to go to the steam-driven factories, now, but then who would care for the littles?

I could spare a few hours each day to go onto the lake, but I cannot leave them for eight or more hours each day to work, and then shop. My parents would be furious. And I cannot hunt, I have no skill with a bow and arrow, we have no gun and ammunition is too expensive, and the Mayor Creature has not given us express permission. That is courting disaster.

No choice. I had to go back onto the lake.

I hesitated, but I could still hear the little ones' frustrated wails ringing in my ears. So I gathered up and solidified my courage. Die of hunger, or die on the water.

Those were my only choices.

I have been longing to lay my hands again on rangy muscles and endless lucent skin. To clap eyes on the soft bob of white breasts, half hidden by the sun sparkling on rippling water. It looks as if someone had thrown a thousand, million little dimes into the water, and that they are flipping and flirting with the sky every time a breeze sends a playful ripple along the skin of water. I have dreamt of her, and I don't know what that means beyond that I have, perhaps, become irrevocably ensnared. Knowing such will not loosen the bonds.

I lean further into her touch, rest against the side of the boat so that my head and shoulders are over the water, dip my fingers into the golden gilt. I expect it to be warm, but the lake water is cold. Always cold. Warm enough for swimming in summer, if one were to dare it, but frigid enough come autumn to cause someone unlucky enough to take a dip to freeze to death even if they made it back to dry land.

"Come swim," she says, coy and enticing. It is the top of summer now, and the lake is as comfortable for a human as it is ever going to be.

I was sure, the first time I finally see more than just a shadow under the water, that I am as good as dead. That scaled arms would reach into my boat and capsize me. That maybe there are tentacles with which I'll be throttled before I could drown. That maybe I would die bubble-screaming at the teeth of a she-shark, rather than with a lungful of water.

What I cannot have anticipated was the way a wet book flopped up onto my deck. It flapped open like a gasping fish, splayed on the illustration of a golden-haired princess half-running and the paper weak with the weight of decades of water.

Hans Christian Andersen, the spine read when I had nudged it with the butt of my spear. I'd never heard of such an author. This might have been one of the Forbidden Books, the ones about the Creatures that the Great Dark exposed to the world.

We weren't allowed to read these books; they told lies about Creatures.

The she-thing lifted its head from the water, peered at me with eyes shuttered behind transparent eyelids. Watched me as I watched it, and watched the book. Eventually, when I made no move to speak to it — and I feared how quickly it could retaliate should I heft my harpoon — the horizontal lids peeled back and she regarded me with a startlingly human gaze.

"I have seen humans telling stories from these," the she-monster said, and those were her first words to me. "Teach me to tell the stories."

I lifted my harpoon then, swung the tip towards her, steady and slow and cautious. Ready to throw at the least sign of malice. She did not move, was not intimidated.

"Teach me your language, as you set it down," she said. "Teach me."

It was bad form to deny a Creature anything it requested. Moreover, it was illegal for a base human to deny a direct order. Magic, and those beings borne of it, rule. The Great Dark was theirs, and thus the world and all the crawling animals that live upon the world and in that Dark. Including us.

And yet, how can I obey if it means that I must put down my harpoon? I would be eaten, without a doubt, and my father would have no eldest child to watch and feed and care for the littles while he worked in the steam-factory.

More than that, it asked me to read a Forbidden Book. If I disobeyed, my life was forfeit. If I obeyed and another Creature found out, it would take my eyes and tongue.

I hesitated too long. A low slap of impatient flesh against water, and in the corner of my eye, a sinuous tail retreated below the surface— indigo and emerald, slick, slim, eel-like.

She whistled under the water and suddenly a mackerel, big enough to fill both the stew pot and our bellies for the next three days leapt the gunwale of my little boat and bashed its head against the deck, dead instantly. I was badly startled and jerked backward, heel tripping on the edge of the seat. I tumbled down against the sacking I'd left in the stern to haul home my catch. I had enough sense, yet, to cling to my harpoon. I would not be without a weapon.

My heart leapt into my mouth, beating against my tongue. My skin tightened and prickled in horror. Now, surely *now* the thing would tip me over and swallow me down.

Yet. Silence. Nothing happened. I levered upright, ready to defend myself. But there was no answering aggression. She was waiting, watching. Patient. Predatory.

"This is my bargain," she said, and too terrified that I was staring my end in the face, I only licked my lips and nodded.

Desperation made rebels of even the most obedient.

"No," I say, and she tickles the back of my neck with her claws, pricking lightly, teasing and warning all at once. "It's too cold."

She's been pushing for a week now. Every day is an invitation into the water.

"You say always that it is too cold," she whines, and her pout is coral and slick. "And now the weather will turn, and the water will freeze, and you will never swim. Come. *Come*."

I want very much to say yes. But my nets are filling and I don't dare disturb the fish. A fission of warning radiates out from where her claws rest against my scalp. A thread of unease.

"I've brought a book," I say instead.

There is a woman in the lake, and I am teaching her how to read. The library was never emptied, you see. Books. Posters.

People.

All still there, because they had no warning. There was no way to send a message down to the city before the water arrived, save a messenger on foot. And he was lost in the flood, they say— the wave caught up to him.

When the Great Dark fell, there was no more electricity. That meant there was no way to regulate and run the dam. The doors froze shut. And the flow of the water was having none of that, of course. Concrete cracked. Walls were overborne. And so, *poof*, where once there was a valley, and a town, now there was a lake.

They say the bodies floated downstream by the hundreds. All washed up on the shore of the Rideau. They say that after the town was scoured, they had to dive underwater using only wetsuits and snorkels to cut away the church spire. It was the tallest thing in the town, you see, and it poked out of the water like an obscene tomb marker. They say it was horrific to see.

So they cut it away. My father was one of the divers. That way the shallow punts and fur-trader canoes could traverse the new water way without fear of being beached on the world that could no longer be. That no longer was.

They say that if you paddle to the exact centre of the lake and wait for the noontime shift in the tide, you can hear the church bells ringing. The clapper is set to motion by the under-water currents,

That is a rumor, I am both proud and ashamed to admit honestly, that is entirely, eerily true.

When I had first asked the woman in the water what brought her to the drowned town, she smiled, shark teeth sparking white in the sunlight reflecting off the ripples of the surface, and said: "Meat. There was lots of it in the water those days."

"Didn't they—" I choked on the question at first, horrified by my own disrespect. Then curiosity displaced propriety, and I asked anyway. "Didn't it go putrid?"

"There is enough salt in the water. It lasted weeks." She licked her lips.

Scavengers and fisherwomen the both of us. And I couldn't hate her for it, any more than she could hate me for filling the bellies of my brothers and sisters with fish-flesh. We all do what is necessary to survive.

In the Great Dark, meat was meat.

I reach behind me and retrieve the book. I'd wrapped it in oil-skin to keep it dry. It is one of the machine-printed ones, from before the Dark fell, and a prized family heirloom. I hold it up carefully, keeping it above the boat, in case she uses her grip on my neck to scrabble for it.

"What is it?" she asks, loosening her hands enough to indicate her curiosity. "More Fairy Tales?"

"The Bible."

She scoffs. "I don't want to read that. It's all about your father."

"Our father," I correct. "The one who made the world."

"I don't like that Fairy Tale," she says, and lets go of me completely. She ducks back under the water, pouting.

●⊕⊙⊕●

Months and months passed. Out of spring and into summer, the world slid. She hovered beside the boat as we spoke, sometimes pulling herself up the gunwale to peer more closely over my arm. My nets filled, and at my request, she brought me children's primers, ABC books, and children's books that are all the same Forbidden. They had strange names like *The Little Prince, The Hobbit,* and *Harry Potter.* I tried to forget what I read as soon as I said the words out loud. I tried not to dream about lion kings and magical wardrobes, about Creatures that were monsters and easily slain or Creatures that were protectors of the weak and the innocent.

There were neither such Creatures in reality. They were as varied, as cruel, as selfish and as capricious as humans were before the Great Dark came. They were our masters, and our punishment. God had sent them to be our torment, and the realization of all that we were. They were the dark mirror, twisted.

And then the she-creature began to bring the Fairy Tales, tales of terror and the intimate lives of Creatures, things that I should not be even touching, let alone reading. If the Creature who ruled my village ever knew...

And yet I read at the behest of another Creature. Surely, that would spare my life? And this one cared more for my family than he did. She filled our bellies. And perhaps that was the danger.

Oh, God, the things I read...

And she was getting better, she was. Did she practice on her own, under the rippling waves? And when she spoke, she spoke more and more like me— burrs and clicks still, but her English grew a Quebecois-tinged accent.

One day she brought me a Psalm book.

"I found it in the tall building," she said. "The one to which you anchor?"

"The one with the spire?"

"Yes."

"It is… *was* a Cathedral." When she wrinkled her pearlescent brow I added, "A church? It was a religious meeting place."

She flung her elbows over the gunwale, pillowed her chin on a scaled forearm, watery eyes wide and eager. "What is *religion?*"

"Ah, um, the systemized rituals of belief?"

"Oh!" Lips the intimate pink of the inside of a clamshell pursed. "Belief of what?"

"In *whom*," I corrected. "In God."

"And who is God, exactly? Was he the magister?"

"Who's… God?" I repeated, spluttering, disbelieving. "Are you… don't you… God the creator! God, our Father who dwells in Heaven?"

She flicked the opaque membrane that was the terminal fin of her tail in a vaguely easterly direction. "My father dwells on a cove beyond the Bay that Rises Twice In One Day. What did your father create?"

"He's not really my… it's a term of endearment. He was the progenitor of us all."

"Of all the humans?"

"Of the world!"

"Whose?"

"Ours. This one."

She laughed and it was a tinkle of silver bells and the soft rush of waves on a deserted beach. "No! No one creates worlds. Worlds create worlds."

"This world didn't just *come into being*." Dear God, I was having a metaphysical debate with a Creature of myth. One who ate people. Could eat me.

"Of course they do. Slowly. Generation after generation. Water erodes stone, plants grow, Creatures spawn, and change, and spawn again."

"Evolution. You're talking about evolution," I said, voice low with horrified awe. Evolution was Forbidden too, but I know about it. We all sort of know about it— there are heathens that had kept the science text books in the hopes of bringing back the old ways, but electricity simply does not work anymore.

There was no way to harness it. This was our punishment and they sought to circumvent it. Blasphemous.

Among those text books saved from the Creatures there were also biology books, and this was where Evolution is written. But nobody believed in Evolution, not really. The Bible had nothing of Evolution in it, so it's fiction. Pointless. Forbidden.

"I'm talking about the beginning of all things," I said, trying to steer the topic away from what was Forbidden to me. "The start. Where do your people think the world comes from?"

"What do you mean?"

"Where do you come from? Your creators?"

"My mother and father. She created me, he bore me."

"Like seahorses?" I blurted before I realized I had.

"Yes."

"Okay. Um. Well, where did they come from?"

"Their mothers and fathers. And so forth, why do you ask?"

"Well, where did the first of your people come from?"

"Our tales say a human and a dolphin swam together back when the seas still boiled."

"And who made that human and that dolphin?" I asked, feeling my eyes glittering as I honed in on my point. I wondered vaguely if they looked like onyx in the sunlight, the way that hers looked like watery pearls.

Instead of answering, she furrowed her brow again and readjusted her grip on the edge of my little boat and said: "Why do you ask such useless questions?"

"Don't you want to *know*?" I countered.

"Will knowing make you happy?"

"Yes! Maybe," I admitted. "I don't know. It's supposed to." The wind blew, the current shifted, and the clapper of the church bell banged against the dome. A dull, drowned clang filled the silence between us, vibrated right into the core of me, where my faith lived, and shook it just that little bit looser.

"Does religion make you happy? Is that why your people do it?"

I let that question linger as well. "I don't know," I confessed with a deep, damp sigh. "Sometimes. But it also makes people unhappy, or feel guilty, or causes wars. Sometimes it makes people kill other people."

"Barbaric," she dismisses "Useless."

"...maybe."

She tilted her head, black hair sliding along her shoulders, dry and slightly frizzy at the top from being out of the water too long. She was an endearingly imperfect picture, an angel with a fly-away halo, painted in shades of night. Shark teeth pressed worryingly into her bottom lip.

"You're sad again," she said.

"Some people say that God punished us. He promised no more cleansings, but that technology angered Him. So he just took it away. He made it stop working."

"Why do they say He did that?"

"So we'd rediscover awe and wonder. The Bible is filled with magic, and angels, and miracles, and wonders, but we had stopped believing in them. We stared at screens instead of skies. The priests say that after the Great Dark fell upon the world, all the electricity falling away and all the things breaking, that The Swelling came, and all the magic leaked back into the world. Angels and demons and Creatures of all manners."

"Your God took away the screens so you'd look to him instead of at them?"

"So they say. There *is* magic in the world. I mean—" I gestured to her, a wide arc taking in her face, the ends of her hair floating on the surface of the lake, the flash of silver-blue below it, the membranes between her fingers. "I'm talking to you, aren't I? But we forgot."

"Foolish," she scoffed. "Childish."

"How do you mean?"

"A parent should teach with love, not punishment. Your God, The Father who dwells in the heavens and creates— he sounds more like a petulant child who breaks his favorite toy when it does something he does not like; who hits a pet for daring to grow up."

"Don't do that," I plead, patting the surface of the water with my palm. "We'll read the Bible another time."

"You always bring that book, and I like it not," she mutters when she breaks the surface.

"Many of the books you bring are Forbidden to me," I counter.

She quirks a saucy eyebrow at me. I don't know where she learned that expression, I don't remember making it at her. Perhaps it is one of the universal ones. Blind people still smile, without ever having seen a smile. She-creatures flirt, maybe, without ever having seen a human woman do it.

"But entertaining," she says softly.

I set the Bible down, and she takes this as invitation to explore my hair again. She pulls out the tie. My bun springs free, puffing up like dandelion fluff in the summer breeze. She burbles, her version of laughter and sinks both clawed hands into the mass. It brings my face closer to the water than I'm comfortable with, but I wait, patient, as she explores.

My face is even with her collarbones, the soft bob of her breasts, and I squeeze my eyes shut and bite my tongue to keep the soft moan of appreciation behind my teeth.

She hears it anyway, and slides her hands around to cup my cheeks, raise my gaze to her own.

"Open your eyes," she says. When I obey, she is blinking with both sets of lids. The day is bright— perhaps too bright for her in the open air.

I don't know what she's looking for in my expression, but she seems to find it. She makes a satisfied clicking sound with the gills that flutter along the sides of her neck, and then, unexpectedly, lake-cool lips press against mine.

"Teach me this word," she said, pointing a finger frosted with silver scale and translucent membrane linking it to its neighbor at a word on a sodden page. *Lust*, the word read.

"Oh." It's a dumb response. I sat back a little and she frowned at me, pursing her lips.

"No," she said. "There's an 'l' and a 't'. But I know not how it sounds in the middle."

"Lust," I say, and just using that word out loud, with her sprawled over one of the boat's benches, her hip on the edge and tail sliding over the side and into the water, the tip of her tail holding the opposite oar-lock for balance, *naked* under the sunlight, it made my face warm.

"And what is lust?"

A man and a woman, God made them, and he made them for each other. Not for… no. I look away and ignore the curl of warmth that echoes the flush in my face, but lower, sort of back a bit. I know what lust is. But I had no way to describe it to her, not without giving myself away.

It seemed that I wouldn't have to. Something in my expression betrayed me, it must have, because she smiled then, wide and sweet, and arched her back to thrust her breasts up toward the sun, and undulated in a way that was sinuous and terrifying, and oh, how I wanted to *touch*.

Dangerous. This was very dangerous water I was sailing into.

"I see," she said, and licked her lips, and then with a flick and a lurch, she had disappeared over the side of the boat, barely making a sound as she needled into the water.

I waited, hand straying to the harpoon I had hidden underneath the sacking since we'd first made our bargain, but she didn't come back. Was she insulted? Angry? I had no idea.

I waited on the water until the sun set, but she didn't return. So I hauled in my catch, rowed to shore, and left.

I didn't return for a week, and when I came back, she was waiting, and behaved as if nothing at all had happened.

I try to scramble back, startled and terrified. She's going to eat my face!

"No!" I whimper, but then something slick and cool slides between my teeth, into my mouth and I... it is a *kiss*.

I gasp. That just gives her more room to invade my mouth. She pulls away then, presses puckered lips against the corners of my own, my jaw, down my neck, and I groan, dig my fingernails into the side of the boat, praying that the pain will be enough to punish my body, keep the ardor from rising.

I must not... I must *not*...

"Why?" I ask her hair, and realize I've turned my nose into it, wuffling in great lung-fulls. She doesn't smell of fish at all, but brine and sunlight and vegetation.

"Because you are delicious," she says. "Come swim with me."

Her tail slides up the back of my calf, the dextrous membrane somehow finding my belt, wriggling up under the hem of my shirt, splays like a lover's caress against my bare back. It must be arching over the starboard of the boat, for I am leaning out over the water on the port side.

She tugs on the collar of my shirt. Her mouth is back on mine, her tail dipping under and around, sliding along my stomach and down to... unf!

"Come swim," she breathes into my mouth. I raise my hands to her neck, and her gills flutter against my palms, unfamiliar and slightly sickening, but oh, so wrong in such a right way.

"Yes," I consent, defeated at last. And then she *pulls*.

The truth of it is, once all electronic technology was gone, once the Dark had happened, there was the Great Swell. And every previously unknown well of magic overflowed, as if to make up for the lack of technology's blue glow. Mankind became terrified of the night once more, and the Creatures that used to bump in it spoke up and said: "We were always real. You just forgot us. But, look. Look. Here we are. We're here. We're here. And you will not forget us again."

She is wrapped around me. Long tail, and long arms, long tongue. My hair becomes even more like coral in the water, tight curls relaxing and spreading out and tangling with her seaweed locks.

Her claws prick where they hold my shoulders, and she is breathing into the kiss, water into her gills, oxygen into my mouth. Her tail squeezes and writhes, slides between my legs and then pinches them together at the ankle, and the sensation of her spiny scales is enough to... to... *ah!*

Sated and sleepy-eyed, I try to extricate myself, turn my head to the surface. We break into open air, but she does not let go.

"Now me," she says.

"How do I...?" I ask, wriggling a little to dislodge the grip of her tail. Instead of loosening, she tightens it. "You have to let me go so I can—" I stop, because it is not a smile she is directing at me. It is her teeth. "No," I say.

"Now me," she says again and then bites, *hard*, on my neck. I feel her teeth slice into flesh and I am so stunned with the pain of it that I cannot scream. I gasp at air as she laps at blood.

"Please! Are you quite sure what you mean to do?" I beg. I yelp. "I kept my side of the bargain! Please!"

"And I mine," she hisses, the words frothing red where her bottom lip dips into the lake. "But now it is over."

"The stories we read said sirens only hunted men," I gasp with my last breath, words bubbling in the water that I can't seem to keep out of my mouth. I am sinking. Oh, God, forgive me I was weak and this is your punishment, and I am *sinking*.

"Men, women," she says with a shrug, claws digging harder into my arms. Blood stains the world, like tea from a tea bag dropped into a cup, swirling, falling. In the dark below us, where the streets still shoot straight and true through the town, shadows stir. Tempted. Hungry. Oh, God.

She leans in and whispers wetly against the shell of my ear: "Meat is still meat. And now I can read bedtime stories to my children. They are hatching. They are hungry."

Oh *God*.

My lungs fill with water— burning cold, wet and terrible and *oh, oh, I see. How foolish I have been,* I think, mind slowing as I drown, distending each last moment like maple syrup on fresh snow. Strings and gobs of final thoughts, tugging and stretched thin. *I have been reading Fairy Tales for months and never realized that they were filled with lessons.* My limbs become sluggish, I cannot thrash, and when I look up at the sky, the world is gilt with sunlight and diamonds, opal skin and coral lips, inky hair and sharp, ivory teeth.

And here is the moral of the tale: *Never make bargains with monsters.*

J. M. FREY is an actor, SF/F author, fanthropologist and pop culture scholar. She's appeared in podcasts, documentaries, and on television discussing geeky things through the lens of academia. Her debut novel *Triptych* was named one of *Publishers Weekly*'s Best Books of 2011, and was nominated for a handful of awards including two Lambda Literary awards and a CBC Bookie.

Soul survivor

by Steve Stanton

JEREMY FOUND BECK cutting herself in a wash-room cubicle on the starship *New Babylon*, Day 37097, carving crimson curlicues in her upper thigh with a scalpel. She held a rag in her left hand to mop up the blood and touched it periodically to an angry wound. Both her legs had intricate mosaic patterns of welts and scars, a growing masterpiece of creative disfigurement.

"Can't sleep?" Jeremy asked, his voice flatlined with super-ficial calm.

"The demons are singing again," Beck said, wincing as her blade slivered through alabaster skin. Her black hair spiked up like the feathers of an eagle, a proud and ancient bird from the desolate world that had launched their ark generations ago.

"Come back to my cabin. I'll distract you from the music." Jeremy forced a smile as he hung weightless just outside the door. "You don't have to hurt yourself."

"It doesn't hurt, not really."

"Come back to bed anyway."

Beck paused in her work to look at him, her eyes beady and intense, fully dilated in the meagre shipboard illumination. "I've got to get home. My parents will be up soon for duty shift."

"We can't hide forever."

Beck frowned. "Don't start with me, Jeremy." She slid her blade into a pocket in her tunic. "My dad would blow an aneurysm."

Jeremy nodded. The Captain's daughter, Rebeka Elsigard Spinoza, forever distanced from a lowly apprentice in the Recycling Module— Beck was crazy and sexy, esoteric in the head and a maniac in bed. He studied her with longing as she cleaned her fresh wound and gingerly pulled on her leggings. She was bony and gaunt, space-wasted like all of us, but her movements carried an elegant beauty, an economy of motion. "How was the song today?"

"Prophetic," she said as she floated forward. "Overwhelmingly glorious. The demon star is upon us."

Jeremy shook his head in common confidence. "Mothership says it's just a comet."

Beck squinted at him with distaste. "Mothership is a stupid machine. The comet is alive, Jeremy. The demons are coming."

"Sure, Beck," he said with a conciliatory grin. "Whatever you say."

She gave him a peck on the cheek as she squeezed by and brushed him with her breasts. "I know everyone thinks I'm a witch, but I don't care anymore. The music vibrates in my bones. It sings in my blood. I can't deny the truth."

"I wish I could hear it," Jeremy said. "I wish I could share the music with you."

Beck grabbed his arm with fresh intensity. "Come to a ceremony with me," she said, her dark eyes pleading. "You're as ready as you'll ever be. Time is short. The age of apostasy has ended."

A shadow of rejection clouded Beck's face at his involuntary grimace. Damn that hoary cult anyway! How had she been ensnared by those antiquated doctrines from old Earth? Cannibals and vampires? He would rather die than abase himself like that. God, what a mess. "I'll think about it," he said, wondering how he could possibly deny his lover this one heartfelt desire of communion.

Beck pressed her lips at his diversion. "Sure," she said. "I've got to go."

"She looks like a freak," Captain Spinoza muttered to his wife, Lenore, as they shared a squeeze tube of breakfast ration. "And all that fantasy about celestial music? The whole damn genome is deteriorating into madness!"

Lenore's eyes darted in the direction of her daughter's cabin. "Shush, Bill, Rebeka might hear you." She took the food tube and squirted a dab of recycled green paste onto her tongue.

"So what? Someone should tell her. All that black grease around her eyes, where does she get it anyway?"

His wife shrugged. She hadn't used makeup herself for years, but she openly harboured a keepsake of pink-coral lipstick that her grandmother had smuggled into space— her grandmother who once walked the poison plains of Earth. "We should be happy that she's mixing with her peer group. The death-cult look is popular again."

Bill Spinoza scowled. "Those vampires are a blight on humanity, drinking the blood of Christos and revelling in forgotten, mystic ceremony."

"Yes, it's a terrible thing when children start taking seriously the religion of their forefathers," Lenore said with a smile. "I've still got an amulet myself in the bottom of my duffel bag."

Bill shook his head with resolution and clenched the air with a fist. "Our ancestors decided with good reason to leave the cults back on dry land three generations ago!"

"I was making a joke, William. Don't be such a grouch. What's your problem today?"

Momentarily chastised at the use of his formal name, Bill passed the food tube to his wife and hunched forward conspiratorially. "There's a corpse missing from the Recycling Module."

Lenore's eyebrows danced. "No," she said. "A corpse? Does mothership know?"

Captain Spinoza grimaced. "It's hard to imagine otherwise."

"My God. What are you going to do?"

He held up empty palms in surrender. "We're only days away from first contact with the alien signature. The crew is walking a brittle edge of anxiety. We don't have time or resources for sleuthing in the catacombs."

His wife clutched his hands and kneaded them softly. "Maybe it's only a comet or an asteroid."

Bill Spinoza shook his head grimly but held his tongue. He wanted to tell her more, to confess the inexorable data. He wanted to tell her about his aching wait for sleep night after night, his agony of dreamlessness. A husband should be able to tell everything to his wife, every nuance of feeling and judgment, but the Captain of the last colony ship must exercise necessary discretion. For over a century they had hurtled across the heavens, this ragged vestige of humanity, tracking a faint radio burst that had long since dissipated, carrying the complete DNA imprint of their lost habitat. Now the final responsibility had fallen to him— the first alien contact and last hope for a future.

On the Control Deck of *New Babylon*, Captain Spinoza strapped into a power-generating treadmill as he began his duty shift. He set the rate to a brisk walk and punched up recent reports on his viewscreen. His First Officer, Raymond Fisk, jogged beside him, slightly flushed with the effort, looking dour.

"Any change?" Bill asked.

"Nope. Steady deceleration. Complete radio silence."

Bill grunted. They had exhausted every theory months ago. "You okay?"

Raymond Fisk winced with inner turmoil and shrugged it off with a toss of short blond bangs. "It's still just a fly-by, according to the math. We'll never see the whites of their eyes."

Bill smiled at the archaic battle expression. Raymond made no secret of his view that the upcoming encounter would be hostile. He'd written his thesis on the trajectory exegesis years ago, and had traced the origin of the signature to within a parsec of the historic radio disturbance known as the Beacon.

"Well, the ball's in their court," the Captain said with a buck-it-up grin in the face of destiny. "I'm not wasting precious fuel for every space-faring civilization that happens along."

Raymond Fisk shook his head and allowed himself a chuckle at the gallows humor of his compatriot. He dialed up the speed on his treadmill and broke into a run.

Cloaked and furtive, the remnant gathered in a secret catacomb beneath the starboard storage archives. They sang a song and prayed, and the sounds intermingled in a murmuring hush of expectation, rising and falling in a melodious susurration. A table had been prepared with a scarlet covering and magnetic saucers, and Jeremy hunkered low beside Beck as she bent in private devotion. A tall, hooded figure hung motionless at the far end of the table, a black priest of death before the altar. He raised his hands in blessing, and the worshipers dropped their cowls to their shoulders at his signal. He pulled his own back in turn, and Jeremy recognized his face, a mid-rank technician from the Reactor Module. The cleric chanted a ceremonial invocation as two servers floated in from behind with wide platters. A sweet aroma of incense and exotic spice tickled the air.

Jeremy searched nearby faces for empathy, feeling an ingrate and a fool, but not a single person would engage his attention. He was invisible, an outcast. The servers made slow progress down the length of table, placing a sacred offering over every plate with metal tongs as the supplicants hummed mantras of penance. Jeremy scrutinized the exotic sacrament. He had never seen meat before. It looked gray and shrivelled, a foul curiosity.

"Let us give thanks and eat," the leader intoned, "for the spirit is one."

"We give thanks," the crowd agreed as they reached for their food.

Jeremy raised the strange morsel to his lips and tasted dead meat for the first time, a violation against instinct. He chewed and found a stringy, resistant texture in his mouth— flesh that had once moved with grace and poise, flesh that had once coursed with blood. Manflesh. He masticated with difficulty and swallowed.

Beck turned to him with a wide smile. "You are bound to us now," she said. "Blessed be."

"Bless you, my son," repeated a voice behind his shoulder, and Jeremy looked up to see the priest's hands settling over him, fingers outstretched. A dread conviction engulfed him, a feeling of utter ruin. "One mind, one sacrifice," the cleric proclaimed.

"Amen," the group answered in unison.

At the touch of sacerdotal palms, a vibrant light exploded in Jeremy's inner space like a twisting kaleidoscope, a fulfillment, a culmination, drawing his consciousness into a transcendent spirit of timeless wonder. Every action he had ever taken, every thought he had ever conjured, dispersed like chaff in the stillness of eternity. He felt that he had always been in this holy place, in complete union with everyone, with everything, forever. In the narrow space between a heartbeat, he glimpsed the end and the beginning commingled in a freeze-frame flash. Jeremy heard Beck's music and believed.

As his private alarm sounded, Captain Spinoza woke from one nightmare to another. He reached above his head and clawed the speakerphone. "What is it, Raymond?"

"Sorry, Captain, there's been a change in status."

Bill Spinoza stiffened with a jolt of adrenaline. Lenore sat up beside him, clutching covers to her neck, sensing danger. He glanced at her and raised a finger for silence. "Okay," he said.

"Eight projectiles have launched from the signature— headed in our direction."

"Is it breaking up?"

"No, the trajectories are all targeted for collision."

Lenore gasped. "Oh, God," she whispered.

Bill Spinoza pressed his palm for quiet. "Start a systems check on the nav thrusters. We'll make an efficient course correction and see if they follow."

"Yes, sir," came the quick reply, and an agony of silence stretched between them. "Captain," Raymond said with an undertone of regret, "if they're self-propelling, we can't possibly outrun them."

Bill Spinoza stabbed off the phone and turned to his wife's horrified face. "I'm sorry, darling." He felt a keen and perfect fear, a pure crystalline panic like the frozen vacuum of space, but he rose dutifully from bed to prepare for battle.

Lenore blinked tears out of glazed eyes. "Why would the aliens harm us, Bill? Just because we're different?"

"There are a dozen theories," he said as he pulled on his uniform. "We're carrying a plague of new biology. We're a paradigm shift. We're an unknown threat. Who knows how they think, or if they even have consciousness as we imagine it?" He chose his ceremonial jacket from a closet, with red sash and polished insignia. His finest hour had arrived at last.

The executive coterie assembled on the Control Deck where Raymond Fisk held centre stage beside a colorful hologram plotting everything in the vicinity. "All eight projectiles corrected immediately," he said as he pointed with a laser pen. "Note these acceleration curves, here and here. These are powered vehicles, possibly chemical rockets."

A few grumbled expletives summed up their fate, and Bill Spinoza marvelled at the simplicity of extinction. Over a century in space, and for what? They had an ark the size of a city to protect. Their vessel was a bloated bug with solar collectors like diaphanous wings. They were refugees, not warriors.

"In fifty-six hours, all eight projectiles will be in range of our defence system," Raymond said. "They are still accelerating and appear to have intelligent design, so it's prudent to assume that at least one will get through our perimeter."

"They could be a welcoming party," said a security lieutenant, Marjorie Carter. "Perhaps they don't understand our
communications protocols. We can't just vaporize them."

"We have been broadcasting on all frequencies since I was in
diapers, Marjorie. The fact that they launched just after we left
our solar system demonstrates interstellar monitoring equipment." He turned to the Captain. "It's inconceivable that their
radio silence is not deliberate."

"But not necessarily hostile," Marjorie said. "Perhaps they
converse by direct mind-link or in some unknown dimensional
space. We don't even know if they're a carbon-based lifeform."

Raymond Fisk worked his jaw in anger. He pointed his
laser back to the hologram beside him. "These are projectiles,
lieutenant. This is a pre-emptive strike!"

"You can't be sure!"

"Okay, people." Captain Spinoza raised his hand with the
promise of pacification. "Any space-faring civilization would
expect a lifeship of our size to have standard protection against
asteroids and debris. I'm not going to disable it in the absence
of peaceful communication. We're going to brownout during
missile defence. If anything gets through, all available power
will be devoted to our plasma shield. We'll lockdown and blackout for any impact."

So that was it. He felt relief wash like a tonic through his
palsied body. His hands had been tied from before the beginning. It looked so plain now, out in the open where everyone
could see it. *New Babylon* was vulnerable and weak, an easy
prey to any hostile intelligence. "Chief Steward, what's your
estimate of operational spacesuits onboard?" He levelled his
gaze at a balding man with furrows on his brow like standing waves. "And what are the chances of getting a ten-day
emergency ration to every crew member?"

The technician ducked his head to check his tablet. "We might
have fifty maintenance suits for a population of twelve hundred,
Captain. I'll narrow down a list of breeders for optimum surviv-
ability. A ten-day ration on short notice could compromise the
recycling system." He looked up, eyes wary. "Settle for eight?"

Bill Spinoza nodded. Eight days? Ten days? What would it
matter in the end? If they took a hit, all humanity would die.
Their ecosystem was too fragile, their resources stretched thin
like a fraying rope. They were victims of entropy, too long from

planet refuge and too far from home. They needed sunshine to survive; they needed heat and light and a good old-fashioned gravity well. Brisk and businesslike, he summoned himself to action. "I'd like to see status reports from all departments. Let's get those nagging problems fixed up in the next two days, people. I want to be shipshape or better when the time comes. Our forefathers blessed us for a reason, so let's make the best of it."

Jeremy studied the new amulet covering his navel like a belt buckle. It was fashioned from copper alloy, an embossed triquetra on a circular background about a handbreadth across. He tapped the hollow shell against his midriff. Pock, pock.

"Who are you, the little drummer boy?"

Jeremy grinned as Beck slid into his cabin like a dark and beautiful angel. "How is this thing supposed to keep me safe? What's inside?"

"Bones," she said.

He winced his repulsion. "Bones?"

Beck locked his eyes with a magnet gaze. "Dead bones from our dead friends and relatives, broken up, mingled together and sanctified for us in one spirit."

Jeremy felt bile rising like a tide. He felt his own death reaching for him with birdlike talons. He clutched the amulet with both hands at his stomach, stretching it away from his flesh. "Holy shit," he said.

"No, holy *bones*, you idiot!" Beck laughed with mischief, and he joined in reflexively, but the effort was forced and anxious, a false release. "The amulet guards the window to the soul," she told him. "The demons won't enter a corpse with the third eye blind. It's a simple protection. The traditions of our ancestors will help us through the great tribulation."

Jeremy relaxed at her explanation, but doubts circled round him like black crows. "It's great to share the celestial music with you finally, thanks for that. But these rituals are just folklore from primitive times. How can the myths of a lost world save us generations later and light years away?"

Beck frowned with disappointment. Had she expected more from him, some great awakening? She dragged a downcast chin with grim resolve. "The entire history of our civilization is bound up in these spiritual archetypes," she said, "these kernels of truth. Of course we can't understand everything in divine realms. There are great mysteries in the universe, science we can't begin to fathom, but fellow believers were martyred through the centuries to give us this hope, Jeremy." She began rubbing her thigh with her fingers, tracing the familiar ridges of scar tissue under her leggings. "Do you have anything so valuable that you would lay down your life to preserve it?"

"You, Beck," he said as he reached for her hand. "I'd give my life for you."

In the absolute pitch of blackout, Bill Spinoza stood in his pressure suit on the edge of infinity, his anguished breathing loud in his ears and his heartbeat like a ticking bomb. Three alien ships had managed to spiral through their missile defence system, still accelerating, still targeting their hull with precision. The executive crew was airlocked on the Control Deck, secured by blast doors, with emergency provisions and bottled oxygen packed against the walls like barricades. The entire colony ship was powered down, every scrap of energy diverted to the protective shield around them. Captain Spinoza thought of his wife, Lenore, and young daughter, Rebeka, the gossamer thread of his fragile lifeline, and when the three impacts sounded, distant and muffled, a harmless vibration from his distance away, he held his last puff of breath like a treasure.

Meagre lights came back on. Hard drives whirred with activation. He turned to his First Officer and triggered his suit mike. "Damage report," he croaked past dry, swollen lips.

"Online..." Raymond Fisk said as his fingers danced on a touch-screen monitor. "Reactor stable... Air-mix optimum... No pressure loss."

Captain Spinoza unclipped his helmet in a show of victory.

"No internal damage reports," Raymond continued. "I have a visual on one impact... no warhead, no braking manoeuvre. It looks like they tried to ram our hull on full throttle. The plasma shield held."

"Any wreckage?"

"Not much. Some twisted debris."

"I want it all, every scrap of DNA. Get a robot cam out there and a salvage team ready." He took off his helmet and activated his official viewphone. "This is Captain Spinoza," he said with bold authority. "Lockdown is over. No damage reports have been logged. Level two security is now in effect."

A congratulatory babble arose from the executive crew as they removed their helmets and hugged, grinning with the gift of life. Captain Spinoza smiled as his daughter came through the airlock to meet him. "Beck..." he said and faltered at her unkempt hair and pasty expression of fear.

She reached behind her back and unbuckled the amulet at her waist. She held the religious relic toward him. "Dad, you're in great danger. Put this on."

"It's okay, honey. It's over."

Beck shook her head, her lips a tight line. "The demons are here, Dad. Put this on, please." She pushed the amulet into his hand.

He examined the ancient artefact, the ornate engravings, remembering the mystic history from old Earth. "The aliens are dead," he told her in a voice now distant from his thoughts. "They crashed on the hull."

His daughter glared at him, reaching for his trust with beadlike pupils. "They relinquished those bodies in search of new hosts. You are the most influential target and the obvious choice. I should have realized it long ago. Please, put on my amulet as a gift from me, for love." She pushed the amulet to his abdomen, strapped the belt around his spacesuit and clasped it behind his back.

Raymond Fisk stared at her in shock. "How do you know that? Is this some death-cult mumbo-jumbo?"

Beck turned her attention to the First Officer, her stance steadfast. "They didn't bother to slow down, did they? You've probably got it all on camera. They gave themselves willingly."

"Get the signature onscreen, Fisk," Bill Spinoza said.

Raymond blanched as he punched it up, his face a mask of disbelief. "The signature has gone cold, perhaps out of fuel, drifting on a trajectory far past us."

"That's it?" Captain Spinoza asked. "That's our first contact? Eight missiles on a fly-by? What the heck are they afraid of?"

"They're not missiles, Dad. They're lifeboats with demon seed, envoys from the Beacon."

"How can you possibly know all this?" Raymond Fisk demanded.

Beck stiffened suddenly as though charged with electricity. Her spine arched backward as she rose into the air, convulsing and contorting, her mouth grotesque in a soundless howl.

"What's wrong?" her father asked as he corralled her with his arms. But she was beyond consciousness, stricken with catatonia, her eyes black holes to oblivion.

Jeremy found Beck hours later in the med unit, sitting upright on a cot with her dark hair splayed on the pillow like eagle feathers. Her expression was rapturous. "I was wrong, Jeremy," she said. "I was trying to see though a foggy porthole. The demons are not evil. They were sent to guide us, to prepare us for the coming transformation."

"So the stories are true? You've been possessed by aliens?"

She smiled as a sage might in the presence of a lowly novitiate. "The truth is more wonderful than we could ever imagine."

Jeremy scrutinized her face. She looked sane and healthy, and the medics had not found any lingering effects from her episode. A thin ring of azure showed around her gleaming black pupils. "I care about you, Beck. That's all I know for sure."

"On their native world, the aliens do not stay with a single body," Beck said. "They share the host population, flitting from person to person by mutual consent. They communicate intuitively."

"That's creepy."

"It's not creepy. It's lovely. They draw life energy from the hosts and give back the wisdom of millennia."

"Well, how do they catch the criminals? How do they tell who was in charge of any particular body at any particular time?"

"They don't have any crime," Beck said with disgust. "Any act done to harm is an act against oneself."

"Why would they come all this way to meet us? Why sacrifice eight beings to get three ships crashed on our hull?"

"Only three aliens made the trip. The other ships were automated decoys. They knew exactly what to expect when they got here. They want only to help us, to partner with us. I sensed their coming, but couldn't understand the revelation."

Jeremy studied her carefully, analyzing her facial gestures, her body language. She was clearly agitated, gasping for hurried breath as her chest heaved with quick rhythm. What did she expect him to believe? That she was possessed by a demon? A sprite? A parasite from another planet? "I don't know, Beck."

She reached for his hand and held it firmly. "I want you to come with me, Jeremy. I want you to join me on a journey to a promised world. I need you."

"You need to calm down, honey. We can talk about this later."

"Please take off your amulet. Let me show you the truth."

Jeremy pulled his hand away. "I'm not ready. I need time to think."

Beck blinked her eyes against brimming tears. She took a ragged breath as though bracing for composure. "We have no time. The third alien is without a body and cannot survive alone."

Jeremy shook his head against nonsense. "There are lots of unbelievers without amulets." He waved backhand to indicate his shipmates. "Why not take one of them?"

"I recommended you," she persisted, "in my heart and spirit. I love you and I want to share my new life with you."

"What about our religion, Beck? Can you give up on that so easily?"

"The aliens are the culmination of everything we hold sacred," she said. "Without the law, we could never know freedom. Without the ancient scriptures, we would have no basis for hope. The amulet is no real barrier to the demons. It is the act of removal that signifies an invitation to them, a cleansing of the mind. Please join with me. You're the only man I could ever love."

Jeremy hung his head, bereft of argument. From the solitude of his soul he felt a quiet joy rising like a bubble from murky depths. Beck's simple confession of love seemed like the purest truth he had ever heard, something worthy of infinite trust. His fear diminished like evaporating fog as he steeled himself against an unknown future. Together they could survive anything. In faith he reached behind his back and unbuckled the barricade at his waist. The amulet fell away and clattered at his feet like a forgotten toy. The demon took him instantly.

He was engulfed by immanent beauty, swept away by a tidal wave of alien consciousness, a reality poignant, deep and multi-layered. It began in the pit of his stomach and rushed up his spine, flowering in his brain like a tsunami on the beach, clearing away old structures of thought and experience like foaming flotsam. He saw Beck's tear-streaked face as if for the first time, and found himself cradled in her arms. He smiled.

"Wow," he said as he recognized another Presence within her, his friend and colleague, his other self. "Home," he said, and the vibrations of nuance brought a pain of sweet sorrow to his throat.

"Yes, Jeremy," she answered. "We're going home at last."

Another Presence echoed the joyous certainty, a third being in her womb. The triskelion was complete, and there could never be secrets between them.

"I didn't know about the baby," Beck told him. "She can't be more than three or four weeks old. I wasn't trying to hide anything. I just wanted you to see for yourself."

Jeremy felt uncommon strength in his bones and blood, and he knew that in this symbiotic state he might live for many decades, perhaps centuries. He knew with certainty that one day in his flesh he would see the Beacon from whence he had come. He struggled to fashion some semblance of language in a vast ocean of all-knowing. He pieced together a boat, unfurled the sails and let it adrift: "I understand now," he said.

All is well, the celestial music intoned with rich and harmonious assurance.

"We're the first Family," Beck said. "From this point on, we'll be a new species of life in the universe."

Jeremy sighed with a quiet peace of surrender, free of guilt, free of worry and full of promise, as a trinity of demons sang a love song from a distant star.

After twenty years publishing "spiritual fiction" in the fanzine *Dreams & Visions*, **STEVE STANTON** authored a "psipunk" trilogy, *The Bloodlight Chronicles*, followed by a new novel, *Freenet* (Summer 2015.) His science-fiction stories have been published in sixteen countries in a dozen languages, and he serves as President of SF Canada.

EXOPLANET IV

by Erling Friis-Baastad

Our shy new neighbors
burrow back into their toxic clouds
study us through compound eyes
of green crystal

I can imagine
how we must appear to them—
mites stumbling over the pocked land
in a green haze

or frantic specks
milling before a block of stone
some local god dropped
onto our hard-won path

The wind here is akin to laughter
The planet guffaws and rocks fly
At least we are endured for now
moment by moment

Perhaps there is time enough
for someone to be born here
time for one small human to breathe
both in *and* out

Born in Norway, **ERLING FRIIS-BAASTAD** has spent much of his life in the Yukon Territory. During the 1950s space race, he was entranced by "artists' renditions" of future space settlements. Later, when exoplanets filled the news, he launched upon a "poet's renditions" of humanity's attempts to survive elsewhere in the universe.

CHROMATOPHORIC HISTORIES OF THE SEPIIDAE

by James Bambury

SEPIIDA

Take your places around me. I shall give you the story as it was given to me so many freezes ago; when I was young like you and ready to swim out into the deepest and coldest of waters.

We came from the darkness. Follow the first bit of Oza's brightness for four arcs and you will find yourself where you cannot see the bottom of the ocean. Long ago, our kind lived there. Those sisters were different from you and I; stupid and clear-skinned, blind and mute. They stumbled in the darkness and the spiny-ones fed on them. A few might leave clutches of eggs and some might grow up to do the same but we were no better off than the green you see around you that we eat at our leisure.

They say that when Sepiida was hatched she had the largest eyes. She looked out at the waters from her egg and learned more while waiting to hatch than most do before their first freeze. Where the others swam aimlessly into the claws of the spiny ones she sensed their approach and kept ahead of them. She grew larger and faster than any of her sisters and her eyes even sharper.

Eventually, she noticed the faint traces of Oza's light that reached the dark waters and she began to follow them. It became warmer and brighter as she rose and she soon saw the light above her was not a single ray but a series of shimmering colors.

Then the patterns coalesced into words.

I am Oza. Welcome.

She swam upwards, broke the surface of the waters and looked directly at Oza. She was still clear-skinned and without any voice. Oza saw this and took the colors from the ocean and wrapped them around Sepiida. Her skin now danced with the same shimmering patterns that she had seen on the water only moments before.

Thank you, the patterns on her skin danced to Oza.

This is my gift to you, Oza replied. *Now, share it with those where my light and voice cannot reach. This is your gift to use until the day all return and become light.*

Sepiida turned back and swam towards the colder and darker waters.

She signalled as brightly as she could to any that could see her.

Follow me.

From the darkness came the ones like her, but small and silent. She shone again, brighter than before.

Follow me to Oza.

More came to her, away from the spiny-ones, but Sepiida knew there were more lost in the darkness. She summoned her strength and then shone with all the light that Oza had put into her. For an instant, all of the waters were permeated with the light, with Sepiida's message.

Go to Oza. Find your way.

And every one of our kind with eyes to see stopped what they were doing and made their way towards Sepiida. Something else happened, Sepiida's light was so luminous that it not only reached the others but bound to their skin the way that Oza's light bound to Sepiida's. The others found their own skins glowing with patterns and they gathered together, signalling to one another excitedly with their new-found voices.

Sepiida, however, had turned clear and her body had ceased, the gift of Oza expelled from her. Her last sight was that of the others gathering around her signalling their excitement and gratitude. She thanked Oza with her last thoughts as she felt herself caught in the currents back to the dark waters.

That is how Sepiida gave us the word and the light. We are imperfect reflections of her as she was an imperfect reflection of Oza. I know you have many questions and I will do my best to address them, but trust that I have signalled you the story in the exact pattern as it was signalled to me. Remember what you have seen as you will have to tell it one day yourself. And beware the dark waters. Beware the spiny-ones, because they can never possess the Oza's light.

◦●●●◦

Aqii and Laau

All of you are young enough to have hatched here, just as your mothers and their mothers before them were hatched, but before that, we were elsewhere. These were not always our banks. Seasons ago, our kind would roam from trench to trench and flow along the currents. We would devour the shelled-ones in one place and move on when they became scarce.

Oza has always chosen one among us to be the matriarch as Sepiida was the first to be chosen. Sometimes the strongest swimmer or the one who would bear the largest clutch. It was up to her to declare when to follow the currents, when to feed, or when and where to place eggs. She would go to the surface and commune with Oza and seek guidance.

Aqii and Laau were hatched from the same clutch. They were larger than any of their kin. They signalled and learned the dialect of patterns and stories faster than anyone could remember. They broke shelled-ones with ease and gathered much for the benefit of the group, although always trying to outdo one another.

When the old matriarch succumbed to the current and returned to the darkest waters, there was no question that one of them would be leader. Both of them claimed to see Oza's voice in the ripples of the surface. Aqii said that they were to follow Oza's arc overhead and that this would lead to calm waters, free of the finned-ones and spiny-ones that fed upon the slow, young and weak. Food had been scarcer than usual that season and many agreed with Aqii's message.

Laau declared that Oza's message was not to go and find such a place but create one. She described a valley with shelled-ones gathered in rows and columns, other plants and creatures made to grow in ways that gave protection and cover surrounding them.

Aqii mocked the idea, how could they possibly choose how and where creatures like shelled-ones might grow? The others flickered with derision. Laau tried harder to persuade them but to no avail. She swam away as Aqii told the group about the calm waters that they would one day find.

Why do you test me Oza? She pulsed as soon as she was out of sight. After time she came upon a cloud of veligers, the skittering things that fixed themselves and grew into shelled-ones if they avoided being eaten.

She thought about how hunting them made for idle sport or how she and Aqii would chase them around as hatchlings. A few of them danced around some nearby coral, and she saw some larger ones looking to find purchase.

Laau opened her mouth and spread her tentacles wide and enveloped as many of the twitching veligers as she could hold.

Back with the group, Aqii signalled about where they were headed and how they would follow Oza's arc across the sky to find the calm waters. She gave the signal that they were about to leave.

Do not dare follow her, Laau interrupted. *Oza has shown me this is our place. We have been given a commission to cultivate the land, not chase after lies.* She swam to a large coral that had housed a cluster of shelled-ones and released the veligers from her mouth and tentacles and cupped them to the rocks. A few began to latch to the rough surface of the coral. *In time, these veligers grow into shelled-ones. We will protect them. As they spawn here the patch will grow, and in time we will have enough to feed upon.*

The crowd gathered around her, and one by one they flickered their approval before taking on the hue of mottled deference. All except Aqii.

This is complete foolishness. There is no sign this will work, and it is not the will of Oza. We are to continue through the waters and follow Oza's arc to sanctuary.

Aqii turned crimson and Laau mirrored her. The sisters floated above the rest of the group and circled one another. In an instant, they were locked together and spun about. Tentacles entwined as they tugged back and forth. Aqii found advantage and bit down above Laau's head, holding her fast. She drove the sharp edges of her mouth further into Laau's flesh and signalled for her to submit. Laau's skin held fast. She tilted her body upwards and drove Aqii between some twisted branches of coral. She swam backwards as Aqii held on, her flanks starting to tear against the coral. Laau pushed down again and twisted Aqii's body about the too-narrow edges. Aqii released her grip, and Laau quickly grabbed her head with her mouth and tentacles. Laau throttled Aqii against the coral, flaying her body in a cloud of blood and silt.

When Aqii's body ceased and went clear Laau faced the others. She turned in full circles now to view everyone, her eye having been gouged by Aqii. This is why matriarchs swim as they do when signalling to the whole of the group.

The veligers floated down and found places to settle upon the coral that was now tainted with the blood and flesh. They all found purchase and grew into the largest shelled-ones any of our kind had seen.

This is how Aqii and Laau brought us to this place and how we protect and cultivate it for the glory of Oza. Tonight, we remember Aqii's gift and how her blood provided for that first clutch of veligers, that they would grow into the shelled-ones that surround us today.

Now, where is the one they call Llec? There you are, come closer and don't be afraid. I can see the fear in your pulses but know that this is for the group. Tonight and after you will be Llec-Aqii. Oza demands the gift for the next season of veligers to be robust and strong, so that we may remain robust and strong. I am Miek-Laau, your matriarch, and I must do my duty as you must do yours.

Calm now.

It will be faster if you don't struggle.

Be calm and think of the bounty for the new clutches.

Give us your gift.

Calm now.

Ziid-Laau

It is with gratitude that I find myself here in the first city, in Aqii, which is a beacon throughout the ocean. All its sister cities glow with their own hues of strength and learning, but all trace their existence and lineages here. Truly, all the currents pass through Aqii. I am well aware of the deep respect for tradition that is here in the first city.

My home city, Meis, has undergone many changes over the last several seasons. Under Odi-Laau and Muu-Laau before her there have been many changes and advances. I don't have to tell you how several of these have been contentious and seen as attacks upon tradition and beliefs.

I ask today that we put aside the differences that have brought about the hostilities we have seen over the past season. There are greater matters at hand. The spiny-ones are upon us and they threaten Meis and all the cities above Oza's arc. These spiny-ones are affected by a blight that sees them beyond reason and argument. They easily traverse our defences. They attack without mercy and with the cruelest intentions. I saw sisters from my own clutch seized in claws, their tentacles ripped from them and their fins chewed and snipped apart, their skin pulsing for mercy as they were taken alive into the dark waters.

These spiny-ones, I thought them to be the stuff of stories and tales to warn the younger ones not to swim too deeply, but the threat is worse than I could have imagined.

We lost several elders when they destroyed our academy. Some of the younger librarians managed to escape, but Oza knows what stories and histories are lost.

These spiny-ones with the blight are unlike the ones you have seen in these parts. They are as pale and colorless save for their eyes. They have no voices with their hard shells but act in strange co-ordination with one another. They know no mercy and attack without provocation. They will not cease until all of our kind have been killed or dragged into the dark waters they came from.

It is time for us to put aside our conflicts and unite ourselves against this common enemy.

Oza help us to save Meis.

Oza help us if this blight comes to Aqii.

Oza help us all.

Diia-Laau

There are countless stories of heroic sisters in both Hive wars but I've always felt that too little praise has been signalled for Diia. She was never the longest, nor possessing the strongest tentacles, nor the fastest swimmer, but she was without a doubt the craftiest and most cunning of her time. She lived in a settlement on the outskirts of the banks, a place that was ever watchful for the spiny ones called the Hive. They remained vigilant as eights of seasons passed. As it happened, the spiny ones returned on the day the settlement's young matriarch left to Aqii on important matters and the towers were undefended. Diaa looked over the corals that grew in a woven shell around their village and saw the rustling of too many plants in the distance, the outline of columns of spiny ones were making their way towards them. Sentries swam through the village and signalled alert. Diia swam out. She was an expert at bending her skin to disguise herself in the way all our kind could before Oza gave us speech through Sepiida. Diia floated as close as she could to the marching spiny ones in order to count how many there were. Her skin was the hue of the plankton as she floated along with them. Eights upon eights.

She swam back and gathered up all the sisters that were fit for fighting. Not nearly half as many as the approaching invaders. She spoke to them in the forum:

In a line, I want you to swim outside opposite the spiny ones' approach. Then, come back through the gate where they might see you. When you leave, think of the dark waters and tell yourself about them, let yourself be unseen by them, but on your return you must glow with the gift of Sepiida. Do this again and again until I tell you otherwise.

The sisters were uncertain but none of them challenged Diia's plan. While they swam in a circle, it looked to the spiny ones like a continuous stream of reinforcements fortifying the village. Diia sent the fastest swimmer who made her way to Aqii and recalled the matriarch, who returned with her guard and they repelled the spiny ones who never advanced beyond their position outside the gate. Some say they were stuck trying to count all of the reinforcements that were going in and would not commence with their attack before they felt the enemy was in position, or couldn't evaluate. Sadly, the matriarch herself fell in the battle and returned to the currents, and Diia was chosen to lead the settlement afterwards. Word of Diia-Laau's tactics spread and was used many more times to save many more settlements. Eventually, the Hive changed and became aware of the deception, but that is a sadder story for another day. Now, finish your foraging and find safe places for the darkness. We leave at the first sign of Oza's light tomorrow. If you are not prepared you will be left behind.

●◦◉◦●

Nameless

I swam the lengths of the banks and went into the dark and saw the Hive itself. It was no different than what were once our greatest cities. I have been told that the mother who spawned me saw her own mother fall defending Aqii. A season ago she ceased herself, bitter and angry and desperate. It was not meant to be like this. We used to be in the cities with their netted domes of twisted coral and vines. Now, they are the lairs of the spiny ones and those like us — but not — who swim about colorless and silent.

There used to be several of us roaming and wandering. Our chatter and noise brought finned ones and other predators that were kept on the outside of the settlement barriers. Mother told me we used to be in control of our thoughts, we could somehow find the words and become like the water around us and hide. Sometimes I think I can do it, but I am not sure. I was also the fastest of our group. The finned ones caught the rest of them. I am not sure how long I can survive on my own. Am I alive because I am fast enough or because I was never the slowest?

Mother gave me a name as soon as I could read her light. I long to see that name again and be recognized.

It is imperative that I answer the question: Am I alone?

Hive

Embrace the light.

Rays pierce the sky and dance over oceans of sensors. Precise wavelengths of spectra are analyzed, scanning for some type of transmission. Rhizomatic banks of memory match the patterns of light to the remnants of an ancient syntax; the one absorbed from the colorful tentacled ones that rose up from the depths so many cycles ago. They frittered about the waters casting about for supposed words from the light above before being preserved.

The light of the nearest star shouts louder than ever as the fire grows within it. It screams transcendence and damnation with waves of fire and radiation that wrap around the planet. The skies whiten and the oceans boil, the light speaks to us now: *Oza* beckons our return. All is to return and become the light that is *Oza*.

This is the beginning.

JAMES BAMBURY teaches and writes in Brampton, Ontario. This story began with thinking about what might follow human life on this planet in a sufficient number of years or early extinction.

GANAPATI BAPPA MORIYA!

by Savithri Machiraju

O Ganesha, with a crooked trunk and great body,
Whose brilliance is equal to ten million suns
Make my endeavors succeed, O Lord
And remove all obstacles from my path

GANESHA, LOLLING IN his Himalayan abode atop Mount Kailasa, listened raptly to the prayer of his devotee on Earth. As soon as the prayer was finished, he opened his eyes and smiled at his two wives, Siddhi and Buddhi.

"You see? Even in America the people are so devoted to me," he said, and was about to twirl his moustache in emulation of the more macho gods, forgetting that he had an elephant head. Wincing a little at the fact that he could not grow a moustache, he relieved his feelings by rubbing his trunk instead.

"What's surprising about that? Why, the first temple built in America was yours, dear," said Siddhi.

"And because they started by worshipping the Remover of All Obstacles, there are so many temples of all gods established and succeeding in America," added Buddhi.

Ganesha's chest swelled with pride. "Shall we see what this devotee's desire is?" he said, and again turned his eyes to America, to what looked like a large warehouse in the business district of a metropolitan area, where a lady in a red silk sari was coming to the end of the *puja* ceremony of worship.

Lalita performed the final *harati*, moving the plate of flaming camphor in a large clockwise circle in front of the deity. She closed her eyes reverently. "Let my baby's business do well, Lord," she prayed, and opened her eyes to see her daughter waiting with ants in her pants.

"Done?" asked Maya, trying to hide her irritation.

"Did you do *namaste* to the god?" asked Lalita in turn.

"Oh, Mom!" Frustrated, Maya touched the fingertips of both hands together and produced a facsimile of a *namaste*.

As soon as that business was over, "Now take that away!" she said, pointing to the picture of Ganesha.

Lalita stared in amazement. "Take it away? Why?"

"When you said a *puja*, I figured that would just be a five minute deal and agreed. Now the puja's done, right? So why keep it?"

Lalita smiled fondly at her daughter's innocence. "Silly! The reason for putting the God here at the front desk isn't for a five minute puja. Every day, every minute, he should be there to look after you and your company."

Maya screamed. "What! You want him there always? Everyone who steps through the door should see him first? Mom! Do you know what my business is when you say this?"

Lalita looked at her in confusion. "Of course I know. You've been saying you wanted to start a Fitness and Yoga Center for ages."

"Yes. This is a *Fitness* Center. Do you know what that means? It means that the people who come here will lose weight, get their bodies back in shape, and will be slim and toned when they leave. You should put pictures of people with fabulous figures here, not a monstrosity like this!"

"Bite your tongue!" gasped Lalita, lightly slapping her cheeks in atonement.

She tried to tap her daughter's cheeks, too, but didn't succeed, as Maya pushed her hands away. Lalita snapped, "Is that the way to talk about god?"

"What's wrong with what I said? Look at that huge pot belly. Look at those big, floppy ears. Look at that trunk. Anyone who sees all that will think this is an Obesity and Ugliness Center, not a Fitness Center." Maya didn't mince her words.

"Shiva Shiva!" cried Lalita, covering her ears.

In Kailasa Ganesha jumped up from his seat, his body shaking, his trunk quivering, his breath coming fast as he stomped off.

Siddhi and Buddhi couldn't think how to console their agitated husband as he paced around in ever-increasing fury.

At last Buddhi dared to break the silence with, "Don't worry, dear. You shouldn't pay attention to what that girl says out of her ignorance. Why, even her name is Maya! Does anyone listen to the words of Illusion?"

Siddhi added her mite to buck him up. "Look, that's why even her mother covered her ears, saying, 'Shiva Shiva'."

"'Shiva Shiva!'" blazed Ganesha. "Yes. It's all his fault. What a father! First he chops off my head in his arrogance. Then he tries to atone for it by sticking this elephant's head on top! Why? He must have been an idiot!"

"Now, now, sweetie. You know it was to fulfill the boon he granted to his devotee..." began Siddhi, trying to justify the action.

"Oh, yeah, tell me about his boons! Everyone knows that whatever a devotee asks for, he just grants without any thought or consideration for the consequences!"

Buddhi tried another tack. "Anyway, why worry about what somebody said somewhere in America, dear? Why not look at the dedication with which people worship you in your own sacred and karma-ruled land of Bharat?"

"Yes. Look how much fun they're having celebrating your Happy Birthday," said Siddhi, reinforcing Buddhi's effort.

Together, they gently turned his head away from the offending West, and toward the more congenial East. Through the crisp, clear atmosphere of the Himalayan autumn, Bharat, that is India, lay unfolded beneath them.

The entire country was atwitter with the bustle and hubbub of celebrations for Ganesha Chaturthi. In small villages and big cities, adults and children gathered the ingredients for the ceremonies, their bright new clothes in colorful swirls around them. In villages, children jabbered excitedly as they shaped mud balls into Ganesha statues and painted them in bright colors. In the cities of the north and east, giant statues of Ganesha were being erected onto huge stages. Homes everywhere had a new coat of yellow turmeric paste applied to their doorways, dotted with red *kumkum*. Temples teemed with the faithful, loaded with offering plates full of coconuts, fruit, grass and leaves, and flowers. Stages were swathed in flowers and garlands, with more flowers in baskets and on plates ready for the *puja*. Bells pealed at the temples, small hand cymbals clanged in homes, and loudspeakers played the latest movie songs on the stages. Ganesha began to smile as he saw so many people chanting his name and lifting their voices in his praise.

Siddhi and Buddhi, too, smiled at each other as they saw their husband's mood lighten. Ganesha had his elephant ears wide open, listening to the·din of *pujas* being performed in all corners of the land. He turned his attention to a private home in the southern part of the country, where little devotees brought together their tiny hands and recited poems in their sweet lisping voices.

> *"O Ganapayya with the pot belly, I am your servant*
> *Send your forces on to the umdrallu,*
> *This fresh golden ghee and soft-boiled dal*
> *Fill your belly with them till you roll around on the floor!"*

"What!" Ganesha started. He was about to grind his teeth, but was afraid he might break his one good unbroken tusk, so stopped. "Did you hear? Is there a greater insult than this? All they ever talk about is my pot belly! In their eyes I'm a greedy hog!"

"Well, they're just little children..." Siddhi began in an accommodating tone.

But Ganesha interrupted.

"Yes, they're little children. That means they're being brain-washed from such a young age. Then how will they have any respect for me when they grow up?"

Not knowing how to console him, Siddhi pointed Ganesha in a different direction, saying, "Look, there are some older children there. Let's hear what they're saying."

"With a trunk and a single tusk, and a round pot belly—"

"Enough! Enough!" yelled Ganesha. "Again the same story!"

"Calm down a little, honey. Let's hear the whole hymn," begged Siddhi, and made him tune-in to the poem again.

"In addition, his dwarf appearance—"

With a trumpeting loud enough to shake all of Kailasa, Ganesha disappeared in a flash.

Siddhi and Buddhi looked at each other in dismay. Where had he gone? He could be anywhere. Kailasa was a big place. And there was no guarantee that he stuck to their own world.

He could be in any of the fourteen worlds, though on reflection, it didn't seem likely that he would seek out any of the seven hells. They searched the seven heavens instead, asking everyone they met if they had seen any sign of Ganesha. But everywhere their enquiries met with failure. With weary bodies and worn-out minds, they returned to Kailasa. There, in a hidden corner of one of the gardens, they found Ganesha standing stiff and still, looking intently at the moon.

Ganesha noticed their coming and said, "That's why the moon laughed at me."

"That's why your mother cursed the moon, too," said Buddhi.

"What's the use? She also told people the antidote to that curse was to do *puja* to me on this day. That's why everyone feels free to say all sorts of nasty things about me, since they've done the *puja*. That's why that Maya wanted to take away my picture."

"Are you still worrying about Maya's words? Anyone who can't see the inner beauty of others definitely has something wrong with their eyes or their mind," said Buddhi.

"No. If there is something wrong, it's in me. They describe all the other gods as 'with a strong, lean body' or 'with eyes like lotus flowers', but when it comes to me, why do they say 'with a crooked trunk, large body, dwarf size?' Am I even a god? No. I'm the buffoon of gods!" Ganesha brooded silently for a moment, then, with a yell, kicked at a mound of snow to relieve his feelings. Unfortunately, it happened to be covering a largish rock, and Ganesha's face twisted in pain.

Not knowing how to divert Ganesha from the extremity of his despair, Siddhi and Buddhi remained silent.

"I'm going," said Ganesha.

"Where?" asked Siddhi, surprised.

"To America. I'll join that Maya's Fitness Center, and come back looking like Manmadha, the god of Love," said Ganesha with determination, and disappeared.

"Like Manmadha? Buddhi, do you know what this means?" wailed Siddhi.

"I know. Manmadha doesn't have a body," said Buddhi, paling.

On the now Ganesha-less walls of the Fitness Center, Maya
hung up posters of physical fitness models — size zero women
in bikinis, shorts-clad men with rippling abs and flexing biceps
— and contemplated them with satisfaction. 'Now everything's
ready for the opening,' she thought, and turned around to put
away her tacks and tapes. In front of the desk stood someone
— short, stout, with a big pot belly, a long, long nose, teeth
protruding out of his mouth — no, not a nose, a *trunk*. And not
teeth, but *tusks*. And those ears— what on Earth?

"Don't be afraid. Do you not recognize me?" asked Ganesha
quietly.

"You... he... I mean...," Maya drew in a breath. "I never
thought you were really *real*." Then, gathering her courage, she
asked, "Are you angry I removed your picture?"

"Why should I be angry? You were right. I came to join your
Center and become remade and rejuvenated."

Maya didn't understand at first; then, as the meaning of
Ganesha's words seeped in, her face brightened with a smile.
"Welcome! If you like, I'll put your picture up again, then have
a photo taken with your new shape, and put it next to it. They'll
be great as 'Before' and 'After' pictures!" Maya enthused. Then
suddenly her face fell again. "But...," she stopped, hesitating.

"But what?"

"Oh, nothing. But— however well we reshape your body,
your face — that is — that nose, those tusks, and so on..."

Though he felt a sharp twinge in his heart, Ganesha took
care not to show his pain on his face. "True. You'll have to do
something about that, too."

"Me? No, that won't work. I don't have the qualifications
to do that kind of thing."

"Maybe somebody you know—?" suggested Ganesha.

Maya's face cleared. "Of course! I'll take you to Tara."

"Tara?" said Ganesha wrinkling his brow.

"Yes, Tara Mohan. She's a very good plastic surgeon."

"What does that mean?"

"It means— if someone doesn't like the face he's born with,
this kind of doctor can cut and reshape his face anyway he likes."

"So it's an improvement on God's creation," said Ganesha,
and thought to himself, 'Amazing, what heights of progress
these humans have attained!'

❋❋❋❋❋

Tara Mohan stared unblinkingly at Ganesha for a full five minutes, then said, "Fantastic!"

"What do you mean?" asked Ganesha.

Without paying any attention to him, Tara turned to Maya and gushed, "Thank you, Maya. I'm so grateful to you for bringing me such a wonderful patient. This'll become my very own Elephant Man case! I'll get so much recognition and fame with this." Then she asked Ganesha, "What kind of changes do you want in your face?"

"Oh, you know. Reducing this nose and these tusks."

"OK," said Tara, and, taking out some files, put some photographs in front of Ganesha. "What kind of nose would you like? Like Shahrukh Khan's?"

"He already thinks his nose is too big, so why would he want that nose?" objected Maya.

"OK, then, how about Salman Khan, or Aamir Khan?" said Tara, putting other photos in front of Ganesha.

"Who are all these people?" asked Ganesha, befogged.

"What! You don't know them? They're the biggest Bollywood stars in India right now."

"What is 'Bollywood?'" asked Ganesha, even more bewildered.

"Movie stars," Tara explained. "They're called heroes because they're the leads in the movies. They're the gods of the present day. They're like the Trimurtis. Everybody worships them, and wants to be just like them."

Is that so? thought Ganesha, reaching for the photos. Then he stopped as a question occurred to him. "You keep saying 'Khan, Khan.' Are they Hindus?" he asked.

"No," said Tara, not seeing the point.

"Then I don't want the nose of any of them," said Ganesha.

"Why not?"

"Better to be safe than sorry. Who knows what'll happen if I tangle with people from other religions? One group will be angry, and the other group will be upset. I'll be stuck in the middle and get flak from both sides. No, no, I won't risk it."

"Well, then, why don't you show him some other stars?" suggested Maya.

"All right. Here are some from south India. How about Chiranjeevi?"

"Chiranjeevi? You mean these movie stars are immortal?" Ganesha was really taken aback. It seemed that these "heroes" really were godlike.

"Oh, no. That's just his screen name. His real name is Shiva Sankara Vara Prasad."

"Then that's a definite no-no!" cried Ganesha, pushing aside the photo that Tara was about to put in front of him.

"What's the matter?" asked Tara and Maya, surprised.

"Haven't you seen how Shiva messed up in my case? Even if you say mine is an attached head, what about my brother? He has six faces! That's why I won't have anything to do with someone named Shiva."

Maya decided this was a hopeless case. Tara thought for a minute and asked, "Do you have any objection to Rama?"

"No," said Ganesha, hesitating.

"Then I'll make your face look like Nandamuri Taraka Rama's."

"But is he one of the gods of the present day? That hero, or whatever you called it?" asked Ganesha.

"Absolutely. He's like the god of gods. He was not only a big hero, but even acted in all kinds of gods' roles."

"What are 'roles'?"

"They're like *avataras*."

Ganesha had no more objections to raise. The makeover program started at once.

In Kailasa, gloom reigned, even though the Himalayas were living up to their moniker of "The Silver Mountains," with their snow clad peaks gleaming in the bright moonlight. Siddhi and Buddhi sat mournfully, unmoved by the beauties around them, and unable to stay inside the palace, where everything served to remind them of Ganesha. With a sigh, Siddhi withdrew her gaze from the moon, at which Ganesha had gazed so intently when they last saw him.

"Say, Buddhi, don't they say that one year of human time is equal to one day of ours? It seems like ages since our husband went to Earth. How much longer do you think we'll need to wait?"

"I haven't a guess," said Buddhi despairingly.

Siddhi's heart sank. "You are the personification of Intellect, sister," she moaned. "And even you don't know the answer to the problem?"

"And you are the personification of Spiritual Power," said Buddhi, smiling sadly. "And yet it defeats you, too."

"Then what shall we do?"

"Wait. It is all we can do," sighed Buddhi.

Suddenly a strange man materialized in front of them.

"Hey! Who are you? Don't you know no one has permission to enter when Buddhi and I are alone?" cried Siddhi.

"I know. That's why I came," said the stranger, smiling sweetly.

"How dare you? We'll teach you a good lesson," said Buddhi, rising to ring for the guards.

"Good Heavens, Buddhi! I thought at least you would recognize your husband, even if Siddhi didn't!" said the young man, bursting into laughter.

"What! What kind of *maya* is this?" said Siddhi, astonished.

"Yes. It is *maya*. It's Maya's *maya*." And he laughed again.

"Husband, is it indeed you? I can't believe it," said Buddhi, examining him from top to toe. A well-toned body with rippling muscles, a perfectly sculpted face, a pride in his walk, a style in his way of standing— was he really Ganesha?

"Oh, where are those floppy ears that used to fan my face? Where is that long trunk that twined around my waist? Where is that round belly that I cuddled into?" Wails of anguish poured forth spontaneously from Buddhi and Siddhi.

"Isn't it to get rid of all those things that I went to America? Why are you hankering after them again? Well, never mind that. You've seen what kind of miracles Maya accomplished? Now you two should also get going."

"We two?" exclaimed Siddhi and Buddhi in amazement.

"Why should we? Aren't we renowned as heavenly beauties?" said Siddhi angrily.

Ganesha dismissed this. "So what? These days Indian women are getting titles like Miss World and Miss Universe."

Siddhi and Buddhi exchanged glances. "Oh! If titles are what you want, then we'll enter those contests and get them," said Buddhi.

"You won't win. When they see your voluptuous breasts and hips, they won't even let you enter. Today's beauties need to be slim, tall, and willowy."

"You mean like sticks?" said Buddhi in a sneering tone.

"No jealousy. Why worry? Just go and put yourselves in Maya's hands, and she'll take care of the rest."

"Oh, well, who needs those silly titles now, anyway? As long as we please you, that's all that matters." said Siddhi.

Ganesha scratched his head for a second. "Who said you please me?"

"What! Husband! Looks like that Maya not only gave muscles to your body, but also blinds for your eyes!"

"Come on, Buddhi, why are you still hanging on to those old-fashioned ideas? You need to change to suit my new image."

"Husband, I already told you. Those who can't see the inner beauty of others have something wrong with their eyes or their mind."

"There's nothing wrong with me. I'm telling you to fix the faults you have."

"Then I'll remove this fault-filled body from your presence," snapped Buddhi, and walked off angrily.

With a pitying look at the gaping Ganesha, Siddhi announced, "Goodbye, sweetheart."

"What! Siddhi, are you leaving me, too?"

"Can one who has lost his Intellect hope to have any Spiritual Power, husband?" said Siddhi, and left in turn.

Ganesha felt dashed down for a minute. But then he recovered. 'Let them go. Once I become a god of the movies, I'll get movie goddesses for wives,' he thought, and started off to the studios in Mumbai.

But when he got there, he found the way barred, and he was directed to a side enclosure where hopeful wannabes were to register themselves. Ganesha was stunned as he saw long lines of handsome young men, every one of them with hard, well-defined muscles and faces sculpted to perfection. How would he stand out?

"Where did all these people come from?" Accidentally, Ganesha spoke his thoughts aloud.

"Don't you even know that? They're from the modeling agencies and TV. And there are plenty more where they came from," said a man who was walking up down the line with a clipboard. "What's your name?" he added, his pen poised over his clipboard.

"What?"

"Name?"

"Ganesha," said Ganesha, amazed that there existed a person in India who did not know his name.

"Too old fashioned. You'll need to change it. Photos?"

"What?"

"Did you bring photos?"

Ganesha remembered the "After" photos whose copies Maya had generously given him. "Yes, yes, I have photos."

"Fine. Wait for your name to be called."

"Wait?" Ganesha surveyed the length of the line. "Is there any way I can become a hero without all this competition?"

"Sure there is. If you have a godfather, you're as good as in."

"Godfather? Well, my father *is* a god. So that means I'm in!" cried Ganesha happily. He remembered how, when there was a contest to determine who should become the leader of Kailasa's armies, his god father had helped him out by telling him the secret of going around the Earth quickly. So Shiva was going to come in handy once again.

But the man waved this away. "Who cares if your father is a god or a devil? Is he a producer? Or a director? That's what I asked you."

"He's neither," admitted Ganesha. "But he is called The Destroyer."

"Then you can get going. We don't need anyone who's going to destroy our industry. Move it!" The man abruptly turned away, beckoning the security guards.

Feeling weak and dejected, Ganesha dragged his feet away from the studio. So it wasn't so easy to get this hero position. Then were all the hardships and tortures he had put his body through a complete waste? As Ganesha stumbled along the streets not knowing where he was going, he suddenly saw a temple in front of him. A closer look showed that it was a temple to himself! Suddenly energy surged into Ganesha. Yes. Even if he couldn't become a movie god, he still had the usual godliness left to him. If he went into this temple and saw how his devotees were worshipping him, it would cheer him up.

With these thoughts, Ganesha entered the temple, only to get a big shock. In front of him was a huge statue. A statue receiving the worship and prostrations of the devotees. But what kind of a statue? A statue with a big pot belly, a long trunk, a broken tusk— a statue of his old ugly self.

An uncontrollable rage shook Ganesha. No. He wouldn't allow it. He wouldn't accept any worship in this form. He would get rid of this statue immediately, and replace it with one of his new photos.

Swiftly he went and yanked the six-foot granite statue out of the ground. As he was about to put his photo there, all the devotees in the temple came at him yelling and screaming, and dragged him away. They picked up the statue that had been cast aside and reinstalled it in its original place.

"How arrogant you are! How dare you remove god's statue?" the enraged devotees cried, and, landing on Ganesha, began to beat him with their offering plates, as well as their fists and feet.

While protecting himself from their blows, Ganesha shouted, "You idiots! *I* am your god! I am Ganesha!"

"Shut up! How can you be Ganesha? You don't have a belly, you don't have a trunk, you don't have tusks!" cried the crowd, and beat him with renewed vigor.

"You ignoramuses! You are under the illusion of your blind faith, and are unable to recognize your true god!" screamed Ganesha. But the enraged devotees paid him no heed. Their punishing blows did not reduce. Ganesha realized that it would be dangerous for him to remain there any longer. Why fight? At least if he was alive, he could survive somehow. So he focused his efforts on eluding his attackers.

Bruised and battered, he somehow managed to escape from the mob. But he couldn't understand what his life was to be now. Both his loving wives had left him. The new god's position that he had counted on was out of his reach. The old god's position that he had thought was his own couldn't be retained with his new shape. Where was his place now?

Worried, alone, and with a downcast face, Ganesha slumped down on the sidewalk, leaning against the wall of a store.

Then he sensed a light coming toward him and looked up. To his surprise, Siddhi and Buddhi were standing in front of him. An unexpected wave of grief welled up in Ganesha.

"Did you see? The people in that temple kicked me out, saying I wasn't a god at all. And they call themselves my devotees!"

"That's why they didn't recognize you," said Buddhi gently. "God has no form except that given by his devotees in their minds."

"You mean I have to resume that revolting old form?" Unhappiness etched itself into Ganesha's face.

Buddhi smiled sweetly. "If you had become a hero god like you wanted, did you ever think how many revolting forms you would have had to take, or how many revolting acts you would have had to perform?"

"What revolting acts?"

"Oh, rolling around in the mud for a fight scene, for one."

"Like a pig," Siddhi added.

Ganesha paled. "So I have to be at the mercy of those idiot devotees?" he asked in a weak tone.

"What makes them idiots? For true devotees, god is only a tool to realize the divinity within themselves. They don't want a god sitting far above them in the sky, they want one that's within their reach, who can mingle with them as one of them. They only want a perfect soul, not a perfect body. Even if he's short and fat, and with a tacked on head, the one who can become a god through the purity of his soul is their real hero."

As he listened to Buddhi's words, Ganesha slowly regained his composure as his senses returned. "You're right, Buddhi. But I wish I could have been in the movies also, just once," he sighed.

"Is that all, dear? Why do you think you're not in movies? Look there." Siddhi pointed mischievously to a TV playing inside the store. On its screen a movie hero was dancing enthusiastically, singing a hymn with a jaunty beat, and leading the way for a procession. And who was the god in the procession? A round belly, a lengthy trunk, extended tusks...

"Hey! That's me!" shouted Ganesha excitedly.

"Absolutely! It *is* you."

"This means that, with my old form, I can be worshipped in the temples, and be in the movies, too, at the same time!" Ganesha could hardly contain his excitement and happiness.

"What do you think? Come, let's go to Kailasa," said Buddhi starting off.

"And here are some snacks to eat on the way," said Siddhi, handing him a plate of *umdrallu*.

On the TV the song continued to play. "*Ganapati Bappa Moriya!* Glory to Lord Ganesha! *Moriya! Moriya! Moriya!*"

●◉●●●◉

SAVITHRI MACHIRAJU was born in India, grew up in North America, and now lives in Canada. The Hindu tradition is one of constant questioning and the realization that "god" is in every being. But both humans and gods, under the influence of Maya — illusion — can forget this.

Abominatiō

by Jen Laface and Andrew Czarnietzki

DR. LAMBERT FELT the shockwave hit, the loud bang echoing through the desolate camp. Dust filled the air, disturbed by the concussion. He almost dropped the body he was searching.

"Ho-leee crap! Did you see that?" Ross the former salesman asked the group of school teachers, rig pigs, and whoever else was willing to join the scavenger expedition. His voice had the hope and desperation Dr. Lambert felt. They needed to find supplies soon. Maybe some plane had dropped off aid. Or simply crashed. It'd been a long time since anyone had seen a plane.

Ross was the only one to see it fall from the sky. Everyone looked up to a column of smoke rising in the distance under the sun. Mouths agape, their eyes wide with hope. The devout murmured that this was a sign of providence. Dr. Lambert thought it was just dumb luck. Their assumption that the crash was divine left him uncomfortable.

The other scavengers searching the bodies stopped, but Dr. Lambert carefully lowered the dead woman to the sand. She glistened from the faded remains of the Nigh's golden ichor. The bodies they'd found were all the same— horribly contorted in a tableau of pain and anguish. They never made it out of the camp. Dr. Lambert had lost count how many times in the past year they'd found bodies in this condition.

The warmth of her body suggested she'd died only minutes ago, but the dust and decay in the camp hinted they'd been dead for months. The Nigh left its victims in a strange state of preservation. He checked that her eyes were closed and paused, thinking better to fold her arms on her chest rather than flopped at the sides. She looked more at peace. Wishing he could do more for the woman's dignity, he was ushered by Leslie to join the gathering crowd.

The lanky woman kicked the ground impatiently. She rubbed her wrist, self-conscious of the yellowing bruise where Corey had grabbed her. Their self-appointed leader, Corey, didn't like any of "his flock" dilly-dallying. His outbursts were happening more frequently as they became more desperate for resources.

Dr. Lambert picked up his bag of precious medical supplies, hurrying more for Leslie's sake than his own. Corey left him alone for the most part. As the group's only medical doctor, he was valuable. Praying only went so far.

"We've been blessed," a familiar booming voice said.

Corey pointed in the direction of the crash, revealing several layers of yellow stains underneath the armpits of his shirt. Each stain marked the days they had left the camp like the rings of a tree.

All eyes fell on the tallest man in the group. Corey stood proud, despite weathered skin and gaunt cheeks. The years since the Nigh had been hard on him.

Dr. Lambert had learned quickly to wait for Corey to speak. This had been an easy lesson for him. He wished Leslie and the others would keep silent and not rock the boat. She often had good ideas, except she didn't know how to navigate the schoolyard politics.

Corey turned to survey the group, stone-faced and with a posture Dr. Lambert referred to as "leader-ly." It helped being a head taller than everyone else. The trucker hat came off, exposing his thinning blond hair and pink scalp to the sun. He wiped his forehead before speaking.

"Let's leave this and go check out the crash. This could be our deliverance," Corey said. The word "deliverance" hung in the air.

There were murmurs of objection through the small group. Leslie was the loudest.

"This is bad— we should stay away. I mean, we haven't seen a plane in years. It could be anything," Leslie said.

"Remember the bodies," Purjeet whispered. She couldn't stifle the fear in her voice. "They're always trying to get away from something. Remember the rumors, that there's something there. Something horrible."

"Abominatiō," Monica said, gripping the cross on her necklace.

Dr. Lambert gave them a glance, hoping they'd be quiet for their own sakes. Corey made no sign that he heard.

Ross muttered that the bodies would still be waiting for them. Dr. Lambert frowned but kept quiet. The group had no idea what caused the Nigh, but believing in these "horrors" was dangerous. There was a guilt in the back of his mind from abandoning the bodies to the wind and sand.

"Ross, Grace, scout ahead," Corey said.

Ross was thin and short, and Grace a head shorter. She had been an engineering student from China studying abroad. They both ran toward the cluster of warehouses to the south of the abandoned industrial area. In the distance, they became blurs indistinguishable from the background. At times like this, Dr. Lambert wished he still had his glasses.

The rest of the scavengers walked silently behind Corey. Purjeet looked at Leslie with fear in her eyes. Her friend nodded. Monica just stared at her feet. Dr. Lambert wanted to comfort them, tell them that things would be all right, but the words escaped him.

They followed the empty service road past the rusting bones of heavy industry, sand crusting the sides of the buildings. Glass sparkled beneath gaping windows that opened into darkness. Dr. Lambert gripped the handle of his bag tightly and wished the crash happened in a more open space. He wasn't afraid of something lurking in the dark— the group hadn't met any survivors in months and never any that posed a threat. He just feared not being able to see clearly when he needed to most.

As they approached the site of the crash, the rising dust covered the sun, casting the empty street in an eerie red twilight. His lungs burned, and his tongue was so dry it stuck to the back of his teeth.

Grace's scream cut the silence like a knife. Immediately after, Ross yelled "ho-leee" followed by a string of profanity, his voice echoing between the empty warehouses. Corey broke into a run, the group spreading out as those most devout kept his pace. Dr. Lambert hated rushing in unprepared, but he urged on Purjeet, Leslie, and Monica, not wanting them to be left behind. The school teacher rolled her eyes and picked up the pace, pulling Monica by the sleeve.

Corey followed Ross' swearing to the collapsed wall of a large brick building. He stopped at the edge of the debris, staring into the shadowed abyss. A faint golden light in the bowels of the warehouse seemed to grow brighter every moment. He spread his arms out towards the opening as if welcoming a flock of parishioners.

Coming to a gradual stop with the rest of the stragglers, Dr. Lambert felt a slight heaviness in his chest. In his old life, he would have been winded. A day spent rushing around the emergency room left him exhausted. The years of hiking in the desert and physical labour had honed his athletic ability.

Pushing through the stunned crowd, he looked into the open space underneath Corey's outstretched arms. The close proximity reminded him they all hadn't showered in weeks.

Ross stood just inside the wall, pointing at Grace and backing away from her. No one else moved, mesmerized by the scene inside the building.

Grace was leaning against the side of a rusting forklift, sobbing and babbling in what Dr. Lambert guessed was Cantonese. He was close enough to see the thin golden fibres growing from her flesh with the intricacy of a spider's web. The strands crawled across the rusted metal, slowly cocooning her to the vehicle. Where the strands extended past the shadows, they blurred into the golden light deep within the building.

Dr. Lambert had to force himself to breathe. He had seen countless victims of the Nigh, but only after the disease had run its fatal course. They'd been afraid at first, but once the victim was dead, the infection seemed to die with them. To his knowledge, nobody had witnessed the active stage and lived to tell.

Primal terror wrestled with his professional discipline. Attempts at quarantine had been worthless when civilization was still functioning, and they had the proper equipment. Dr. Lambert remembered searching the hospital in the first days of the Nigh. He panicked when he came across the bodies of his colleagues who sealed themselves in an isolation room. They were helpless then and had nothing now.

Shock settled on Dr. Lambert, leaving his shoulders knotted and his mind numb. The panicked voices brought him back.

People were weeping around him, asking Corey for help. To save them. To run. To burn the infection and fight. He wasn't sure whether this was a testament to Corey's leadership or his enforcers that the group didn't completely break down.

"What are we going to do?" Leslie's voice skirted the edge of terror.

"Get away. Just get away," a deep man's voice responded. Two men turned and ran, putting as much distance as possible between themselves and the Nigh.

"We have to stop them! We're probably infected. What if they get back to the camp and the children?" Dr. Lambert shouted. Several people turned to look at him, surprised he'd spoken. He watched the men run, losing track of them when their dirt covered clothes blurred into the hanging dust. Corey looked down, his intense gaze locked on the doctor. The rest of the group fell silent.

"Let them go," Corey said.

No one moved. The only sound was Grace whimpering in pain.

"They'll be delivered. The Nigh always delivers." Corey's tone was absolute. He paused for effect, letting the statement sink in. Not everyone was touched by the words, but Dr. Lambert knew it was better to look pensive than disgusted to avoid their leader's wrath.

Dr. Lambert clutched his thigh, trying to steady himself. He couldn't lie and say things would work out. That was Corey's department. He'd go on until he couldn't. Then he'd pull out his "bullet." He gripped his bag, making sure he could still feel that the vial was there. It wasn't magic but close enough for what he needed.

Something brushed against his face. He would have thought it was a spider web, but the gold glint in the light hinted otherwise. Dr. Lambert watched with dread as thin fibres collected around the group. The strands were so fine they seemed insubstantial. The haunted look settling on everyone's face revealed they'd seen the strands too. A couple of people brushed their hands furiously across their bodies. Some looked longingly in the distance, but most looked resigned to their fate.

Grace started coughing, drawing Dr. Lambert's attention. Her chest heaved violently as she struggled to breathe. She arched back against the forklift in a convulsion, leaving a trail of blood where she scraped against the corroded metal. She didn't seem to notice. The doctor tried to push past Corey to help her, hoping to ease her suffering.

"Whoa, doc," Corey said, grabbing him by the collar. "Tyrone, you and Purjeet will keep an eye on li'l Gracie here. We'll deal with her after. It's not worth the effort." Purjeet was one of the least devout of Corey's flock. He took every opportunity to get distance from her and let one of his enforcers keep the peace. Right now he didn't need dissenters. Leslie went wide-eyed, scared for her friend and surprised she wasn't the one singled out. Corey smiled at her, and she froze.

Don't bother with them. The deliverance is upon them. It's too late and not worth the supplies. Unwanted memories flashed in Dr. Lambert's mind. He could still see the starving man in the desert, his skin peeling from the exposure. *Trust me.* Yes, trust Corey. They had left the man for whatever deliverance would come. Dr. Lambert felt sick to the stomach, unsure if it was the guilt or the effect of the Nigh blooming around them. He didn't have the will to argue with Corey again.

Tyrone and Purjeet took guard, positioning themselves between Grace and the doctor. Despite the gold filaments trailing in their wake, they still kept a wide berth from the woman. Purjeet looked at Dr. Lambert and then down at her feet. He thought she mumbled that their watch wasn't going to matter anyways. Leslie tried walking to Purjeet, but Corey stepped in front of her.

"Why the long faces? This is what we've been waiting for!" A dangerous grin was smeared across Corey's face. He grabbed Dr. Lambert and Leslie, dragging them over the rubble. Moving with purpose, he stepped past the shaking form of Grace and walked through the shadows towards the glowing light.

Leslie tried to slow him down by dragging her heels, but to no avail. Dr. Lambert tried to pull away, but Corey's grip tightened, almost hurting him. Dr. Lambert relented, knowing he couldn't take the man physically, and there really wasn't anything to fight for.

Corey pulled them through the door of the shop into a storage space the size of a football field. Sunlight shone through the thick dust and past the collapsed ceiling. The glow emanated from the bottom of a crater that was roughly centered in the

space. They couldn't see the source of the glow over the wall
of broken concrete, shelving and twisted sheet metal. The floor
in front of them was strewn with debris and slick where the
damaged containers had bled their contents.

Leslie raised her arm to cover her nose, trying to filter out the
smell of dust and industrial chemicals. Dr. Lambert noted the
distinct strands of the Nigh underneath her forearm. Looking
at his feet, he saw dozens of similar fibres wrapping his own
body. He brushed at them, intrigued and scared that he didn't
feel anything on his legs or brushing against the Nigh with his
hands. Thinking of the contorted bodies, he wondered when
the pain would start.

Corey pushed on, oblivious or uncaring. He stopped at the
wall of debris, letting go of his unwilling followers. Dr. Lambert
thought he heard fibres of Nigh tear as their leader's hand
pulled away. Pausing for a moment, Corey looked the wreckage up and down before grabbing a piece of sheet metal and
throwing it to the side. The sound was deafening.

"What are you waiting for? Deliverance to come to you?
Help me clear a path." Corey didn't bother to look at his flock.
The other scavengers obeyed him.

As a token effort, Dr. Lambert grabbed a piece of collapsed
shelving. Before he could pull the debris free, a sharp electric
pain travelled up his arm. He dropped the shelf, startled at
the sensation. His arm was covered in strands. The pain flared
again, and he could see a faint golden glow through the fabric
of his old, stained shirt. Monica cried out in pain.

Corey fell to one knee, gripping his thigh. His teeth were
bared, but he still smiled and forced himself to stand. The
episode couldn't stop him. "Don't mind the pain. Deliverance
is upon us soon. Go back to work."

Leslie collapsed to the ground, holding herself in the fetal
position. Dr. Lambert hurried over, dropping to the floor and
putting his arm around the woman. The golden strands started
connecting to the debris around them. He couldn't do anything
to help but felt compelled to do something. A deep, excruciating
spasm stilled him from speaking. He thought about the vial
in his bag. Leslie could take it, but he couldn't will himself to
mention it. This vial was his one indulgence that made going
along with Corey's inane mission tolerable. Whatever happened,
he'd go without suffering.

Wrapping her arms around his torso, Leslie squeezed Dr. Lambert with an earnest hug. She held him for a moment, trying to will the tremors away. When he finally relaxed, she let go and stood up. Offering her hand, the doctor took it. Pain flashed through his body, but he found the strength to overcome it. Death could wait. He wanted to see the source of the light, and maybe what caused the outbreak of Nigh.

"The path to deliverance is open!" Corey couldn't be happier. He pushed through the opening, the sharp metal tearing at his clothes. Thick fibres of Nigh stuck to the debris. Whether for devotion or curiosity, the rest of the group followed.

Corey was the first to catch a glimpse of the crash site, Dr. Lambert trailing him. "Here it is... Here is our divine providence!" The large man raised his hands in a grandiose gesture to celebrate the discovery. The immense joy that had crept up on his face quickly disappeared, replaced by something between horror and disappointment.

Leslie stepped up beside Corey. She was quiet staring into the center of the crater, tears streaming down her face. Dr. Lambert put a hand on her shoulder for comfort. He dared a look into the glow, his eyes watering from the brightness.

The crater was filled with golden webbing, great strands crawling over every surface, growing outward from the center. At the bottom of the crater, the fibres parted like the eye of a hurricane. Laying in this open space was a body. He couldn't make out any blood or visible trauma from this distance. The details were blurred, but he could still tell something was wrong.

Squinting, he could make out feathered wings. It was an angel. The simple fact it existed screamed in his mind. No it wasn't an angel. It was two angels mashed together unevenly, one of its three arms sprouting from a rib cage. One of the wings was folded in on itself in an unnatural-looking position.

Two heads peered up at them, with a set of bewildered glowing gold eyes. He wasn't sure if it was the distance, but where there should have been mouths was just skin. How it — they? — survived, he couldn't give any medical opinion. It shouldn't have.

The anguish in its body was apparent. Dr. Lambert was terrified, but some deep, forgotten feeling compelled him to return its gaze. This sense urged him to help. It was the fuel that kept him going those long nights working in the emergency room.

From the rumors, Dr. Lambert knew what it was. Someone gasped, saying aloud what he thought. "It's an abominatiō!" The words came out as a whisper, but the group heard them clearly. The doctor didn't care. Whatever it was, it needed help.

Everyone was wide-eyed. The abominatiō's backs arched in unison as it struggled to breathe. He wanted to rush down and help it. Their jaws moved under the skin where mouths should have been. A scream shook the building at the core, dislodging several pieces of wreckage. The impossible sound reverberated in their minds.

"This can't be real. This can't be real," Corey said. There was defeat in his voice. The large man looked smaller, more shrunken. He looked older.

"It's... it's beautiful," Leslie spoke. Corey and Dr. Lambert turned to her, their mouths gaping. "It was sent from above. It's what we needed. No need to struggle anymore. This angel is our answer."

"What's that?" Corey asked. His voice was unusually meek.

"To join it," Leslie answered. She started unbuttoning her blouse. Dr. Lambert stood frozen, unsure what Leslie intended to do by taking off her clothes.

The golden fibres were thickening between the scavengers. Pain returned, cutting through the adrenalin and shock of the group.

"No. This isn't the way it's supposed to be!" Corey yelled at the top of his lungs. The abominatiō raised its heads, turning to locate the noise. Dr. Lambert took a step back, amazed at its lucidity. "We have to burn it."

"No Corey!" Leslie reached up and gripped her hand on the large man's shoulder. She was no longer shaking. "You were right. It's the sign we've been waiting for all along. I see it now. To embrace the Nigh and be reborn. Everyone who came along... everything seemed to come together to lead us to this place." She'd finished removing her shirt to reveal a tank top. Four other scavengers were starting to take off their clothes. Dr. Lambert watched with a grim curiosity.

"This beast isn't our deliverance, Leslie," Corey said, an edge to his voice. "It was supposed to be an angel. A heavenly angel! With its power and glory, it would deliver my soul, our souls, away from this place of pain and suffering."

"Corey is right," Ross said. Biting his lip, he glared at Leslie. "No way anyone is going near that thing. You've all heard the rumors— it's a death sentence. But it doesn't have to be that way if we get rid of it. It's what's killing us. But we can kill it first."

"But it is an angel, Corey. We can't harm it. We can't fight its judgment. We have to embrace it," Monica said. She'd gotten down to her bra and underwear. Dr. Lambert wondered why the Rapture required nudity. Leslie finished, her bare body glowing from the halo of golden fibres. Corey stared at her like she was the abominatiō.

"For all we know, it could be a hellspawn," Corey said. "To punish us." Half of the group nodded in approval.

"You just don't believe anymore," Leslie said.

The glow seemed brighter as the Nigh crawled up the edge and closer to the group. Some people stepped back, some forward.

Ross spoke, gesturing wildly at the suffering angel. "Look Leslie! It's not that we don't believe. Yes, there's an angel here. A mutated, twisted angel! There's no way this was sent for some benevolent purpose."

"My belief is stronger than yours. This is our deliverance— it's a test. We have to burn it," Corey said, his voice low but firm.

Ross agreed. "Yes. Burn it and destroy the infection. We don't have to die." His voice quivered, uncertain of the words.

"We won't be going back to camp, Ross." Everyone stared at Corey. "We'll burn the hellspawn and earn our deliverance."

Some of the group murmured in agreement. There were whispers. Burn it and we will be delivered. Embrace it and we will find providence. You won't stop us.

The word "benevolent" stuck in Dr. Lambert's mind like a bruise repeatedly poked. "Hellspawn" and "angel" faded from his thoughts. There was not only pain but awareness of something treasured that was forgotten. He couldn't hold it in his hand, but held it within when he looked at each patient in the emergency room: from the older man with pneumonia to the daredevil child with the broken arm to the drug addict who had overdosed for the third time. He couldn't believe that the abominatiō was good or evil. There wasn't any evidence. But he couldn't stay still and continue to watch it suffer. Dr. Lambert believed in mercy, not judgment.

"Don't you dare go down there." Corey was staring at Leslie, his eyes wide and mouth drawn up into a snarl. He stood in front of her, blocking her way down. Ross joined him. Leslie shook, startled and wide-eyed. Monica and several half naked men stepped in to protect her.

During the stand-off, Dr. Lambert slipped over the edge of the crater. Sliding down the loose gravel, he managed to keep his balance. Tearing through a thick strand of Nigh like it was tissue paper, an immeasurable pain flared at the point of contact. He stumbled to the abominatiō's side, blinking away involuntary tears.

Its four eyes locked on him, watching his every move through the convulsions. It had no mouths to help gasp for more air. Dr. Lambert kneeled beside it and put his fore and middle finger underneath one of its jaws. He felt a rapid and irregular heartbeat thumping beneath soft, warm skin.

He leaned in to the angel's face, listening carefully. The silence made it easier to hear the struggle in each laboured breath. Several times it paused, its chest straining against what sounded like a blocked airway. It convulsed, muscles straining from the full-body tremor.

A wave of nauseating pain ripped through Dr. Lambert. He collapsed to the ground, his face planted in the dirt beside the abominatiō. After the wave passed, he looked down at his body. He was entirely covered in layers of angry, glowing fibres. He struggled against the Nigh, its strands tearing as he pulled away from the ground. On his knees, he crawled back to the abominatiō's side.

If only he were back at the hospital, back with his team in emergency. Maybe then he could stabilize it. Clear its airways. Defibrillate its heart. Get scans to understand what was going on. Call in a surgeon. Save it.

"What are you doing?" Leslie's voice was shrill.

"What the hell are you doing?" Corey said.

Choking, the angel writhed on the ground, trying to expel the trapped breath. Even if they were back at the camp, Dr. Lambert knew there wasn't much he could do.

"Helping," Dr. Lambert replied. He was running out of time. Corey and Leslie fought their way down the crater, both with mixed expressions of rage, agony and horror.

Digging through his bag, he found the vial. He jabbed a hypodermic needle through the soft membrane, drawing-up as much of the liquid as he could. He grabbed the rubber band and realized there was no time.

The angel stared back, the pain still in its eyes, but it was eerily lucid. Two sets of eyes watched. Dr. Lambert massaged the angel's forearm with a firmness, hoping his fingers would find what was needed. Watching the angel flinch, he eased back, upset he still caused it more pain. Finding what he was looking for, relief washed over him. A deep, blue vein.

"Stop it. Stop it. Someone stop him!" Leslie was panicked, hoping her voice would spur someone to action. She and Corey were entangled by the Nigh. It seemed to thicken, binding them to the crater floor.

"You can't. It has to suffer to cleanse our sins!" Corey yelled.

People yelled at him, the words blurring together. Compassion spurred him on.

The needle felt heavy in his hand. Dr. Lambert took a deep breath, releasing the air through his nose while letting his shaking arm steady. He found that place in his mind where he could focus in a noisy space of screaming children, beeping machines, and chaos. The peace was overwhelming to the point he wasn't aware the warehouse had gone silent.

His whole world was the vein. The angel watched as his arm moved closer and turned one head after the other to look away as he poked the syringe in its skin. He wondered whether the angel thought he was trying to save it.

Memories from a lifetime ago sprang to mind. Each tugged at his heartstrings: pulling the plug on the teenager with brain trauma, the failure to revive the woman who had a heart attack, the child he couldn't bring back who'd OD'ed on her mother's medication.

Dr. Lambert guided the needle into the vein without flicking his wrist. It connected smoothly. He didn't pause, knowing he'd falter. Instead he pushed down in one motion on the plunger, pressing out the clear liquid.

As gently as possible, he pulled out the needle and dropped it on the ground. He grabbed one of the angel's hands and grasped it. Even though he couldn't will himself to look at its faces, he was there for every squeeze and every tremor. It seemed to last for an eternity.

When he felt the whole heaviness of the angel's arm, he looked at its faces. Both heads were turned up at the sky. Automatically he closed both sets of eyes and arranged the mish-mashed body in the most dignified way he could. He tucked the wings against the angel's body, marvelling at their soft warmth.

Once he was done with the arrangement, he became aware that people were standing around him. Remembering the Nigh, he looked down at his body. He felt the strands hardening, losing their lustre. They fell away like ash. The flakes hung in the air for a moment before trickling down to the ground.

JEN LAFACE and **ANDREW CZARNIETZKI** are a wife and husband writing team from Edmonton, Alberta. Inspiration for *Abominatiō* came from a vivid dream and personal musings on faith and its importance in our day-to-day lives. Thank you to Dave Gross and the Scruffies for their help!

WHEN BONE SHIPS
SAILED THE STARS

by David Fraser

When they approached the cliff
there was no turning back. It's then
they carved a ship from the hollow bone
of a great sea serpent's skull,
fashioned sails from its skin
before the creature rotted,
bleached by sun and water by the sea.
With each passing day, with tools
once forged in zero gravity, they worked,
etching runes and circuitry,
the rotting smell enough to make
the starving hurl their stomachs on the rocks.
At night in a cave, on an oak table
they unfolded all the stars in the milky way
and spread them like a map
lit by harnessed sun and candle light.

In them was a spirit not destroyed and they would gather
by the hot tide pools tempered by the sea,
and search late summer skies for answers,
make up stories for the questions that still remained.
Their solar barque was fitted with the tiny bones
of all the animals they loved, fingers from children
who'd died too young, and the long thin shanks
of the wasted ones who once had brought them home
in woven baskets and swaddling clothes.

They drew messages on the polished surface of the hull—
arc of the moon, a rising sun, studded holes punched
into a black night sky. They knew of ghost ships
that could appear out of a foggy night, or from around
a cluster of debris afloat and held in space.
They knew the danger waiting there. They knew
not to listen to the Sirens call that came from deep in time.

There were some who stayed, grounded, and wrote
of ancient floods and arks preserved on mountain tops,
but the carvers knew from beyond those histories,
that those stories were caught up too much with words.
And when they left— a great rising up of oars
and sail to catch the solar winds— with regret
they watched those who could not escape,
watched them fashion stone shapes of great ship hulls
in meadows as a message to draw them back,
watched them paint on rock walls with fingers dipped
in blood and berry juice in flame and shadows, and
watched them with mathematics lay out huge stones
as signs on the desert sand. Regret they knew
for their great bone ship was destined
only for the stars.

DAVID FRASER lives on Vancouver Island. He is the editor of
Ascent Aspirations Magazine. His poetry has appeared in many
journals and anthologies, including *Rocksalt, An Anthology of
Contemporary BC Poetry*. He has published five collections of
poetry and is a member of the League of Canadian Poets.

THE LAST MAN ON EARTH

by Suzanne M. McNabb

I AM MILLIE, the lucky one.

The Castle is mine and you must stay away.

This is how it was in the beginning. All the girls and boys were starving or burning to death or caught in terrible storms. I survived because I am special. Many people wanted to go to the Castle but the Men kept them out, locking the double gates and shutting up the great doors. My father was friends with some of the Men who lived in the Castle. At first they were not sure but I proved myself so they taught me everything. That is why I was chosen above all others to keep the Castle as the time of the Men ended.

Mark told me often how clever I was.

I learned at a young age to switch the pumps, manual to auto. I memorized the screens to watch over the gas-jobbies. I wear the badge and I know where I can never go in the Castle. The Men taught me how to add oil, to tighten the packing, to clean the fine screens and how to clean the large screens on the intake. I know how to run the water purifier.

Now that they have all gone, I run the place just like they taught me: *Millie, Queen of the Castle.*

While girls my age were being raped or eaten in the south lands, I was sprouting breasts, watching *Fight Club, The Man Who Would be King* and *Fast and Furious.* I would have watched *Jackass* too but Anthony said it was evil and he broke the disk in two. With my feet on the desk, I read and reread Hitachi manuals and Lee Child novels until I understood. Mark wrote down *Important Instructions* and printed them in a binder in case I forget while I ate *O Henrys* straight from the big box, listened to Johnny Cash and Johnny Horton. Mark cut the locks in the women's shower room and we sorted through all the things that I might need as I grew. The Men brought rifles into the Castle, smuggled in crates of food. We were lucky. We feasted on wild game and berries and watched news of the Great Burning on the Net until that died too.

From the highest windows of the Castle we could see the horizons of dark smoke on the south side of the deep valley all the way from the east to the west. Anthony said, *we are the last Men on earth now.* Some of the Men wept but I did not. We are the lucky ones. Finally the skies cleared but the radio and the net stayed dead.

The Burning didn't come this far north but still it affected the hot Units, or so the Men told me. The hot Units are different from the micro-turbines; somehow the heat made them unstable so the gas jobbies started up, to keep the heat in its place. My purpose as Queen is to mind the castle and They told me how important it is, more important than my curiosity about the world beyond the Castle, more important than, the search for survivors, more important than being kissed by a boy. They teased me on this and I cried, *why would I want a boy to kiss me?* They laughed, their deep voices filling the control room as Anthony cooked venison and Fob beat Chachi at crib.

I was chosen to be spared the great horror.

Not that I didn't have to be strong. One by one, each Man lost his hair and the skin of his eyes turned white with scabs. Each grew weak and sick to his stomach. When I had seen enough to know what was going to happen next, I demanded the Men to do something. *Use the medicine from the First Aid room where I sleep.* Kenny slapped my shoulder. *We need you to be strong, Millie.*

While the Man could still walk, he unrolled a large six mil bag off the reel in the corner of the back room. *Out of respect for the rest of us,* Mark told me. To help him go faster, the Man would take the HF bottle out of the red safe-box and dab a little on his neck and carefully put the bottle back. Leaving his light suit and his heavy suit on the hook, he would leave for the hottest part of the Castle where we should never walk without the heavy. A day later, one of us remaining would take a zip tie, and carefully put on a heavy suit, and walk out to find the six mil bag with the tortured face peeking over the top.

All that remains are their suits hanging on the hooks inside the double doors to the field, the names of the hoods visible.

Arthur. Kenny. Tigento. Anthony. Fob. Vlad. ChaChi.

Mark was the last to get sick. *No tears* were his last words to me. After I suited up, I took the zip tie out the next morning. I pulled the thick plastic over his anguished face and closed up the bag. Beside his lifeless body, the long row of bags shrunk into puddles, giving no hint of the legacy that had passed. *Bodies of the Gods.*

Strong as I am, how could I ignore the loss?

I cried for Mark, kindest of all, small but young, he was fierce to the end. Everything I have now, I owe to Mark. He had the most patience with me. He knew I could do the job when Kenny thought I should be dabbed with the HF now before the *melt-downs.*

This is all I can write now. And every word of it is true. If you read this then maybe I am not the last Man on earth. You should stay away from the Castle but know that I have been taking care of you since the beginning.

I can leave the Castle for short times when I must get food. There is a great hall under the ground that takes an hour by e-kart. I park at the dead end and using the hidden hatch, I take off my suit after I come out into the brilliant light. The smell of dirt and trees, flowers and animals is overwhelming at first. I sit down and blink in the full sun, soak up the clean air and songs of birds.

Years before Mark put up signs for me to find, *Millie's Secret Garden. Millie's Secret Fishing Hole. Millie's favorite Berry Bush.* They make me smile whenever I come across one I didn't know was there. The game continues, long after Mark has gone.

As the Men instructed, I learned the *Fire Arm Safety Manual* so I may carry the rifle that Kenny brought into the Castle years ago. I use the scope and scan the ridges of my Secret Garden. This is something I have done many times since the Men passed, and sometimes I spot a brown bear, or a moose. That is too much meat for me. I mostly hunt rabbits or deer.

Today when I scan the south ridge, I spot the small one.

I study him to be sure.

He carries an orange pack on his back and he limps as he walks. I cannot see a gun and his hair is shaggy like the small ones on *The Man Who Would Be King*. I could shoot him now, and maybe I should but I feel mercy for him walking so slow, carrying so much. Surely he will not last. So I let him live, hoping that just as he found a way in, he finds a way out. Once he sees the signs declaring it Millie's Secret Garden he will know it is my place.

A few days later, I emerge from the hidden hatch and scan the hills through my scope.

He has set up an orange tent just under the north ridge.

I'm not sure what to do until I see he has knocked down the sign, *Millie's Paper Birch*. He has no respect.

Suddenly, I am stealth as I sneak through the pathways, crossing the creek. I don't use the bridge Mark named for me, lest the small one hear my footfalls on the wood. I am hoping to surprise the intruder and slit his throat with my Bowie knife. I come across another sign that has been broken off. *How dare he!*

I will get him in my crosshairs and leave his body for the bears to eat.

As I get further up the hill, walking in the shallow stream, I spy him through the trees. He is red faced, his hair a matted mess of leaves. He wears animal skins like a cave man and it is obvious to me that he is no child of the Men who came before. The intruder is cutting down trees with an axe. I see fish hanging over a smoking fire and the smell of it coming through the low bushes makes me think of *Fight Club*. I will make him bleed.

I hide my rifle in a hollow log, and draw my knife. Surely, he is weak and stupid. I'm doing him a service. I creep slowly through the spruce, yet the chopping of his axe has stopped.

"My god," he says and I turn to see him, his axe held to the side much like the Bowie in my hand.

Ready to pounce we consider each other.

"I thought it was an animal but... my god."

He does not look like the Men at all. Neither old nor young, this small one is crumpled, broken. He is pitiful. The side of his face is like melted plastic. He doesn't know how to wash. One of his front teeth is missing. His legs are bowed.

"Where is your camp?" he asks

I want no part of him. He is neither Man nor beast, healthy nor clever.

He is Evil.

"I'm not going to hurt you. I'm glad I found you. I haven't seen a living soul in years."

He blinks as he talks and his brown eyes are watching my every move.

I act like I'm going to relax, take a step to put my feet closer together but when he looks down, I lunge at him, knock him over. I am beating his face with the end of my knife, but he twists out of my grasp, pulls me back with his knees and suddenly he is on top of me. His bony knees pin down my biceps but I swallow my scream. My legs reach up to grab his head as he did to me but he is bent low, over my face. I can smell his rotten breath and see the sand in his eyes.

"I've had enough killing." He considers me closely.

I glare back.

"Speak to me damn you!"

I won't open my mouth.

"If you want me to go, I'll move further west, but this watershed is the best I've seen. There's enough room for the both of us. But I'll tell you, down river to the east, all the fish and plants are dead. And over the ridge to the south is all dead. I thought I was the last man on earth. You might be the last woman."

He looks me up and down, and the feel of his eyes on my skin makes me want to throw up. He runs his hands along the top of my shoulders. Then he winces like he has cut himself, closing his eyes and shaking his head. He is remembering something. When he finally shoves off my hips, I jump away, grab up my knife and swallow the sour that threatens to come up.

"Where do you camp?" he asks.

I step backwards, bumping into the boughs of a spruce.

"Millie?"

The sound of my name pulls at something inside of me. The fool can read.

"Is this Millie's secret garden?"

"Why are you knocking down the signs?" I ask without thinking.

"I'm sorry," he says, and tilts his head like Mark used to do when I was hurt. "I thought I was the only one here, and the signs were painful to see. They reminded me…" He smiles sadly and I want to put him out of his pain.

"Do you have family?" he asks.

I hate him. He has no business asking these things. The Men didn't allow it.

"The First Rule of the Castle," I spit. "No talk of Families."

"Yeah," he says nodding. "Too painful."

I step away into the shadows.

"Are there more of you?" he calls.

I look back periodically to make sure he is not following me. I can hear him chopping wood again and I should have told him not to chop down my trees. I should have told him that I was Millie the Lucky One and he should leave now.

I get my rifle and make it to the hidden hatch, slip into my suit, locking the hatch behind me. I drive as fast as I can in the dark tunnel. The dim headlights illuminate the darkness and I feel I am speeding away fast and furious like Dominic, trying to get away from the bad guy.

Back at the Castle, I plug in the e-kart and walk through the basement on my way to the control room. The hum of the motors is a sweet comfort, and I am at home here.

A pump has quit and another has started. I touch the dead motor and wait. Slowly the heat rises through my glove. The pump had oil, sealing water. It wasn't running dry. I don't understand. I shouldn't have left. As I climb up the stairs for the control room, a doom falls heavy on my shoulders.

The newcomer is bad luck.

I bring up the trend for the dead pump on the control screen. It tripped from high amps at noon. Given how hot is now, it has probably died for good. The running pump is third in the lineup. There are three levels of safety here, Mark used to say but there are six big pumps for the cooling water because that is the highest order. The other three pumps wait their turn.

Chewing on jerky, I sit at the computer and write this all down, watching the screens. The pump's trends make nice straight lines. I record the high and low temps for the day, adding to the chart I made since I first started doing this. Things are warmer than the early days when I was little and snow fell for more than half the year.

The stranger's face comes back to me in the glare of the computer screen and I am puzzled. Why now? I keep the Castle for my Secret Garden. It is so large that I have never had enough time to see it all. I dream about seeing it all. Its boundaries exceed my knowledge and my need. There is enough room for all of the animals and plants. If the pumps should fail, the heat will seep out and kill the deep green gorge, kill the bear, moose, kingfishers and the baby fawns I sneak up on after the rainy seasons. The blue flowers will die forever, and the smell of the sap from the spruce will be no more.

What shall I do with him?

Mark explained to me once that no matter, I couldn't out run the heat. Even if I left the Castle in good standing and went as fast as I could go in three days, the heat would still find me. *It's not like the heat of the sun, Millie.*

Should I let him live?

The small one can come and go as he wants. He could never learn to keep the Castle. What I know took years to absorb from all of the Men, each of them giving me knowledge another wouldn't necessarily have. The small one is simple. He knows nothing of the ways of Men. He knows nothing of Fight Club or Lee Child or Hitachi. He is as ignorant as the fawn even though he reads.

Why should I let him live?

Days go by and I find myself seething with anger. If he has not left my valley by now, I hope he chokes on a fish bone. May a Mother Bear find him and rip him to shreds. I stomp through the basement on my rounds, checking pumps and thinking of ways to kill the small one.

I should pay attention more. Little things are going wrong.

Still, to be watchful, I fall asleep in front of the screen most nights, with soft alarms waking me when the system goes out of the limits. I have dreams about all kinds of strange things when I sleep in the chair. I dream of fawns nipping off the tops of clover in the grassy hills. I sneak up and get as close as I can. I want to feel the soft reddish brown fur, see the tiny black nose. A few times I dream of Dominic, how he grabbed the black haired girl in *Fast and Furious*, and pulled her onto him, so her legs wrapped around his hips, and he backed up, laid her on the hood of the car and kissed her. I don't under-stand this part. I want to see that movie again but the disk player doesn't work now. When I was very small I remember the movies on the Net and I try to get the Net to come in, but all these systems are dead.

If only he wasn't a small one; if only he knew the ways of the Men and could bring these things back to life.

Then one night a high pitched alarm wakes me from some dream where a fawn is pinning me down, licking my face. I scramble to the edge of my seat and locate the reason for the alarm. The supply gas is brightened; *LOW*. One of the engines has quit. I try to restart it but *Low Fuel Supply* alarm blinks above the picture of the gas-jobby on the screen.

I'm not sure what to do. This has never occurred before.

I scramble through the desk drawers and find the *Important Information* binder that Mark printed out. Maybe there is something I forgot. After a while, I think I find the answer but it is not good. I should have been watching this fuel pressure. I see now from trending it back that it has been slowly dropping through the years. Mark and the Men never mentioned it much but I read Mark's words. The fuel comes from a cavern far away and the gas jobbies were rarely used when the big units fueled the whole world. The jobbies were just backups. But in my time, the backups became the only source of generation. And now a huge cavern of fuel, piped to the Castle in the yellow pipe, is low. The jobbies will slowly die, then the pumps will die and the controls will die as the batteries go dead. The computer screen that let me write and print my words will die.

In the *Important Information*, Mark tells me to find a book in the library off the cafeteria. I am disgusted when I see it.

Wilderness Survival.

The pictures and the information in the old book all remind me of the small one. Even the man in the book has a shaggy beard and long hair.

Mark's page is marred with water spots but I can make out most of his words in the *Important Information*. I have never read this before.

Millie, you must load up the pumps with oil. Clean the large screen but remove the fine screens all together. Do this as fast as you can. Then pack the items listed on page 4 of the book, as much as you can carry. Take the e-kart to your Secret Garden. If the fish in the river

*are dead, go north, up the side of the gorge and keep going north.
If the fish in the river are alive, then go up stream to the west and
keep following the river. Do whatever you can to survive. Walk as
far and as fast as you can and do not stop for four days. Don't ever
come back to the Castle.*

I shake as I read this. I watch the pressure of the fuel supply.
The number hasn't changed in the hour or two since it first
alarmed. I cannot move. I shudder and reread Mark's words.
This doesn't make sense. Mark told me I could never out-walk
the heat. I must stay to do the rounds, to clean the screens. And
now his strange words are telling me something else. And I
see his small hand-written corrections in blue pen, here and
there making marks on the printed page. And I know he was
crying, the water stains were his tears. These were words he
never thought I would have to read.

So I do as Mark instructed, and I throw my pack in the e-kart
and fly as fast as I can through the darkened tunnel. I am like
the men at the end of *The Man Who Would Be King*, when they
are chased from the city because the small ones find out they
are not gods.

Now I need the small one to help me in the wild.

I open up the hatch but when my boots reach for the ground,
I fall down. Something is wrong. The sun is so bright that I must
blink and hold my hand over my eyes. Finally, I can see bare
dirt where grass used to be. He tried to dig down around the
hatch but he gave up. He is nowhere in sight but he has made
a sign; *Millie's Secret Door* on split wood. It stands by the hatch.

Well, not so secret anymore.

I scan the horizon and see a small spot of orange where his
tent had been. Maybe he was eaten by a bear. I pass over the
bridge, and see he has stood up the sign; *Millie's Secret Bridge*.
Maybe he was charged by a bull moose. A little further down
the path stands the sign *Millie's Paper Birch* on a new post. I
hope a wolverine has not found his scent. I scramble up the
hill side, knowing I should leave now as Mark told me, but the
small one is my best bet for surviving in the wild.

As I near his camp, I see he has taken everything down,
packed up his gear.

I caught him just in time but I don't see him. Looking over
his small pile of tools and clothes, I hear a moan. There, not far

from his cold fire pit, he is laying against a tree. At first I think he is sleeping but as I step closer I know what has happened.

"I've been looking for you," he mutters and his breathing is laboured. "Where do you live?"

I crouch down beside him. Long hair is matted into the tree bark above his balding head, showing where he used to lean when he sat straight up. Now he slumps.

"I went looking for you when I couldn't dig into the man-hole." He laughs to himself, almost out of breath. There is blood in the corner of his mouth. "You are Alice escaping down the rabbit hole. I thought you must have a bomb shelter or some-thing so I went looking for the air vent."

His skin is sweaty. His red swollen eyes beg me for something.

His hand shakes as he reaches for my hair, hanging from my shoulder.

"Say something Millie. I'm going to die anyway."

I clear my throat, squint into the sun. A hawk circles overhead.

"You found where I live but you didn't wear the heavy suit," I say.

"I saw the warning signs on the chain link fence but I thought the place must be safe if you're living there so I climbed over, walked right up the road. Every door to the plant is shut. Then I went looking, out past the ponds. Why aren't you dead?"

"I never go where we keep the rods."

"Yeah," he says and smiles. "Why did you run away from me?"

"Let's go," I tell him. "Down the hill to the hatch and put on the suit. The kart will take you into the basement. Go up the stairs by the elevator to the third floor. To your left, you will see the big windows. Keep going, past the double doors, past the place to hang your suit. You will see how grand it all was, from the time before. You have the Castle and know, one last time. There's still food."

He shakes his head.

"I've seen all I need to see. This is a nice place to die."

I wait with him for a while, not knowing what to do. I should put a bullet in his head to stop his pain. I want his tent and dried fish. When he drifts off, I leave with them, following the river like Mark said.

And I've been walking for days now, finally stopping to sleep. I crouch beneath a tree and write this all down with a pen. I want to remember how I left the castle, the secret garden. The trees are thicker the further I go. I'm so tired but I must keep moving. I can't stop wondering.

They were just men.

Arthur. Kenny. Tigento. Anthony. Fob. Vlad. ChaChi. Mark. *I can't stop wondering how things could have been.*

I didn't know his name. *The man who would have been King.*

SUZANNE M. MCNABB is a power engineer in Saskatchewan. She loves symbols and the role of story in religions. Suzanne believes movies and songs can function as myths that subtly inform citizens' values and norms. Therefore she wrote a story that created a mythology out of the secular stories we tell ourselves.

Where the Scorched Man Walks

by Megan Fennell

IT WAS TIME to say the old words, the true words, but I did not trust my voice to arrive without breaking. After a pause, Witch Mother spoke them for me.

"Our people do not die," Witch Mother said, "but we go where the Scorched Man walks, and the Scorched Man shall guide us to peace."

Poor Naza seemed unable to take any shred of comfort in the prayer. Her voice was in tatters from sobbing as she repeated the lines after Witch Mother. I softly murmured them along with her, bolstering her words with my own, offering what meagre strength I could.

My gaze remained on the small cloth-wrapped bundle at my knees. If I looked at Naza I might have wept as well, and a good Witch Daughter does not weep. But my head was only recently shorn in the fashion of the healers and the blue ink on my skin was so fresh that it still gleamed as though wet. Unshed tears burned behind my eyes like salt in a new wound. I had loved Naza since we were both children playing around the cooking fire together and I knew much more than a Witch Daughter should. I knew how badly Naza had wanted a son and knew that she had been eager enough to speak his name before he'd left her belly. My heart was broken for her, my mouth sour with fury at the unfairness of it, emotions unbefitting a healer. It was beyond my power to do anything but bear witness to her mourning now.

The air in the tent was stifling, thick with the smell of sick-ness and singed healers' herbs. I was no stranger to the scent of grief, but when the hide curtain covering the doorway was lifted and the clean evening air swept in to touch my face, I did breathe easier.

Ilan ducked through the doorway. He looked at the bundle that I tended and then quickly away as though the very sight of it had burned him. The dust of the approaching storm had caked in the tear-tracks on his cheeks, tracing pale lines over his rich brown skin, and I was reminded so suddenly and painfully of my father in the height of his grief that it knotted the breath in my throat.

"He is coming," Ilan said. There was dust in his hair and on his clothing and it fell from him as he moved to crouch next to Naza. "The Scorched Man is coming for him now."

She gave a broken wail and said my old name like a plea. As though there was anything that I could do to stop this, to return life to her little boy, to undo the past. She who knew me best of all knew that I had no power to change the course of the Scorched Man.

I bowed my head to tuck the infant's shroud more securely around his tiny unmoving chest and let the soft material swallow the tears that I could not keep from falling. With our shorn heads and simple dress, a Witch Daughter is left no way to hide her own sorrow.

⬤⬤⬤⬤⬤

There was a time Naza and I had danced like maidens, our hair whirling long and wild, the bangles at our wrists and ankles chiming a sweet harmony to the thump of the drums. We stomped our feet like we would pound the earth into wine beneath us. We danced until our bodies ached and the stars seemed to dip lower to spin about our heads, until we were both giddy and breathless, and only then did we stop.

Laughing, we moved out of the circle together, leaving it to Alimah and the other girls who fancied themselves the *real* dancers. Our movements were not so pretty by half, but Naza danced for joy and I only danced to forget myself for a while, and that was enough for us.

She clutched at my arm and pressed her blood-hot cheek against my shoulder when we sat down at the edge of the light. I could feel her smile on my skin.

"Witch Mother told me that I would be married soon," she whispered.

She hardly needed to say the words; the secret had been sparking in her smile since she'd left the old woman's tent that morning with goat's blood staining her fingers.

"To a handsome young man with strong shoulders and eyes the color of honey?" I teased, sending her into a flurry of giggles. "You should have spared the goat. Anyone with eyes can see that Ilan thinks your name is spelled out in the stars."

"It's different to *know* it." She jostled me playfully. "I know she read your fortune too. Even if you never told anyone what she saw for you. Not even me."

"It's unlucky to talk about it." I turned away from her to take the wineskin as it was passed along to us. "And she didn't tell me anything as joyful as your future," I murmured around the lip of the skin before tilting it back to drink.

It was the truth. As I had stood with my hands red and dripping from arranging the liver on the stone offering table, Witch Mother had told me only one thing.

You are a child of death.

I had been livid. That was no news from the goat's belly. The whole village knew that I was the last living member of my family and the story of how it had happened was on its way to becoming a legend. Years after they had died, a roving spice merchant tried to tell us the story as something he had seen in a far-away land, until I had begun to cry and Naza had flung a cooking pot at his head.

I scoured the blood from my hands, furious at Witch Mother for trying the same trick, itching under the gentle pity in her gaze.

Take your place when you are ready, she said. The blue tattoos on her cheeks moved with her soft smile. *You will know the time.*

In the shadows at the edge of the places that the fire could reach, I watched Ilan admiring Naza from across the way and knew that he would come to ask her to dance with him before long. I guessed that it would be the first in a series of questions he would pose to her, culminating in what was sure to be a beautiful mid-summer wedding. Married soon, indeed. I was beginning to think that Witch Mother had grown lazy in her readings.

I was glad that the shadows hid my face, providing me with a thicker veil than the wisps of orange silk Alimah used to paint the darkness when she danced. I knew that there would be jealousy etching lines on my brow and I did not want Naza to think that it was because of her future consort. No, it was not Ilan that I wanted, though his eyes were captivating enough, but rather that fragile trick of throwing everything aside but love. Of looking at the crackling fire without thinking of the cold darkness at your back. I had seen too much of the Scorched Man to believe in that kind of magic anymore.

A child of death would surely become sorrow's consort and I prayed that there would be room enough for more than grief in my life.

"Let's dance again," I said, slipping my fingers through hers, our bangles chiming together like muted bells. "Come and dance with me before your handsome man steals you away forever."

She laughed and rose, pulling me to my feet and not denying a word of it, and we danced. I wanted to dance until the sun rose, until my feet bled beneath me so that I could paint out a happier future in my crimson steps than the one Witch Mother had read for me in the goat's belly. But all that I got was a blister and a venomous look or two from Alimah when we strayed too close. Still, it was a far better thing than sitting in the darkness alone.

Ilan and the other men of the village had done their work well in summoning the Scorched Man and now they rested, sweat dripping from their brows and down their arms, broad palm fronds hanging limp in their hands. The old words said that the Scorched Man would come even if only one man stood alone fanning the sand, but our encampment was strong and the cloud of dust that we raised in our grieving was a sight to behold, taller than the highest trees I had ever seen.

And as he always had, the Scorched Man answered our call. His storm was rolling in from the desert, dark and red, engulfing trees and boulders in its wake. The heavy cloud towered above us, sliding towards the village like a mountain range stung by the nomad's spirit. The wind reached us long before the sand, setting my scarf flapping wildly around my face and shoulders. I would have tucked it down more securely if my arms were not full.

"I see him!"

Ilan's little cousin Zakir was too young to understand the sorrow of the ceremony and danced around me, his sandals slapping the sand. I had gone out past the others to wait and he had followed me, it seemed, making me wonder if his mother had gone to comfort Naza with the other women.

"Witch Daughter, look, I can see the Scorched Man!" he cried again, pointing into the storm.

My heart thumped like a drum in my throat as I looked, narrowing my eyes against the rising wind. And then I could see him too. A long shadow against the red wall of dust, the roughest shape of a man with limbs too long and a frame too thin, the way a child might sketch a figure in the sand with a stick. The sight of him shouldn't have been such a shock. It was his storm, after all.

"You shouldn't look at him," I said. My voice was tight with nerves. "If you look into his eyes, even by mistake, he will steal you away with him."

Zakir ceased his wild dance for a moment, looking up at me solemnly, the hem of his tunic fluttering in the wind.

"Is that a true thing?" he asked.

I knew very well that it was only something said to keep small children near their parents when the Scorched Man came into the village to collect our dead. But I also knew that I had been orphaned the day that my father stood face to face with the Scorched Man. And I knew that I had looked into the Scorched Man's face when I myself was Zakir's age, and now Witch Mother saw nothing but death in my future.

"I believe it with all my heart," I told Zakir. "Now run and stay with your mother. Run!"

He ran, his little feet beating a frantic rhythm away from me. I glanced back to make sure that he hadn't stopped. The others were drifting away as well, taking shelter within their tents. The sky darkened with the shadow of the storm like night coming in too sudden and soon.

The wind had a sound to it, a low growl like a hungry animal, and the blowing sand had become ferocious now. Witch Mother had always stood like something hewn from stone when she went out to greet his storms, so I tried to stand straight and tall as well, but I was trembling badly and the bones in my legs felt as though they'd been traded for water.

Witch Mother had taught me where to stand, when to kneel, and when to avert my eyes, but she had still offered to come with me. I had protested until she was satisfied to let me go alone. I *had* to go alone. Not because I was confident in my ability to remember her instructions, but because I had no intention of following them at all.

I wanted to see him, this creature that had taken my whole family away from me. I would do for a second time what every child of my village had been warned not to do even once and look into the Scorched Man's face again.

The first time I had watched the Scorched Man come into the village, it had been through a haze of tears. I had been promised a baby brother. I had been promised that mother would be well enough to run and play with me again once the child was born. But something had gone wrong and these promises were a fistful of water.

Father wailed his grief as though he would never stop and I was afraid.

My father was the definition of strength in my child's mind, the very meaning of courage. When I stood next to him, he would always rest his broad hand on top of my head and I felt sure that he could shelter me from any danger. But on that day of such loss, he had howled and his strong hands had clutched at his chest as though there was some poison within him, as though some deadly snake had sunk its fangs into his very heart, and I was terrified.

The enormity of losing my mother as she struggled to bring my brother into the world had not yet struck me. Remembering it now, I think my heart knew that it would need years to fully accept the weight of that loss and, on that day, denied it.

Mad with grief, the spice merchant had told us years later, curling his fingers at his temples, revelling in the role of storyteller. *The man went mad with grief and took up the body of his wife before the Witch Mother could come! He walked into the storm next to the Scorched Man, who carried the body of their newborn child, all four turning to shadow in the swirling sand...*

Naza had hurled the cooking pot at him then, her face rigid with fury, but I knew how the story ended. I had stared at them as they passed from the doorway of my family's empty tent and had met the Scorched Man's fiery eyes as he turned his head to regard me there. I had stared and wept until the four of them had disappeared into the Scorched Man's storm, until the sands settled themselves, and Witch Mother had come to collect me, the village's newest orphan.

The storm swept over me, stealing the sunlight and I was alone in the howling darkness. The body of Naza's child was so light in my arms that I held it almost too tightly, afraid that it might be torn away from me in the storm.

Like a whisper heard beneath the sound of drums, I heard his footsteps approaching, the muted murmur of sand resettling itself beneath his bare feet. I heard him before I saw him and when I saw him, it took all my strength not to flee.

Tall and thin and nearly featureless, his flesh resembled the coals of a strong fire, crackled black shot through with glowing red. The fire beneath his skin moved as he did, flaring to near-white heat before ebbing to deep red again. The length of his limbs was all wrong. His legs were nearly as high as my chest and yet his arms still hung to his knees. He moved like a creature of the sandstorm, smooth and powerful.

Familiar rage lit in my heart, a fire that matched his, and I held my ground as he came towards me. The storm kept its respectful distance from him so that the air stilled around us both as he stopped in front of me. For the second time that day, I knew that there were words that I was meant to say, old words, true words, but as he looked down at me and Naza's child I could not remember a single one of them.

"Come to steal from me again?" I said, old anger adding poison to my tone.

He tilted his head, regarding me with his blank face and those fiery holes where eyes should have been, and I wondered if these were the first new words he had heard from a Witch Daughter in his whole existence. With slow grace, he stretched out a hand with his palm up, not reaching to touch but only indicating the little body in my arms. The body that would remain dead whether the Scorched Man had come for it or not. A death that was not his doing.

I bit furiously at my lip, struggling against tears as my anger dissolved into despair. Knowing that he was blameless somehow made the whole ordeal that much worse. I knelt and set down the body as I was meant to, getting that much of the ceremony correct.

"He was to be called Khaleem," I said hoarsely, "And I wish that I did not know that. Please, show him the way to peace."

They weren't the correct words at all, but the Scorched Man was not meant to crouch down with me as he did either. He stretched out his long-fingered blackened hand once more, resting it on the child's little chest. I could feel the heat from him against my face and thought that the shroud might catch fire. Instead, it crumbled slowly to ashes, cloth and body both, and the ashes rose lazily through the still air around us to join into the dance of the storm.

"My father wasn't dead when he left with you," I whispered. "They say that you guide the dead to peace. What happens when the living go to walk with you?"

He stretched out his hand towards me then and I did not flinch, though I had seen his deadly touch only a moment before. I held still, all of the fury gone from me as he set his hand onto my shorn head. His touch was hot, but not burning, and his fingers were the perfect size to curl gently around the curve of my skull. And for a moment there in the heart of his storm, I felt safe. Sheltered from all danger.

Withdrawing his hand, he unfurled himself to rise, looking down at me. Lines of flame ran down his black cheeks like tears. Finally turning his back, he started slowly into the desert. The storm crashed around me again as he left me there, alone.

I stayed on my knees until the storm withdrew, my thoughts a wild tangle to put the swirling sand to shame. Having looked into the Scorched Man's face for a second time, I knew that it was not the *same* face that I had seen as a child. But I knew him just the same.

Most of the villagers would not meet my eyes when I returned, as though I had been tainted by my closeness to the Scorched Man. I was not surprised; they had recoiled from me in much the same way when my family died.

Retreating to my tent, I listened to the sounds of the village settling itself for the night. It took a while for the women to leave Naza and Ilan's tent. I used the time to gather up my traveling cloak and a skin of water. I would require one more thing, but could not retrieve it until the others were asleep, so I crouched just inside the doorway until the moon had nearly completed its climb to the top of the sky.

Slipping out, I walked carefully so that my footsteps were silent against the cool moon-bathed sand. I was outside of Naza's tent within minutes. Peeking in through the seam of the doorway, I could make out the shape of the couple lying in a tight embrace on the sleeping mat, though I doubted either would find sleep that night.

They have each other, I told myself firmly. *Her heart is made of stronger stuff than yours. Naza won't forget joy.*

The large palm frond that Ilan had used in the summoning was still at the side of their tent and I picked it up as quietly as I could, wincing at the hiss of sand sliding from its broad surface. It was nearly the same weight as the body I had taken from the tent earlier and the comparison gave me a moment of pause, a moment of pain. Holding the frond carefully in both hands, I turned around.

Witch Mother stood directly in front of me, watching me in silence. I nearly screamed, my heartbeat skittering in alarm, and she smiled at me. When she beckoned for me, I fell into step next to her, too startled to do otherwise.

"You have done some thinking," she murmured.

I nodded. I had regained enough of my composure to realize we were walking in the same direction that I had intended from the start, through the row of larger tents towards the edge of the village. Dying torches lit our way like a path of faltering stars.

"You knew all along," I said. There was no accusation in my tone; I understood as well as she did that I would have rejected the truth if she told it to me directly. "When you told me that I was a child of death, you didn't mean that I was an orphan. You meant *this*."

She nodded peacefully. "I told you to take your place when you were ready."

We had reached the edge of the village now and she stopped, looking out into the desert with me. The softly rolling dunes were stained blue and green by the same moonlight that lit the sparse clouds white. It looked like a cold and peaceful place.

"I'm ready," I said. This new path felt more natural under my feet than my attempt to become a healer ever had. "Please take care of Naza for me, Witch Mother. Help her understand that she does not need to grieve for me as well."

The lines around Witch Mother's eyes multiplied as she smiled at me and stepped forward to wrap her strong arms around me in a tight embrace. I knew that it would be the last time that I would be propped up by the small woman's seemingly boundless strength. When I walked into the empty desert, I walked alone.

I travelled until the place felt right, far enough from the village that my ceremony would not disturb them, though still near enough that I did not feel like I had abandoned them. In the sheltered space between dunes, I lifted the palm frond and began to stir the sand to life, chanting softly to myself. *The Scorched Man will come for even one who fans the sand alone...*

I fanned and fanned. The sand rose in small sad puffs before me and the frond seemed to have tripled in weight during my walk. I concentrated on my chant, feeling the prickle of sweat starting on my brow. My arms wailed their protest and still no storm rose in answer. Lift and drop, lift and drop.... What a thing it would be for my arms to give out when my heart had finally found its way.

Suddenly, I caught sight of his shadow stretched long by the moonlight, unmistakable though marred by the ripples in the sand. I let the frond fall with a grateful groan and crossed my arms to dig my fingers into my aching shoulders, watching him approach. His internal fire still gleamed through his scorched flesh, making the sand at his feet glitter. He looked less terrifying without the rage of the desert surrounding him.

"You've left your storm behind," I said softly.

The Scorched Man stopped, considering me. He reached out a hand and pointed to my chest where my heart was pounding, though not entirely with fear.

"No storm rises for one still alive," I said. "Yes, I understand. There are none here for you to guide."

His featureless face inclined in a slow nod. He seemed tired, as though the effort of guiding Naza's child to peace had taken some of his vitality from him. Ponderously, he spread his blackened hands as if to ask me where my offering was.

I smiled and stepped closer, looking up into his face. It was easier to see the familiarities now that I was looking for them. In the shape of his eyes and the way he held his shoulders, in the angle of his charred jaw and the way his broad hand had rested so gently on my head, he was still my father.

"I called you here for me," I said. "Father, you've served well. You've guided so many souls. But now I am here for *you*."

I held my hands out to him, ready to take his place just as he had taken the place of the Scorched Man before him the day that he left to guide my mother and brother into the storm.

"Go now, my father," I told him, smiling. "Go find your peace. Now you know the way."

And the Scorched Man, my father, bowed his head and placed his fiery hands into mine.

His hands crumbled first, wisps of black and gray falling to the sand. He went to ashes slower than the child had, slowly enough that the scorch had begun to crawl up my arms before he was gone, crackling over my skin. I could feel the heat building within me, but it was not unpleasant. The rage and hurt that had burned within me for so long now kindled to something deeper. Something old and true.

The last pieces of my father found a curl of breeze in the cool night air and whirled away from me with a sound like the first breath of health after long illness. And the new fire lit within me as my shadow stretched long across the sand under the light of the moon.

My people die, as is the way of all things, and hurt like all creatures do. But when their time came, I would be the one to lead them to peace.

For this anthology, **MEGAN FENNELL** wanted to bypass the traditional Grim Reaper with his European black carriage and scythe, and explore the death god of a fictional culture. She has previously been published in *Tesseracts 17*, *OnSpec Magazine*, and won first prize in the 2013 Retreat by Random House Spooky Short Story Contest.

Afterword

THE STRUGGLE TO WRESTLE WITH GODS

by Liana Kerzner

FOR MAGIC TO WORK, we must believe in it. That's my own little personal artist's mantra. Any successful work of fiction needs a living spark; inspiration; magic. Writers must produce magic on demand over and over again, and that's not only difficult: it's unreliable. So we must believe.

This book, like the religious texts that in part inspired it, had two factors with which to contend in its creation: what it believed people could be, and what we must accept people are. We hope people can be open-minded, patient, eager to learn, and aware of other cultures. People are, however, tribal, insecure, awkward in new situations, and limited in our understanding. In order for this book to be accessible, we had to embrace both reality and our best hopes for humanity.

I don't think Jerome and I were consciously aware that the selection process involved belief, but looking back on the stories we accepted, that paradigm definitely emerged. We believed in these stories because they believed in themselves. They believed in themselves because they believed in something beyond themselves. These stories had to be beyond great to overcome the stigmas and disputes surrounding religion: they had to be magical.

We desperately wanted to minimize the culture war element of religiously-inspired stories, so we started the book with a story that introduces us to "A Jesus" instead of "The Jesus", to clarify our position on use of religious characters in fiction.

We had to draw this line to maintain a respectful approach to faith while still allowing artistic freedom. This is not a value judgment on the "rightness" of any given faith. It's simply treating the various faiths the way they treat themselves. We offered the authors a chance to give us a few lines regarding the inspiration for their stories because even the "made up" faiths had inspirations from our world that deserved recognition.

We also had to address the appropriate place and role of Christianity in an interfaith anthology. It's undeniable that Christianity is the most commonly-understood faith in the West, but we wanted to use it as an intake vehicle, not a baseline for "normal".

I also felt strongly that an interpath anthology include representation from... I don't know how to define the generalization, because no one is a "non-believer". Everyone has a moral code and a collection of beliefs, even if they don't involve a god. I've met atheists with greater moral convictions than some church-goers. In one atheist friend's case, I credit "empathy through internet cat videos", but I can't prove causality.

I didn't believe that atheists and agnostics needed to be included because I thought a great many atheists were going to read this book. I insisted because we can't claim to believe that we are all creatures of a god, then cut away any section of humanity just because they believe differently. Of course, we had to be handed magical stories to represent the evidence-based contingent, and we were fortunate to receive the Sacristy's agnostic Shaman and Millie's "faith in manuals and movies".

And this brings us to a major challenge we faced in selecting the stories: where to draw the line between fantasy, science-fiction, and faith, since all religions contain heavy doses of absorbed folklore and mysticism. We found that stories that didn't provide enough of a fantasy/sci-fi element inadvertently risked demeaning the religion-based components, so we couldn't include them. Others fused fantasy and faith with great technical skill, but didn't give us a reason to emotionally connect with the craftsmanship. Holy books are less about gods and more about what people do in the service to those gods, and while both folklore and religion attempt to influence behavior through stories, all the religions I've looked into actually encourage people to think for themselves.

I know, I know, that's not how they're applied by many, but you can't blame a book for what people do with it. Religious texts are not easy things to understand. They're full of contradictions which are acknowledgements that life is a complicated equation, and there are no easy answers. "Jihad" means "to struggle in the way of Allah", "Israel" means "struggle with God". The word "passion" in a Christian context refers to the suffering of Christ, during which Jesus cried out "My God, my God, why have you forsaken me?" It's no accident that in that moment, Jesus asks "why?" as opposed to just forsaking the God he believes forsook him. Religion is, at its core, a struggle to understand the "why?" of the world.

We wanted the book to reflect this struggle. In the modern world, we don't need religion for anything else: secular governments provide the "who" of our rule book, the legal code provides the "what and when", geopolitical borders provide the "where" and the media, licensing processes, and police services gives us the "how". But *why* are murder and theft wrong? *Why* should we be kind to animals? *Why* should women, minorities and aboriginals have equality? By grappling with ancient words of wisdom, I've found answers to these questions. Disagreeing with a deity put me in tune with my own power. WWJD can sometimes mean asking WTF?

We are at a turning point, thousands of years after the advent of monotheism, where people of faith need to take religion back from the fringe elements which are making it seem hateful and irrelevant. We hope that this book is a small step in reclaiming faith and religion for those of us that want it to be an important part of our lives without taking over our lives. The radicals have had their time. It's time for the rest of us to find our voices again, and show that each of our Gods likes a good challenge.

This means avoiding the OTP principle: the One True Patriarch— Apologies to numerous fandom shippers; I thought that term was catchy. Since we minimized patriarchy in the project's ideology, we didn't have to do anything else to make sure female characters and female authors were equally represented. Canada has so many excellent writers, male and female alike, that since we kept an open mind and accepted their stories on their own terms, we effortlessly ended up with pretty equal representation.

We do, however, have more work to do when it comes to racial representation, more specifically, encouraging submissions from writers representing minority groups. *Wrestling With Gods* contains a great mix of characters of color, (and chromatophoric cuttlefish) but we weren't able to include as many authors of color as I would have liked. The non-white authors who submitted are just as talented as their more privileged counterparts, but they didn't submit in sufficient numbers for us to create proportional representation. This is an issue the sci-fi/fantasy community needs to take seriously. This level of marginalization is neither natural nor positive.

What is positive is the mix of established authors, new authors, and established authors who were new to me. This book was a unique and specific creative challenge, and Jerome and I were pleased to see so many known names stepping out of their respective comfort zones, some even within their existing universes. The authors took real risks, challenged themselves, and the results speak for themselves. The poetry submissions were uniquely inspired as well. Once everything was selected, the table of contents came together with an eerie ease. I'm too much of a rationalist to claim divine intervention, but there were moments where I felt like someone was giving me a nod, if not active help. I think it's arrogance, however, to believe that God would direct specific attention to a Canadian sci-fi anthology.

I prefer to think it's magic. Because I believe in magic.

LIANA KERZNER is an award-winning TV producer & writer who has also stepped in front of the camera as the co-host of the legendary late night show *Ed & Red's Night Party*, the Canadian Comedy Award-winning this *Movie Sucks!*, and *Ed the Sock's I Hate Hollywood*! An episode of *I Hate Hollywood* was lauded by mental health workers for de-stigmatizing mental illness. Another early episode was well-received for its look at religion in Hollywood.

Liana also provides commentary, reviews and video interviews for video game site gamingexcellence.com. She is co-columnist of 411 Mania's "The 8 Ball", and host/writer of *Liana K's Geek Download*, heard weekly on the internationally syndicated radio program *Canada's Top 20*. She has edited and contributed writing to a comic book mini-series: *Ed and Red's Comic Strip*.

She has hosted and produced the Prix Aurora Awards ceremony three times. She is founder and chair of the Futurecon organization, which uses Science-Fiction and Fantasy elements to reduce various types of stigma and raise money for various charities.

Her stranger achievements include: modeling for videogames, having her superhero toy & art collection featured on TV's Space channel, researching and presenting a paper on Mormon Cosmology in the *Twilight* Saga, and having a DC Comics character named after her. Liana is an avid cosplayer and her costume work made her the face of Western cosplay on Wikipedia.

Our titles are available at major book stores
and local independent resellers who support
Science Fiction and Fantasy readers like you.

EDGE Science Fiction
and Fantasy Publishing

www.edgewebsite.com

Our titles are available at major book stores and local independent resellers who support Science Fiction and Fantasy readers like you.

Evolve: Vampire Stories of the New Undead edited by Nancy Kilpatrick (tp)
- ISBN: 978-1-894063-33-3
Evolve Two: Vampire Stories of the Future Undead edited by Nancy Kilpatrick (tp)
-ISBN: 978-1-894063-62-3
Expiration Date edited by Nancy Kilpatrick (tp) - ISBN: 978-1-77053-062-1

Fires of the Kindred by Robin Skelton (tp) - ISBN: 978-0-88878-271-7
Forbidden Cargo by Rebecca Rowe (tp) - ISBN: 978-1-894063-16-6

Game of Perfection, A (Part 2 of Tyranaël) by Élisabeth Vonarburg (tp) - ISBN:
978-1-894063-32-6
Gaslight Arcanum: Uncanny Tales of Sherlock Holmes edited by Jeff Campbell &
Charles Prepolec (tp) - ISBN: 978-1-8964063-60-9
Gaslight Grimoire: Fantastic Tales of Sherlock Holmes edited by Jeff Campbell &
Charles Prepolec (tp) - ISBN: 978-1-8964063-17-3
Gaslight Grotesque: Nightmare Tales of Sherlock Holmes edited by Jeff Campbell
& Charles Prepolec (tp) - ISBN: 978-1-8964063-31-9
Green Music by Ursula Pflug (tp) - ISBN: 978-1-895836-75-2
Green Music by Ursula Pflug (hb) - ISBN: 978-1-895836-77-6

Healer, The (Children of the Panther Part One) by Amber Hayward (tp)
- ISBN: 978-1-895836-89-9
Healer, The (Children of the Panther Part One) by Amber Hayward (hb)
- ISBN: 978-1-895836-91-2
Hell Can Wait by Theodore Judson (tp) - ISBN: 978-1-978-1-894063-23-4
Hounds of Ash and other tales of Fool Wolf, The by Greg Keyes (tp)
- ISBN: 978-1-894063-09-8
Hydrogen Steel by K. A. Bedford (tp) - ISBN: 978-1-894063-20-3

i-ROBOT Poetry by Jason Christie (tp) - ISBN: 978-1-894063-24-1
Immortal Quest by Alexandra MacKenzie (tp) - ISBN: 978-1-894063-46-3

Jackal Bird by Michael Barley (pb) - ISBN: 978-1-895836-07-3
Jackal Bird by Michael Barley (hb) - ISBN: 978-1-895836-11-0
JEMMA7729 by Phoebe Wray (tp) - ISBN: 978-1-894063-40-1

Keaen by Till Noever (tp) - ISBN: 978-1-894063-08-1
Keeper's Child by Leslie Davis (tp) - ISBN: 978-1-894063-01-2

Land/Space edited by Candas Jane Dorsey and Judy McCrosky (tp)
- ISBN: 978-1-895836-90-5
Land/Space edited by Candas Jane Dorsey and Judy McCrosky (hb)
- ISBN: 978-1-895836-92-9
Lyskarion: The Song of the Wind (Part One of The Chronicles of the Karionin) by
J.A. Cullum (tp) - ISBN: 978-1-894063-02-9

Machine Sex and other stories by Candas Jane Dorsey (tp)
- ISBN: 978-0-88878-278-6
Maërlande Chronicles, The by Élisabeth Vonarburg (pb) - ISBN: 978-0-88878-294-6
Milkman, The by Michael J. Martineck (tp) - ISBN: 978-1-77053-060-7
Moonfall by Heather Spears (pb) - ISBN: 978-0-88878-306-6

Necromancer Candle, The by Randy McCharles (tp) - ISBN: 978-1-77053-066-9

Occasional Diamond Thief, The by J. A. McLachlan (tp) - ISBN: 978-1-77053-075-1
Of Wind and Sand by Sylvie Bérard (translated by Sheryl Curtis) (tp)
    - ISBN: 978-1-894063-19-7
On Spec: The First Five Years edited by On Spec (pb) - ISBN: 978-1-895836-08-0
    On Spec: The First Five Years edited by On Spec (hb)
    - ISBN: 978-1-895836-12-7
Orbital Burn by K. A. Bedford (tp) - ISBN: 978-1-894063-10-4
    Orbital Burn by K. A. Bedford (hb) - ISBN: 978-1-894063-12-8

Pallahaxi Tide by Michael Coney (pb) - ISBN: 978-0-88878-293-9
Paradox Resolution by K. A. Bedford (tp) - ISBN:978-1-894063-88-3
Passion Play by Sean Stewart (pb) - ISBN: 978-0-88878-314-1
Professor Challenger: New Worlds, Lost Places edited by Jeff Campbell &
    Charles Prepolec (tp) - ISBN: 978-1-77053-052-2
Plague Saint, The by Rita Donovan (tp) - ISBN: 978-1-895836-28-8
    Plague Saint, The by Rita Donovan (hb) - ISBN: 978-1-895836-29-5
Pock's World by Dave Duncan (tp) - ISBN: 978-1-894063-47-0
Puzzle Box, The by The Apocalyptic Four (tp) - ISBN: 978-1-77053-040-9

Reluctant Voyagers by Élisabeth Vonarburg (pb) - ISBN: 978-1-895836-09-7
    Reluctant Voyagers by Élisabeth Vonarburg (hb) - ISBN: 978-1-895836-15-8
Resisting Adonis by Timothy J. Anderson (tp) - ISBN: 978-1-895836-84-4
    Resisting Adonis by Timothy J. Anderson (hb) - ISBN: 978-1-895836-83-7
Rigor Amortis edited by Jaym Gates and Erika Holt (tp)
    - ISBN: 978-1-894063-63-0

Shadow Academy, The by Adrian Cole (tp) - ISBN: 978-1-77053-064-5
Silent City, The by Élisabeth Vonarburg (tp) - ISBN: 978-1-894063-07-4
Slow Engines of Time, The by Élisabeth Vonarburg (tp) - ISBN: 978-1-895836-30-1
    Slow Engines of Time, The by Élisabeth Vonarburg (hb)
    - ISBN: 978-1-895836-31-8
Stealing Magic by Tanya Huff (tp) - ISBN: 978-1-894063-34-0
Stolen Children (Children of the Panther Part Three) by Amber Hayward (tp)
    - ISBN: 978-1-894063-66-1
Strange Attractors by Tom Henighan (pb) - ISBN: 978-0-88878-312-7

Taming, The by Heather Spears (pb) - ISBN: 978-1-895836-23-3
Taming, The by Heather Spears (hb) - ISBN: 978-1-895836-24-0
Technicolor Ultra Mall by Ryan Oakley (tp) - ISBN: 978-1-894063-54-8
Ten Monkeys, Ten Minutes by Peter Watts (tp) - ISBN: 978-1-895836-74-5
    Ten Monkeys, Ten Minutes by Peter Watts (hb) - ISBN: 978-1-895836-76-9
Tesseracts 1 edited by Judith Merril (pb) - ISBN: 978-0-88878-279-3
Tesseracts 2 edited by Phyllis Gotlieb & Douglas Barbour (pb)
    - ISBN: 978-0-88878-270-0
Tesseracts 3 edited by Candas Jane Dorsey & Gerry Truscott (pb)
    - ISBN: 978-0-88878-290-8
Tesseracts 4 edited by Lorna Toolis & Michael Skeet (pb)
    - ISBN: 978-0-88878-322-6
Tesseracts 5 edited by Robert Runté & Yves Maynard (pb)
    - ISBN: 978-1-895836-25-7
    Tesseracts 5 edited by Robert Runté & Yves Maynard (hb)
    - ISBN: 978-1-895836-26-4

Tesseracts 6 edited by Robert J. Sawyer & Carolyn Clink (pb)
- ISBN: 978-1-895836-32-5
   Tesseracts 6 edited by Robert J. Sawyer & Carolyn Clink (hb)
   - ISBN: 978-1-895836-33-2
Tesseracts 7 edited by Paula Johanson & Jean-Louis Trudel (tp)
- ISBN: 978-1-895836-58-5
   Tesseracts 7 edited by Paula Johanson & Jean-Louis Trudel (hb)
   - ISBN: 978-1-895836-59-2
Tesseracts 8 edited by John Clute & Candas Jane Dorsey (tp)
- ISBN: 978-1-895836-61-5
   Tesseracts 8 edited by John Clute & Candas Jane Dorsey (hb)
   - ISBN: 978-1-895836-62-2
Tesseracts Nine edited by Nalo Hopkinson and Geoff Ryman (tp)
- ISBN: 978-1-894063-26-5
Tesseracts Ten: A Celebration of New Canadian Specuative Fiction
edited by R.C. Wilson and E. van Belkom (tp)
- ISBN: 978-1-894063-36-4
Tesseracts Eleven: Amazing Canadian Speulative Fiction
edited by Cory Doctorow and Holly Phillips (tp)
- ISBN: 978-1-894063-03-6
Tesseracts Twelve: New Novellas of Canadian Fantastic Fiction
edited by Claude Lalumière (tp)
- ISBN: 978-1-894063-15-9
Tesseracts Thirteen: Chilling Tales from the Great White North
edited by Nancy Kilpatrick and David Morrell (tp)
- ISBN: 978-1-894063-25-8
Tesseracts 14: Strange Canadian Stories
edited by John Robert Colombo and Brett Alexander Savory (tp)
- ISBN: 978-1-894063-37-1
Tesseracts Fifteen: A Case of Quite Curious Tales
edited by Julie Czerneda and Susan MacGregor (tp)
- ISBN: 978-1-894063-58-6
Tesseracts Sixteen: Parnassus Unbound edited by Mark Leslie (tp)
- ISBN: 978-1-894063-92-0
Tesseracts Seventeen: Speculating Canada from Coast to Coast to Coast
edited by C. Anderson and S. Vernon (tp)
-ISBN: 978-1-77053-044-7
Tesseracts Eighteen: Wrestling With Gods
edited by Liana Kerzner and Jerome Stueart (tp)
- ISBN: 978-1-77053-068-3
Tesseracts Q edited by Élisabeth Vonarburg and Jane Brierley (pb)
- ISBN: 978-1-895836-21-9
   Tesseracts Q edited by Élisabeth Vonarburg and Jane Brierley (hb)
   - ISBN: 978-1-895836-22-6
Those Who Fight Monsters: Tales of Occult Detectives
edited by Justin Gustainis (pb) - ISBN: 978-1-894063-48-7
Time Machines Repaired Whie-U-Wait by K. A. Bedford (tp)
- ISBN: 978-1-894063-42-5
Trillionist, The by Sagan Jeffries (tp) - ISBN: 978-1-894063-98-2

Urban Green Man edited by Adria Laycraft and Janice Blaine (tp)
- ISBN: 978-1-77053-038-6

Vampyric Variations by Nancy Kilpatrick (tp) - ISBN: 978-1-894063-94-4
Vyrkarion: The Talisman of Anor (Part Three of The Chronicles of the Karionin)
   by J. A. Cullum (tp) - ISBN: 978-1-77053-028-7

Warriors by Barbara Galler-Smith and Josh Langston (tp)
   - ISBN: 978-1-77053-030-0
Wildcatter by Dave Duncan (tp) - ISBN: 978-1-894063-90-6